**What we were not facing was a robot or an alien or a Ghostie or any of the other things rumoured to wander around inside baubles.**

"You want to take a breather there, cove," Prozor said, as the figure came closer. "We can parlay just fine without gettin' in each other's faces."

"Pass me my bow," Fura said.

Strambli reached over and extracted Fura's crossbow from the rig on the back of her suit. The bow was already cocked, the way Fura preferred it. She took one hand from the bottle and took the bow in the other, levelling it down the corridor. The figure straightened up a bit, just enough that we could start to see its face coming into view through the curve of its visor.

That was when my shivers turned to cold terror.

# Praise for Alastair Reynolds

"An adroit and fast-paced blend of space opera and police procedural, original and exciting, teeming with cool stfnal concepts. A real page turner. The prefect of this title is sort of a space cop, Sipowicz in a space suit, or maybe Dirty Harry with a whiphound."

—George R. R. Martin on *The Prefect*

"[Reynolds is] one of the most gifted hard SF writers working today." —*Publishers Weekly* on *Beyond the Aquila Rift*

"[Reynolds is] a mastersinger of the space opera."

—*The Times* on *Blue Remembered Earth*

"A swashbuckling thriller—*Pirates of the Caribbean* meets *Firefly*—that nevertheless combines the author's trademark hard SF with effective, coming-of-age characterization."

—*Guardian* on *Revenger*

"*Revenger* is classic Reynolds—that is to say, top of the line science fiction, where characters are matched beautifully with ideas and have to find their place in a complex future. More!"

—Greg Bear

"A leading light of the New Space Opera movement in science fiction." —*Los Angeles Review of Books*

"A fascinating hybrid of space opera, police procedural, and character study." —*Publishers Weekly* on *The Prefect*

"Reynolds has sketched in a galaxy littered with the relics of former civilizations (human and alien), with plenty left to the reader's imagination, and room for a sequel."

—*Library Journal* on *Revenger*

"*Revenger* is tremendous fun." —*Locus*

"An expert mix of the fantastical and horrific."
—*Publishers Weekly* (starred review) on *Revenger*

"Reynolds' newest action-packed science fiction novel is a tale of sisterly devotion, heartbreaking loss, and brutal vengeance.... Fans will enjoy the well-developed characters and detailed world building." —*Booklist* on *Revenger*

"A blindingly clever imagining of our solar system in the far flung future." —*Sun* on *Revenger*

"A rollicking adventure yarn with action, abduction, fights, properly scary hazards, very grisly torture and even ghosts of a sort."
—*Daily Telegraph* on *Revenger*

"By far the most enjoyable book Reynolds has ever written."
—*SFX* on *Revenger*

"The world of *Revenger* is undeniably fascinating, and with Reynolds as your storyteller, a journey into it is definitely worthwhile."
—*SciFiNow*

"Reynolds makes the human story compelling in a narrative that, spiced with bizarre characters aplenty and propelled by vengeance, smacks intriguingly of everything from Robert Louis Stevenson's *Treasure Island* to *Mad Max*." —*Nature* on *Revenger*

"A delightful romp through the spaceways."
—*Interzone* on *Revenger*

"A must-read...an unexpectedly personal and emotionally-driven tale of determination and retribution—with some great twists along the way and a gutsy heroine..."
—*Starburst* magazine on *Revenger*

"A layered star-spanning odyssey filled with drama, adventure, and, yes, revenge." —*AudioFile* on *Revenger*

"An excellent, gripping piece of work."
—sfandfreviews.blogspot.com on *Revenger*

"Basically, it's *Treasure Island* meets *Moby Dick*, set in space, with a nice *Blade Runner*-ish color palette and a cast of characters worthy of a Terry Gilliam movie. I loved it."
—Joanne Harris on *Revenger*

"One of the giants of the new British space opera."
—*io9*

"It's grand, involving and full of light and wonder. *Poseidon's Wake* is one of the best sci-fi novels of the year."
—*SciFiNow*

"Reynolds blends AIs, mysterious aliens, intelligent elephants and philosophical ruminations on our place in the universe in a well-paced, complex story replete with intrigue, invention and an optimism uncommon in contemporary SF."
—*Guardian* on *Poseidon's Wake*

"Few SF writers merge rousing adventure with advanced futuristic technology as skillfully as Alastair Reynolds."
—*Toronto Star* on *On the Steel Breeze*

"Reynolds is a master of the slow build up leading to apocalyptic action, and *On the Steel Breeze* is no exception."
—National Space Society

"A book of great fascination, rich description, and memorable action." —*Locus* on *Absolution Gap*

"His writing mixes spartan style, provocative ideas, and flashes of dark humor.... Reynolds excels at weaving different threads together." —*Los Angeles Review of Books* on *Slow Bullets*

"Alastair Reynolds is a name to watch. Shades of Banks and Gibson with gigatons of originality."

—*Guardian* on *Blue Remembered Earth*

"If you like hard SF...with fast-paced action and hard-boiled characters...you're in for a great ride."

—*SF Site* on *Redemption Ark*

"Reynolds has a galaxy-sized imagination allied to a real storytelling ability."

—Bernard Cornwell on *Blue Remembered Earth*

"Heir to writers like Isaac Asimov and Arthur C. Clarke. Reynolds keeps up the tradition of forward thinking.... An immensely thrilling, mind-bending piece of work."

—*The A. V. Club* on *House of Suns*

"[A] tour de force...ravishingly inventive."

—*Publishers Weekly* on *Revelation Space*

"Reynolds takes quests for vengeance and redemption and places them on a galactic stage." —*Locus* on *Redemption Ark*

# SHADOW CAPTAIN

## By Alastair Reynolds

### Novels

Century Rain

Pushing Ice

House of Suns

Terminal World

The Medusa Chronicles *(with Stephen Baxter)*

### Revelation Space

Revelation Space

Redemption Ark

Absolution Gap

Chasm City

### Poseidon's Children

Blue Remembered Earth

On the Steel Breeze

Poseidon's Wake

### Revenger

Revenger

Shadow Captain

### The Prefect Dreyfus Emergencies

Aurora Rising *(previously published as* The Prefect*)*

Elysium Fire

### Short Story Collections

Diamond Dogs, Turquoise Days

Galactic North

Zima Blue

Beyond the Aquila Rift

Slow Bullets *(novella)*

# SHADOW CAPTAIN

Alastair Reynolds

orbit

www.orbitbooks.net

This book is a work of fiction. Names, characters, places, and incidents are the product of the author's imagination or are used fictitiously. Any resemblance to actual events, locales, or persons, living or dead, is coincidental.


Cover design by Blacksheep and Lauren Panepinto
Cover photo by Depositphotos


Author photograph by Barbara Bella



Orbit
Hachette Book Group
1290 Avenue of the Americas
New York, NY 10104
orbitbooks.net

Simultaneously published in Great Britain by Gollancz and in the U.S. by Orbit in 2019

First Edition: January 2019

Orbit is an imprint of Hachette Book Group.
The Orbit name and logo are trademarks of Little, Brown Book Group Limited.



Library of Congress Control Number: 2018961293

ISBNs: 978-0-316-55570-8 (trade paperback), 978-0-316-55568-5 (ebook)

Printed in the United States of America

LSC-C

10 9 8 7 6 5 4 3 2 1

To Mum, with continued love and gratitude.

# SHADOW CAPTAIN

# 1

"Tell me what you think you saw."

"It wasn't nothing," Surt said, squeezed next to me in one of the two adjoining seats in the sighting room. "I oughtn't have mentioned it, not with your sister being so jumpy."

"Never you worry about Arafura. If you saw something, we all need to know about it."

"But if there was another ship scuttlin' about out here, we'd have seen it on the sweeper, wouldn't we?"

"The sweeper isn't infallible, Surt. That's why we watch for sail-flash. If the conditions are right it can show up across a much longer range, especially through a telescope. You were sighting through one of the high-magnification tubes, weren't you?"

Surt looked abashed. "I wasn't even trying to find a ship. Just looking out at the worlds, hoping to get a squint of my home. Fura won't get cross at me, will she?"

"Of course not," I answered softly, making an adjustment to one of the aiming wheels. "We've all done it, and it's nothing to be ashamed of. A bit of homesickness doesn't make us any less committed to the crew."

"I probably wasn't even squintin' in the right part of the sky. Never could get my head around all those tables and charts like the rest of you. Got a noggin' for machines, not numbers."

"Don't feel too bad about it. Those tables aren't easy for any of us, except maybe Paladin."

She tipped her head down, silent for a few seconds.

"Do you ever look, Adrana?"

I nodded, picking up on her meaning. "For my homeworld? Yes. Now and then. But I don't think I've ever seen it, not so I'd stake my life on it."

"It was Mazarile, weren't it?"

"Yes."

"Sounds a pretty place."

"It wasn't, not really. Just a brown rock with some green bits. Too dark and dowdy to show across more than a few thousand leagues. Our parents moved there when they couldn't afford to stay somewhere nicer, down in the Sunwards, and I don't think it ever really felt like home to them."

"Is your parents both back there?"

"No... not exactly. Our mother died quite a long time ago. She got sick when one of those illnesses swept through the worlds, and we didn't have enough money to get a good doctor or go to the aliens. Maybe they couldn't have helped her—"

"And your father?" Surt asked sharply, cutting across my ruminations.

Something in me went as tight as rigging under a full spread of sail. Since we'd taken over the running of this ship, my sister and I had both had to deal with some difficult changes. Her being what she'd become, and me being what I'd been on the way to becoming, thanks to the unpleasantnesses that had been visited on me in the kindness room. For the most part, we squared up and discussed these things openly, at least between ourselves. Given that we'd once got to a point where I had a knife to her throat, talking was the only way to rebuild the trust we'd shared since childhood.

But even then, even after all this healthy openness, Father was a subject I dared not go near.

"Which tube were you using when you saw the flash?"

Surt blinked at my non-answer, but she was clever enough

not to poke at that subject. "It was this one, Adrana," she said, swivelling one of the tubes around, thumbing open the cover on its eyepiece.

"It's plausible, I think. The optics on all of 'em are all top-notch, and the mirrors nicely silvered, but she must have had that one re-calibrated quite recently. I wouldn't mind betting it's one of the best sighting pieces on any ship anywhere in the Congregation."

"Pity she couldn't think of anything pleasant to do with it, 'cept butcherin'."

"She did have her character flaws," I said, smiling so that she understood that my understatement was most certainly ironic. "But at least she had excellent taste in equipment."

Until recently our ship had belonged to a woman called Bosa Sennen. Bosa had called her ship *Dame Scarlet,* but among her enemies it had long earned a second, nearly official designation: the *Nightjammer.* It was by way of allusion to both its favoured haunts, in the darkness beyond the worlds, and the blackness of its hull and sails. Bosa employed it to hunt down other crews, stealing their prizes and murdering their crews, save the very few that she took for her own purposes. She had done this for much longer than an ordinary lifetime, because Bosa Sennen was as much an idea as a person—an idea that could attach itself to an individual, to use or be used by that individual, before moving onto someone else.

Less than a year ago, Bosa had made the first of two serious errors. She had stalked and taken a ship, the *Monetta's Mourn,* on which my sister and I were serving: our first time away from Mazarile, and our first experience on any such ship. Arafura had escaped but I had not, and Bosa only decided to use me rather than kill me because of my skill with bones. So she had taken me aboard the *Nightjammer* and started turning me to her ways, using psychological, chemical and electrical methods of torture, coercion and personality-adjustment.

Months later, she had made her second error. She had gone after another crew and tried to take them, not knowing it was a trap put together by Arafura. My sister's plan had been ruthless and clever. She had saved me and captured Bosa, and between us—and her crew—we had gained control of the *Nightjammer*, making it ours.

A new ship needed a new name, and so we gave it one.

*Revenger.*

It had been ours for three months; three long months which took us from one year into the next, and because the old year had been 1799, and the new one was 1800—eighteen hundred years since the documented founding of the Thirteenth Occupation—it was a new year as bright and shiny as a hatpin and felt like the propitious time to be starting a fresh enterprise. We were going to make something of ourselves. Not as butchers or pirates, but as honest privateers—those who wanted to remain in this life, at least, rather than going back to our homeworlds. Exactly who wanted what was yet undecided—and not much spoken of. But whatever our decisions, collective or personal, there was no possibility of just waltzing back into the busy commerce of the Congregation.

We would be shot to splinters at the first glimpse.

The problem was, we knew what we were, and what our new ship had become. But the rest of civilisation was not yet reliably acquainted with the facts. As far as the other ships and captains were concerned, and so far as the rich worlds, cartels and banking concerns behind the organised expeditions knew, Bosa Sennen was still alive and active. It would take more than just a helpful transmission from us to set things straight—especially as Bosa had a long record of just that sort of duplicity.

So for three months we'd had no choice but to skulk.

In truth, the time was usefully spent. First we had to learn how to operate *Revenger*, and that took weeks—plenty of them. We had to hook what was left of our old family tutor and mentor into the nerves of the ship, Paladin's robot mind gradually taking control of the navigation, sail-gear and weapons. Then we had to keep up our basic stocks of consumable materials, including fuel, and that meant cracking a few easy baubles, going into them and scooping out such treasures as remained unplundered. We had done so, and proven that we could operate the ship and function as a crew. But still, every time we took the launch back from the surface of a bauble, we were reminded what our ship looked like from the outside.

A predator.

A black-hulled, black-sailed monstrosity, cruel in her lines and entirely incapable of being mistaken for anything but the *Nightjammer.* We meant to change her disposition, but that would take time, and for now we dared not be too hasty about it. If someone did chance upon us, even in these dark, distant orbits, and made a decision about us, then we might require all the weapons presently available, merely for our own self-defence.

Thus we loathed Bosa, while at the same time being cynically grateful for the quality of the fittings she had left us.

Her long-range telescopes were the equal of anything in any museum on Mazarile, and certainly superior to the optical instruments on the *Monetta's Mourn*, which was itself very well equipped. They were properly cared for, too. Their tubes had engravings on, their leather-work was still fine and black, and the movable gaskets—where they pierced the glass bubble of the sighting room—were still tight against vacuum and nicely lubricated. There were many tubes too, clustered together with their eyepieces aimed back at us like the point-blank muzzles of a firing squad.

Surt ventured: "Do you really think it was sail-flash?"

"I think it more than possible." I pressed my eye to the lens and worked the focus dial. "If there is a ship stalking us out here—or at least trying to get close enough to this bauble to jump our claim—then her captain will be doing her utmost to control the disposition of her sails, with respect to the Old Sun, while not caring to cast light in our direction. But sometimes it can't be avoided." To begin with I swept the scope quite widely, picking up the red glimmer of the bauble around which we were orbiting, and I considered the chances that some of that glimmer might have got caught up in the optics and thrown a confusing trick of light across Surt's eyepiece. It wasn't that likely, I decided. The optics were good and Surt would have needed to be staring almost directly at the bauble to pick up any of its blush.

Satisfied that the answer lay elsewhere, I swept the scope back and forth along a narrower arc, patrolling the area in which Surt thought she had seen the flash. "Or it could be something else. Space debris, or a flash from a rogue navigation mirror that's drifted free of the main commerce routes. Or it could be a hundred other things, none of which are of consequence."

"I should've taken more pains to note down the position when I saw the flash."

"You did all that you could, Surt. The main thing was to bring the matter to my attention, which you did."

"You've always been kind to me, Adrana."

"We're all just trying to do our best."

"I know, and I think Fura knows it too, but she can be sharp with me when I get things wrong."

"Pay no heed." I adjusted the sighting angle again. "Without you, we'd still be trying to get Paladin to speak again, never mind run this ship. Arafura knows that perfectly well."

"Would she like it better if I called her Arafura, do you think? Only I thought Fura was the name she preferred."

"It is. I think she believes it more suited to her current calling. Shorter and harder."

"Like Bosa," Surt said, pleased with herself for making this connection.

"No," I answered firmly. "Not like that. *Never* like that."

"I didn't mean no disrespect, Adrana. There I go, getting things wrong again. I'd be better off shutting my gob completely. And keeping away from pens and paper. All I ever leave is a mess of smudges."

"You're serving this crew, Surt, and serving it capably."

I vowed not to be too harsh on her for failing to record her observation. Only a little while since, Surt had been unable to read or write, and the use of pens and log books was still not second nature to her. When I checked over the observational watches, hers were the blemished, crossed-out and incomplete entries.

She was becoming more proficient, though, and needed no chastisement from me. Not when we were hardly spoilt for spare hands.

"Do you see anything?" she asked expectantly, as I switched from one eyepiece to another.

"Nothing," I said, when I had swept a few more sectors. "I don't doubt your sighting, not for a second. But I don't think we need trouble Fura on the basis of a single flash." I had used my sister's shortened name deliberately, thinking it might put Surt better at ease, and had made a private decision that I would try and think of her by the same means. "Perhaps, when we have what we've come for, and are debating our next course, I'll mention it to her in passing. But there'll be no slight on your actions."

"I hope not. I don't really mind that sharp tongue of hers… but that's just words. There's a wrong side of her I never want to see."

"Nor do any of us," I said under my breath.

*

Our launch broke away from its berthing rack with a jolt and slipped neatly between the teeth of the upper and lower jaws of *Revenger*'s maw and into clear space. Through the portal I watched the jaws hinge shut on the red-lit docking bay, the only light and colour for millions of leagues. Until Fura touched the jets and sent out a pulse of rocket thrust, lighting up the hull in brassy highlights, that sharp-toothed grin was the only part of the ship to be seen.

She used the rockets sparingly, knowing we were low on chemical reserves. From my seat behind her control position I watched her with a quiet, sisterly admiration. She had come a long way since Captain Rackamore took us up in his launch for the first time, at my instigation.

"And you're sure no one will have cleaned the place out before we got here?" she asked, twisting around in her seat for a second before snapping her attention back onto the controls.

"Sure as I can be," Prozor said, sitting opposite me, clutching her notebook—scrawled full of her bauble maps and auguries and reminders to herself—as well as a very expensive pocket chronometer, which she had in the other hand, her thumb clicking down on the starting and stopping buttons as if she needed reassurance that they still worked. "Rack came back here over and over, and there was never any sign of anyone else showin' interest. Mainly 'cause there wasn't much worth salvagin', at least not in the shallow layers, and there never was time to go deeper. Not even for a crew on their game, like we most definitely was."

Slowly the bauble came round in the nose windows of the launch. It was hard to see, even though we were less than twenty leagues out. The field was still up, cloaking the lump of rock, but unlike some we had seen it was gauzy and dim, like a layer of smoke clinging to the rock's surface.

"The question I'm stuck with," Strambli said, "is what this place is worth to us, if no one but Rackamore ever bothered with it. You just said there's no treasure here." She was exercising her fingers, squeezing on a little contraption made of springs and metal.

"Depends what you mean by treasure," Fura said, craning around to look at Strambli. "My book, treasure's whatever a cove needs most in the here and now. Don't matter whether it's a million years old or a month, it's the immediate value that counts. All the gold in the Congregation's no use to someone gasping on their last drop of lungstuff. We ain't in that boat just yet. But what we do need badly is fuel."

"Rack used this place as a supply drop," Prozor said, looking around at the rest of us besides Fura, which amounted to Strambli and myself. Just the bare minimum for an expedition into a bauble, with Surt and Tindouf staying behind on the main ship. Paladin counted as crew as well, I suppose, but none of us were in the habit of thinking of him in quite that way. "Propellant for his launch. A handsome stockpile. Rack's philosophy was to run a light ship—minimal armour, minimal armaments. And a nice, lean crew, so we didn't have to split a prize too many ways. He didn't want to be luggin' a hold full of rocket fuel around, so the *Monetta* only ever carried just enough to do the job, Rack always knowin' he could come back to the Rumbler when he needed a top-up."

"So we're using up precious fuel," Strambli said, frowning so hard she made her lopsided face even less symmetrical. "In order to get more fuel."

"Not so hard to get your grey around," Fura said, directing a fond if exasperated smile at our Opener. "Like depositing a quoin in a bank, so it'll turn into two quoins."

"I'd thank you not to mention banks," Prozor said, rarely missing a chance to remind us that she had lost her savings in the crash of ninety-nine.

"You'd need a lot of faith in banks to deposit your last quoin," Strambli muttered. "Which is what that fuel is to us."

"It isn't," Fura said. "Not by a good margin. But we do need more propellant, and if we've got to burn some to get our mitts on Rack's stockpile, so be it." She directed her glowy face at Prozor and me. "Besides, I'd say it's *our* stockpile now, wouldn't you? We're the last of Rack's crew, so it's not as if any other cove has a better claim on this place than us."

"I suppose not," I said.

"We'll get in fast," she was already saying, while working the controls, steering us nearer to the bauble. "Take as much as we need, and no more. What made sense for Rack makes sense for us, too. Agreed, Prozor?"

"No truer thing ever said," Prozor answered, which was her way of managing to sound equivocal. She snapped shut her bauble book, did up the fancy clasps as if she had no expectation of ever needing to open it again between now and the last gasp of the Old Sun. "Usual margins, I take it?"

"However Rack liked to play it," Fura said.

"Well, Rack had a few advantages we lack," Prozor said, meaning (if I knew her at all) a crew he'd picked by hand, rather than one that had been shoved together by chance, but she left the rest of her statement tactfully unvoiced. "Usual margins'll cut it. The rest of us, we may as well finish gettin' suited." She gave a squint to her chronometer. "We've got five minutes until field drop."

So far so practical, and we'd already donned most of our vacuum gear, apart from the helmets and final connections. We'd inherited a very capable ship, full of fine equipment, but you wouldn't have guessed it from the motley look of our party. Our suits were a jumble of parts, brown and rust-coloured alloys cut and welded together with care and attention, but not much thought as to whether the final result was pretty to the eye. We were ugly and lumpy, like the contents of a junk shop thrown together in the approximate shapes of people. Why didn't we use some fancy suits that Bosa had left us? Because there weren't any, or rather there weren't any that were suitable for this sort of work. Bosa didn't soil her hands scrabbling through baubles. She let other crews have the pleasure of that, and then jumped them for their pickings. Bosa had left us some handsome black vacuum suits, but they were for boarding and gutting other vessels, leaving us to salvage our mongrel gear from the hulk of the *Queen Crimson*, Captain Trusko's ship.

We checked each other's suits, locking down helmets, tightening faceplates, making sure all the hoses and seals were secure, swinging our arms and legs, making squatting and flapping motions. Strambli went around with a little squirt-can, dribbling oil into the moving parts. I worked my gloves until my fingers bled inside them. We checked the suit-to-suit squawk, me giving a thump to the side of Prozor's helmet until she came through clearly. Fura was still operating the launch, but she allowed herself to be fussed over from her seated position, stretching out an arm like a queen expecting to be kissed on the fingers. It was her right arm in this instance, which was mechanical from the forearm down to the fingertips. She would wear a normal pressure gauntlet on the other hand, but on the tin one she had a pressure-tight cuff around the elbow, keeping her metal hand free of any encumberment and allowing her to touch and sense things in vacuum with a great discrimination. The cuff was bothersome and hard for her to adjust, so Strambli was checking it for pressure integrity.

Prozor examined her timepiece again. "One minute," she said, this time coming over the squawk, so that her voice sounded distant and near at the same time, because there was still atmosphere in the launch.

Fura slowed us down for the final approach. It was like a restless, sooty sea down there, blanketing the world beneath. The field was fidgeting around, growing tenuous in places. Bits of the surface began to show through, prickly with jagged, upright rock formations, like the quills of some armoured animal.

"Thirty seconds," Prozor said. "Maintain descent rate."

"Don't look like it's quite ready to pop," Strambli ventured.

"It will," I said, knowing how unlikely it was that Prozor would have made an error in her auguries.

In the last fifteen or twenty seconds the field seemed to shiver, and that shivering sped-up like the flicker from a coin spinning on the table, that fast whirlygig flutter just before the coin topples over. That was the death song of a field, and when it went it went instantly, just vanishing, so that what was below was now just an uncloaked rock, spines sticking out all over, bristling from pole to pole.

It was dark. One side was facing the Empty, the other the Old Sun. We were ten million leagues beyond the outer orbits of the Congregation, so that the Old Sun's light had already fought its way through the gaps between thousands of worlds—millions, more likely—growing a little dimmer and wearier with each exchange. When that light flopped onto the bauble like an exhausted traveller, about all it could do was daub a few red and purple highlights across those quills, hinting at the gloomy secrets trapped between their roots. On the side facing the Empty—where the only dependable illumination was that from the distant stars, too far away for any monkey mind to comprehend, even those of us who've ventured as far out as Trevenza Reach, the bauble was nearly as black as *Revenger*'s own sails.

"Do you see anything you recognise?" Fura asked, directing her question at Prozor.

Prozor had started one of the stopwatch dials on her timepiece, measuring out the hours from the moment of field drop. "Drift north. That clump of spikes over there is a landmark."

"They all look the same," Strambli said.

"Not to me," Prozor answered.

Fura levelled us out just above the tops of the spines. I looked over her metal-clad shoulders at the fuel gauges, watching the needles twitch every time she had to use a pulse of thrust to stop us drifting in too close. Prozor had already told us there was a swallower inside the Rumbler, which added to our difficulties, especially as we were going to be hauling out heavy reserves of propellant.

"Keep talkin', Proz," Fura said.

"Take us lower. Cut between that pair of spikes."

"Won't be much clearance."

"No more'n we need. Our launch ain't any bigger than the one Rack used, and he squeezed through any number of times."

"Take your word for it," she said, and although I could only see the back of her helmeted head, I imagined her biting on her tongue as she concentrated hard.

We slid between the spikes, angling down. It got darker, shadows criss-crossing until they squeezed out the last, meagre traces of light. Fura turned on the launch's own lamps. Yellow beams crossed vacuum and danced across the swelling roots of those stony spines.

"I see the landing zone," Prozor said. "Dead ahead. Hold this descent and you'll be golden."

"Why's this place called the Rumbler, anyway?" Strambli asked.

"Adrana," Fura said, turning to me. "Call out the heights, please."

"Why, certainly," I mouthed, moving to the side of her console, where I was able to read the slowly revolving digits of the altimeter. The instrument was similar to the sweeper on *Revenger*, only instead of whirring around it pinged pulses straight at the ground, measuring the delay before they bounced back. "One hundred spans," I said, when the digits hit that round number. "Ninety. Eighty."

Something buzzed on the console, a red light flashing. Fura snarled.

I recognised that light. Fuel warning.

"Don't tell me you cut it that fine," I whispered.

"No point going home if we don't find Rack's stockpile," Fura replied, in the same low voice.

"I can't believe—"

"Maintain those call-outs, sister."

I wanted to snap back at her for voicing her request as if it were a demand, but since I was just as keen for us not to crash as Fura, I forced myself to swallow my pride and intone the numbers.

"Sixty."

"Lateral drift," Prozor said.

Fura nodded. "Correcting."

"Fifty spans," I said through dry lips. "Forty."

Fura worked another control. From the belly of the launcher came a clunk and whirr as it put out its spidery landing legs, too delicate and cumbersome to be deployed before now. Now the stutter from our engines was lighting up more and more of our surroundings, the spikes rising up around us like the huge, petrified trees of some fairytale forest.

"Backwash," Fura said. "Transitioning to landing jets."

"Steady as she goes," Prozor said.

"Twenty spans," I called out. "Ten... five..."

The landing area came up fast, a flat circle of blasted stone, scorched by multiple rocket exhausts. The legs were the first to touch, springing down to absorb some of our momentum.

"Contact light," Fura said, as another indication lit up. "Motors stop."

The launch settled down on its legs, landing belly-down. The engine rumble died away, leaving only the hiss and puff of our breathing mechanisms, the leathery bellows squeezing in and out.

The red fuel warning light was still flashing. Only now that we were down and stopped did Fura reach over and flick her finger against it, making it turn off.

"Faulty indicator," she said, turning around with a big grin on her face. "You didn't think I was *that* desperate, did you?"

Through the barred-over window of my faceplate I smiled tightly. "Sometimes I wonder."

"How much time, Proz?"

Prozor's visor tipped down to study her timepiece. "Six hours, eleven minutes."

Fura pushed back her control seat, rising from the console. "Then we'd best not stand around bumpin' our gums, had we?"

We helped Fura complete the last of her suit checks, gathered our equipment—we were all carrying something, not just Strambli with her particular box of tricks for getting through doors and other sundry obstructions—and then went through the launch's airlock in pairs, which was the most it could take at a time.

When there were four of us outside we stood next to the launch, swivelling around with our helmet lamps on to get a better view of things. The launch only just fitted on the landing zone, hemmed in by the roots of the rocky spines, their tops lost to darkness. The level ground under our feet was new, which was to say it wasn't more than a few centuries old, rather than the millions of years that this bauble had been ticking around the Old Sun. Some other captain had put it there, making it easier to come and go.

"What was that?" Strambli asked.

We'd all felt it, too. Like a little shudder going through the ground under our feet, there and gone almost before we had time to notice it.

"Reason it's called the Rumbler," Fura said. "That's some sort of deep activity which—I'm reliably informed—ain't anything we need to poke our noses into. Right, Proz?"

"Right. We'll keep to the shallow levels. What goes on under 'em isn't our concern. They say it's the swallower, getting fidgety in its magnetic cradle."

"If I never see a swallower up close, that'll suit me just fine," Strambli said.

None of us contradicted that sentiment, especially not Prozor.

# 2

We set off.

At one end of the landing area was a steep ramp leading down into the surface of the bauble, with a doorway at one end of it. The aforementioned swallower was putting out half a gee at the surface, which sounds very little if you've spent your entire existence on a civilised world like Mazarile, Graubund or Metherick. You might imagine we were bouncing around like puppies, hardly feeling the weight of our suits.

It wasn't like that at all.

In the three months since we took *Revenger,* we'd only set foot outside that ship to visit baubles, and only a couple of them had swallowers. The rest of the time we'd been floating around inside the main ship, hardly weighing a feather. Even when she was under sail or on full ions, *Revenger* never got above a few hundredths of a gee, which was just enough to be a nuisance but not enough to give your bones and muscles any sort of trial. Now, Surt—who was back aboard the main ship—knew her way around the medicine cabinet, and there were pills and potions that could keep our hearts from getting too lazy, or our bones from crumbling away like stale biscuits.

But the short time we had spent under the press of the launch's rockets had been no sort of preparation for surface operations.

By the time we grunted and shuffled our way to the bottom of that ramp I was sweating like a horse. We weren't even inside.

One consolation was that the door into the bauble was open, exactly as Prozor had promised. The frame was a heavy arch of stone-coloured metal, marked with black symbols and with controls and indicators set into recesses up and down both sides. Those symbols meant nothing to me. There might have been thirteen Occupations—thirteen times since the Sundering when people had spread out and made homes in the worlds of the Congregation. But some of those civilisations had been thousands of years long, sufficient for many languages to come and go just within a single Occupation.

Conventionally, it was an Assessor's business to know the ancient tongues and scripts. But we were presently lacking a full-time crewmate in that position, which meant that such work fell to our Bauble Reader or Scanner, Prozor, who had been around the worlds long enough to be able to double as Assessor or Opener in a pinch.

"Eighth Occupation," she said. "Time of the Two-Headed Princes, I think. Turbulent's the word for them days. Baubles were starting to pop open left, right and centre and everyone was making a scramble for loot and power. Lots of lawlessness, lots of wars and revolutions, in just that one Occupation."

"So we just...walk through, is that it?" Strambli was asking, before any of us had crossed the dark threshold of the doorway. She was about to act on that statement, stretching a hand into the gap.

"Wait," Prozor said, and reached to pick at something on the left side of the frame.

"What?" Fura asked.

"Just checkin' this is still in place. Which it is." She was pinching something between her fingers, too small or fine for me to make out. "Rack stretched a line of riggin' across the door, criss-crossed from top to bottom. Did you cotton onto it?"

"No," Strambli said, sounding slightly put-out.

"That's the idea. Wouldn't have known if you'd broken it, either. But Rack would."

"So he'd know if anyone'd trespassed, while he was away," I said, nodding and thinking that Bosa wouldn't have been averse to a similar trick. Except in her case—if I had learned anything during my time as her protégée—the thread would have been rigged to set off a bomb or weapon.

You could never be too particular, in baubles.

"Any other little mementos Rack might have left us?" I asked, as we filed through the door.

"No, just that one—and it nearly slipped my grey, too." Prozor pulled a gadget from her belt, a thing the size of a thick thumb, and passed it to me. "But this didn't. Clamp your lamps on that. Surt helped me lash it up from the gubbins we pulled from the *Queenie*."

"It's meant to mean something, is it?"

"Short-range squawk localiser. When we're near the supply—assuming old Proz hasn't forgotten the frequencies—it ought to start flashin'. There's a transmitter stashed in with the fuel, where your average thievin' cove wouldn't think to look. Rack didn't want anyone lootin' his drop to get too far with it."

I stared down at the cobbled-together device, which was doing a perfectly creditable job of looking totally dead.

"Then we're in trouble, aren't we?"

"Have some faith, girlie."

The doorway led into a sort of corridor, sloping gently into the bauble. We lost squawk contact with the main ship as soon as we ventured a few paces into it, but Prozor said that was to be expected, and nothing out of the usual for baubles.

There were alcoves on both sides, with plinths where statues had once stood. They were all gone now, except for some rubble and a handful that were so pitifully broken they were not worth the trouble of moving. From what we could see of the remains, picked out with our helmet lamps, they were all soldiers, dressed in scaly armour, their hands clutching invisible armaments.

We carried on down. I looked at the localiser, willing it to light up. But so far there was nothing.

The rumble came again, just as it had before. I thought of the swallower having some sort of indigestion, grumbling as it wolfed something down. Swallowers were not meant to swallow anything once they were chained and harnessed in the middle of worlds, but occasionally things shook loose and fell into them, and once in a while that could start a chain-reaction that reduced a whole little kingdom to hot rubble as the swallower gorged, getting fatter and heavier.

"This isn't looking too encouraging," I said, eyeing the still-dead localiser.

"It was just a precautionary measure," she said, breezily. "And maybe I did get them frequencies muddled around. My noggin's had a few leaks in it since Bosa put a fresh dent in my skull..."

The device started flashing.

"Prozor," I said.

"...or Jusquerel swapped 'em without tellin' me, or the juice has drained out of Rack's transmitter, or..."

"Prozor," I said, firmer this time.

"What's it say?" Fura asked, leaning over.

There was a pattern of lights on the top of the thumb, a fat central one and a ring of smaller ones around it. The main one was flashing the brightest, but one of the outer ones was giving off a faint pulse as well, pointing down the corridor.

"We're on the right scent is what it says," Prozor said. "And there was you all doubtin'—"

"Keep walking," Fura said, cutting her off.

I kept the thumb raised up in front of me, the lights flickering in and out now and then, but generally getting brighter and steadier as we got near the base of the corridor. As the floor levelled off we went through another arched doorway like the first, and then we stepped into a much larger chamber, too big for our lamps to illuminate. We paused for a few moments then carried on walking, our labouring bellows the only sounds coming through our squawk receivers.

"This is the place," Prozor said.

Fura turned to our Opener. "Light it up, Strambli."

Strambli opened a little box on her belt and reached in as daintily as anyone could while wearing vacuum gloves. She pinched out a light-imp, a star-shaped thing about the size of a marble, then held it up before her with a sort of fond regret before squeezing it. The stellate object shattered and a flicker of light played between Strambli's fingers until she stepped back and the flicker stayed where it was, suspended. It wavered and got brighter, pushing out a fierce yellow light that quickly exceeded the contribution from our lamps. The yellow light flooded the chamber, brightening all the while.

Strambli had let the light-imp off between us, so our own shadows produced hard spokes which reached all the way to the walls. We shuffled around as the yellow light wavered and danced.

The room was circular, with a domed ceiling. It was at least twice as wide as the landing zone on the surface, with more alcoves around the rim—a few holding toppled or broken soldiers but most of them empty. Above the alcoves were long inscriptions in the same ancient language as the doorway we'd entered through.

I paused to take it all in.

I had been thinking about the deep antiquity of things almost constantly since we had taken to this new life among the worlds and baubles, pondering numberless aeons and the thin scratches of civilisation we have made against that vaster darkness. I had spoken to Paladin of the things he had seen, and pored over the learned histories and charts, trying to reach a point where such contemplation left me feeling settled and comfortable, rather than dizzy and bereft. But I could not—the means was not within me.

Somewhere out beyond the Empty there now shone stars that had been born in gas clouds after this room was decorated. There were stars that had been alive then that were just corpses now, if they had left the least trace of themselves. There was just too much past, too much time that had already happened, and our lives were as nothing against that endless black conveyor belt, ceaselessly rolling, stretching and stretching ever further backward into a dread eternity.

If any person were to say that they stood in such a place and did not feel the abyssal press of those discarded ages, I can state with confidence that they were either lying or deluded.

"Um, Prozor," Strambli said, coughing a little delicately. "This is the place, isn't it?"

"This is the place," Prozor said. Then, with a bit less assurance: "It has to be."

"Then where the hell is my fuel?" Fura demanded, almost breaking into a shout. "If it isn't in this room, and there's only one way in and out of this room..."

"That thread on the door wasn't infallible," I said. "Someone could have put it back the same way after they left."

"No. The localiser's still picking up a signal," Prozor said. "If some cove pilfered the fuel, they'd have pilfered the transmitter as well."

The light-imp was still giving off its yellow radiance, hovering in the vacuum like an obliging fairy. I could understand Strambli's reluctance to crush it. Light-imps were often found in baubles, but they weren't so common as to be worthless.

"There's another doorway," I said quietly, because I had only just noticed it for myself, and none of the others were directing their gazes in the same direction. "Between those alcoves, it's darker than the others. There's a way out of here."

"Deeper into the bauble, you mean," Strambli said.

"Deeper into the bauble, yes," I answered.

"That door was always sealed," Prozor said. "We never opened it, never went through it, never even tried opening it. Rack never had cause—this place was only ever a supply drop to him. All the rumours said it had already been cleaned out of anything valuable."

I walked over to the black aperture between two of the alcoves, compelled to inspect it though every bone in me was screaming otherwise.

"You got a fix?" Fura asked, as I waggled the thumb back and forth.

"Not exactly. Could be under us, it could be off to one side behind those walls. What's clear is that it wants us to go down that shaft. Are those gouge marks in the floor?"

Prozor came over to join me, bending down to shine her lamp over the patterns. "Not gouged," she said. "It's metal, scraped off the fuel bottles." She knelt down carefully, knee-joints squirting oil as they compressed. "Flecks of paint, too." She looked at a chip of colour perched on her fingertip like a petal. "Can't be too far away, or the localiser wouldn't snag it."

"I don't like it," Strambli said.

"You ain't *paid* to like it," Fura retorted, which was rich considering that none of us were on anything that could be called a regular schedule of payments. "If cracking baubles was easy, any monkey'd do it. We're here precisely 'cause it ain't easy. Proz: how much time's left?"

Prozor inspected her timepiece. "Five hours, on the nose."

It had taken us an hour to shuffle this far. Any crew could take a risk once or twice and not be punished for it, but going in and out of baubles over and over demanded restraint as well as fortitude. Crews that aspired to be long-lived as well as profitable always allowed as much time to exit a bauble as they spent getting in, plus a handsome margin to allow for fatigue and equipment failure. More still if they planned to lug loot out of a gravity well.

"Then we go deeper," Fura said, making a clenching gesture. "That fuel wasn't just sitting here, minding its own business, waiting to be claimed. It was put here by Rack, 'cause it belonged to him, and now it belongs to me."

"And by 'me,'" I said, "you mean 'us.' Just so there's no confusion."

"We ain't equipped," Strambli protested. "Not properly. We ought to come back, with winches and ropes and anything else we might need."

As Fura gave a shake of her head behind the barred-over window of her helmet, the glowy made it easy to see her face. It was flaring brighter than usual, stoked by her anger and indignation, producing catlike stripes around her nose and brow. "We'll burn more fuel doing that, and sit around for three months waiting for the next window." She turned around on her heels, looking at each of us in turn. "Have you all forgotten who we are? This is the crew that took down Bosa Sennen—the crew that cracked the Fang! And we're getting our drawers in a twist about a little stroll down a tunnel?"

"We are going to need that fuel eventually," I said, admitting it to myself as much as to anyone else.

"What a surprise," Strambli muttered, shaking her head. "The Ness sisters agreein' with each other, when it suits 'em."

"Only they do have a point," Prozor said. "And since I used to crew with the man who stashed the fuel here, the cove who never took nothing that didn't belong to him, I also can't help taking it sort of personal."

I confess that I took exception to the idea of someone else pilfering it, too. For those of us who had known Rackamore—and I counted that association a privilege, even though our acquaintance had not been lengthy—this injustice was a grave personal slight. It would hamper us, too. *Revenger* hardly needed fuel, provided its sails and ion-emitters were in tolerable order. A big, delicate ship like ours seldom wandered close enough to a gravity well to do itself harm.

But to visit baubles, as well as trade with the settled worlds, a crew needed a launch, a little runabout with rocket motors, and those motors gobbled up propellant like it was going out of fashion.

We could have argued about whether or not to split up the party, but in the end we stuck together, moving away from the wavering glow of the light-imp and into the dark. Now it was just our lamps again, and our shadows pushing ahead of us, and long rows of alcoves and broken soldiers, stretching down and down. But on the floor, unmistakably, were lines of scratched metal and paint where our fuel had been dragged, and none too cleverly.

We let the thumb lead us on. That corridor went down and down, getting steeper in places. I visualised the way we had come as a sort of dog-leg with the empty chamber in the middle, and now we were about twice as far underground as at the start. The localiser's lights were starting to point off to one side, almost back the way we'd come, except horizontally.

The rumble came again, shortly before we reached the end of the corridor. It felt stronger, as if we were closer to the swallower. We were, too, but only a tiny distance compared to the size of the bauble. Now that rumble was starting to make me think of the snoring of some big coiled monster, sleeping in its cave while we tried to creep around it.

"Rack had some funny ideas about the best places to leave his hard-earned," I said.

I was still pondering the decisions that had brought Captain Rackamore to his inglorious end when we came out into a huge sort of tunnel, too big to be properly called a corridor. Strambli dug out another of those precious light-imps and, after some muttered misgivings, cracked it open. In its hovering, wavering light we took in our surroundings. The size of the first chamber had been impressive enough after that long corridor, but this was something else again, and for a few moments none of us could find any words that seemed worth the bother of uttering.

The tunnel was perfectly circular, like a drainpipe. We had come out of a doorway set into the curvature of the wall, almost at the lowest point where it formed a floor. The ceiling was about eighty spans above us, so even if we had made a tower of ourselves, each standing on the shoulder of the one below, we wouldn't have reached much more than halfway up.

What was almost more striking than the height of that tunnel was the way it stretched away in either direction, curving down ever so slightly as it diminished, until swallowed up by darkness. I guessed, without needing to do the mathematics (which would have been knotty, without a pen and paper) that the tunnel went all the way around the bauble before joining up with itself again.

Unlike the corridor, the tunnel lacked any alcoves or ornamentation. It gleamed back at us with a sort of oily sheen, the walls unbroken by any doorway except the one behind us and another, much further along, just at the point where the shadows took over. We could all see that doorway, a fair stroll from where we had emerged, and the thumb clearly telling us *that* was the way to head.

"How long?" Fura asked, breaking that long silence.

"Four hours, thirty-three," Prozor said. "And from what I know of us and our suits, we'll need twenty minutes to huff and puff our way to that door, never mind what's on the other side of it."

"We can still make it," Fura said.

Prozor laid a hand on her shoulder, before she started striding off. "That's as maybe, girlie, but I still suggest we plant ourselves here, just for a while."

"Why?" Fura asked.

"Because…I've got a hunch and I don't much care for it. Those rumbles were always here when we came before, but they were under us and faint and Rackamore never needed us to go any deeper. But now I've taken the bother of timin' 'em, which is what I should've done long ago, timin' being second nature to a Bauble Reader."

"Go on," Fura said, willing to let her speak.

"They come too regular-like to be the swallower, unless it's doin' something that swallowers never do. Once every thirty-eight minutes. And you'll notice it got stronger, the closer we got to this tube. I reckon there's a reason for that."

"Something's coming around," I said, looking up and down the darkening length of the tunnel with a new foreboding. "In this pipe, or whatever it is. That's what you think's happening."

"Maybe I'm wrong. I'd like to be. But I figured it wouldn't do us too much harm to wait and see what happens in…" Prozor glanced down at her timepiece again. "About seventeen minutes, now, I reckon."

"We'd have had time to reach that door," Fura said.

"Or maybe we wouldn't," I said, reminding myself that although she had rescued me, and put herself through a great deal of nastiness to do so, I was still meant to be her older and wiser sister.

"I've heard of baubles with things like this in 'em," Prozor said. "Just never run into one myself, or for that matter met a cove who has. Rat-runs, they call them."

"Ain't we lucky you remembered now, and not when we're halfway to that door," Fura said.

"It was the rumbles that set me thinkin' it over. These rat-runs, most of the time they're not workin' as they were meant to. The things that go around, they get jammed up, stuck fast. Means the tunnel's blocked at a certain point, but all that means is that you might need to go the long way round."

"But not this one," Strambli said.

We were still standing on the floor of the tunnel, the light-imp wavering.

"Seventeen minutes, we could still do it," Fura said.

"On Mazarile," I said, "when the trains were coming into Incer Station, they'd make a big breeze ahead of them. You'd see rubbish moving, and newspapers, and the hems of dresses would start fluttering, and ladies would reach up to hold their hats in place, and then you'd get a big warm draught of wind as the train was approaching. And that's without the sound. But there'll be none of that here. No warning, 'cause there isn't any lungstuff here. No breeze, no rubbish. No sound, unless you count that rumble. That thing's going to come around the bend and our first sight of it will be too late."

"I never had you down as the cautious one of us."

"If caution had anything to do with it," I answered my sister, "I wouldn't be within a million leagues of a bauble in the first place. But now that we're here, I do quite like staying alive, while there's a choice."

Fura gave a grunt, plainly disappointed in me, but my view prevailed over hers and we squeezed back into the last part of the sloping corridor, with just our heads inching out into the wider volume of the tunnel.

"We don't even know which way to look," Strambli complained.

"Toss a quoin," Fura said.

"I want to see it," Strambli answered. And I understood her perfectly. Anything that happened in a bauble—anything that you survived, anyway—was a useful experience, doubly so if you ran into something a little out of the commonplace. More than useful: remunerative. You could sell that intelligence to other crews, to start with, but even if you chose not to, you would always know what you had seen or done, and it would do no harm at all to your reputation.

"We ought to divide it up," I said, smiling Strambli's way. "Prozor and me looking left, Fura and Strambli right. When one of us says something, the others can look. But wind your necks in swiftish. If that thing trundles around the circumference of this bauble once every... how long did you say, Proz?"

"Thirty-eight minutes. Of which eleven are remainin'."

"Then it isn't going for a nice stroll in the park. I reckon it's going to be moving about exactly as fast as a train."

Little more needed to be said in the minutes left to us. Prozor kept up a running countdown, telling us when it was down to two minutes, one minute, thirty seconds, fifteen, and then—collectively, I think—we all stopped breathing, just for the interval. Two of us gawping one way, two of us the other.

In the end it was Prozor and I who had the first sight of it.

In my mind's eye I had been thinking of something like a flat-faced train, a sort of blank piston, filling the tunnel from side to side and bottom to top. In the event, I could not have been further from the mark. The rumbling thing was simply a big ball, covered in mottled metallic patches, rolling toward us. It was eighty spans in diameter—one of the grand old mansions on Jauncery Road would have rattled around inside it with room to spare.

A big, rolling thing like that ought to slow down eventually,

I found myself musing. There might not be pressure inside the bauble, but the ball was rolling along inside the corridor and there must have been bits of it scraping against the walls all the time. Its surface was rough-looking, not smooth-polished like a ball bearing. Over time, by all that was right and proper, it should have ground to a halt. Yet something was evidently keeping it going, whether in the ball itself or in the corridor, some sly force that compensated for the meagre increment of momentum it should have been losing with each roll around the bauble.

I didn't care for it at all.

We watched as it struck the hovering light-imp and rolled right over it. It ought to have crunched the light-imp right out of existence but on the next roll the imp was still just visible, stuck to the ball as a sort of glowing smudge. On the next roll it was fainter, and on the one after that there was no trace of it. Then it was past us anyway, rolling off around the great lazy curve of that tunnel, disappearing back into the darkness, which was deeper now that we lacked the imp.

Prozor started another of her timers.

"Thirty-eight until it rolls around," she said, poking her head out into the tunnel.

"Are we certain it's the only one?" Strambli asked.

"There ain't another," Prozor replied.

"What if it gets faster, once we're in the tunnel?"

"It won't, Stram. I might not've seen one of these before, but there's rules that they play by. They don't get faster."

Prozor was trying to settle Strambli's nerves. There had been rather a lot of that lately. It wouldn't be fair to say that Strambli was cowardly—she signed onto her earlier crew as an Opener, after all—but she was the least steady of us whenever events departed even slightly from the anticipated plan. That in turn made the rest of us jittery, and jittery people make mistakes.

No one needed to remind Prozor of that.

"Stram," she went on, forcing her point. "This is a queer place to come for fuel, I'll grant you. But it's just a bauble. It was dug out by different coves than us, for reasons we can't speculate.

There's things about it we won't ever fathom. But that don't mean it's takin' a personal interest in you, me or any of us. Anything that's clever in a bauble, anythin' that *might* react to us, adapt to our presence, try and trick us, that'll have broken down or gone wrong long ago. What's left is dumb stuff like a rumbling ball, and I'd bet you a bag of quoins it don't know we're here, and even if it did it wouldn't be capable of changin' its behaviour to suit. I'll bet you a second bag that if we came back in a million years it'd still be takin' thirty-eight minutes to go around."

"I ain't got the shivers," Strambli said, a little resentfully.

"Wouldn't blame you if you did," Prozor said. "Shivers is helpful. But you've got to know when you can trust a bauble."

Strambli would not be persuaded to waste another light-imp, so we made do with our helmet lamps, beams bobbing up and down as we shuffled. It took us fifteen minutes to get to the other door, better than Prozor's estimate, and all the while the signal on the localiser was getting firmer and more insistent. The second doorway was set on the same side of the tunnel as the first, but instead of leading to a corridor sloping up, this one faced another descending shaft. It was not so steep as to hinder us, though, and before long our lights were picking up signs of another large space ahead. The shaft levelled off and we stepped through another doorway.

The fuel was there. We had taken only a few paces into the chamber before our lamps picked up the ribbed casing of a propellant bottle, and then another, and another after that, each painted metal drum about as tall as a person, with valves and gauges on the outside. They were stacked on top of each other, upright in piles of between three and five bottles. It was done haphazardly, none of the bottles lined up too neatly, so that the higher stacks looked fit to wobble over without much persuasion. We walked around them, and then eased through the gaps between the piles, not saying much.

We were all arriving at the same thought, which was that things had taken a tricky swerve.

"Is this how would've Rack left 'em?" Fura asked.

"No," Prozor said. "Wasn't no need."

Most of the room was empty, with the piles of fuel gathered in the middle like a kind of sculpture or shrine. Other than that, there were alcoves with broken statues in, most of them just rubble with the occasional foot or part of a leg, and a couple of dark doors leading into deeper parts of the Rumbler.

"We'll need to come back with heavy gear," Strambli said resignedly. "Ropes and tackle. Power winches. Hydraulics. If not this window, then the next."

"This is what we came for," Fura replied. "This is what we're taking. It'll take more'n a jolt or two to set that fuel off, won't it, especially if there's no atmosphere?"

Prozor scratched a glove against the side of her helmet, leaning back as she looked all the way up one of the piles. "Depends on your idea of a jolt, girlie."

"We'll take our chances," Fura said, as if it were a settled thing. "Ain't got the muscle to take down one of those stacks piece by piece, so we're just going to have to topple one and keep our fingers crossed."

"I wouldn't stop at fingers," Prozor said.

Fura brushed her metal hand against the side of one of the three-high piles, reaching high enough to press the second bottle, hard enough to make the bottle rock slightly, and the one above rocked a bit more. "These bottles are dented enough as it is. I reckon they'll take a few more knocks." She stepped back, hands on hips, eyeing the stack until it stopped wobbling. "This one'll do. That top bottle's just waiting to topple off, and a quoin says it'll roll away from the others when it hits the floor."

Whatever misgivings I had, and there were several, I had to admit that we were scarcely spoilt for choices. So I joined my sister, and we started pushing hard on the second bottle, waiting for it to wobble back before giving another shove, the way you might assist a child on a swing. Each push we gave added a bit to the wobble, and then that wobble started spreading like a rumour to the bottle above, until that was tilting back and forth in the opposite direction.

None of this made any discernible sound, but I could imagine the creaking and groaning as our efforts made the pile increasingly unstable. The top bottle was wobbling more than the one under it now, because it had nothing above it to weigh it down, and with each lurch I wondered if it was going to come down on our heads.

Fura's timing was impeccable, and she stepped back from the rocking pile a second before it gave way. The bottle toppled as it went, and clouted the floor on its rim, denting itself but not bursting. It bounced once—up half the height it had already fallen—before landing again and rolling away from the other fuel bottles, and us.

"Now the next one," Fura said, before the first bottle had come to a halt, and she was already setting the second bottle rocking back and forth again.

Before long we had three bottles for the taking, which—under the circumstances—struck me as a fair haul. Given the time left to us there was no hope of working any more than these three back up to the top chamber.

"Here," Prozor said, and she was holding the localiser up to the side of one of the bottles still in a pile. "This is the one. Rack opened it up, welded in a little compartment, fixed the transmitter inside. Clever gubbins. Runs off a little thermal engine—just takes a sip of fuel when it needs to, not enough that you'd ever miss it."

"Sly old Rack," I said, feeling proud and sad at the same time, and thinking Fura must be having similar thoughts.

We took stock. We still had three and a half hours before we needed to be off the bauble, but there was the additional question of that big rolling ball to consider. It was due back again in four minutes, so there was no hope of making it back to the far doorway before it arrived.

"We can still get a headstart," Fura said. "We'll roll the bottles up to the top of the slope, one at a time, without concerning ourselves with the ball."

Even the dented bottle still rolled nicely enough, but it took three of us to begin shoving it back up the slope, and even then we could have benefited from another helper. But three was the most that could squeeze alongside each other and not get tangled up, so while Fura, Prozor and I did the hard grunting, we sent Strambli up to the top of the slope to keep a watch on the big tunnel. We worked carefully, knowing it would only take one slip to have the bottle rolling back the way it had come.

That shaft was shorter than the first and after four minutes we were nearly at the top. Strambli was waiting for us, hand on the doorframe, ducking her head in and out of the open space like a nervous chicken.

"Here it comes," she said.

The rumble grew. We shoved the bottle onto an area of level floor at the top of the shaft and I only let go once I knew it was safe. The ball came past, the rumble juddering through to our bones. Quick as I could I jerked my own head out into the tunnel, looking toward the huge object as it rolled away from us. I regretted it, as the beam from my helmet lamp picked out the ball's scabby patterning, plastered over it like the territories on a globe. It was just a flash, even then, but I saw more than the first time.

Those patterns were imprints. They were what was left of things that the ball had rolled over and squashed, the way it finished off Strambli's light-imp. Not merely squashed, but absorbed into itself, with a layer of them stuck onto it as it rolled away. And those patterns were not as random as I'd initially fancied. They were bodies, stamped onto the ball, arms and legs and heads all spread-out and distorted but unavoidable once your eyes had figured them for what they were. Monkey shapes, sometimes, but not always.

Other, stranger coves than us had ended up stuck on that ball.

"What you were saying earlier, Proz," I said. "About how balls like that usually end up jammed, stuck in the tunnels. I think I see it now."

"Does you, girlie?"

"It's because they get bigger and bigger, isn't it? Whenever they roll over someone who doesn't make it between those doors in time."

"Didn't think you'd care for all the details."

"That's a lot of time, a lot of dead coves," Strambli said, with a dawning horror in her voice.

The rumbling had passed. The ball was off on its next lap, as single-minded on that course as the drooling, mad-eyed greyhounds they used to race at Jauncery Field. "Right," I said, pushing aside thoughts of the poor folk who'd been rolled over already, and nodding in a matter of fact way back to the fuel bottle. "Let's get this to the other doorway, shall we? If we can get it rolling, it shouldn't take us much longer than when we came."

"No, we'll fetch the other two bottles first," Fura said. "Get them here, all together, then we'll worry about rolling 'em the rest of the way."

We gave Strambli the choice between guarding the one fuel bottle or coming back down with us, and after a bit of deliberation she decided she would sooner remain with us. So with Prozor keeping an eye on the time, we went back down to the lower chamber and began to roll the next bottle up the sloping corridor. It was harder this time, the sweat dripping salt into my eyes. According to the gauges there was just as much fuel in this one as the previous bottle, no more and no less, but we were more tired and our suits offered no sort of mechanical assistance.

I stumbled when we were halfway up, and as my fingers came off the bottle Fura and Prozor only just had time to stop it rolling back.

"You tired?" Fura asked, breathing heavily.

"We're all tired," Prozor said. "Be a miracle if we weren't. Won't hurt to take a minute to get our breath back."

Strambli was a few paces ahead of us and looking back over our shoulders and down the length of the corridor, back to the room where we had found the fuel. No part of it was visible now, just a blackness beyond the limit of our lamps.

But Strambli made a sort of clicking noise, the way some people do in their sleep when they have not quite reached the point of snoring. "F—" she started to say, and I knew she was trying to call Fura's name.

Prozor twisted around as far as she could without letting go of the bottle.

She looked back down the corridor, the way we'd come.

"Hello, cove," she said.

Something was shuffling out of the darkness, coming up the corridor behind us. It was a shadowy thing emerging from shadows, puzzling at first, but a second or third glimpse was all it took to recognise the essentials. A boot, a knee, a chest-pack, hoses and pipes, a gloved arm reaching out to us. Slowly more of our light fell on it, picking out the details of a spacesuit, older in its parts than any of ours, but just as jumbled and motley. The helmet—what we could see of it given the figure's stooping, down-looking gait—was all rusted and scabbed, like something that had been underwater for centuries.

The figure kept shuffling up the corridor. It moved as if it were stiffer on one side than the other, meaning it had to shuffle sideways, and something else was compelling it to bend down, as if doubled-over with laughter or gut-cramps.

I suppose I had the beginnings of a shivery intimation even then, but it started small and built slowly, because at first I was relieved to see that our thief—because who else could it be—was a regular bauble-cracker just like us. There were still some questions that needed settling, such as how long this person had been in the bauble, and how they had got past Rack's tell-tale without breaking those threads. But I supposed all that would come clear in the fullness.

What we were not facing was a robot or an alien or a Ghostie or any of the other things rumoured to wander around inside baubles.

"You want to take a breather there, cove," Prozor said, as the figure came closer. "We can parlay just fine without gettin' in each other's faces."

"Pass me my bow," Fura said.

Strambli reached over and extracted Fura's crossbow from

the rig on the back of her suit. The bow was already cocked, the way Fura preferred it. She took one hand from the bottle and took the bow in the other, levelling it down the corridor. The figure straightened up a bit, just enough that we could start to see its face coming into view through the curve of its visor.

That was when my shivers turned to cold terror.

# 3

There were two realisations, striking almost simultaneously. The first was that there was no glass across that visor, so the figure couldn't be breathing. The second was that, in all frankness, not breathing was rather the least of their problems. Not having any skin was the more pressing issue. No skin, no muscle, no nothing. There was just a bony skull, with black caves where there ought to have been eyes.

Two nose-slits, a grin of a mouth, a jaw lolling open on a few gristly shreds of tissue.

Fura shot the crossbow. It went straight into the chest-pack, and perhaps that was the sensible place to aim when you were dealing with a living cove. I was less sure that it made any difference now. Had it been me, I would have directed the bolt through that open visor and shattered that skull like pottery.

Still, it had an effect. The chest-pack gave off a silent crackle of sparks, then some black emanation came belching out of it, and the figure toppled forward with its arms stretched before it, much as if it were offering itself up in supplication.

It remained still, prostrate on the sloping floor. The black smoke was still coming out of it, curling out from under the body, and there were still sparks lighting it up from underneath, but there was no trace of movement.

"Seen some wrong things in my time," Strambli said,

speaking low and slow. "None of 'em were a tenth as wrong as that, though."

"You ain't been around much," Prozor said.

Fura walked slowly to the prostrate form, taking the time to drop another bolt into her crossbow. The figure didn't move as she neared, and when she gave the helmet a kick the body twitched once but gave no other reaction.

Fura looked at Prozor. "You got a theory for this as well, I s'pose?"

Prozor made her own way to the fallen form. She knelt down, squatting as well as one could in one of our suits, and scooped a hand under the empty rim of the helmet, tugging it higher to bring the skull back into view.

Prozor craned down so she could peer deep into the empty sockets.

"Mm-mm," she said, like a doctor about to deliver the bad news about an illness.

"What?" I asked.

"Cove's a twinkle-head. Or used to be."

I had rattled around with Prozor for long enough to pick up a good measure of her spacefaring cant, but that was a new one on me. Since I did know what the "twinkly" was, though, I ventured an educated guess.

"Something to do with the gubbins inside skulls?"

Prozor nodded behind the bars of her faceplate. "Some crews get greedy, or lazy, or can't find a Bone Reader that's a match to their skull. So they scoop out the twinkly from inside the alien skull, and plop it into their own noggins, cutting out the middle-girl, so to speak."

"How—why—would they do that?" I asked.

"How's the easy part," Prozor said. "You girlies had your Neural Alley. Places like that all over the Congregation, and there isn't a service someone won't offer, for the right price. They drill little holes in you, like mineshafts, and they drop the twinkly into your grey at various depths and leave it there. The holes seal over and the twinkly takes root."

"All right—and the why?"

"Once in a while, it gives a cove the ability to speak to bones—and more—without any sort of extra apparatus." She allowed the helmet to fall back to its resting position, standing up as she did. "But generally there's a cost. Occasionally the twinkly gets a will of its own. Starts whispering to things it oughtn't to. Like spacesuits, 'specially the clever sort, with gubbins of their own. It comes to a sort of arrangement with the suit, mutually beneficial."

"And the cove?" I asked.

"Superfluous. The twinkly don't need it, and neither does the suit. Usually only one way that ends." Prozor gave the helmet a kick, firmer than the one Fura had delivered.

"Is it worth us bringing back the suit and the corpse?" Fura asked, replacing her crossbow in its rig, now that it had served its purpose.

"Best left to rot," Prozor said. "Ain't anything we can't find somewhere else."

"What did the twinkle-head want with our fuel, do you think?" I asked.

"That suit can run off fuel, just the same as Rack's transmitter," Prozor said. "More'n likely—and knowin' what I do about twinkle-heads—it had plans to lure us in then keep us down here, in the bauble."

"What use are we to that bag of bones?" Strambli asked.

"None at all, girlie. But our suits, our gear, that's another story. Things break down, wear out, especially down here. The twinkle-heads can always use new parts to keep 'emselves goin'."

"It was going to cannibalise us, that's what you're saying," Fura said.

"Good job there was the just the one of them," Strambli said.

"I was gettin' to that..." Prozor said. "What are the chances that one twinkle-head managed to take all our fuel and stack it in those piles?"

"Send some more our way," Fura said. "We can spare a few more crossbow bolts, if they all go down that easily. Let's get this fuel to the top of the slope."

Leaving the sparking, smoke-belching twinkle-head where it had fallen, we resumed our progress up the slope. The rest had done our muscles some good, but it was more than rest that made us work faster now. I felt as if an extra pair of hands was helping us roll the bottle, getting us to the top faster. I had my back to the darkness behind me, and that suited me very handsomely.

With a final grunt and shove we got to the top of the shaft, rolling the second fuel bottle to a halt next to the first, which was just where we'd left it.

"How long until the ball comes around again?" Fura asked, not even catching her breath.

"Eighteen minutes," Prozor said, meaning it had taken us twenty to fetch the second bottle and roll it to the top, allowing for the interruption caused by the twinkle-head. I had no reason to doubt her, but it had felt about twice as long.

"That's just time to reach the far door if we move now," I said, remembering it had taken us fifteen minutes the first time. "We can push both bottles at the same time, if you like. Once they're rolling on a level surface, they shouldn't slow us down too much."

"And the third bottle?" Fura asked.

"Forget the third bottle," I said, meeting her glowy-framed eyes with my own, and putting as much authority into my voice as I dared. "Two's better than nothing. We don't want to run into more of those things."

"I ain't going back down there," Strambli said, giving a little shudder behind her visor. "Not for all the quoins in all the banks in all the Congregation."

"While we're bumping our gums," Prozor said, "the ball's rolled closer. Nearer to seventeen minutes now. We *could* still make it, but it's gettin' tight. Depends how fine you want to cut things."

Fura looked at each of us in turn, and I could see some dark calculation working behind her eyes. It was less about the minutes and seconds that were preoccupying the rest of us, and more about loyalties and command, and how far she could presently push, given that none of us had scratched our names under any sort of agreement that she was in charge.

"All right, we stick with what we've got. But we ain't chancing the ball this time round."

"I could go ahead," Strambli proposed. "Make sure the way's clear."

"It'll take four of us to lug that fuel," Fura said. "So we all stay put." She hefted her crossbow again, ready to use it if something came shambling up the shaft. "Tell us a story, Proz. You've always got a story."

"Not today," Prozor said, unshipping her own crossbow.

Strambli and I did likewise.

*

"Five minutes," Prozor announced, and I couldn't help but take a deep breath, as if we were already on the point of moving. I touched the fabric of the bauble, trying to feel the faint but growing rumble of the ball, the promise that it was on its way. But there was nothing, and I ought not to have expected it.

I spent the next couple of minutes pondering our plans beyond this bauble, given the limited likelihood of our getting more fuel out of it on this visit. So far, since taking *Revenger,* we had contented ourselves with the margins of the Congregation, holding to the shadows and generally not doing anything that might attract attention. But we could not go on like that indefinitely. We were not outlaws, exactly—at least, we did not think of ourselves as such. But then I found my thoughts returning to Surt, and the sailflash she thought she had seen from the fighting room, and our automatic assumption that we were being stalked by another ship.

It was not how we thought of ourselves, I knew, but what others did.

"Three minutes," Prozor said.

I touched the wall again, unable to stop myself, and this time there was something.

"I can feel it."

"I doubt it, girlie. It's still a way off."

"I'm not imagining it."

Fura looked at me then touched the wall with her metal hand. To begin with it had been much clumsier than her old one, with hardly any feeling in it. But the longer it was a part of her, the more sensitive it had become, and now she said she could feel vibrations through it that were much too subtle for her other hand, especially cased in a gauntlet.

"Adrana's right," she said. "There's something. But I don't think it's..."

"*That's* what it is," Strambli said, calmly enough.

They were shuffling into the range of our helmet lamps, a sort of moving barricade of them coming up the corridor like a plug, shuffling and shambling and knocking against the walls as they approached. They were all twinkle-heads but no two of them were exactly alike. Some of them had a limb or part of a limb gone from their suits, and a few still had a bony part hanging down where the suit had been ripped away, flapping around like a gristly pendulum. The only thing they had in common was that most of them still had a skull, or part of one. As their heads bobbed up and down in what was left of their helmets I caught the twinkly behind the eye-sockets, pretty glinting colours that had no place in such a horrible setting. Some of them had jaws and some of them didn't, and some of their skulls were staved in or almost completely gone above the sockets, so that the twinkly was much more visible.

There were so many of them, and so many squeezing in behind the ones at the front, that we would have been dead if they had possessed any sort of massed weaponry. That was the one blessing. If they had a plan, I supposed it was to overwhelm us, then pick us apart like a carrion.

We were frozen for a few moments. Fear played a part in that, but there was also indecision.

Fura broke the paralysis. She put a bolt into the middle of the mass, and was loading another when Prozor took a shot of her own. Strambli and I were soon joining in. We just aimed, shot, reloaded. There was no strategy to it beyond that, and the suits and body parts of the twinkle-heads were such a jumble that it would have been quite futile to concentrate our attack on any one weakness. The skulls were the obvious target, but putting a bolt through the front of a visor was anything but straightforward. Still, we tried our best, aiming for the ones who had little left of their helmets, and out of those, favouring the ones whose skulls were already half-shattered. When the bolts found their mark, the twinkly exploded like silent fireworks, and the twinkle-head went stiff as their suit lost its governing control.

But the mass of twinkle-heads was continuing its advance, and although we were doing some damage they were soon going to push us out into the main tunnel. Some of them were giving off black smoke now, just like the first one, and that was making it even trickier to aim our crossbows.

"Strambli," I said. "Help me with this."

I fired one last shot then dropped my crossbow. I got both hands on the second bottle, the one we had just sweated all the way to the top of the slope, and began to shove it back to the lip of the incline, Strambli joining in as soon as she got my intention.

"No!" Fura said, realising what I had in mind. "We need that fuel!"

"No," I said, patiently as you please. "What we need is to stay alive long enough to use the other bottle of fuel."

Before she could offer any objection I gave the bottle a final heave and momentum took it over the lip, Strambli and I letting go as it began to roll toward the twinkle-heads. I snatched my crossbow up from the floor and was loading another bolt into it when the bottle ran into the twinkle-heads.

It went through them like a fist through skittles. The first wave got the brunt of it, bits of them exploding under the impact, metal and bones and twinkly splintering out of the smoke, but as the bottle's own passage cleared a path behind it, I saw it rumble over the second and third waves pressing in behind the forward party, and the effect was just as devastating.

They were not stopped, though, and nor was that an outcome I had been counting on. The twinkle-heads who had suffered the least damage fought their way through the remains of their comrades, shoving them aside or picking up pieces to use as bludgeons. But we had slowed the advance, and now it was easier to direct our bolts at the survivors, taking careful aim through visors or going for joints and other vital suit components.

That minute and a half since Prozor's last update took its sweet time passing, but I felt we had tipped the balance in our favour now and when the ball came sweeping past us in the main tunnel, rumbling by in a few seconds, I was certain that we had made the right decision. Now we had thirty-eight minutes to get to the far doorway.

Common sense said to abandon the remaining fuel bottle or send it trundling after the twinkle-heads as a follow-up gift. But I had to bend my thinking to Fura's. We could roll it on the level easily enough, so it was foolish to waste it now. So we spilled out into the main tunnel, Prozor and I propelling the bottle ahead of us, wheeling it through ninety degrees, and then pushing and pushing until the hard part was keeping up with it.

Strambli and Fura, meanwhile, kept up a rear-guard attack on the twinkle-heads, decimated now but still advancing. It was pitiful, glancing back to see them shambling, shuffling and crawling out into the main tunnel. There must have been twenty or thirty of them, not that it was always easy to tell where one twinkle-head ended and another began.

We ought to have got ahead of them very easily, but the queer thing was that the more broken or dismantled the twinkle-heads were, the quicker they were able to go, shuffling or wriggling after us such that there was never a point where we could catch a breath. I saw one that was just the upper half of a spacesuit, with nothing below the waist except a bony pelvis and two twigs of legs. There was another that was just some legs joined at the hip, with no skull or brain to be seen, as curious as that sounds, and a third made up of a helmet, a shoulder, and most of an arm. It had found a way to move itself in sudden twitching convulsions, like a snake being repeatedly electrocuted. What it meant to do to any of us if it caught up was something best not dwelt on.

Twelve minutes, it took us, to reach the sanctuary of the second doorway—three minutes less than on the way down. Sweat was pooling in our boots, our breathing like the rasping of saw blades. We had got far enough ahead of the twinkle-heads for them to be lost in darkness, but we all knew they were still behind us, still staggering and twitching their way along. That tide of broken suits and mangled body parts was not going to turn back just because we had slipped out of range of whatever passed in them for the gift of sight.

As exhausted as we were by then, our labours were nowhere near done. We still had to heave the bottle up two more sloping corridors, always thinking of the twinkle-heads closing in on us, and by the time we got to the top of the first corridor—to the intermediate chamber where Prozor had expected to find Rackamore's fuel store—my arms felt about as useless as those grasping bony twigs. The only saving grace was that if the corpses did show up in our lamps, we always had the option of flattening them with the remaining bottle.

We were nearly back at the surface lock when the rumble came again. I thought it quite likely that some of the twinkle-heads had still been in the main tunnel, adding their impressions to the markings on the ball. It seemed to me that they must have had some dim cognisance of the ball's regularity, to have managed to pilfer the fuel in the first place. Equally, I believed, a mindless, scavenging lust now drove them on, regardless of the consequences.

I was very glad not to see them again.

Breathless and weary, we made it back to the launch with just the one bottle of fuel, and none of us were in any sort of rush to linger on the bauble. Prozor neglected to rig another thread across the entrance, and Fura poured on the rockets almost before she was in her seat, the rest of us grabbing the handholds as we climbed away.

"That went well," I said, once we were into clear space, the Rumbler dropping away like the memory of a dream that had started well and then turned sour. "I'm sure there isn't a plan in the history of the Congregation that went off as smoothly as that."

"It did," Prozor said, taking off her helmet and working her hair back into its normal mass of bristling spikes. "Four of us went in and four of us came out. We didn't die, and we've got a bit more than we went in with."

"One bottle," Fura said, twisting around from her controls while Strambli was helping loosen the pressure-cuff on her right arm. "Hardly worth the fuel we burned getting here. We're going back, next opportunity. Give those twinkle-heads a dose of something shivery and see how they like it."

"Or we could just look for some fuel somewhere else," I said.

"I thought you'd have shown more loyalty to Rack's memory," Fura said, wriggling her shoulder to extract her right arm from the suit sleeve. "That was his property down there, and now it's ours by right. How can you rest knowing it's been stolen from us?"

"Everything that ever comes out of a bauble was someone else's property once upon a time," I said.

"That's different," Fura said, shrugging out of the rest of her suit. "It's been millions of years. No one cares after all that time."

"You'd best hope," I said, drawing a dark glance from her.

Before very long, the jaws of the docking bay were cranking wider, a red grin in the darkness. Fura used the steering jets to turn us around so that we were able to back into the mouth tail-first; a little fish letting itself be swallowed up by a bigger one. We latched onto the berthing clamp and the jaws sealed up on us. A few seconds later, Surt and Tindouf appeared outside our windows, wearing suits. They were checking over the launch and completing the docking connections so we could float aboard the main ship without getting back into our own suits.

It took us a few minutes to gather our gear and float out through the connection into the galley of the main ship, which was linked directly to the docking bay and was the only area large enough to serve as a staging point for our expeditions, where we could gather to plan an expedition, assess treasure or take our suits on and off without jabbing our elbows in each other's faces. It was still a tight squeeze, what with the galley table taking up half the room, as well as instrument consoles, equipment racks and storage lockers, which was why we did so much suiting-up and suiting-down on the launch. Surt and Tindouf had already come inside from the docking bay, their helmets off and ready to greet us.

Judging by their hopeful looks, Fura hadn't taken the time to signal ahead.

"If you'd come back quickly, I'd's've been worried," Tindouf was saying. "That would've meant someone had already stolened that fuel, and there wouldn't have been any point in stayings, would there? But you've been *hourses* and *hourses*. We takesd that to be a good sign, didn't we, Surt?"

"Until we saw their faces," Surt said, puncturing his optimism like a harpoon through a balloon. "Ask yourself, Tindouf. Do they look like a happy crew?"

"You know I's not the best judge of that, Surt."

"They don't look contented to me at all, Tindouf," she said, confidingly. "They look like they've been through seven kinds of hell."

"Hell don't begin to cover it," Strambli said. "The things we saw..."

"Did you get the fuel?" Surt cut across, evidently in no mood for one of Strambli's long-winded accounts.

I shook my head. "Some. Not as much as we'd hoped. Turns out Rack's supply store wasn't quite as theft-proof as he'd imagined."

"Twinkle-heads got to it," Strambli said, giving a shiver.

"Except we both know they're not really real," Surt said. "So whatever it was..."

"It was twinkle-heads," Prozor said, in the kind of tone that silences any further disagreement. "I know. I looked 'em right in the face, just before we flattened them with a fuel bottle. About twenty, thirty of the grinny devils. Probably hundreds more in the lower levels. We were lucky to get out."

"What would they have done?" Surt asked.

"Nothing pleasant, is what," Prozor answered. "Be glad we got out like we did, with some fuel rather than nothin'. Now can we all agree to put some leagues between us and this bauble, before any of us get bad ideas about goin' back for a second helping?"

"Seems reasonable to me," I said. "No point sticking around, anyway, with the window about to close."

"They took what was rightfully ours," Fura said, her metal fingers opening and closing slowly. "That ain't sitting well with me."

"What we've got will tide us over," Prozor said soothingly. "Rack only ever took a bottle or two out at a time, anyway."

Surt made a beckoning gesture toward the galley table, its magnetic surface already set with lidded tankards and bowls, hot buttered bread steaming out of one of them. "Get some food and ale into you, that'll take the sting outta the day. Tindouf and I'll get that fuel unshipped from the launch and prepare the sails for departure. You did well, bringin' back what you did. Count myself lucky I've never seen a twinkle-head. Don't plan on seeing one, neither."

"Very wise," I said, smiling at Surt.

Surt had a famished appearance to her, all sucked-in cheeks and hollow eye-sockets, and that could look like hardness or even meanness at first acquaintance. She was kind, though, and very clever with machines, and over time we had come to consider each other good friends.

"You sits yourself down," Tindouf told her. "I can take care of the fuel for now. I'll call when I needs the special touch."

"Save some bread for me," Fura said, moving in the direction of the control room. "Some of us have work to do."

I floated myself onto a seat at the table, strapping a loose buckle around my waist to hold myself to the seat. Prozor had gone to the forward toilet before joining us, while Strambli was over at one of the store cabinets, rummaging around for some extra salt, as was her habit. Before she joined us, Surt tore me off a chunk of bread and leaned in to pass it over. I took the bread and bit into it, not realising until that moment quite how hungry I had become. The bread was turning a bit stale, and the butter was thinned-out, but it was vastly better than nothing.

Then Surt said, in a very low voice: "It's back, Adrana. I saw it again, when you were down in that bauble. We've got company."

# 4

The sighting room was a little bubble-shaped chamber situated high on the back of the ship. It was constructed mostly of glass, the only point of ingress being a rib-pinching door that looked as if it would be a tight squeeze for a very skinny child. Once the door was sealed—even Tindouf got through that opening by some means—the whole sighting room could be raised out of the body of the ship, pushed up on the end of a stalk that ran off the same hydraulic circuits as the sail-control gear, but which might also be operated manually, using a hand-pump in the room itself. Thus extended, the sighting room afforded an unobstructed view of a greater area of the sky, without the bulk of the ship blocking half the panorama.

Alone in one of the two seats that faced the banks of clustered eyepieces, I employed a small red lamp to read through the most recent set of entries in the sighting log. The first time she saw the sail-flash, if that was indeed the cause of it, Surt had been searching the sky in an unmethodical and slipshod manner. By the time she realised the possible significance of that flash, the telescope had swung on its well-oiled gimbals and she had lost any sense of the transitory pointing angle. I had swept the suspected area while she sat in the adjoining seat, but there had been nothing to confirm or refute her observation. Not surprisingly, perhaps, for if it *had* been sail-flash it would still have been an exceedingly momentary event.

But Surt had seen something like it again, and this time she had been diligent in her observation and note-keeping. Her hand was still not the neatest, but she had laboriously entered the time and coordinates, as well as appending a commendably legible note to the effect of what she had seen.

*Poss. flash, duration one half sec. or less, not repeated.*

Surt still had difficulty with reading and writing, but she was improving, and there was a formula to the keeping of these log notes which meant she need only refer back to what had been written previously, and adjust as she saw fit.

She made mention that this was the second such flash seen from that area of the sky, and perhaps that would have been better kept between Surt and I. With the lamp extinguished, I allowed my own eyes to adjust to darkness, selected a telescope with medium magnification, and began scrutinising the same area of sky, with a certain margin of error to either side. There was sense in that, because if the origin of that flash were indeed another ship, it would have had time to move with respect to the fixed stars, and by quite a margin if it were close to us. Of course I very much hoped it was not close, but I had to consider the possibility.

I saw nothing. I had not doubted Surt the first time, though, and I did not doubt her the second.

I glanced back through the earlier entries, in our varying hands. No one else had reported anything, not since we had been in orbit around this bauble, but again that offered no reason to think we were safe. Equally, the flash could still have some alternative origin, or it might be from a ship that was engaged in some innocent pursuit, with no improper designs against us.

But as I settled my hand on the lever that would return the sighting room to the ship, I knew where I stood on the subject.

*

"Adrana," she said, sitting at her desk—strapped into it, I should say—and bent over as she wrote something in one of her journals, with the only significant source of light being the red glow of Paladin's head, fixed to the desk like a curious lantern. "I'm very glad you came. I wanted to show you something—a little puzzle I dug out of Bosa's things."

I studied her for a second or two. Even though she had acknowledged my presence, and in friendly terms, her face was still fierce with concentration. The glowy, which could at times shine from her skin with great prominence, was subdued now, and rendered nearly invisible under Paladin's dusky glow. Her wild black hair billowed around her head in our near-weightlessness—we were under sail, escaping the bauble's pull—but aside from that detail I might have been looking back at my younger sister lost in some childhood reverie of intense but inconsequential concentration, composing a story or tinting an illustration.

She had taken over Bosa's private quarters. It was a chamber with angled walls, situated next to the main control room, where we attended to the larger and more complicated navigation and communication devices. Both of these rooms were in turn accessible from the galley, being located above the mouth and jaws of the docking bay. Now Fura spent many hours at Bosa's desk, surrounding herself with the former pirate's belongings, many of which were exceedingly cryptic.

Numerous control circuits ran through this part of the ship, making it the most convenient place to install Paladin. What remained of him was wired into the desk, which was in turn connected to the navigation, squawk, ion-emitter, sail-control and coil-gun batteries, meaning there was almost no part of *Revenger* that Paladin could not operate for himself. But Paladin was damaged, and it had required patience and kind attention to help him relearn his capabilities. Fura had always been fonder of him than I, although I had taken strident pains to revise my ways, and now regretted my earlier disdain, so it was natural that she should be the one nearest to him, helping him rebuild his logic pathways and adjust to this vast and unwieldy new body he had now inherited.

That arrangement—innocent and agreeable at first—had hardened into formality now, though, with Fura assuming residence of this room just as if she were our captain, properly appointed.

"Surt's seen something," I said.

She dipped her pen back into a pressure-tight inkwell. "In the sighting room?"

"Yes. A scintillation, consistent in length and brightness with sail-flash."

"She mopes around trying to find her homeworld. I expect she saw a flash from the Congregation."

"No," I answered carefully, feeling I needed to stand up for Surt. "It was toward the Empty, with the Old Sun well over her shoulder when she made the sighting. I've consulted the Glass Armillary, as well as the charts and almanacs. There are no worlds or baubles that she could have mistaken for the flash."

"If there were another ship out here we'd know it. We'd have picked up squawk and skull chatter and glimpsed much more than a single sail-flash. If she'd seen it on more than one occasion I might credit it, but—"

I interjected: "It was seen on more than one occasion."

She looked at me sharply. "During the same watch?"

"No. When I saw Surt's observation I swept the same area of sky, just as a precaution. I believe I saw something as well."

"Then you made a note of it?"

I had drawn myself into a lie, both to protect Surt and to impress the seriousness of the situation upon Fura. But I did not wish to make it worse for myself. "It was a momentary thing, and not bright enough to merit an entry in the sighting log. Under other circumstances, I would have made nothing of it. But Surt's earlier observation makes it harder to dismiss. I'm minded to think another ship is stalking us."

"Sail-flash is very hard to range, even if I accept that this phantom's real. Under the right conditions, with sufficient magnification and dark adaptation, a flash like that might be seen across ten million leagues—far too far away to be of any concern to us."

For someone who had never left a world a year ago, my sister was prone to act if she'd been born and raised on a sunjammer, with a life's worth of experience in all matters of navigation and spacefaring. She spoke with certainty about things that were doubtful, and yet when I voiced a similarly confident opinion she would be the first to pick at it, shaking her head like an old hand.

"Or," I answered patiently, knowing I had practically as much experience as she did, "it could be very much nearer."

She turned her gaze to the glassy globe that was Paladin's head. "Did you understand all that Adrana just reported, Paladin?"

"Yes," he replied, in his deep, dignified voice, which I now knew to belong to a robot that was once a soldier, as well as a friend and protector to people, who had served his masters with loyalty and courage and then been punished for that fealty. "I understand sail-flash. When one or more elements of the mass of sail is out of alignment, or damaged, or subject to deliberate deflection, it may serve as a mirror, disclosing the presence of a vessel beyond the usual methods of detection."

"It needn't indicate indifferent mastery of a ship," I said.

"Not at all, Miss Adrana. Under ordinary circumstances, it is all but unavoidable—an occupational hazard of celestial navigation. But a captain or master of sail, should they seek stealth, will do their best not to allow sail-flash to intercept the line-of-sight of another vessel."

"Paladin," Fura said. "You'd have reported if we'd been hailed, or swept in the usual sense, wouldn't you?"

"No sweeper has been detected, Miss Arafura, nor have we been using our own instrument at anything but the lowest setting. Nor have we intercepted squawk transmissions, encoded or otherwise, which appear to be meant for any other vessel in our locality."

"And we certainly ain't been putting out squawks, other than the low-gain communications we use for bauble operations," Fura said. "And *our* sails don't flash. So there's no way another ship could have smoked us out, even if they had an inkling we were operating in this sector."

"There is the bauble," Paladin said, in a diffident tone, as it were bad form to remind us of this point.

"The bauble's always been here," Fura said.

"But we have not," Paladin replied. "When its field was raised, the bauble was the brightest object in the vicinity, and we have been orbiting it. Might you have the coordinates of the sail-flash incidents, Miss Adrana?"

"Yes. Both sightings were close to one hundred and sixty-six degrees east, twenty-two south."

The lights in his head spangled with a sudden flurry of computation. "Then it is possible we were seen as we passed across the face of the bauble. Our sails may be dark but they are not invisible, and even with a reduced spread of sail we are much larger than the bauble. There is another factor, too. If that other ship was paying close attention to this bauble it may have seen the rocket plume from our launch, as we came and went."

I chose my reply carefully, making no mention of Surt having seen the first sail-flash before we sent out the launch. "Someone fixating on this bauble for a reason, you mean?"

"If one wished to find a ship operating on the margins of the Empty, it would be much more efficient to maintain vigil on a number of carefully-chosen baubles, rather than trying to search every cubic league of empty space."

"I don't care for this," Fura said, shaking her head. "One ship stumbling on us blind out here, I'll curse my bad luck but accept that it happens. But the way Paladin's speaking, it's as if there's a deliberate plan."

"If that's the case, then we may pick up a hint of it from the skull. I know you've been reluctant to use it lately..."

"With excellent reason. It's our only skull, and it is damaged. I should rather ration our time on it, while it still functions. We might also risk giving away our identity, even an unintentional disclosure of our position."

"I know those dangers, but if we don't use one of our primary assets, we might as well smash it to pieces ourselves." I looked at her sharply. "What is is that makes you so resolved not to go into the Bone Room, Fura? You were so keen, when we crewed under Rackamore—always trying to prove your abilities over mine. If one of us should be reticent, it ought to be me."

"It was not a competition," Fura stated coldly. "And if I have reticence, as you put it... you cannot know what it's like, having *this* in me." As her temperament darkened, so the glowy began to flare out of her skin, where it had been subdued before. "I can—will—control it. But I do not need alien spectres screaming through my dreams, when I already have a headful of phantoms to contend with. Are you not satisfied, to have this role to yourself? A ship really only needs one Bone Reader, does it not? And you are so very capable."

"As you say, it is not a competition." But wishing to put matters into a less troubing light, and dissuade her mood from further deterioration, I added: "It *was* just sail-flash, and there are other things that can produce a similar phenomenon. We haven't been swept, and no one's tried to jump us. We're moving into open space now, and we'll soon set a definite course. More than likely we won't see another trace of that ship."

"I'm sure you're right, Adrana." She reached across the desk and moved a magnetic paperweight off the back of a heavy, rectangular book whose pages were wider than they were tall. "No point dwelling on it now, in any case, not until we have more information." She looked at me with apparent concern. "I see that you're unsettled. Would you care for something else to puzzle over?"

I wondered where she was leading, but at the same time could not ignore my curiosity.

"I take it this is another of Bosa's things?"

"One of her possessions, yes, although I don't think she had any part in the writing of it." She slid the heavy book over to me and opened it at a page that was set with a bookmark. "Something she came by, looted from another ship."

"Or a bauble?"

"No, it's the work of the present Occupation, as you'll see, so I reckon it doubtful that it was written, then put in a bauble, then found again, all in the last few hundred years."

The book was spread wide. The left and right pages were both of the kind that could be unfolded out several times, but for the moment Fura was directing my attention to the one on the right, made of denser, creamier paper than the other, which looked thin and translucent.

"Open it. Tell me what you see."

I lifted an eye. "Giving me orders again?"

"No—giving you a gift, something to take your mind off our other troubles." She studied me with an increased intensity. "Do you think I'd be so full of myself as to treat you as an inferior? It was me that came for you, Adrana—me that quite literally risked life and limb for your salvation. Would I have done that if I didn't love you as any sister would?"

"Of course not," I said, chastened to one small degree, and irritated to another. "I shan't ever forget what you did."

Nor stand much chance of forgetting, I added silently.

"Very well. Now do as I insist: open the book."

I obeyed her, taking pains not to tear the stiff paper as I straightened it out. It unfolded to four times its original width, nearly spilling off the edge of the table, and I had to jam a paperweight on it to prevent it springing back. I recognised it instantly, and wondered how it could be any sort of puzzle. It was the timeline of the Occupations, perfectly familiar to us from the long wall at the Hall of History in Mazarile. Familiar to any cove from almost any world in the Congregation, too, because there were museums like that all over the place, as well as thousands of books in schools and libraries, with the same representation.

A red line went from left to right, marked with big ticks and little ticks—gradations of millions of years, then hundreds of thousands. Rising up from this line at irregular intervals, like the last broken posts of a rotten fence, were the thirteen Occupations—the thirteen times since the Sundering that people had spread out into the Congregation and established a civilisation. The uprights were very narrow, as they had to be. The Occupations only ever lasted a few thousand years at best.

Normally in such figures there was some annotation to the uprights. The third Occupation, for instance, was sometimes called "The Epoch of the Baublemakers" because no one had ever found any bauble older than that. The eighth Occupation was often referred to as "The Time of the Two-Headed Princes." The eleventh was either "The Council of Clouds," or "The Empire of the Ever-Breaking Wave," or both, depending on who was speaking. It was complicated, because crews had their own terminology and historians several others, and they didn't always marry up.

No such annotation here, though—just those uprights, inked in the same red as the baseline.

"I suppose there's a catch," I said. "Or you wouldn't be asking me to identify something we both know as well as the alphabet."

"Unfold the page on the left, dear heart. It's made so that it spreads out over the page you've already extended."

I pinched the edge of the translucent sheet and unfolded it, using the same paperweight to anchor it down once it had reached its fullest extent. Then I frowned.

"What is this?"

"The puzzle I was hoping you'd be able to explain. 'Cept it isn't really a puzzle, I suppose, as the meaning of it's plain enough. But I don't quite get the meaning of the meaning, so to speak."

"Neither do I."

The translucent sheet had a red baseline as well, and its tick marks lined up exactly with the ones on the underlying page. The same span of time, in other words. But rising up from the baseline on the translucent sheet was a veritable forest of uprights, far more than the paltry thirteen on the main timeline. They were marked out evenly, too, not in step with the ticks, but still with an equal spacing between them.

"There are hundreds of these," I said.

"Four hundred 'n' forty, near as it matters," Fura said. "Paladin's examined the same figure. Remind me, Paladin, how far apart those intervals are?"

"Each vertical stroke is twenty-two thousand, five hundred years from the preceding one," he said.

"Now do you see how they correspond with the thirteen big marks below?" Fura asked me.

"Most of them don't."

"But thirteen of 'em do, and very handsomely at that. Paladin confirms it, too."

It was true, as near as my eye could judge, squinting through the translucent sheet to the one below it, and allowing for folds in the paper, the thickness of the inked uprights, and so on.

"I don't know what to make of it," I said. "The thirteen Occupations seem to fit these ticks quite nicely. But what about the hundreds that don't match at all? They just fall in the gaps between Occupations, where we know there wasn't any civilisation."

"That we know of."

I nodded slowly. Historians sometimes spoke of "Shadow Occupations" as a theoretical possibility—little false dawnings of civilisation, happening between the known Occupations but leaving no trace of themselves, or whose traces had been confused with the relics of the known Occupations. It was possible, I suppose, and it gave historians something to argue about, which suited their temperaments ideally. But so far as I recalled, not even the wildest of them had ever suggested that there might have been hundreds of Shadow Occupations.

Let alone in the region of four hundred and twenty-seven.

"It can't be," I declared firmly. "We'd have known of such a thing by now. Assessors would be tearing their hair every time we cracked a bauble. Nothing would make any sense. But the thirteen Occupations *do* make sense, most of the time. Paladin: which Occupation made you?"

"I am a robot of the Twelfth Occupation, Miss Adrana, as well you know."

"And you'd know if there'd been dozens and dozens of Shadow Occupations between then and now, wouldn't you?"

"I cannot say with certainty, Miss Adrana. I was confined within a bauble for much of the time. I must also depend on the historical records compiled by people."

"Tinheads only know what we tell 'em," Fura said, which was a little unkind given that Paladin was listening.

"Somewhere there'll be older robots, or ones with a better memory, won't there?"

"Good luck finding 'em, or persuading 'em to blab when you do. This is dangerous knowledge, sister. It wouldn't surprise me at all if the tinheads would sooner pretend not to know anything about it, if they know what's good for 'em."

I stared at the sheets, part of me certain that she had thrown me this puzzle as a diversionary tactic, knowing how much I liked such fancies, while the other part of me could not help but be drawn into it. "Those thirteen lines seem to match up pretty well," I allowed. "But I'm not sure it tells us anything. If you asked me to find a pattern of lines that fitted our timeline, I'm sure it wouldn't be too hard. Finding patterns is what we're good at, but it doesn't mean there's any deeper truth to it."

"This ain't like looking into some tea leaves in Neural Alley," Fura said chidingly. "Some cove went to a lot of trouble to find that regularity, and I think there's something to it."

"So you really think there are all these Shadow Occupations, hundreds of them, that no one's ever found any trace of?"

Her answer was more considered, more guarded, than I'd been expecting. "No, not really. But if something didn't happen at all those intervals, when it did thirteen other times, that's just as puzzling to me."

Curiosity gripped me and I removed the paperweight, folded back the extending sheets, and leafed through the rest of the heavy volume. The pages were full of knotty little diagrams, numbers and calculations and curious squiggling types of algebra, and lots of drawings similar to the ones on the extending pages, complete with timelines and notches.

It was all handwritten, I realised. Inked and tinted very carefully, without so much as a smudge or correction, but not printed. It was all too neatly inked, I decided. Only a lunatic could keep up that degree of orderliness page after page, scribbling down their addled theories like a manic printing machine, never once committing the tiniest slip.

"This is either the work of a genius, or someone just as insane as Bosa herself. She shredded every book in Rackamore's library. Why didn't she do the same to this one?"

"Spite drove her when it came to Rack," Fura said. "But she wasn't averse to a little scholarship, when it lined up with her own interests. She took her whims and obsessions seriously and she had time to dig into them. Much more than one ordinary lifetime, if you think of all those bodies she burned through. Once she started pondering the meaning of quoins and baubles and aliens, and these little Occupations of ours, what makes 'em start as well as what makes 'em end, it was natural that she'd follow that to the beginning, and the question of what makes us what we are. In her own mad mind she still had room for curiosity, like the rest of us. But you'd know that, wouldn't you?"

"I was her prisoner, not her best friend."

"Still, some of her obsessions must've rubbed off on you, this being one of 'em."

I was in no immediate mood to go back over my time in the presence of Bosa, so I made a very strong effort to ignore Fura's digging and twist my mind back onto the immediate subject at hand.

"I accept that it's interesting."

"I knew you would."

"But if there's a glimmer of truth in any of this," I said, tapping a finger against the heavy volume, "wouldn't the simplest thing be to ask the aliens?"

"The same aliens that Bosa said have been busy trading in

dead souls, stuck inside quoins?" Fura flexed her fingers. "I wouldn't trust one word that rattled out of a Crawly."

*

Near to a bauble—or any world, for that matter, which contained a swallower—a ship like ours was always in the prudent habit of reducing its spread of sail, sometimes folding and retracting all the sails completely, so that all that was left of the ship was the tiny hard husk of its hull. There were other considerations, too. Debris got caught up in a world's gravity well, pulled into it like dirt around a plug-hole, and even a small amount could do prodigious damage to a spread of sail, and that was before you considered the easy opportunities for sabotage by rival parties. Crews spoke of hauling-in to a world, by which they generally meant a close approach or low orbit, but the deeper intention of the phrase lay in the act of pulling in some smaller or larger fraction of a ship's spread of sail, which was a very cumbersome and delicate process at the best of times.

We had reduced our sail as we neared the Rumbler, but not completely, since a ship with no sails must depend on ions alone for speed and is therefore vulnerable to ambush. Now, as we shrugged off the Rumbler's influence, we were once again running under five thousand acres of collecting area. We were just barely able to achieve that, though, since we were still operating without a dedicated master of sail, and much of the control gear and rigging arrangements on *Revenger*—setting aside the question of her night-black sails themselves—were of unfamiliar or unorthodox disposition.

We had Paladin, of course, and he was wired directly into the sail-control systems, so he could, in principle, operate all necessary aspects of the rigging. But Paladin had no innate understanding of celestial navigation, or the particular quirks of this ship. Like the rest of us, he was having to learn on the job. We had furnished him with such operational documents and manuals as we could find, but Bosa's crew had been so well-schooled that they seemed to have had little need for any instruction beyond word-of-mouth.

What we did have was Prozor and Tindouf. Neither was a master of sail but both had crewed on enough ships to pick up something of the art, vastly more than the rest of us, and when they bashed their heads together on a particular problem it was pleasing how readily they came up with a solution. They had hauled-in and hauled-out the sails each time we got near a bauble, getting better at it each time, and they had made such alterations to the trim and arrangement of the rigging as suited our changes of course.

This work would have been difficult at the best of times, using the ordinary reflective sail. Ours were a singularly different proposition. These catchcloth sails were tuned to an invisible flux, a ghost-gale blowing right out of the Old Sun's core. They had a peculiar way of behaving, flapping and billowing according to their own capricious moods, and they needed a constant careful eye on the sail-control gear. What made them trickiest of all was that the sails were black on both surfaces, and this was an order of blackness beyond anything in our common experience.

Fura had shown me some small scraps of catchcloth in the ship's stores, and wafting them through my fingers was like trying to hold a shadow composed of ink. It seemed to slither out of my grasp like a thing with its own volition. You could make no crease, and a piece of catchcloth folded over itself twenty times still felt as thin as a single layer.

Out in space, strung on lines of molecular-filament rigging that themselves went out a hundred leagues or more, catchcloth was the literal fabric of nightmares, especially when you were depending on it for your existence. Tindouf and Prozor could only see the catchcloth by the things it concealed, and for the most part that meant trying to assess when a piece of black sky was covered over by something even blacker. Of necessity they placed their reliance on strain-gauges on the winches, as well as the ship's inertial compass, to verify that our infernal sails were behaving as they ought.

We cursed them, but they were also our salvation. We had every reason to hide, and by having catchcloth sails we made it practically impossible for another ship to sight us at anything but close-range. It was the advantage that had allowed Bosa to surprise and murder other crews. If Surt's sail-flash did indeed betoken the presence of another ship, and they had spied us as we eclipsed the bauble's light, then at least the sails had delayed this reckoning as long as possible. Now we had to hope that they would carry us back into the shadows, and we could speed away from that interested party as effortlessly as we slipped the bauble's pull.

As to our next destination, that was not a settled matter. There had been a plan—unstated, but I think mutually accepted—to continue along a string of baubles for a few more months, picking our targets shrewdly and generally staying out of anyone else's sphere of operations. The holds of *Revenger* already contained a sizeable amount of quoins and treasure, no doubt most of it plundered from other crews, but it could always be added to and each bauble was a crucible in which we became a little harder as a crew. More than that, we enjoyed the challenge.

Now that plan was looking untenable, even if Fura still clung to it. We didn't have enough fuel to run the launch as freely as we would need. We could haul-in to one bauble, perhaps two if we ran our reserves down to the knuckle, but doing so would only be avoiding the inevitable. We still needed the worlds.

It must have applied to Bosa as well. She had made her living stealing from other ships, but there must have been occasions when she needed something from a world, some rare but necessary commodity beyond the scope of her usual plundering. She could not have stolen from a world by force, so she must have been compelled into something resembling legitimate trade, although doubtless facilitated through intermediaries and disguises. Indeed, there were rumours of such activities. They only ever concerned worlds on the edge of the Congregation, where lines of communication were strained and the rule of law weaker than in the lower processionals.

Dared we follow her lead?

"We're not outlaws," Strambli was saying, as the crew gathered in the galley between shifts. "We just took an outlaw's ship. That doesn't stop us returning to the worlds and doing honest business. We need fuel, to begin with, and we definitely need more help. You Ness sisters are always harpin' on about what a fine cove your Cap'n Rack was. Would he have run a ship with so few hands?"

"He had a few luxuries we don't," Fura answered patiently. "Like friends, and monetary reserves, and the ability to trade whenever it suited him."

"Well, we won't get any friends, skulking around out here," Surt said, pausing as she sucked in her cheeks, which vanished into the sides of her face more than was pleasant to look at. "We've got the reserves, ain't we? Maybe not in banked credit like Rackamore, but with the quoins and relics we've already got. We sure as apples ain't *poor*. And we do need a master of sail, and an Assessor, and one or two spare hands wouldn't kill us."

"We've run the ship by ourselves until now," Fura said. "We may continue to do so. There are still many baubles within easy reach, and if we are careful with our fuel and supplies..."

"We nearly got caught by those twinkle-heads," Strambli said, giving a little shudder as she shuffled a deck of metal-coated cards. "If we'd run into real bother down there, do you think Surt and Tindouf would've been able to help us? We're short-handed for bauble work, never mind how much fuel we have. We can't go on like this."

"If there were more of us," Surt said, "we'd be able to keep a permanent watch in the sighting room."

"You saw one flash," Fura said coldly. "It was noted."

Trying to stay on convivial terms with both my sister and the three others, I said: "In practical terms we can sail back into the main worlds of the Congregation whenever we like. But we ought to be aware of the risks in doing so. You had the right of it, Strambli: we took an outlaw's ship. That doesn't make us outlaws in our own eyes but we have to think about how it looks from the outside. Besides ourselves, no one really knows what happened."

"Then we'll tell 'em," Strambli said, fixing me with her lop-sided stare.

"Easier said than done," I answered, with an understanding smile. "We could squawk our side of things all we liked, transmit our good intentions, even put it out through the bone room, but it would only take one doubter to put a coil-gun broadside across us, and even a brief squawk transmission would give away our position very easily. Until we're in port, and explaining ourselves, no one's going to trust a word we say—and the risk is we'll get peppered long before we make port."

"One of us sees sense, at least," Fura said.

"I'm trying to see both sides," I replied. "I don't like the idea of not seeing the worlds again. That's no life, even if we were able to stay alive. We didn't set out to be fugitives, did we? And even if we go with your idea and continue working baubles, short-handed as we are, and hoping our luck doesn't run out, there's no guarantee that we'll find enough to live on."

She held her silence before answering, taking in all of us in turn, even silent, amiable Tindouf, who seemed content with whatever fate threw at him, provided it did not take him too far from his beloved ion-emitter.

"If your minds are set on this," she said, sounding very much as if she was having a tooth drawn, "then I shan't be the one to stand in your way. But at least accept that it would be madness to sail into the lower processionals, or to any world where we're likely to run into other ships and crews in any numbers."

"Agreed," I said provisionally, glancing at the others for their assent, which seemed to be offered. "But there are worlds on the edge of the Congregation, the same sorts of out-of-the-way places where Bosa must have done some trade."

"What about Trevenza Reach?" asked Strambli keenly, her

larger eye brightening like a miniature nova. "I wouldn't mind seeing Trevenza Reach, and we could always recruit some new crew there, couldn't we?"

"It's no good to us," Fura said, with blunt dismissiveness. "I was there once, but its orbit's taken it closer to the Congregation since then. It's highly populated, swarming with spies and agents, and a common stopover for crews working the high spaces. Corrupt, as well. Vidin Quindar was able to get out there and smuggle me back to Mazarile with only a scrap of paperwork."

"There are twenty thousand other inhabited worlds," I said. "It oughtn't to be too hard to find one that fits our requirements."

"If you think it trivial, sister, be my guest." But some cautious impulse showed in her face. "No. If you'll allow it—all of you—I'll take a gander at the *Book of Worlds,* and the Glass Armillary, and find us a few candidates. You'll admit that I have a good knowledge of the worlds, won't you?"

None of us could contradict her on that score. She'd had her nose in one or more volumes of the *Book of Worlds* since she could read, and she was still pining for the beautiful editions she had seen in Rackamore's library. She could reel off the names of two hundred worlds before I got to twenty.

"Then it'll be your choice?" I asked.

"No! I'll just present the options I think are worth your consideration, and the final selection will be yours and yours alone. I'll accept your collective decision, but that ain't to say I'll endorse it." Fura folded her arms. "Still reckon this is a suicidal course of action. But far be it from me to stand in the way of my own crew."

# 5

Five days later I was up in the sighting room when the Old Sun began muttering and complaining to itself. The magnetic compasses started to gyre, while a pale fire—sometimes lilac, sometimes indigo—chased along the great cobwebbed leagues of our rigging, occasionally dancing on the distant perimeter of a sail, defining a rectangle or a hexagon of perfect starless obscurity.

I watched with only a distant concern, struck more by the beauty of the spectacle than the chances of it doing us harm. It was silent and rather lovely, with the fire moving with a kind of playful animus that I found charming rather than threatening. In truth, and as I reminded myself, there was little cause for worry. The solar storm might impede the temporary functioning of some of our instruments and equipment, but it would have to be much stronger to do lasting damage. Paladin was safe, since Surt had installed blockades in his wiring, so he could not be overloaded by an induction surge.

A normal ship would have been wise to reduce its spread of sail, and that could be treacherous if the sail-control gear was already immobilised by the storm. Our catchcloth sails put us at the mercy of different winds, though. Sometimes the fluxes rose and fell in synchrony, but as often as not the weather boiling off the surface of the Old Sun bore no relationship to the moods of the invisible gale surging from its core. The fire itself showed that the rigging was holding its configuration, and that the sails were under no excessive load. Tindouf, down in the ship, would be monitoring the strain-gauges as a matter of routine, while Paladin would be consulting the inertial gyroscopes and star-trackers to ensure we held our course.

During my watch I had been looking through the telescopes, searching the whole of the sky, but also—methodically—returning to the sector where Surt had seen her sail-flash. I had the sighting log open on my lap, but also the book Fura had shown me in her quarters, with the strange pattern of Shadow Occupations. I had taken it with her glad permission, and between intervals of peering through eyepieces I let my eyes recover by switching on my red lamp and examining the book.

I was drawn to the book as an itch draws a scratch, or a sore tooth draws a tongue. That did not mean I was convinced that there was sense in it, let alone some vast, disquieting truth that made a mockery of all that we had been taught as children. I thought, rather, that the book was the work of some mad or mischievous person, intended to promote further madness or confusion, rather than to illuminate some submerged truth. My intention was to find the mistake or lie and return the book to Fura, proud that I had put to bed any silliness about hundreds of unknown Occupations.

But I could not. Not to begin with, at least, and when my red light flickered out—impaired by the storm—I had not really begun to see where I might start.

The intercom buzzed.

"I am detecting elevated solar activity," Paladin said. "It would be advisable, Miss Adrana, if you were to return to the shelter of the main hull."

True enough; the storm might not be capable of doing much harm to the ship but that glass bubble offered much less protection for a living organism than being down below behind spans of armour and lagging. I signed off the log, closed up the telescopes, and used the hydraulic lever to return the sighting room to the safety of the hull like an eyeball being wound back into its own socket. I climbed out through the narrow connecting door, clutching only the mad journal as I left.

"Is it a blowy one, do you think?" Strambli asked me, as I passed her along the way to the control room. "I ain't ever been one for storms. There was a ship once, somewhere down by the Daughters of Blood and Milk, I think it was, got caught with their sails run out in a Niner, heavy on the ions, too, and they couldn't get one of their winches to work, so they sent out half their number to slice the rigging with yardknives, or else they'd be shredded in the pull of the Daughters, and when they got 'em back every one of 'em poor coves was cooked alive in their suits—"

"I've heard that story as well," I said, gently interrupting her flow. "Only it was out by the Vault Keeper, not the Daughters. Tindouf told me something similar about the Drooling Dog. Ask Prozor and she'll have her own version of it too, and you can bet it'll be a different ship and crew." I smiled and laid a hand on her wrist. "Just scare stories, Strambli. Besides, this isn't a Niner, not even close, and even if it was our sails wouldn't need hauling in."

She looked at me with mild resentment.

"I ain't jumpy, don't get that idea."

"I didn't think you were. Besides, we all have the right to be a little jumpy now and then. I'd say it's a very worthwhile survival trait, wouldn't you?"

Her expression was non-committal. "I looked through the sighting log, after what Surt said to Fura. Did she really see sail-flash?"

"She saw something, and perhaps it was real, but we'd be very unwise to make too much of it. The chances of another ship finding us out here are very small, and the likelihood of one taking an interest in us is even smaller. I shouldn't lose too much sleep over any of it. Besides, we'll soon be on a definite course, with a new plan. If we see a hint of sail-flash behind us then, we'll have to consider our options. But I doubt we'll see any more of Surt's phantom."

"And this new course of ours—does that mean Fura's come up with her suggestions?" She dropped her voice. "It's been five days, Adrana. How long does she need to pull some names out of the *Book of Worlds*?"

"That was what I was going to see her about."

"I'm glad one of us still gets an audience. Won't be long before we'll need permission to catch her eye, let alone have a chat."

"She's got a lot on her mind, Strambli, especially after our difficulties in the Rumbler. She takes responsibility for everything that's happened to us, and that weighs heavily on her now and again."

Strambli gave a slow nod. "Just as long as her ladyship favours us with her selection somewhere between now and the end of the present Occupation, I s'pose we'll be grateful for what we can get."

"We'll have made our choice by the end of the day, I'm sure of it. And forget about this storm. It's not going to cause us any trouble." I tried to lighten her mood. "Are you finished with your shift?"

"I was just going to wash some pots and pans."

"I'll let you know as soon as I have something from Fura."

"Captain Ness, you mean," Strambli said, turning from me.

*

For once Fura was in the control room, rather than her own quarters. She was at the Glass Armillary, which was much too big and cumbersome—not to say delicate—to be moved to any other part of the ship, even if it had been desired.

"I thought you were still on sighting duty," Fura said to me, as I made my presence known.

"Paladin called me in. Anyway, the static-discharge makes the whole ship light up like a lantern, so it isn't very good for dark adaptation anyway. I'd already swept all the sectors several times, and seen nothing."

"Well, it's handy that you're here," she said, stroking a metal finger against the edge of the Glass Armillary. "I've got the choices I'd like to present to the crew, damn their insistence."

We had our charts and maps, and they were useful for baubles and their insides. We had our star charts as well, and they helped with celestial navigation. But such records were of little use in the three-dimensional space of the Congregation, where the worlds were in constant movement with respect to each other. In a month any fixed representation of those world's positions would have been dangerously out of date. In half a year, many of those worlds would have been on the other side of the Old Sun, making a nonsense of any attempts to plot crossing times or plan an expedition. A navigator would have been better off throwing dice than trusting to that. But they needed something.

Hence, the Glass Armillary.

If you squinted, it looked like a lacy glass sphere, about three and half spans across, cumbersome and delicate as an ornamental chandelier, contained within a frame that was only bit less fragile-seeming than the glassy structure itself. When it was packed away, though, the Armillary's "sphere" turned out to be made out of a series of concentric rings, thirty-seven in total, each of which could be tilted at an angle to its neighbours.

The angles of the rings were set with reference to tables, and then locked, creating the sphere-like impression. The innermost ring represented the innermost processional of the Congregation; the first processional; and indeed was numbered as such. Within the inner circumference of that ring lay only empty space and the central jewel of the Old Sun. The outermost ring was numbered thirty-seven.

Mazarile—our homeworld—lay in the thirty-fifth processional, which meant it was on one of the rings of greatest diameter, furthest from the middle.

So were a lot of worlds—hundreds and thousands of them, although only a few hundred were named and settled.

Each of those worlds had its own orbit. But the way the Congregation was organised, those orbits tended to be bunched together in families, like the lanes at the greyhound track. All the worlds in the thirty-fifth processional minded their own business and kept to the thirty-fifth processional. They might pull apart from each other now and then, but they would never drift too far from the confines of that ring.

The worlds nearest the Old Sun moved in the fastest orbits, going round quicker than the ones on the outer edges. These were in the low-numbered processionals and were usually called the Shallows or the Sunwards. They were warmer, drawing the full benefit of the Old Sun's ailing energies and, generally speaking, they were desirable worlds on which to live, but it could be challenging to navigate between them, lending them a certain exclusivity. The bulk of people, though, made their homes in the mid-processionals. No one agreed on precisely where those began and ended, but it was commonly held to be somewhere between the tenth to the thirtieth. Beyond that lay the outer processionals, where worlds travelled further apart, commerce was sparser and more difficult, the economies slower, fashions a little behind the day, and so forth. The last handful of processionals (including Mazarile's own) were sometimes called the Frost Margins.

Of course, being able to name the processionals—even having glass circles with numbers on—was still only partially useful.

Within each ring, then, were a number of secondary rings given their own tints and sub-numbering. These sub-rings were very cunningly inlaid and could be slid around by hand or adjusted minutely using something like a glass clock-key, so delicate that it needed to be locked away with a different key all of its own. There were a few of these sub-rings in each processional, and each could be assigned the designation of a particular world of interest, and marked accordingly, using coloured wax pencils. The exact position of that world could then be fixed and altered from day to day. It was still tiresome as someone had to use ephemeris tables to make the initial setting; but once marked, it was relatively easy to keep track of a world's position, at least over the typical span of a crossing or expedition.

There was no hope of marking all twenty thousand settled worlds, and for most purposes there was no need to, anyway. The fortunes of worlds shifted all the while. What was an important trading stopover in 1650 might be a negligible backwater by 1750. In this bright and shiny new year of 1800, most captains and crews might only need to concern themselves with a hundred or so probable destinations, excluding baubles, and a hundred worlds could be marked onto the circles, with care, and their evolving positions tracked from day to day, week to week.

Baubles were a different, but related case. They tended not to move with the processionals, and their orbits could be irregular. They often swung out far beyond the outer worlds into the Emptyside. It was impractical to mark them in the same way as the settled worlds, so—if they were indicated at all—it was with red marbles on the end of long stalks, fixed into holes drilled into the Old Sun. There were baubles all the way down to the Sunwards, though, not just up in the Empty. Privateer crews tended to avoid those deep-orbit baubles, though, preferring to leave such easy pickings to the combines.

There were gradations etched onto those circles and stalks, indicating how many minutes it took a squawk signal to travel from one point to another. That was sometimes useful to know for the purposes of negotiation and signalling, but mainly it was shorthand for working out approximate crossing times. Sailing out from the Old Sun was easier than moving inward, but as a rule of thumb a ship might require six months to cross from one side of the Congregation to the other—sixteen light-minutes as a photon travelled. With a ship the size of *Revenger* (about four hundred spans nose to tail) and a crew numbering in the single figures, it was easily practical to carry sufficient rations to keep everyone healthy. In reality, captains would replenish stores at a settled world, then plot an expedition that took in a string of baubles, visiting each in a logical sequence based on crossing times and opening auguries, spending between three and nine months away from civilisation.

Now, with all those worlds I alluded to—squeezed into a volume only sixteen light-minutes across—and remembering that there are *millions* of such worlds, not thousands—you might be forgiven for wondering how such a tricky piece of clockwork could keep ticking for millions of years, without any sort of mishap.

No one can say for certain, but collisions must be very rare. There is certainly rubble out there, and some have speculated that it represents the dust of worlds that got in the way of other worlds. Others, though, hold that such dust is merely the material that was left over when the fifty million worlds were forged. Still others hold that the rubble is evidence of the Intra-Congregational war they claim happened between the Second and Third Occupations.

But the best explanation—from what I remember of the Museum of History—is that the worlds have an in-built aversion to colliding. Just as there are swallowers inside some of the worlds, so there are mechanisms—instincts, you might almost call them—which deter the worlds from wandering out of their tracks. Since these correcting mechanisms only have to apply a tiny alteration to forestall a collision ten thousand or a million years in the future, we have never sensed their direct influence, and perhaps we never shall.

For the sake of completeness, I ought to say that there's another theory, which is that, between the Occupations—when there are no monkeys around to witness anything—*something* comes along and gives all the worlds a tiny nudge, correcting them just enough to keep them out of trouble for a few more thousand years. Maybe that is so, but I prefer the first explanation, as it removes any possibility of this being done as a favour.

Because the thing about favours is that they can always be withdrawn; and the other thing about that second explanation is that it tangles itself up in a different mystery altogether, which is why we even have the Occupations.

Dwelling on these complications couldn't help but send my thoughts drifting back to the mad journal, which I was still carrying, and which troubled me more than I liked.

"Are you day-dreaming again?" Fura asked gently, snapping me back to the present, and the control room. "You've been staring into the glass like someone hypnotised you."

"I was just thinking what an awful shame something this rare and beautiful got to be in the possession of Bosa Sennen."

"It ain't hers now, which is all that matters. She took good care of it, though, didn't she?" Fura was using the little glass key to make a tiny adjustment to one of the Glass Armillary's circles, holding an ephemeris table open in her other hand.

"She had a rage on her," I said, thinking back to my time as her prisoner and understudy. "But she'd always prefer to direct that rage into slow cruelty, rather than mindless violence. Besides, she knew how valuable all this glass was to her. She was like a spider, waiting on the edge of a big black web, and this was her guide to where and when to move in."

Fura extracted a bauble and its stalk and repositioned it carefully, threading it through the narrow gaps between the circles.

"Did she ever involve you in her deliberations?"

"No," I answered, trying to be truthful while saying what Fura wanted to hear. "She listened to my reports from the bone room, and occasionally she'd bounce a question or two off me, when she was making up her own mind. But I was never the one that swayed her. I only ever got a glimpse or two of this gadget, on the few occasions she allowed me into this room. I think she was worried I might smash it, out of spite."

"Even after you'd seen what she did to Garval?"

"I thought I was going to die one way or the other." I swallowed, thinking of the vile punishment wrought on our friend

Garval, who was captured at the same time as me. "But I could think of easier ways to go than at Bosa's hands. I wasn't in a rush to see her bad side."

"You speak as if there was a side of her that *wasn't* bad." Fura went to a cabinet and slipped the glass key back into its place, locking up after it. "We daren't go into the deep processionals, not until our name's cleared, and Trevenza Reach is out of consideration. That leaves a handful of suitable worlds that we might risk a peek at, after taking some precautions."

I had no idea what sort of precautions she had in mind, but my curiosity was pricked. "Go on."

"This is us," she said, touching a stalk with a black marble on the end of it, not too far from the red marble of the Rumbler. "And these are three candidate worlds I've come up with, in the thirty-sixth and thirty-seventh processionals. Forget the bright lights, 'cos none of these places is what you'd call bustling, even compared to dear old Mazarile." She moved her hand to the outermost pair of disks, touching the places where she'd made a wax inscription. "But they'll serve us, I think—or one of 'em will. The combines rarely come out this far, so there's little chance of running into corporate trouble. There won't likely be too many other ships in the vicinity, either, and if we need to make a run for it, there's a lot of clear space we can lose ourselves in. First is a little spitball of a world called Metherick, or sometimes Methrick, depending on which edition of the *Book of Worlds* you consult. It's in the thirty-sixth. Sphereworld, not too unlike our own dear home. Couple of ports, a few cities—towns, more like—total population around three-hundred-thousand, although that may be a little out of date."

"You're right—makes Mazarile seem like the centre of the Congregation."

"We can't go near anywhere too teeming. It's backwaters or nothing, dear heart. But any one of us who doesn't like this new life can stop off there and wait for a ship going somewhere more lively."

"And the likelihood of recruiting the hands we need?"

"Who can say? Chances are there'll be people who're fed up with Metherick and willing to take a chance with a new crew, provided we're not too picky. Being a sphereworld, it will cost us what little fuel we have left to get the launch in, and the ship will need to stand off at quite a distance..."

I pulled a doubtful face. Given the choice, it would be better to find a world that did not have a swallower in it, so that we could come and go more readily.

"And the next place?"

She moved her hand along a bit, but still on the same processional. "Kathromil. Tubeworld. Population around one-hundred-and-fifty-thousand at the last census. Just one major settlement, but I hear it's not too bad a place to do business. No swallower to trouble us, so we can haul-in close on sails without ripping ourselves to shreds, and we won't burn too much fuel shuttling over."

"Sounds ideal."

"It's my favoured choice out of the three, in so far as I'm forced to approve of any part of this plan. I would still rather we confined ourselves to more baubles, rather than risking contact with civilisation. That said, I feel duty bound to point out that there is one small drawback."

"Which is?"

"They've got some bad blood where Bosa's concerned."

I shrugged. "Who doesn't?"

"More than the usual. After the crash of eighty-one Kathromil ended up on hard times, not being on anyone's obvious trade circuit. To dig themselves out of that hole, the chamber of commerce invested almost all of their surplus in an expedition of their own. Sponsored a ship and a crew, in the hope they'd turn up something to change everyone's fortune."

I nodded. "The same bright idea our chamber had with Captain Lar."

"At least Captain Lar came back. The Kathromil expedition

wasn't even that lucky. They ran into Bosa, down near the Dargan Gap. She picked 'em apart, leaving just enough evidence to make it plain that the handiwork was hers. Butchered the expedition and bankrupted its backers. As you can guess, the city elders on Kathromil have been nursing some bad feelings ever since. Once a year they have a parade through the streets, after which they make a big bonfire and burn an effigy of Bosa. Still, we're not Bosa, are we?" She held her gaze onto me for a second longer than was comfortable, as if daring me to dispute this last point. "So long as we don't give them any cause to suspect otherwise, there's no reason for 'em to treat us inhospitably. I just thought I'd mention it, is all, so you knew there was that fly in our stew."

"I don't know, Fura. Seems to me if there was a place we'd be wise to avoid, it would be a world with a particular grudge against Bosa. What about the third possibility?"

"I don't think it's as viable."

"Tell me anyway."

Her finger skipped to the thirty-seventh processional, and landed next to a wax inscription. "Wheel Strizzardy. Wheelworld, as you might've cottoned. Just as easy to haul-in to as Kathromil, all things considered. Population about three-hundred-and-fifty-thousand, so a shade busier than the other places, although we oughtn't to put too much stock in that, the census being so out of date..."

"As long as there's people, it serves our needs. I'm sorry, but I'm thinking I like it a bit better than the other two. Metherick's all right, apart from the fuel and trouble'll it'll cost us, but I'd still sooner do business with a place in the thirty-seventh than the thirty-sixth. It's only one processional further out but things thin out quickly in those outer orbits."

"That they do. And so does the experience of ships and trade. But is Wheel Strizzardy too far into the backwaters? Anyone who decides to leave us, they'd be at the arse-end of nowhere."

"We'll make sure everyone has the facts before they decide whether to leave us or not," I said. "Besides, what you said about Metherick applies just as well to Strizzardy. If there are coves stuck there, we'll be able to pick and choose our new recruits."

"Mm," Fura said doubtfully. "I'm still favouring Kathromil."

"Then why did you consider Wheel Strizzardy, if you're so set against it?"

"I'm being fair about it. I know there's a mood about the ship—some of 'em thinking I'm getting above my station, that I've always got to have my way." She made a convincing show of regret, dimples appearing either side of her mouth. "This ship's had its share of monsters. I don't care to be the next one. So I will be flexible."

This surprised me, in a good way, but I did my best to accept it without fanfare. "I'll put your arguments fairly and squarely—you have my word on that."

"I don't need your word, sister. I trust you to do right by me—and all of us."

The intercom buzzed. Fura snapped to it with a scowl of irritation. "What is it?"

"Miss Arafura," Paladin said. "The solar weather event is abating. According to the latest advisories on the general squawk we shall not be troubled by another disturbance for at least a week."

"Adrana and I will listen on the bones, just in case there's anything more on the horizon. Was that all, Paladin?"

"No, Miss Arafura. There was something else."

Fura switched the intercom to the private channel, so that it was only coming through into this room.

"Proceed, Paladin," she said.

"During the peak of the storm, when our operational systems were suffering the greatest disturbance, I detected a troubling indication from a number of our hull receivers."

"Connected to the storm itself?" I asked, thinking how the

electromagnetic interference had already played havoc with our compasses.

"I cannot be certain, Miss Adrana. It is possible that the storm created rogue signals in a number of my sensory circuits, and I have allowed for those wherever possible. But there is also a chance that we were swept by another ship."

# 6

Paladin was right about the storm, but the clearing of the weather left our minds more unsettled than before. I wished we could know for certain what had happened, but like Surt's two sail-flashes (only one of which was in the official record) the event only sowed further anxiety. To begin with, the storm might have tricked the hull receivers into generating a false reading, giving the impression that we had been swept when in fact nothing had occurred.

But if one ship *were* stalking another, and wished to sweep them to improve their positional and distance fix, then a solar disturbance was exactly the time when that sweep might be risked. If it were done quickly, just a single ranging pulse, then from our standpoint it would be hard to distinguish from a false indication caused by the storm and the other ship would only run a small chance of giving away its own location. Since our own equipment was already providing confused readings, and our more delicate instruments had been pulled into the hull, it was a gamble well worth taking. I imagined the sweeper-operator in our phantom pursuer, hunched over a glowing screen, one hand on the thumb-control, waiting for the opportune moment when the storm would provide maximum confusion, and then transmitting that ranging pulse. A second or so later, our ship would have shown up on the sweeper screen as a faint, fading blob. Our sails were dark and our hull all the shades of charcoal and black, but our ship would only have to reflect a small fraction of that ranging pulse to give away our position.

The situation was perfectly balanced. We could have used the cover of the storm to send a ranging pulse their way, and benefited from the same confusion. But we had not thought of it, and now the storm was fading, and to run the sweeper now would confer little or no benefit. Quite the contrary. We would both know exactly where the opposing ship lay, which was a kind of parity. But if we had in fact *not* been swept—and we were not sure that we had been—then running the sweeper now would discard whatever stealth advantage we now retained.

If indeed there was another ship out there at all.

But Paladin's sensors had detected that sweep from the same general part of the sky as the sail-flashes. While I believed in a growing number of curious things, coincidences were not among them.

*

I spun the locking wheel, opened the door, entered the cramped, windowless space, and then fastened the door again from the inside, tightening the wheel as far as it would go.

The skull filled most of the room, suspended from the spherical wall by a series of cables, each of which had springs interspersed along its length to dampen any vibrations. It was long like a horse's skull, but much larger, and if there'd been a large enough hole in it I might easily have wriggled inside and used it as a cot. Not that I had much inclination to do that. Through the fist-sized eyeholes lay a cavelike structure of thin ridges and partitions of bone, as well as gauze-thin curtains of tissue, and several hundred tiny twinkling lights, sprinkled around the interior and sewn together with a fine cobwebbing of connective strands, the lacy remnants of alien neural circuits. Those lights had made me uneasy long before I ever saw my first twinkle-head; now that uneasiness produced a shudder. The lights flickered because some obscure process still went on, even though nearly all the organic matter in that skull had been scoured away. It was like a city where all the people had died, all the purpose for the city's existence gone, the buildings gutted and windowless, wind chasing rubbish down the deserted streets, but where the traffic lights still worked, the underground trains still operated and the stock-market machines kept printing out reams of paper babble.

I assured myself that the twinkly was just machinery that no one had turned off, clever enough to do its job but not quite clever enough to grasp that its host was deceased. The twinkly was twinkling because it was in contact—or attempting to re-establish contact—with other skulls, the remote dead brethren of this one-time alien host.

Which was handy for us—crews, I mean—because it meant we had another means of signalling each other besides the squawk, which was to imprint our own messages onto that alien murmuring.

The difficulty was that only a few people had the aptitude to send and receive signals through the skulls.

I was one of them. So was Fura.

Of those who were capable, only one in a thousand ever got really good at it. The problem was that the aptitude gradually faded away as the brain's neural circuitry hardened into the fixed patterns of adulthood. Mister Cazaray, who had taught my sister and I, had been in his early twenties when he started losing his edge. By then his synapses were stiffening, no longer able to adjust to the skull. Cazaray had still been able to read the skull on the *Monetta*, but his faculty had been declining and he would never have been able to tune in to a different one.

I was nineteen; Fura well past her eighteenth birthday. I had to remind myself of that now and then, as the events of the past year were enough for several lifetimes, and there were days when we both carried it in our faces, feeling old beyond our years. But still, we were not yet of the age Mister Cazaray had been, and that meant that we ought to have a few more years of reliable skull-time between us. But exactly how many years—how long it would be before the aptitude began to tail off, gradually or precipitously—no one could have told us.

I went to the part of the wall where the neural bridges were racked, took one of them from its hook and settled it on my head, pressing down to get the induction pads as close to my scalp as possible. There were fold-down muffs to shield the ears, and a pair of hinged blinkers for the eyes. The bridge also had a bulge on the left-side temple, which contained the spool for the contact wire.

I drew out the contact wire, pinching the small, needle-like plug as if I were about to do some darning.

Then I turned my attention to the skull. Apart from the holes drilled into it for the support wires, there were dozens of metal sockets bored into the bone, dotted at random positions from one end to the other. These were the possible input sites, where the contact wire from the neural bridge might be able to lock in to a viable signal.

If it had only ever stayed in one position, the life of a Bone Reader would have been a lot simpler. But half the art lay in chasing that signal around the skull, following it as if it were a rat scampering under floorboards.

Sometimes it was very faint, and sometimes entirely absent. Occasionally it disappeared for good, which was why captains occasionally needed to find new skulls. "New" in the loosest sense: all skulls were ancient, but there was a market in them and now and then some fortunate cove found one in a bauble, and if it was a sound one, that was the cove's retirement taken care of there and then.

This skull might have been good once, but it was getting trickier to use and the evidence for that was all over it. No one drilled so many input sockets into a skull unless the signal was turning elusive. The sockets were marked with symbols, inked onto the bone, making a record of dates and signal strengths. All very methodical, as was Bosa's way. She wanted to know the speed at which this skull was failing her, so she could plan ahead to the next one. When Fura set a trap for Bosa, part of the lure had been the promise of stealing a fresh skull from Captain Trusko. But Trusko's skull had gone dark as soon as we tried to transplant it from one ship to another, and we were forced to continue relying on Bosa's original.

How long it would last was anyone's guess. All these holes risked weakening the skull's integrity. There were grave cracks running the length of it, sutured with metal staples, but it was the hidden flaws that caught you out, the buried stresses that built up internally and invisibly, until the skull cracked wide at the slightest contact.

"Courage," I whispered to myself, for there was still no part of this that I considered natural or enjoyable.

The skull jerked on its springs as I hooked in, but it soon settled down. I disdained the eye-shields or ear-muffs, and did not need to turn down the light. I took a vain sort of pride in that.

Still, I was obliged to offer my empty mind to the skull.

There was more to it than just silencing the ordinary clutter of my thoughts. Any cove could do that, but squeezing even a hint of a signal out of a skull had taken Fura and I days and days of practice.

There must have been times when even Cazaray doubted that we had the gift. It was more than just calming the chatter in our heads. We had to find the secret windows and doors inside our own skulls, the ones that were usually bolted shut—for good reason—and fling them wide open so that a thin, questing wind could find its way into us. That wind pushed its way up from the dark, damp basements of our minds, through dusty chambers and along forgotten corridors, curling its way up secret staircases, until at last it found a way into the conscious mind.

Sometimes the wind was all that came, carrying no message except its own presence. It meant the skull was active, whispering to me, but that no one was using another skull to push a signal through to this one. It was like picking up a telephone and hearing a hum, but no voice.

I moved from one socket to the next. The wind was absent. Judging by the marks next them, these inputs had been dead for some while. But it never hurt to check.

I plugged and unplugged and listened.

And picked up the thin edge of something; a furtive, slippery presence that was there and not there. The input was sensitive, the presence coming and going as I moved my finger on the wire.

And moved my lips without speaking. *Something.*

I had been alone in the bone room until then but now I shared that space with a bodyless guest, one that might well have been mindless, but which was in the same instance fully aware of me, observing and responding.

It was the skull's carrier signal, signifying it was active, capable of sending and receiving. The twinkly was twinkling a little brighter and more insistently than before as I nudged the skull into some state of wakefulness.

Patterns of coloured light spilled from the eye-sockets.

Now I had to listen even harder—to pick out a monkey signal riding the carrier wave, its modulations a hundred or a thousand times weaker. There were dials and sliders on the neural bridges, to amplify the signal. One always did that with caution, and never before locking on to a stable carrier.

There it was.

Words were coming through. It was less like hearing spoken language than being aware of the gaps that would be left if spoken words were taken out of silence, leaving negative hollows of themselves. Cold as newsprint, mostly, and lacking any sort of natural inflection.

My habit was to note down the words, mouthing them to myself first, committing them to memory just long enough to scratch them into the message log, without once losing the train of what was still coming in. That was a skill in itself.

*"... beg confirmation of auguries for Blind Spot, the Barnacle and the Yellow Jester. Will reciprocate with information on incidents of discord and mutiny on two vessels of mutual interest..."*

Neither meant for us, nor intelligence that was of any direct benefit. It was just one unnamed ship sending to another and thinking they had the conversation all to themselves. More than likely it was two ships that had done friendly business in the past and established a history of exchanging information. They might be using matched skulls, sourced from the same bauble; or matched readers—siblings, like Fura and I; or both. Or they might be using loose encryption—codes and misdirection—or simply trusting that no third party was likely to be tuning in at exactly the right time and frequency. It might even be a privateer sending indiscriminately, begging for scraps.

That was only one voice coming through. The strongest, certainly, but there were others, phasing in and out like ripples on water, so that I might catch only a word or a phrase at best.

*"...purchase of ten thousand leagues of triple-filament yardage... would advise that a launch of excise men were last seen... lost the back-preventers on the photon squall...fifteen high-bar quoins by way of salvage... the surgeon's mate to attend with all expediency... as we hauled-in to Black's Talon... bring lungstuff and your best loblolly boys..."*

Different voices, whispering out of different skulls, from different ships. Always ships, with rare exceptions. Skulls never worked properly on worlds, or else the banks and combines would have carved up the market in old bones years ago. Too unreliable for those coves, anyway. Too spooky.

It took a good Bone Reader to pick out those secondary voices, but I counted myself rather better than good. Beneath them was a level that was yet more difficult to read, and yet I knew it lay within my capabilities, when the skull was working well and all other factors lay in my favour. Pressing that higher babble from my attentions, I strained to listen beyond it. The silence rose and fell, roaring its emptiness into my mind. Sooner or later, as I well knew, I would think I heard a voice where none was present. But if I concentrated well enough I might pick up a true communication slipping beneath all the others.

There.

Not a word, not a sound, but the presence of another monkey mind, connected to another skull. I could not say that it was near or far, only that it had been reaching out to me, not because it desired contact—it would have been stronger and more assertive if that were the case—but because it had an interest in knowing something of my nature. Our minds touched at that faint level of interaction, and we each flinched back at the same moment. It had been sufficient, though. I had learned nothing of that other mind, gained not one scant insight into the person who might have been in that other bone room, thousands or millions of leagues away, but they had tried very hard to exclude a word from their own thought process, a word that betrayed entirely too intimate an understanding of our own nature, and yet that word still slipped through.

*Nightjammer.*

*

At the next convenient watch I made tea, rationed out a little more hot buttered bread, and gathered the others in the galley while I laid out the entrails of our darkening situation. Stationed around the table were Prozor, Strambli, Surt, Tindouf and myself. The only one not present was Fura, who had elected to remain in her cabin until she knew the verdict, not wishing to be seen to influence proceedings.

That was prudent of her, I had to admit. Even if she said nothing, she would have found it hard not to chip in at opportune moments with a scowl or a frown.

"If you're here to tell us that she's changed her mind again..." Strambli said warningly.

"No, she hasn't," I said. "She said she'd come up with a destination for us, and that's what she's done."

"I hear we was sweeped," Surt said. "And that the sweep came from the same place as those sail-flashes of mine."

"I thought there was just the one," Strambli said, frowning slightly. "There were other flashes?"

"One flash that we can speak about with certainty," I said. "And a sweeper alert that happened to arrive in the middle of that storm, which is when I'd be least inclined to trust any of our instruments."

"So you don't think there's a ship tailin' us?" Surt asked, folding her arms.

I had made no mention of the incident in the bone room, not even to Fura, and I was in no mood to add to Surt's concerns until we had a better understanding of our predicament. "Paladin couldn't say where that sweeper pulse might have come from with any certainty, if indeed it was real. The same general part of the sky as Surt's sail-flash, yes, but if we started jumping at every shadow—"

"I don't like it," Strambli said.

"You don't like many thingses," Tindouf said, so plainly and with so little malice that not even Strambli could have taken umbrage. "I trusts the Ness sisters. If they say there isn't a ship coming after us, I believes 'em."

"You'd trust anyone," Surt said, shaking her head.

"I woulds," Tindouf said agreeably. "Until they crosses me, which only ever happens the once."

"If there is a ship with an interest in us," I said, "it will follow us. Otherwise, it's just a mirage, or some perfectly innocent ship that just happens to be operating out here as well. For which there's no crime."

"And which do you think it is, Adrana?" Strambli said.

"I think we should put it out of our minds until we've changed course."

Strambli bit into some bread and reached up to wipe butter from her lips. "So Fura's decided our plan, has she, with her years of experience of this sort of thing?"

Tindouf tapped his clay pipe against the table. He smiled gently and in his usual conciliatory tone said: "Let's see what she has to says for herself, shalls we, before passin' judgements?"

Prozor took some tea.

"Can't hurt."

"Fura didn't make her choices blindly," I said, unwrapping a sheet of rough-edged cloth on which I'd marked the names and salient details of our possible worlds. I set it on the table, with four low-bar quoins at either corner serving as magnetic paperweights. "She thought it was best to look to the outer processionals, and I don't think any of us would fault her on that score. Then she narrowed it down by only considering worlds that are a little off the beaten track. We wouldn't want to get too close to a place that does a lot of commerce, because it'll likely be swarming with other ships and crews, some of whom may recognise us for what we are."

"Be hard for anyone not to," Strambli said.

"Fura's given that some consideration as well," I said. "But I'll come to that once we've settled on a choice. Now, I don't want to be seen to be ruling out a place before we've discussed it. But Fura's first candidate is a world called Metherick, and while it seems good enough for our purposes, it's the only one of the three with a swallower, which means a steep gravity well."

"We couldn't get too close on sails," Prozor said. "So our only way in or out would be with the launch."

"If things had gone peachier with Cap'n Rack's fuel, it wouldn't be a problem," I said. "But as it stands we can't be burning it too profligately, and getting to and from a world like Metherick would put a dent in what's left of our supply."

"So I s'pose the other two places are easier?" Surt asked.

I nodded. "Kathromil and Wheel Strizzardy. I don't suppose anyone here has direct experience of them?"

"Met a cove who'd been to Kathromil once," Prozor said, favouring us with no further elaboration on that score. "And I've been to a hundred wheelworlds, but never heard of Wheel Lizzardy…"

"Strizzardy," I said.

"Or that one, either."

"Both are in the thirty-seventh," I said, tapping a finger against the cloth. "Neither's what you'd call the beating heart of civilisation, but then that's not what we want, either. We need a place just quiet and sleepy enough not to cause us difficulties, but where we can still do business. Anyone who wants to leave us, they'll have ample opportunity. Perhaps they'll have a wait of a few months before there's a chance to buy passage somewhere else, but we'll make sure whoever steps off this ship has the funds to cover themselves."

"Just don't go blabbin' about your adventures," Prozor said. "Or we might need to come back and recover those funds."

I smiled at Prozor, taking that to be an indication that, no matter what other people's plans might be, she was sticking with the ship.

"I doubt there'll be any blabbing. But we will need to watch what we say. Fura likes Kathromil, but there's a wrinkle to it that I think you all should know about."

"Which would be?" Surt asked.

"They're no friends of Bosa." I told them about the sponsored expedition, and the fate of it. "They hate her with a passion and we'd unwise to get ourselves snared up in that grudge. They'd only have to think we were something to do with Bosa for it to go badly."

"And I doubts they'ds be in a hurry to hear our sides of it," Tindouf said, before drawing a long inhalation through his pipe.

"It's a problem, to be sure," I said, nodding at the big man. "I wouldn't care to put their sense of fair justice to the test, if I could help it."

"Which means steering clear of Kathromil," Strambli said. "With no guarantee the other place'll be any better."

"We wouldn't know for sure until we got there," I said. "But they don't have that very public history with Bosa, which is one thing. No reason to be fearful at the first sight of us."

Surt folded her arms skeptically. "Is this really the best she's come up with?"

"Sometimes you draw the short straw," I said. "And sometimes all you've got is short straws. I agree that none of them look very promising, but we're limited in the options open to us. Each of us could stick a pin into the *Book of Worlds* and find somewhere nicer, but we have to restrict ourselves to places where we won't get into trouble, or stand a chance of running into other ships. I'm afraid that rules out most of the Congregation."

"Looks as if Wheel Strizzardy it is," Prozor said, "unless there's a disadvantage to that place as well."

"Not that I'm aware of," I said.

The others mumbled and nodded their reluctant agreement. "If them's the choices, Adrana," Surt said, "then I suppose we'll take the third one. Better on fuel."

Strambli rubbed at her neck. "And keepin' our heads glued on. I prefer it. Tindouf?"

"I's take what's given." He tapped the pipe between thoughts. "But here's the thing that's botherin' old Tindouf, Adrana. They might not have a direct grudge against Bosa, but that don't mean they's going to be friendly when they sees our sails—or rather *don'ts* see 'em, which is just as bad. They'll still knows what's we are and what's we did."

"The man has a point," Prozor said.

"They'll see our sails," I said. "Some of them, at least. Bosa wasn't stupid, she knew she might need to pass herself off as a normal ship and crew, so there's a supply of ordinary sail in the holds, not far shy of two thousand acres. It's in poor condition—more'n likely it was looted from the ships she plundered, after they'd been given a coil-gun broadside—but Bosa never meant to use it in place of her catchcloth."

"So what use is it to us?" Surt asked.

"We can run it out on the normal rigging," Prozor said, going with the idea. "Don't matter how peppered or torn it is, if it passes muster from a few hundred leagues."

"Why would Bosa bother with all that sail, if she never went near a civilised port?" Strambli asked.

"She did on occasion," I said. "Besides, the sails take up some room, but not much when they're packed and folded handsomely, and even a thousand acres of sail wouldn't weigh as much as one drum of fuel. The rigging's heavier by far."

"It'll work," Prozor said, frowning hard, as if she was thinking through every detail in her head. "Wouldn't hold up to a second glance, not to someone who knows their riggin', but the trick is not to draw a second glance in the first place."

"In which case," Surt said, "and I hate to break it to you, but it ain't just our catchcloth sails that needs attendin'. Have you seen the state of us?" She leaned forward to press her point. "We look like what we are: a pirate ship! This whole bag of bolts is several kinds of nightmare from the outside, what with all the spikes and grisly *accoutrements* Bosa saw fit to stick on 'er."

"I agree," I said, thinking of the times we'd come back to the ship from a bauble expedition. "It is a significant problem."

"Crossing time to Wheel Strizzardy?" Prozor asked me, in the sensible expectation that I'd have the calculations under my belt.

"Five weeks," I said. "Thirty-five days, give or take one or two. We could get to Kathromil a little sooner, if we had to."

"We ain't going near anywhere that feels that strongly about Bosa," Strambli said, rubbing at her neck as if she could already feel a rope around it.

Prozor ruminated. She knew a thing or two about putting together a knotty plan. "We can do it," she said eventually. "Configurin' the sails won't be child's play, exactly, but then we ain't exactly children, are we? If we tricked Bosa—which we did—than we can trick some sappy coves on Wheel Strizzardy, 'specially as we mean 'em no harm by it. As for the hull, what's been fixed on can be fixed off, if we've a will."

"In five weeks?" Surt asked doubtfully. "Less than that, even, as we'll need to look pleasant through a sweeper or a telescope, once we're close enough?"

"So long as we get a start on it, we'll be golden," Prozor said.

Surt picked desultorily at the bread, sniffing as if she could pick up the scent of mould even with all the butter slathered onto it. "I suppose weeks is better than months, even if we have to work our fingers to stumps. Whether or not any of us jumps ship, it won't be a day too soon to get some new supplies aboard."

"Agreed," I said, allowing myself a small private sigh of relief, feeling that I had won the crew around to the most sensible plan open to us. "We need this rendezvous regardless of anyone's personal intentions. But we need to be clear on the risk, all the same. Maybe not as much of one as sailing to Metherick or Kathromil, but no one's going to welcome us with open arms if they get so much as a hint of a connection to Bosa." I took some more tea before I continued. "Time's on our side for the present, but word will get around, and things will be pieced together. We need to press our advantage while we can, and that means making a fast crossing to Wheel Strizzardy, while doing all that we can to get this ship looking a little less shivery." I nodded at them all in turn. "I concur with Proz. We can do it, if we don't sit around bumping our gums."

"And your sister?" Strambli asked. "She'll take kindly to this little mutiny over her preferred choice?"

"I'll take care of Fura," I said.

*

I met her in her cabin, studying her profile for a few seconds as she worked with her journals, Paladin's lights playing across the outline of her face. For the second time I had the forceful sense that I had wandered in on my sister when she was younger, lost in the rapture of a picture book or jigsaw, her imagination casting itself away to horizons beyond the wallpaper, parlours and stairs with which we were so familiar.

Whatever the adventure she thought she deserved, Fura was having it now. A fine black ship to sail, a crew to do her bidding, a robot with a soldier's mind at her side, and the entirety of the Congregation and all its worlds at her disposal. Yet I wondered if some part of her wished things had come out just a little differently. If you were fierce and determined enough, you could obtain the things you most desired. When those gifts arrived, though, it was often with complications and bedevilments you never once considered.

"They've agreed," I said.

She turned her face to mine and the hardness came back into it like an unyielding mask pushing up from under her skin.

"Then we're of one mind, that Kathromil's the best choice?"

"Not precisely," I said, feeling it was better to get the bad news out of the way. "They agreed Metherick's too risky, all considered, as well as being wasteful of fuel. But I told them about that grudge against Bosa on Kathromil, and that didn't sit well."

"There isn't a world in the Congregation where she'd be welcome, Adrana."

"I know it's a question of degrees. But burning effigies of Bosa was a step too far, and frankly I don't disagree, not when there's a world that serves us just as well and which we can reach just as easily."

Her eyes narrowed. "You weighed in on this, did you?"

I nodded slowly. "I offered my opinion, as I was entitled to do. The choice was freely made, though. There's no point delegating a decision if you won't accept the outcome."

"No," she answered, almost trembling, as if she was keeping some almighty fury just under control, like a bottle of rocket propellant about to explode. "You're right...and I *do* accept it. I would've preferred Kathromil—if we'd kept to a script, we could have dodged any suspicion of being connected to Bosa—but if Wheel Strizzardy is the crew's choice, I abide by it." She glanced down at her own papers, dense with her own handwriting and the spidery workings-out of celestial mechanics calculations. "Five weeks, then."

"Tindouf suggested we disguise the ship herself, in addition to the sails. Prozor's in agreement."

"Then we'll steer immediately for Strizzardy. Did you...gauge the weather, in terms of who means to stay, and who to remain?"

I had noticed that when we were speaking privately my sister discarded some portion of the act she put on for the benefit of the others. She was inclined to speak more properly and not be in such a habit to sound like she'd been born in a space-chest. It was as if, deep down, she recognised that we were still playing a sort of dressing-up game, one that had started the night we abandoned Father at the Museum of History, and which occasionally happened to involve death and mutilation.

"I can't say. I think Prozor's with us for the long haul, and I can't see Tindouf being quick to leave. Strambli and Surt, I'll reserve judgement over. Perhaps being given the chance to leave will be all that they ask for, and then they'll happily remain aboard."

"And you, seeing as we're on the subject?"

"I'm not done with this little escapade of ours just yet, Fura. Like you I'd like to see a little more of things. But looking beyond the next five weeks, it depends on what our purpose is."

"We've got a ship and a crew. I'd have thought our purpose was transparent."

"To you, perhaps."

Her look was inquisitive, but not hostile. "I fail to see where the difficulty lies."

"Here's where," I said. "Other than the fact that we lack a couple of specialists, we're equipped to go into the same game as any other privateer. Cracking baubles, finding treasure, selling it back to the worlds—earning our living that way, with all the ups and downs that come with the profession."

"Which is why I was so keen to get our mitts on that fuel," Fura said.

"I don't doubt that you had plans for that fuel. You'll be wanting to crack a few more baubles, I'm sure. But I think you've got things buzzing around in your head that go beyond common privateering."

"Which would be?"

"Something grander, and likely something more dangerous. I know you, sister. Maybe not as well as I used to, but well enough, and I recognise a preoccupation when I see one. You're thinking of what Bosa told you about the quoins, near the end."

"Be better if I ignored all that, would it?"

"Her business—her madness—doesn't have to become ours."

"Oh, I can keep her at arm's reach," she said off-handedly.

"The glowy's companion enough for me—there isn't room in my skull for a second tenant."

"You'd best be sure of that."

"Oh, I am. It wasn't me that she tried to turn, was it? Beyond that short time near the end of her life, after I rescued you, me and her were barely acquainted."

"No," I said, reflecting on the things she had done to Bosa. "But from her point of view, you more than made up for it."

"Listen," she said, striking a more reasonable tone. "I'm not making any assumptions about those quoins. But if they do exist, that's still stolen money, isn't it? Perhaps all that stuff about dead souls being locked in the quoins is just so much chaff. As you said, she'd have come out with anything if it bought her a few more breaths. But we'd be fools to turn up our noses at a hoard of quoins, if it's ours for the taking."

"Mm," I said, not convinced by this sudden shift to cold-hearted avarice. "And we'd do... what, exactly, with this money?"

"If Bosa was stealing from crews for as long as legend has it, there could be millions of high-bar quoins sitting unclaimed." Her voice gained a reverential hush. "Ours, Adrana. We could split it among the crew and retire to the worlds of our choosing. No one'd know where it came from. That's the great benefit of quoins—they can't be marked or traced. So long as we spent our gains carefully, so as not to devalue the quoins already in circulation, we could live handsomely."

"I'm glad you've given this some thought."

"Just musing on it, dear heart. We could do more than retire, though. The banks treated our poor father shabbily, didn't they? For once we'd have leverage over 'em, sister. Financial power—more than our dear dead parents ever dreamed of. Father always paid his debts—he was too proud not to. But when he needed a loan to help look after Mother, or take care of his own health, do you think they cared? He was a fine, proud man, and the banks rewarded his honesty and loyalty with callous disregard." She sniffed, lines wrinkling the bridge of her nose. "We could be a power in the Congregation that they needed to be fearful of, not the other way around. Now, wouldn't that be a fine thing?"

"You always did have a way of making any action seem like the only proper thing."

"You were the one who twisted my arm to run away."

"And it's turned our lives upside down." I sighed, not wanting to squabble with Fura. Time was I'd have generally won any argument, being ten months older and cannier, but that advantage counted for little now. "All this talk is speculation, though. You don't have the faintest idea where to start looking for those quoins."

"And you are certain she never mentioned them to you?"

I sighed again, wondering how many times we had already gone over this. "She was nurturing me as a possible successor, not unburdening herself of her every secret. She never spoke of them and we never visited any rock or world between the time I was taken and the time you came for me."

"No matter," Fura said, glancing at those journals on her desk. "The operational secret must lie somewhere in this ship. Paladin will find it sooner or later; there's nothing he can't ferret out, given time. He's got to be careful, though—can't rush things. The ship may not be sentient like Paladin, but it's got a slyness about it all the same. There's a chance it'll scramble or erase its secrets if it suspects interference."

"I thought the ship was ours?"

"It is—in the flesh, if not yet fully in spirit. But have no fear, dear heart. We'll bend its loyalty to us soon enough, with care and consideration, and oblige it to cough up its treasures."

"I listened to the bones," I said, off-handedly, thinking I should enjoy a look at those journals, when the opportunity came.

She gave me a sharp, disapproving glance. "I thought we had an agreement."

"We did. Never one of us alone with the skull. But it's dying and you were otherwise occupied. Anyway, I thought you should know that I picked up a mind and word."

Curiosity battled with displeasure in her face.

"Did you?"

"*Nightjammer.* This ship's old nickname. They were trying very hard not to let it slip, especially when they sensed me."

"You should never have—"

I cut her off with gentle assertiveness. "I knew you would not be pleased, and I thought twice about mentioning it. I've said nothing to the others for now, they're rattled enough as it is. But I think we may read a few things into that name. Someone knows what we are, and I'm of the strong opinion that the mind I sensed is on the ship that generated that sweeper pulse and gave off Surt's sail-flash. We are being shadowed by a ship that knows our identity, and I can think of only one reason anyone would be so bold as to do that."

"They wish to take us," Fura said, with a sort of reverence in her voice. "And they must believe they can."

# 7

We turned for Wheel Strizzardy. We were falling back into the Congregation now, chasing a long parabolic course, employing the flux on our sails to alter our angular momentum around the Old Sun, and therefore—by slow and painstaking means—effect the celestial equivalent of tacking into the wind.

For ten days a sort of normality returned to the ship. Despite a heightened period of watches in the sighting room, no more sail-flashes were seen. The Old Sun had settled into a deep and contented slumber, with no eruptions or prominences to meddle with our systems, and therefore no possibility of using the sweeper in a covert fashion. We were not swept, and we did not dare chance a return sweep. I did not return to the bone room, and to my knowledge neither did Fura. In fact, I went so far as to employ Prozor's old trick of placing a thread across the doorway—except that in my case I used a strand of my own hair. Whenever I inspected the bone room door, that strand was still present. In truth I was not surprised by that. Fura cared even less for that crack-ridden skull than I did. I think she was afraid that some of Bosa's madness was still inside it, waiting for a new receptacle. Neither of us would be too sorry when it finally stopped working.

It was a busy time, and that helped settle our collective nerves. Besides the sighting room watches, all hands were required to help with the work of transforming the outline of our ship. We had less than five weeks to complete the job, since we would be falling into sweeper and telescope range long before we actually hauled-in at our destination.

Prozor was right: it only had to pass muster at first glance, but if there was something about that first glance that rang false we would be in immediate trouble.

With only six able crewmembers we all had to weigh-in. Quickly we agreed on a division of labour, with shifts and teams all plotted out by the hour and by the watch. Most of the work would require being outside, in vacuum gear, which meant a lot of taking suits on and off, and coming and going through locks. The more that could be made to run like clockwork, the better we could keep to a schedule.

It was a golden rule that one, or preferably two, people would always remain inside the ship. One to make sure those outside could get back in, if something went wrong with the lock. Another just in case the first one went and died on us. It was why Tindouf and Surt had remained aboard while the rest of us went down to the Rumbler. It was also prudent to have eyes and ears on the sweeper and squawk, and someone had to be in the sighting room whenever practical.

So we organised into three teams, dividing up the watches in a pattern that was equally fair and equally gruelling. Fura and Surt constituted one squad, Strambli and Prozor the next, and Tindouf and I the third. Each team was made up of one former member of Captain Rackamore's crew, and one former member of Captain Trusko's, allowing for some overlap, and sidestepping any question of strained loyalties or favouritism.

It was hard on us all and I won't pretend otherwise. But it was better than sitting around fretting, with nothing on our minds but worry. Now our heads and hearts were taken up with practical matters, preparing for our watches, coming and going from locks, taking care of suits and tools and always, always planning the next step. Curiously, although we were tired, and although there was still a possibility that we were being pursued, our collective moods all went up a notch. There was more laughter in the galley than at any time since our taking the ship, even if that mirth had a ragged edge to it and was never far from turning into yawns.

Deep down, I thought, we were creatures of order—all of us. We liked divisions of work and rest, and felt happiest when we had a structure governing our days.

The pattern of watches proceeded thus. The first team would sleep for six hours, work outside for six, rest for six, then rest again. Twelve hours straight rest sounded easy, but in reality there was never any shortage of chores to be done, including cooking and washing-up, since the usual arrangements were now in abeyance.

Meanwhile the second team's watches would be to sleep, work outside, rest, then go outside again. The third team had the toughest pattern: sleep, rest, and then two consecutive outside shifts—twelve sweaty hours in vacuum gear, with no respite. They got a lot done, though, by not having to come in and out between those shifts.

No one would have put up with that, except that the following day would see the arrangement shuffled around, so that it was the first team who worked the double vacuum shift, and the second team who got two consecutive rest shifts.

You might think it was inefficient that we all slept at the same time. But that was the usual way of things on a small ship, and it made the meal times much easier to arrange, as well as ensuring that the noisy comings and goings of locks and suit checks was never to the detriment of anyone's squint-time. Six hours was more than enough, even given our tiredness after the vacuum shifts. Under the near-weightless conditions of space, the body demands a lot less restitution than it does on a world.

That was the division of watches; what we did in them was a different question. We had no master of sail, but Tindouf was the next best thing, so it fell to our team to tackle the job of making our sails look as normal as we could, using the two thousand acres of ordinary sail. It was a slow and fiddly job, but not especially difficult or dangerous, beyond the commonplace hazards of working in vacuum. Before we commenced, Tindouf found a piece of sail the size of the table and used it to sketch out the work ahead of us, drawing a spidery diagram with *Revenger* like a tiny bug pinned at the centre of a prodigious fan-like spread of rigging and sails. His plan was to haul in some of the catchcloth sails and substitute normal sails in their place, while also adding a few hundred leagues of supplementary rigging, supporting an arrangement of normal sails that had no purposc beyond making us look friendly.

"We won't sail as 'andsomely as we does now," Tindouf said, stroking his chin regretfully. "Torque loading'll be out of kilter, for one, and we'll needs to use ions to smooth 'er out. But at least we'll have the luxury of seeing our own sailses, for once."

"So will anyone shadowing us," Surt said.

"That can't be helped," I replied. "We either do this work or never go near another port, and we need every hour left to us to get it done. But we can minimise the risks, can't we, Tindouf? Keep our reflective surfaces averted from any eyes astern of us, so they needn't see very much more than they already do. If they're even behind us at all. We haven't seen anything since we turned."

"I do like an optimist," Strambli said.

"Sos do I," Tindouf said.

I was content that the shift assignments had thrown us together. Tindouf had little to say for himself when he was outside, preferring to sing to himself—usually childlike lullabies and nonsense ditties. If it bothered me I could turn down the gain on the suit-to-suit squawk, but generally I was happy to hear him mumbling and humming away, because it meant things were going well. I only needed prick up my ears when he went silent, because that usually meant something had got torn or tangled or jammed.

Principally, I was glad not to be in the other two teams. Not because I disliked the people in them, but because by my reckoning we had by far the pleasanter assignment. The other two teams had to turn the ship itself into something easy on the eye, and that was a far knottier proposition than changing some sails.

Not just knotty, but as good as impossible, at least in five weeks. *Revenger* was always going to look mean. Meanness was baked into her lines, and there was little we could do about that. Like *Monetta's Mourn*, she had an "eye" on either side of her hull, just rear of the jaw. The eye was the largest window, and on both ships it was positioned for the benefit of the galley, where the crew spent most of their waking hours. The eye on *Monetta's Mourn* was set a little higher, though, and it managed to look friendly. On *Revenger* the eye was set low, almost in line with the jaws, and the effect was to suggest a subtle form of derangement. The eye was smaller, too, and there was a sort of purposeful frown to it. The general countenance was not improved by the jaws being set with rows of sharpened alloy teeth, or by the many angry spikes and barbs jutting out from the hull like poison-tipped quills.

The plan was to cut away or disguise as many of these ugly additions as possible, but a number of them served functions relating to navigation and sail-control, complicating their disposal. Then there were the hatches and irises related to the coilgun batteries, which had to be re-fashioned to look less like gun ports, or no more than anyone might expect of your average prickly privateer.

They had to go out there with tools, dismantling what they could, cutting through what couldn't be dismantled, all the while vigilant for tricks and traps, and minding not to skewer themselves or cut through a bit of suit when they thought it was the ship. For the purposes of cutting, they had recourse to Strambli's tools and instruments, which ranged from drills and saws to energy-beams and a kind of miniature flame-torch that operated on the same propellant as the launch and would glide through most things like a knife through butter. Still, it was slow going, and there were bits of Bosa's ship fashioned of strangely toughened materials that must have come out of a bauble, resistant to all our conventional cutting methods. It was small wonder she had soaked up all the coil-gun volleys directed at her by her victims. We saved any part that was small enough to bring back into the ship.

None of that would have troubled me, but there was something else that made me glad not to be on those assignments. Over the years—we might as well say centuries—Bosa had been crossed by a lot of people. As with our friend Garval, she had a particular way of enforcing discipline. When she had killed someone—or was in the *process* of killing them—she was in the habit of fixing their bodies onto the outside of the hull. If they needed to be kept alive long enough to make her point, she would arrange it—plumbing life-support into a suit, even as that suit was nailed or welded onto the ship's jagged lines. Garval had been the most recent addition, fixed under the bowsprit spike that projected from the upper jaw—the same spike that eventually did for Bosa herself, when she fell onto it. There were many bodies, though—more than we ever imagined when we first saw her ship. She had been welding and nailing them onto the hull for so long that in places it was three or four layers deep. When my companions peeled those bodies away, breaking them off like scabs of hard-packed rust, they glimpsed the cryptic history of the ship itself. I shuddered to think of the ledger of misery accounted by these corpses, or the length of time that misery had been drawn out. Still, there was nothing we could do for them now, save cutting them away and casting their remains into the Empty. There was scant dignity in that, and perhaps not all of them were deserving of any, but I preferred to think kindly of them while I knew no better.

The shifts went on. We slept, ate, worked, and rested—trading tired stories of what we had faced, or considering our plans for the next day. When one of the other two teams came in, I kept a careful eye on their faces, noting when things had gone to plan or when they had run into something that made them silent or reflective in the galley, unwilling to share the experience except in a guarded glance or suddenly averted eye. I held back from pressing, and so did the others. It was sufficient to know that they had found evidence that Bosa's cruelty went further than we had so far imagined. I had already seen and heard enough to tide me over for one lifetime. The sooner we scoured her memory from this ship, the better.

It was on the eleventh day after we had changed course that the thing with the sails happened, and after that very little was ever the same again.

*

Tindouf and I were working that shift alone. We had been out in the rigging, an easy league from the ship (which looked terribly small from that far out, like a small, dark pip lodged in a greater darkness) and we had completed our allotted schedule of duties. But before we had set out, Tindouf had been troubled by some indications from the strain-gauges, and he wished to conduct an examination of an area of old sail to make sure nothing had become torn or tangled. What he found was instantly disquieting.

A whole spread of catchcloth studdingsail—more than ten acres of it—had been repeatedly punctured, and in places it had separated from the rigging and was furling around like a live thing, a dancing, folding, twisting curtain of impossible blackness, quite awful to behold. We watched it, half-mesmerised, until Tindouf delivered his verdict.

"We's been shot, Adrana. No doubts about it."

"Shot?" I said, understanding him but wishing I did not, because then there might be some explanation for this damage that was more palatable than violent action.

"Sail-shot most likelies, yes. You loads it into coil-guns just like ordinary slugs, but it don't go so quickly, and you don't aims it straight at shipses, neither. Some coves calls it grape-shot, but since it's mostly used against sailses, and not grapeses, I prefers sail-shot."

"Could this have happened some time ago, during Bosa's attack on Captain Trusko, and we're only now aware of it?"

"No, I's quite sure this is new. I keeps a careful eye on them strain-gauges, you sees, and I'd have known if we'd already been sail-shot. I thinks this happened within the last shift."

I activated the short-range squawk. "Paladin?"

"Yes, Miss Adrana?"

He sounded faint and scratchy, but that was as it had to be. We were keeping the power as low as possible, so that our communications would be undetectable to anyone more than a thousand leagues from the ship. "Paladin, it looks as if we've been shot at—what Tindouf calls sail-shot. It's played merry havoc with a whole area of catchcloth. Did you see anything on your sensors that might have been an attack?"

"No, Miss Adrana—most certainly not."

Fura, who could not have been too far from Paladin—I imagined her at her desk, scribbling into those journals—cut across our exchange. "We can't have been shot at, Adrana. We'd know it. We'd have seen coil-gun flash, either visibly or thermally, and surely something would have hit the hull if they sent a volley our way."

"Tindouf believes it happened within the last few hours," I said.

"Then perhaps we ran into debris. We are creeping closer to the Congregation, after all."

Behind his visor, Tindouf gave a slow, grave shake of his head. He dared not contradict my sister to her face, but he was content to let me know his feelings.

"We're coming in anyway," I said. "We were just about done with our shift, and I don't like the look of this at all. No one's going outside again until we've talked it over."

*

There were four of us in Fura's quarters—Tindouf, Prozor, the two of us, and I suppose Paladin as well, making five.

"You most likely won't have seen coil-gun flash," Prozor was saying. "The muzzles never get hot enough to show, because sail-shot hardly needs any magnetic impulse compared to a full slug broadside."

Fura needed persuasion. "Then what, may I enquire, is the point?"

"A disabling shot, girlie. Aimed at your sails and riggin', not your hull. And if it does hit your hull, it'll just bounce off without doin' too much harm."

"To take a ship intact, rather than destroying it," I said.

"That's the idea," Prozor said. "Nothin' more vulnerable than sails. Only thing that stops ships tearin' each other to shreds is good manners, most of the time."

"And yet," Fura said, extending her metal hand. "Here we are. Still alive, and with ninety-nine percent of our spread of sail intact. If that volley was meant to disable us, it's not done very well, has it?"

"I wouldn't sleep too soundly," Prozor said. "If there's a ship behind us, as we reckon, then that might've been a ranging shot, just to get a feelin' for things. Prob'ly they don't have a really accurate fix on our position just yet, or they're a little too far away for a precision shot. But they'll be hopin' to come closer."

Fura could hold to her opinion tenaciously, but if the weight of argument was against her—and it was in this case—then she would usually relinquish her position, albeit after some difficulty.

"You've seen your share of stern-chases, Proz. I won't quibble with your reading of things. The question is, what can we do in response? Send a broadside their way, and hope they get the message?"

"They have a better fix on us than we do on them," I said. "All we have is an area of sky, whereas we know they've managed to bounce at least one sweeper pulse off us. But even if we did know their coordinates well enough to aim our guns, we'd have to think very hard before retaliating."

"And why is that?" Fura asked.

"Because we're going out of our way not to look as if we play by the old rules of this ship." I hammered the heel of my hand against the table to bolster my meaning. "We're innocent privateers. That isn't an act, it's what we are—what we intend to remain."

"We've been *shot at*," Fura's eyes widened as she spoke, as if she were making an exceedingly simple point that I was being too stupid or obstinate to understand.

"Possibly," I allowed. "Even probably. But we can't be sure it wasn't an accident. If we respond in kind, we'll invite an escalation, as well as making it plain to them that they *have* managed to damage our sails, which will be exceedingly useful intelligence. If we strike more forcefully, with heavy slugs, we'll seem to be acting just as Bosa Sennen would have done—with disproportionate and murderous disregard. If we open the squawk and attempt to persuade 'em of our good nature, we'll also be giving away our exact position."

"So what would be your recommendation?"

"I would ask Tindouf to find us some more ion thrust so that we have a chance of pulling out of range. Suspend all work outside the ship, except for those operations either on or very near the hull, presuming that they won't strike at us directly. Increase the watches in the sighting room, and maintain close observation of the sweeper and squawk, supplementing Paladin wherever possible. You and I, meanwhile, will pay close attention to the skull."

"Has you picked up a whisper from the boneses?"

I sighed, accepting that it was time to be more forthcoming with the other members of the crew, starting with Tindouf and Prozor. "Something, yes. I believe I touched the mind of another Bone Reader, someone aware of our nature. I caught the distinct appellation *Nightjammer*, and before that mind sensed my own, I believe it was reaching out to some other Bone Reader. Attempting to report, you might say."

"Speculation," Fura said.

"Yes, and it's speculation that we've been shot at, as well. Everything is speculation when all we have is sail-flash, a sweeper pulse and a few holes in one of your sails. But I know what I felt, and I'm inclined to trust my intuition. That ship, whatever its nature, is not acting independently."

"This changes nothing," Fura said, without being quite able to suppress a visible trace of disquiet. "We must still continue with the alterations. In three weeks we'll be within clear sight of our destination, and the work must be finished much sooner than that." But she met my eyes and I believe I saw some grudging acceptance in her own. "It's too dangerous to have too many of us out in the rigging, if there's a chance of another sail-shot. But we can't ignore the problem, either."

"We could delay our arrival."

"That'd look queer in and of itself, if someone has an eye on us," Prozor said. "No good reason not to sail with all advantage."

"She's right," Fura said, continuing after a very prolonged inhalation. "The only solution is to work more quickly, and more efficiently, so that we may achieve more in less time, and with fewer hands occupied outside. Surt and I took eight hours trying to cut through a single piece of cladding. That's bad enough, but our torches depend on the same fuel we use for the launch, and that's hardly in abundant supply." She set her jaw. "But we know what'll cut through just about anything, if we have the will to use it."

"No," I said flatly.

"We weren't ever going to unlock 'em again," Prozor said. "Not until we were at death's own door."

"If we don't complete this work," Fura answered, "that is very likely where shall find ourselves. We have the Ghostie things. We should not be afraid to use what is rightfully ours."

"I's don't likes 'em shivery things," Tindouf said, speaking for us all. "But if they helps us gets the job done quickers..."

The next morning when we were all awake, Fura and I went to fetch the keys to the Ghostie armour. Ever since we had used the armour and weapons to surprise Bosa, we had kept them locked away in a metal-walled vault near the bone room, tucked above the long gallery of the lateral coil-gun batteries. That arrangement had been arrived at by mutual consent, but not until after one of the most vigorous debates of our new crew. There was a strong opinion that the Ghostie armour should be destroyed, or tossed into space at the earliest opportunity.

None of us liked it.

The Ghostie armour—the suits, the weapons—was age-old technology. It had come out of a bauble called the Fang, where it had been stored in gold-encrusted treasure boxes. Fura had told me of the expedition several times, embroidering the facts only slightly each time. I had also read her account of things in *The True And Accurate Testimony.*

When first they opened those boxes, it had seemed that they were empty.

Ghostie technology had a property that meant it slipped out of your conscious attention when you were looking at it directly. To see it at all, you had to look at it askew, out of the corner of your eye, and even then not try too hard. In those glimpses you saw glass armour, glass helmets, breastplates, gauntlets, shoulder-pieces, and glass knives and swords and guns—or what we chose to call guns, since we knew no better.

Occasionally I had taken the keys to the Ghostie store and risked opening the door and peering inside. My initial reaction was always the same, unwaveringly so. The Ghostie armour was gone. By some furtive means it had escaped, leaving only the bare walls of the store.

But then I would catch myself and force my eyes to stop staring so intently, to slide to one side and focus on some imagined thing far beyond the confines of the store. Then, and only then, I might catch the hint of a glassy edge, the barely-defined shape of something I thought I almost had words for, and I would satisfy myself that the Ghostie armour was still present, still where it had been left.

"We only need the cutters," Fura said after a long silence, during which she must have been going through the same process as me, half doubting that the relics were still present, and then finally convincing herself that they were. "The guns are too risky, and the extra armour won't be of any benefit."

"Maybe now isn't the time to use any of it."

"We're being chased, dear heart," she said in a gentle, pitying tone, as if I might have forgotten about the pursuing vessel. "If ever there was a time, this is it."

"You're frightened," I said, marvelling at the thought that there was still something that could puncture her single-mindedness.

She seemed surprised.

"Yes—aren't you?"

"Terrified. And glad to be terrified, too, and to see that you feel a bit of it as well. It means she can't have got too far into me, and the glowy can't have got too far into you."

Fura reached for one of the knives, averting her vision deliberately so that she was able to guide her metal fingers onto the haft instead of the blade.

"Do you remember the last time you held one of these? I believe it was to press the blade against my throat."

"The ingratitude of it," I said sarcastically.

"Oh, I don't blame you for that—why would I? It was Bosa's madness, still lingering in you. But we flushed her out of you, didn't we? Good and proper." She opened my palm and placed the knife in it, as tenderly as if it were a necklace of flowers. "See? I trust you implicitly, even with a Ghostie blade. Would I do that, if I thought there was even a tiny bit of Bosa still hanging around?"

"I suppose," I said quietly, "that you'd find out sooner or later, whichever way it was."

"Whether you're to be trusted?"

"No," I answered. "Not just me. Either of us."

"Is there something you'd care to get off your chest, sister?"

"You gave in very easily."

"Gave in?"

"When the crew contradicted your preferred choice of destination. I thought you would kick up more of a rumpus, but you accepted it very equably."

"Ah. Then from your tone, I take it that you would have

preferred it if I'd turned against their choice, and forced my own upon them?"

"No," I said. "Not at all. But it makes me wonder what sort of preference it was, if you were so content to discard it."

"They say that the glowy," Fura replied, "is inclined to make one see conspiracies where none exist. It turns whispers into betrayals, and your closest friends to enemies. The curious thing, though, is that I'm the one with the glowy in me, not you."

A silence fell on us. I had said too much, and in doing so concretised a vague feeling into a tangible suspicion. Fura, in the substance of her responses, had done nothing to quell that suspicion. If anything, she had only hardened it. But both of us must have known that any further words would do more harm than good, considerably so, and therefore we said nothing. In that brooding, reproachful state we extracted the rest of the cutting implements, by which I mean the knives and machetes and swords—anything with an edge and a handle. They had to be treated gingerly, because if you slipped with one of those bladed horrors they'd whistle through just about anything, as Bosa's crew had found out the hard way. Once the cutters were organised, we locked the vault again, but not before satisfying ourselves that the other things were still where they belonged. All this was completed in that same wordless condition, our communications—such as they are—effected by cold glances and curt nods.

To begin with nothing bad happened.

The shifts were reorganised a little, so that there were only a few hours in which the sighting room was unoccupied, and Fura and I increased our watches in the bone room as often as we could, sometimes together, Fura setting aside her reluctance if we were jointly present, and sometimes singly, and in that regard usually me rather than Fura. I might have remonstrated with her for not taking her due share of the burden, but my sister was rarely amenable to that sort of persuasion, and in any case I believed that she was sincere in the stated cause of her aversion; that with the glowy in her she already had enough to contend with besides the whisperings of alien skulls. We were both of us mindful of the night-terrors that had come upon our friend Garval, who had been driven to the brink of insanity by the skull on Captain Rackamore's ship, and while Garval had pretended to more aptitude than was the case, neither of us were anxious to meet the same fate.

Other than that, and allowing for a certain elevated state of apprehension, the work soon fell back into its old pattern, except that the pace of change was now accelerated. The Ghostie tools made life much easier. Not having to fight against the fabric of the ship was a significant benefit, and if there was now any aspect of it that was not as we wished, it came off without protestation. Of course, we were careful not to hack away anything vital, and a great deal of what was removed was done in such a way that it could be put back later, if we were so minded.

By the eighteenth day it was plain to all that our efforts were having some benefit. The character of our ship was being visibly modified, and perhaps it would soon be sufficient to meet our aims.

Tindouf and I had rigged a thousand acres of sail, and we were getting nimbler-fingered by the day. Those bright sails stood out against the catchcloth like silvery windows cut into the sky.

"It dont's look quite right to me," Tindouf confessed. "But I do knows my way around riggin', and if most folk see enough ord'nary sails, they won't go lookings for thems that they can't see."

I agreed. It was the best distraction we could hope for, and it would only have to suffice from a distance. By the time we were close to port, we would haul in sails anyway. All the attention would be on the main part of the ship at that point, and the hands had worked a surprising charm on her belligerent lines. They had softened the larger spikes and barbs by tacking sailcloth over them, disguising their nature in the same way that furniture loses its obvious form under dust-sheets.

The sail was thin and easily torn, but it had been painted over using a stiffening caulk, the same preparations we used for patching hull leaks, and that imbued it with enough strength to suit our needs. The same had been done for the coil-gun ports, using sails to mask most of the doors, leaving just enough visible to suggest that our ship still had some modest capabilities of self-defence. The teeth had been disguised by adding an extra layer of sail around the jaws to the docking bay.

Little could be done to remedy the baleful, scowly disposition of that main eye, or the scabbed, disfigured look of the hull after so many of Bosa's victims had been cut away from it. But the hands had stretched more sail-cloth over the worst bits and painted what they could, using colours other than black so as to break up the lines and make the ship look a little more approachable. It was a question of going so far and no further, because no ship ought to be tarted-up too gaily. To me she still had that meanness, but it was ameliorated, even if the mask was perilously thin in places.

Meanwhile, every hour of work brought us nearer to the Congregation. Several times in Fura's testimony she had mentioned how pretty all those worlds looked, especially when one's vantage-point lay beyond them. I supposed it was the same with houses, which always looked more inviting from the vantage of a cold street corner, looking up at the yellow-lit windows of some grand tenement, imagining the lives going on within. Whereas inside, all that cosiness and warmth could get stuffy. Still, I would not deny that it was a pretty sight, and when Tindouf was occupied with something that spared me for a minute or so, I made sure to indulge my share of it.

The Old Sun almost hid itself away. There were too many worlds getting in the way, millions of them, slipping past on their own merry orbits, like shoals of fish swimming past some old lantern still shining from murky depths. Most of those worlds were not only nameless, but also uninhabited and perhaps scarcely ever visited. Out of all the potential worlds in the Congregation, people could only scratch a living out of twenty thousand of them, and without exception they were the ones that could still imprison an atmosphere.

But the Old Sun's light fell on all the worlds indiscriminately, and each time it bounced off one, be it a rock or a bauble, or one of the mirrors that had been put into space to help ships move around, the light got bent or stained in one way or another, shifted from blue to red or red to purple, as if the worlds were fifty million little shards of coloured glass jangling around in a kaleidoscope, their only purpose to make flickers and spangles of light, a constant scintillating dance of them, which was as fancy to the eye as it was hypnotic. The colours of the Congregation were the colours of evening gowns and night-lit parlours and dusky rare gems in velvet-lined jewel-boxes. I will readily confess that it made me a little home-sick, thinking of all the pleasures and luxuries we were now having to forgo. At such moments my conviction wavered, and I would find myself speculating about the possibilities of returning to Mazarile, abandoning this adventurous new life. Maybe not today, maybe not tomorrow, but when we had a few more quoins to our name, just enough to feather our retirement. But then I would bring to mind the huge and empty house awaiting us, if it had not been repossessed by Father's creditors, and the plot of land where he had gone to join our mother, and the pull of home would feel a bit less seductive.

Besides, I would chide myself, we had business to attend to. Even if the exact nature of that business was perhaps clearer to Fura than it was to me.

# 8

Even with the alteration in shifts, there was still a six-hour watch when there were two work parties outside, leaving only two of us inside the ship.

As we went into the fourth watch, one of the rest teams would get suited-up and join the team outside, who were enduring two consecutive vacuum shifts. After due consideration I had judged that this was the best time to sneak a look at Fura's journals.

Fura and Surt were on the double vacuum shift on the nineteenth day. Strambli and Prozor had gone out to join them for the fourth watch and Tindouf and I were inside. We had completed all our chores by the end of the third watch, made tea, played cards, spoken of rigging and sails, and I had endured more of Tindouf's singing and humming than was fair on any sane creature. The ship had shuddered a little, as it was predisposed to doing, and an amber light had come on on one of the status boards in the galley. Tindouf shook his head, more in mild annoyance than frustration—that shudder and status light spoke of a common fault with one of the circuits feeding the ion engine.

"I promise I shant's be long," he said, as if we were in danger of missing each other's company.

"It's all right, Tindouf—I wanted to look up something in the

*Book of Worlds*, anyway. I'll be going to my bed when I'm done—all this not-working makes me tired."

"You can use my *Book of Worlds* if you cares," Tindouf said helpfully.

"Thank you, but there's a copy in the control room, and I know my way around that edition pretty well."

"Suits yourself, Miss Adrana."

Tindouf collected his clay pipe and shoved off in the general direction of aft. I waited until I was certain of no early return. The only remaining sounds were the occasional thuds of magnetic boots stomping around on the outside of the hull as the other four got on with their work.

I went into the control room, and pottered around for a minute or two studying the controls and screens, as well as the Glass Armillary—admiring it the way you would any delicate, precious thing. Principally though, I was summoning up the courage to go into Fura's cabin. Before I did so, though, I went to one of the chained shelves and took out the *Book of Worlds*, just so I could make a show of pondering it if Tindouf were to pop back unexpectedly.

More than that: I actually flicked through it to the entry on Wheel Strizzardy:

*Wheelworld in the thirty-seventh processional. Quarter-spoked, with a fixed hub and ample docking amenities situated at both hub and rim. Nineteen leagues in circumference, of which the whole is pressurised and agreeably disposed for habitation. There is but one principal settlement, which is Port Endless, a continuous thin conurbation strung along the entirety of the rim, and presently home to three hundred and forty thousand citizens. At one time rather bustling, Wheel Strizzardy has in recent centuries fallen on quieter times, and prospective visitors are well advised to…*

Exactly the backwater we had been promised. I snapped the book shut so hard that it gasped out a puff of dust. Keeping it clutched in my hand all the same, darkening the cover with my palm-sweat, I went to the connecting door that led into Fura's cabin. I had never known it to be locked, and there would have been rumbles of grave discontent had she ever fallen into that habit. Frankly, though, I was only half-relieved when the door opened at my push. Had it been bolted, at least I would have had an excuse to abandon my plans.

You might wonder how I could love and admire my sister, and be grateful for all she had done for me, and yet still keep that little knot of distrust in my heart concerning her motivations. You might deem it strange and cold and uncharitable of me. All I can offer by way of defence is my certainty that we had reciprocal feelings about each other, and that this state of affairs had existed long before we ever set to space. It was the product of our childhood, of two girls of similar age being confined together, educated at home, and largely obliged to make the most of each other's company. Our self-made entertainments often depended on the withholding of some information or intent from the other. It meant that from an early age we had become very agreeably familiar with the idea of not entirely trusting the other.

So it carried through into the present, except the games had become more serious. I distrusted what the glowy was doing to Fura and feared its progression, but that was only part of it. The changes she had wrought upon herself had made her less recognisable to me, less easy for me to understand or predict. There were preoccupations that I knew she chose not to share with me. Taking her side of things, I knew she had concerns about the electrical, chemical and psychological conditioning Bosa Sennen had worked on me. I said that I had flushed Bosa out of my system, and I wished to believe it for myself, but that was insufficient assurance for Fura. She must have worried that I was putting on an act, waiting for the right moment to slip back into character. It was no good me pointing out that she was the one living in Bosa's cabin, obsessing over quoins and retribution.

The truth was that we both had Bosa in us to a degree: me because she had imprinted herself deliberately, and Fura because she'd had to become more like Bosa to kill her in the first place. What it meant, though, was that those knots of mutual distrust were hardening and growing, like an echo that amplifies with each return, and I could think of nothing that was likely to help matters.

Sneaking around her possessions would most certainly not assist. But I had to see those journals.

I closed the cabin door behind me, but refrained from latching it. I paused a while to make sure the stomping was still going on outside, and that there was no indication that Tindouf had returned to the galley.

Paladin was the main thing that caught my eye, his globe flickering with tiny lights, serving as the room's sole source of illumination. No lightvine grew around the walls of the cabin, although it was abundant elsewhere. Fura forbade it from this room.

"May I help you, Miss Adrana?"

"I'm quite all right, thank you," I said, quietly.

I moved to him, eyeing the items on the desk, fixed there by magnetic means. Journals and ink-wells and paperweights and quoins, a mixture of things that had originally belonged to Bosa or been salvaged from Captain Trusko's ship. Several editions of the *Book of Worlds*, one of them a much earlier edition than the volume in my palm. Fura's own account of her adventures: *The True and Accurate Testimony*. I opened it idly, as I had done on many occasions, because no matter what I might think of my sister lately, I never failed to be impressed by her industriousness in filling all those pages.

It was bound into the cover of a book that had once belonged to Captain Rackamore, his own edition of the 1384 *Book of Worlds*, and being one of the few tangible links to our former employer, it had a fond significance to me as well. My fingers stroked the swatches of marbled paper on the inside cover, which had already been very old and damaged before Bosa mutilated it. Perhaps it was my heightened alertness, but I noticed something that had never been obvious to me before. There was a patch in the lower corner of the book where the marbling had been rubbed away almost back to the underlying material of the cover. It looked deliberate, rather than an accumulation of small insults. Almost, I thought, as if there had been something written there, which was now effaced.

Setting it aside, because it was not the objective that had drawn me into the room, I turned instead to the other journals. I recognised them easily enough. I had seen them both open on her desk, Fura writing into one while reading from the other. They were both secured by quoins, which I moved, glancing only cursorily at their denominations and marvelling that I could now treat a high-bar quoin with such casualness. The journals began to drift away from the desk, and I reached for them with my free hand.

"Are you certain I cannot be of assistance, Miss Adrana?"

"Has she asked you to keep any secrets from me, Paladin?"

A rapid, agitated chatter came from his relays, just like the sound of the stock-market ticker Father had once kept in the downstairs parlour, when he had shares worth monitoring.

"I am obliged to serve and protect both of you, to the limit of my abilities."

"Which means she might have, I suppose, but that it conflicts with your deep programming. Unless she asked Surt to rewire your basic loyalties."

He chattered and flashed some more.

"My loyalties are unwavering and beyond any external influence. I am at the service of the Ness sisters, not as a slave but as a free machine, a robot of the Twelfth Occupation, soldier and protector, and a verified witness of the Last Rains of Sestramor."

"I know, and I shouldn't have asked. And for what it's worth, I'm sorry about some of the things I said and did to you when we were back on Mazarile. Do you remember the household very much, Paladin, or were those memories damaged when they broke you?"

"I had a life, and then another life, and now I have this life. I remember a great deal, but I have forgotten vastly more. You were never as unkind as you believe, and a great many times I was deserving of your scorn, for I was not fully alive."

Sensing that I wasn't going to get very much out of him by direct interrogation—nor did I wish to put him through undue distress—I scanned the desk for such clues as were readily apparent.

Weighed down side by side were a pair of papers that had clearly been torn out of log books or similar. They were lined and columned, with printed annotations, and had both been filled in by hand. One was in a normal, legible script, whereas the other's entries were in a curious sort of angular writing, a script that triggered no immediate recognition but looked to me like some form of code.

I paid attention to the one I could read, examining the entries.

| | | |
|---|---|---|
| *4/7/96* | *15:00* | *rising flux, eight becoming nine—hauled in sun-gallants as precaution* |
| *19/7/96* | *03:00* | *quietude, but moderate activity forecast for coming watch* |
| *30/7/96* | *09:00* | *eight decreasing to seven—advisory favourable but considered prudent to retain stay-preventers on star-foils* |
| *13/9/96* | *18:00* | *quietude, running under all sails* |
| *14/9/96* | *09:00* | *continuing quietude, turning to moderate lassitude* |
| *21/9/96* | *12:00* | *sudden storm, ten exceeding eleven, squawk and sweeper inoperable—all able vacuum hands charged to haul-in…* |

What I was looking at, plainly enough, was the routine record-keeping of any spacefaring ship. The two pairs of sheets were printed differently, but each had a column of dates running from the top to the bottom, and the legible entries concerned observations on the changing patterns of solar weather and the captain's response to it.

And then I understood.

"This weather journal belonged to Captain Trusko, didn't it, Paladin?"

"I have not been vouchsafed the origin of the document, Miss Adrana. I was merely asked to correlate the entries against those in the encrypted log."

"Which is Bosa Sennen's—the weather log of this ship. Different ships, but subject to the same weather events, broadly speaking."

"It would be unwise of me to comment."

"You don't have to—I can join the dots for myself. Those weather entries don't line up precisely—they wouldn't, unless the ships were operating in the same area of space—but it's enough to give you something to work with, isn't it? She's got you using these weather logs to crack Bosa's private code."

Paladin stopped with his chattering and flashing.

"Have I done something wrong, Miss Adrana?"

"No... not at all. You've done very well. If Bosa made records in code, it's only right that we find a way to read it."

I was still holding the journals. Both had clasps on them, and if they had been locked that would have been the end of it. But Fura had not fastened them. I opened one of them and leafed through pages and pages of the same angular writing, until I came to about halfway through the book and the pages turned blank.

Bosa Sennen's private journal, I thought to myself. Presumably interrupted at the point when she had the grave misfortune to run into my sister for the second time.

I flicked back through the densely-written pages. The shade of ink changed now and then, but it all looked to be done in the same hand. I should not have been too surprised by that. If Bosa had been keeping journals for as long as she'd been stalking ships and crews, she would have needed a lot more than one volume to set down her ruminations. This was merely the most recent of them, and doubtless if I'd been able to look at older versions, the evidence of Bosa's identity shifting from one body to another would have been plain. Without Fura's intervention, it would soon have been my handwriting filling up one of these books.

The text occupied the pages in relentless blocks, without any sort of rest for the eye. Every now and then, though, a small part of it was underlined in red. I knew that shade of red very well—so did we all. It was Fura's special ink, the one she had used to compose *The True And Accurate Testimony.*

I held the book closer to my eyes, squinting at the parts she had underlined. It was always a similar pattern of symbols, varying only slightly.

A particular word, a particular phrase, I decided.

I put the journal back down, setting a quoin over it the way it had been when I arrived.

Then I opened the second book and flicked through its pages. I only had to glance at them to recognise Fura's handwriting. It had changed since our childhood days, but not greatly. Although she had to force her tin fingers to hold and move a pen, that was evidently easier than learning to write with her other hand. The writing was pressed onto the pages, like some declaration scribed into rock. There was a tense, compressed quality to it, as if all the rage and frustration had transferred from her fingers into the ink itself, where it now lay like a primed trap.

I leafed through the pages. In the silence of the cabin, they made a slippery whisking sound, like scissors being sharpened. I listened for the clomp of footsteps on the hull, a warning that the hands were returning to the lock, but no one was moving around at the moment.

The entries were fragmentary, not linear. The latter part of it was blank, but there were also gaps all the way through, and there was never one page that was filled top to bottom. I believed that I understood: Fura was translating parts of Bosa's journal. Not systematically, from the start, but piecemeal.

I opened the first journal again and cross-checked. If there were three underlined sections on one page, then there were three fragments on the corresponding page in Fura's book. If there were no underlined sections, that page was left blank.

I read some of the translated parts, and there was rarely a complete sentence.

*area of catchcloth we discarded today would've bought us a million-bar quoin, if we were so inclined*

*caught secreting quoins in his private quarters, with a clear view to jumping ship*

*between six and seven million quoins at present market value*

*a trinket that reminded her of a quoin, but it was nothing of the sort*

*stuffed his belly with quoins as a reminder not to cross me*

*forced to do business, so rationed out the quoins even though it pains me*

I felt cold. I knew I was holding something that Fura had not been in any rush for me to see, and that I ought to have put it back down on the desk before I saw something I regretted.

But I could not help myself.

"Quoin or quoins," I whispered aloud. "That's how you've been doing it. Looking for any occurrence of those words, and translating around them. Is this true, Paladin?"

"I have only done as I was requested, Miss Adrana."

My hands were starting to shake now. I knew that Fura had an interest in the quoins, and I could scarcely blame her for trying to learn a little more about Bosa's preoccupation. But this was the first I'd seen about cracking secret codes, or making a methodical effort to dig out specific information connected to the quoins. It must have taken uncommon reticence for Fura not to boast about comparing the weather reports.

Still with trembling fingers I turned more of the pages in Fura's journal. A word—a name—started jumping out at me, underlined where it appeared in certain of the translated passages.

*can trust Lagganvor with the quoins*

*if someone's to carry quoins on my behalf, better Lagganvor than Rastrick or Mullery. But I'd sooner do it myself*

*Sent Lagganvor off in the launch, told him he'd be wise to come back with more than one quoin if he doesn't want to see my sharp side. He thinks I'm soft on him, after the gift of that eye. But I only gave him the eye so that he could serve me more efficiently*

I skimmed ahead, a dark intuition beginning to prickle just under my forehead, like a night-sweat.

*Lagganvor has gone to ground, with my quoins. If he's wise he'll never mention my name again. But no one wise crosses me in the first place. He'll blurt, eventually, and I can't have that. Besides, I wouldn't mind having my eye back.*

A picture was forming in my mind from these scraps. I only had the outline of it, but that was sufficient. Bosa had been forced to do some sort of business with the edges of civilisation, some rare but necessary transaction. Not in person, obviously, but through willing intermediaries. Lagganvor was either a crew member, or some agent she thought she could trust. She had given him quoins and sent him off to do her bidding. And he had disappeared, absconding with her money and the risk of exposing her secrets.

What followed was Bosa recounting the steps she had taken to find Lagganvor again. Gathering intelligence by her usual furtive means, listening to rumours and skull-whispers. Lagganvor had wronged her, and she was never one to let bygones be bygones. She wanted to find him again—silence him, most likely, with a side-order of cruelty, just so no one else got any silly ideas.

Find him, torture him, kill him.

From what I could gather from the entries, Bosa had been determined to catch up with Lagganvor, but had at the same time been distracted by other, equally pressing matters. One of them, I quickly realised, had been settling an old grievance—or at least unfinished business—with Pol Rackamore. That had led to one thing, and then another, and eventually it led to Bosa herself dying, with Lagganvor still out there somewhere.

I wondered if he knew his good fortune, not to have those black sails on his back.

Then something else caught my eye and I had to stare at it for a few seconds just to make sure of my wits.

Fura had written down some of Bosa's possible best-guesses for where Lagganvor might be hiding out. They were in a column, etched down in Fura's heavy, laboured hand, each pressed a bit more deeply into the paper.

Most of the names meant nothing to me.

*Proscle*

*Rustrell*

*Zancer*

*Scillmouth*

But one I did know, especially lately. It was the last in the list, and my sister had underlined and circled it in her special ink:

*Wheel Strizzardy*

I closed the journals and made sure they were put back on her desk exactly as I had found them.

"Paladin, listen carefully to me."

"I am listening, Miss Adrana."

"I will not ask you to lie. You have not lied to me, to the best of my knowledge, and I respect that. But unless Fura asks a direct question of you, I would ask that you volunteer no knowledge of this conversation, or of my having been in this cabin."

"That is an unusual request, Miss Adrana."

"I accept that it is. But since I am not asking you to state a deliberate falsehood, nor to withhold information if it is requested of you, I am fully confident that it is within your capabilities."

"Might I ask your intentions?"

I had felt cold spying on Fura's writing, but something hot was rising in me now. I could see how the rest of the crew and I had been turned into unwitting accomplices while thinking we were going against her wishes. That story about the Bosa-hating cult on Kathromil might have been real, but Fura had dropped it into her conversation knowing exactly the effect it would have on us. My devious, deceitful sister was playing us all like shadow-puppets.

I thought of the time I had pressed a knife to her throat, when she first found me in the bone room during the fight with Bosa. The anger of that moment flared back into me. Rather than willing it away I allowed it to linger, letting it warm me from inside; a golden glow filling my ribcage.

"I'm considering them," I said.

I had no plans to kill her for this treachery, or even to punish her badly. She was still my sister. But some hurtful things were going to have to come out. If it was the glowy making her act in this secretive, distrustful way, I would make fair allowances. But it would only double my resolve that something needed to be done about it, before I lost Fura for good.

I double-checked to make sure her things were undisturbed before leaving the room. She would learn of my presence there in the end, but—with Paladin's hoped-for cooperation—it would be my choice when that happened, not hers.

I closed the connecting door and lingered in the control

room, looking at the Glass Armillary again and musing on how Fura had played me so skilfully, setting me up as her instrument to convince the others. I felt disgusted with myself, as if I were in some sense complicit.

"Oh, Fura," I said. "How did we end up like this?"

I heard footsteps again, clanging on the outside of the hull. Not just one pair of footsteps but several of them, moving quickly. I took my leave of the control room and went back into the galley, planning to put on a pleasant face and give away no trace of what I had learned.

Tindouf came into the galley, looking agitated. The knotting of his brow and the set of his jaw made me think of a spoilt baby on the point of mewling.

"Is something wrong with the ions?" I asked, wondering what could be troubling the big man.

"Not that, Adrana, but they's comin' in quicker than I likes. It's not near the ends of their shifts, and that portents somethin' bad. I don't cares for it."

"Have you heard anything on the suit-to-ship squawk?"

He shook his head. "Like most of the thingses on this ship, it only works when it has a mind to."

The footsteps were clanging around the hull in the direction of the main lock. Tindouf and I nodded to each other, a wordless understanding that we had best get to the lock promptly. It was under the galley, aft of the docking bay, squeezed between a storage room and some of the internal machinery related to the sail-control gear. It was a squeeze getting there, even if you were not suited, but I knew my way around the nooks and crannies of the ship.

By the time we got to the lock, my ears had already given a pop as the ship bled a bit of lungstuff into space. That meant that the party was coming back in quickly, not bothering with the usual courtesies. We had plenty of reserve lungstuff, but that sort of haste was never a good sign. *Portents somethin' bad,* I thought, Tindouf's words echoing through my skull.

The main lock was big enough to take four people at a time,

and all of them were in it when the door opened. I took a quick inventory of what I saw. Fura was all right. She was already taking off her helmet. Surt and Prozor were all right as well, near as I could judge. But something had happened to Strambli.

They were carrying her, and blood was bubbling around them, a scarlet froth of it that seemed to be originating from the lower part of her leg. I swallowed hard at the sight of it. Blood still discomfited me. I had seen prodigious amounts of it floating through the ship after Fura's ambush, but as with many things connected with those events, I had pushed them into the dingiest corner of my conscious mind.

"What happened?" I asked, directing my question at Fura.

"I squawked. Where the hell were you?"

"We didn't pick up any squawk," I said, waiting for Tindouf to give a nod of agreement. "But we're here, aren't we? What happened?"

"I think they shot us again," Surt said, her voice coming through the grille under her helmet. "Took out the spritsail, sixty leagues from the ship. None of us were anywhere near it, but the yardage was under tension and it snapped back and caught Strambli in its coils. Lucky it didn't go clean through her, but she slipped with that Ghostie knife—"

"Didn't... slip," Strambli said, grunting out the words, and although she was in obvious distress, I was glad that she was able to talk because that meant she was awake.

"Help us get her to the surgery," Prozor said, sounding breathless.

Tindouf and I took over from Prozor and Surt, giving them time to get their helmets off and recover some of the energy they had obviously spent getting Strambli back to the lock. Fortunately it was only a short distance to the sick-bay, along a narrow passageway tucked behind the sail-control gear, and into a small but well-equipped medical room located immediately beneath the coil-gun batteries and a little forward of the bone room.

Bosa had kept a surgery but that had only ever been its secondary purpose. She had called it the "kindness room" and it was where she dished out most of her punishments, especially those that involved drugs, electricity, knives or some other manifestation of cruelty. It was also where she administered the treatments that helped twist a person's loyalty or shatter their old notions of what was right and wrong. Some of that involved surgery and some of it also depended on electricity and drugs, but the one constancy was that there was nothing charitable about it. I had spent too much time in that room to wish to linger in it unnecessarily: days and weeks in which she whispered into my head, trying to turn me to her way of thinking, trying to push a corrupting shard of her own soul into my own, where it might lodge permanently, days and weeks in which she pressed electrodes to my skin or injected me with burning fluids. Just being near that room brought those long hours back; being inside it was enough to summon cruel and intricate thoughts, ideas of punishment and malice that felt both foreign and fully a part of me. She had treated me quite well, too, seeing in me her natural successor, and therefore keeping her physical punishments to a minimum. Others had not been nearly so fortunate. If she wished to make an example of someone, some poor cove she did not require alive or whole or sane, she would put them in the kindness room and visit unspeakable acts upon them. Their moans or screams or whimpers would radiate out from the kindness room via networks of speaking-tubes, feeding into every part of the ship.

But it was also a surgery, and if it held items that could be put to sensible employment, it would have been wasteful of us not to make use of them. So we had blocked off those speaking-tubes, thrown out or dismantled all the contraptions and instruments that had no purpose beyond torture, and retained the rest so we could treat such minor injuries and ailments as befell us.

"You're going to be all right," I told Strambli as we got her onto the long, leather-clad couch that served as both bed and operating table.

"Didn't... slip," Strambli repeated. "Not my fault. Knife twisted. Wouldn't have happened if that sail-shot hadn't..."

"Were we really attacked?" I asked.

"Yes," Fura snapped, the glowy brightening around her eyes and temples. "And we'll be dishing some of it back, if I have my way. Come to my quarters as soon as you're done here."

"Where is the Ghostie stuff now?" I asked Prozor.

"Still outside," she said, helping remove Strambli's suit piece by piece, even as the blood still frothed out of the leg wound. "Locked in that chest, just as if we were swappin' shifts."

There was a box on the hull, welded there for the purposes of tool-storage while we were altering the look of *Revenger*. "Did you see it happen?" I asked, thinking they'd have been working in close proximity.

But Prozor gave a sharp shake of her head. "No. I was off freein' up some tangled riggin', around the curve of the hull. When I came back I saw Strambli was in trouble. Did Paladin pick up anythin' on the short-range sweeper?"

"No, the first I knew of this was when you came back in."

"Lucky she didn't decompress," Fura said, her cold eyes meeting my own.

"The Ghostie blade's only a few atoms thick," Prozor said. "So even though it went in deep, right through her suit, it only left a hairline gap when she pulled it out."

"I'm sorry, Strambli," I said, and she gave a yelp of pain as I removed the damaged part of her suit leg. Under the pressure-tight armour she had several layers of fabric insulation, sewn with flexible tubes for heat regulation, and they were all sodden with blood. But the bleeding was easing, I decided, probably because the underlying wound was so clean and narrow.

"This'll help," Surt said, drawing up a syringe from one of the medicine cabinets.

"You sure you know what's in that?" I whispered.

Surt nodded, easing my fears that she was about to inject Strambli with one of Bosa's punishment drugs. Prozor, Tindouf and Fura had got the upper part of Strambli's suit off and Surt was able to peel away Strambli's sleeve to get to the flesh of her upper arm. She injected her very competently, and a wave of relief passed through Strambli almost immediately, her eyes losing focus and then fluttering as she slipped into something blessedly close to unconsciousness.

I leaned in to inspect the wound, now that the blood-saturated fabric was being peeled away. It was in her left leg, about halfway up the shin, a little to the outside of the imagined line running between kneecap and foot. It was about the length of my little finger and looked no worse than a long paper-cut.

"It could be worse," Surt said, in a gently questioning tone.

"Yes. She's still got the leg," I answered. "But it's the worst injury we've seen since we took over this ship and we can't take any chances with it. The wound will have to be cleaned and stitched, and then we pray there's no damage to bone, nerves or circulatory structures."

"Didn't know you'd been to medical school," Fura said.

"I haven't." I looked at her for a long, brooding moment, tempted to confront her with what I had discovered in her quarters. "I'm just speaking common sense. There might be bits of suit fabric forced into the wound, and they'd need to come out before they cause any trouble. If Paladin still had his body he could scan the injury, but all we have left is his head." *Which has been doing some sly translating for you,* I added silently.

"I'll clean it," Surt said, fishing in the medicine cabinets for what she needed. "But I've never stitched anything."

"I'm no master of sail," Tindouf said. "But I've done my share of stitchings. I'll sews her up 'andsomely." He thought about that for a few seconds. "But not so 'andsomely that she doesn't have a scar and a story to talk about afterwards." He looked down with a distant fondness at his own elaborately scarred and blemished knuckles. "We likes our scarses, we does."

"Just fix her," Fura said, already turning from the patient.

As she did so I noticed something in the battery of controls on her left sleeve, on the suit she had not yet removed.

"You say you called in on the squawk?" I asked.

She spun back to face me.

"Yes, several times, and no one answered."

"You're on the wrong setting," I said, nodding at the controls. "Either it got knocked when you were going through the lock, or you forgot which one's for the ship and which one's for the launch." I shrugged, content to have proven that Tindouf and I had not been sleeping on the job. "We guessed something was wrong when you all came in at once, ahead of time."

Fura screwed up her face in rage, but I had the sense that most of it was directed at her suit, not me.

"Damn all this."

"Are you serious about retaliating?" I asked. "We don't even know who we'd be shooting at, let alone where to aim."

"We soon will," Fura said.

# 9

I met her in her quarters, as she had requested. She was at her desk, as composed as if nothing of the slightest consequence had happened. No attack, no wounding of Strambli, no intrusion by her sister into her supposedly private dealings. I wondered, under other circumstances, if some alteration to the desk and its belongings might have alerted to her to my activities. Yet while there was anger and determination in her face, the glowy was subdued and I saw nothing that suggested she harboured any fresh suspicions against me, beyond those that had been with us for months.

"I think Strambli will be all right," I ventured. "If the wound can be cleaned, and Tindouf does a good enough job stitching it up. If all else fails, we'll be at our destination in a little over two weeks, and they should have much better medicine than anything on a ship."

"We may be there a little sooner still," Fura said. "Did you glance at the Glass Armillary on your way?"

"Ought I have?"

"You'll recall that there are baubles—red marbles on long sticks, for those projecting into the Emptyside."

"We're not detouring to a bauble," I said, before the idea had a chance to take root.

"Did I say that we were?" Fura looked affronted. "We're

strapped enough for fuel as it is. No, I meant to draw your attention to the small black marble, quite close to our present position."

"I assumed it was another bauble."

"It may have been a bauble once, or an inhabited world, or some nameless rock. It has no name now because it figures in no charts, no almanacs, no ephemeris tables—certainly none that you or I would ever have seen."

"Then I don't—"

"It's a swallower," Fura said, sighing slightly at my laggard comprehension. "A swallower without a world to enshroud it. A naked swallower, drifting through space on its own orbit around the Old Sun."

"No such thing exists."

"By which you mean that no such thing *should* exist, by all that's right. Sometimes they get loose, though. When a world is destroyed—which happens, albeit rarely—the swallower's never damaged. It breaks free of its confinement, a dragon unchained. The only reason we don't hear of more swallowers orbiting the Old Sun is that the violence of the destruction is normally enough to send the swallower off into the Empty, forever beyond the Old Sun's influence. This one remained behind, though." Her hand moved to a bound journal. "Bosa knew of it, and the parameters of its orbit. It must have been very old information, long lost to the likes of Trusko or Rackamore. We're very lucky that she kept track of the swallower's position."

"So we can be sure to avoid it?"

"No. So we can use it to our advantage."

"You're not serious."

"I am perfectly serious. Our course was going to take us quite near the swallower in any case—not close enough to cause us difficulties, but near enough that we might have verified its position. Do you remember those books we used to look over, with the coloured plates? A swallower bends starlight, like a little lens, held up to the sky. I meant to sight onto it with one of the telescopes and prove to myself that the orbital tables were correct. We will still do that, but now I will have Paladin and Tindouf arrange a small alteration to our course, one that brings us much nearer to the swallower."

"You should be doing the opposite. We're already damaged as it is."

"Superficial, according to Paladin. Nothing the hands can't repair in a few shifts, even without Strambli to weigh-in. We will maintain all sail until we are very near the swallower, giving no hint of our intentions to the pursuing ship. Then we must haul-in rapidly—quicker than we've ever done before. Soon after, we shall use the swallower's gravitational potential to our benefit." She jabbed her metal finger against a paperweight and with the other hand scribed a curving course on the desk. "We swing in very tight, and change our tack, much more sharply and rapidly than we could ever do under any plausible combination of sails and ions."

"To what purpose?"

"I would have thought it clear. We will surprise our adversary. Even if they have a fix on our position, they will not anticipate such a turn. It will confuse them, since they know nothing of the swallower, and in the fog of that confusion we will have the better of them. As we turn, we will sweep them once. That will expose our position, but they will doubt their readings and risk a return sweep of their own. By then we will have a very hard fix on them, and we will have the additional benefit of presenting our broadside to the pursuer. We will run out all lateral coilguns and fire 'em until they cook."

"Do you mean to kill them?"

She looked diffident."To punish them, most certainly. They have struck at my ship."

"Our ship. With disabling shot."

"Tell that to Strambli."

I thought of chastising her for that remark, since it was not long since she had affected a chilly indifference to Strambli's welfare. But I merely smiled and said: "It sounds like the sort of gambit Bosa would have tried. Using something dangerous to her advantage, launching a surprise retaliation, and showing no mercy."

Fura lifted an eyebrow. "And what of it?"

"Are you sure you want to be doing something that makes us look more like Bosa, when we're already trying to shake off her reputation?"

"If survival requires us to act in a certain manner, I see no alternative. Unless you have a counter-proposal, dear heart?"

I tightened my jaw. She knew well enough that I had nothing better to add, beyond holding our course and trusting in luck.

"I don't have an alternative. But that doesn't mean I'm persuaded by your plan. We'll need to discuss it with the others."

She made a benevolent gesture with her palm, like a queen granting some minor favour.

"Of course."

"It's a good thing Bosa left a record of this swallower in her unencoded journals, or we'd never have known about it."

"I have made some small progress in deciphering her encrypted records," Fura said, off-handedly. "With Paladin's assistance, needless to say."

*

After that, there were only three possible topics of conversation on the ship, and they were all equally entangled. Strambli's condition, the nature of our enemy, and the gambit Fura had in mind.

"I don't likes the idea, not one bit," Tindouf said in reference to the last point, speaking—I felt—for all of us. "But I don't says it can't be done."

"Why must we haul-in?" Surt asked. "We're short-handed as it is, and they could send more sail-shot our way at any moment."

"The swallower may have attracted debris," I said. "So we'll need to protect the sails just as if we were near a bauble or a world. But we'll also be swinging much closer to the swallower, and the ship will feel the pull, like a sheet of dough being stretched under a roller. The sails and yardage would shred if we didn't bring 'em in."

"I don't like swallowers," Prozor said, a statement that she interjected into the conversation at clocklike intervals, just in case any of us were at risk of forming the contrary opinion.

"I've heard mention of naked swallowers," Surt said. "Never sure I believed in 'em. Definitely never thought I'd be consentin' to sail close to one by choice."

"They're not evil or haunted or cursed," I said. "Just a thing that people made once because it suited their needs, and most of the time they suit our needs as well."

"I heard it was the Clackers made 'em," Surt said thoughtfully. "Or the Tuskers."

Tindouf stroked his chin. "The Stingtails, I heardses."

"It wasn't aliens," I said. "The swallowers are as old as any of the worlds, as old as the Congregation itself. It was us—monkeys like you and I. We took the rubble of the eight old worlds and made all the millions of new worlds out of all that material. But there was still a lot of stuff left over—enough to make lots and lots of swallowers. We put 'em in the new worlds so people could walk around normally, just as they used to on Earth or Mars, before the Sundering."

"I don't like swallowers."

I laid out a sheet of sail, on which had been drawn the calculations for our course and the critical actions ahead of us. Our trajectory was a gradually sharpening curve, tending to a spiral as it neared the black pin-prick of the swallower.

"Paladin verified these figures," I said. "We can depend on 'em, and we gain in two ways. It gives us a helpful shove in the direction of Wheel Strizzardy, meaning we get there sooner—useful, if Strambli doesn't start perking up. We also have the advantage of the other ship, for the few minutes that it'll take 'em to doubt their readings. They'll rumble us sooner or later, but not before we've bloodied their nose."

"I was thinkin' of bloodyin' a bit more than that," Surt said, directing a confiding smirk at Tindouf.

"I know how we all feel about what's happened. We're angry about Strambli and feel we ought to be retaliating. And we will, in kind. But no more than that. We'll show restraint—the one thing Bosa could never have managed. But we're not her crew, are we?" I looked at my companions, inviting their affirmation, which was offered, albeit grudgingly. "That ship isn't picking on us for no reason. It thinks we're the *Nightjammer*, the *Dame Scarlet*. We can't very well blame them for that, can we? They've chanced on us and we look like the most hated and feared ship in the Congregation. There'd be no censure against a captain who destroyed Bosa Sennen—quite the opposite. But our enemy wishes to take us alive and we will extend them a similar civility. We'll send them a full coil-gun broadside, not sail-shot but heavy slugs, only we'll take pains to damage only their sails, aiming away from the hull. Our sweeper fix will be accurate enough for that, and we know that Bosa's guns are very precise at long range. Even if we only graze their sails, our meaning will be plain. They will see that we have demonstrated our kind intentions when it was within our grasp to do much worse, and that will stand us in good stead when we approach port."

"I don't like swallowers."

By turns, despite these objections—none of them easily dismissed—Fura's plan gained traction. It was agreed that veering close to the swallower was better than waiting for another salvo of sail-shot, and there was a general enthusiasm for hitting back at the enemy. If we were to commit to the idea, though, there was not a moment to be lost. We would be at the swallower in three days, and the sails would have to be struck with the expert coordination of Paladin, the sail-control gear, and those of us still fit enough to put on vacuum suits. Which would have been work enough, except that we were not yet done with the other preparations. If we had been busy before, now we were obliged to labour to the limits of endurance.

The saving grace was that it took my mind off anything except the immediate practicalities. It was enough just to be working, eating and sleeping. In the grind of those hours I almost found myself forgetting Fura's deception, or at least wondering if I might have misunderstood the scratchings in her journals. Perhaps she had made the connection with Lagganvor *after* our decision had been cast, and it was merely a happy accident that he had gone to ground in the same place. Deep down, though, I knew this was not how it had happened.

When I was not working, or taking care of my basic needs, I tried to think of Strambli. We all made a point of that, visiting her as often we were able, and keeping her abreast of developments.

Slowly it became apparent to us all that she was not making the swift recovery we had hoped for. Surt, who was the only one of us who knew anything about shipboard medicine, had to spend more and more time in the surgery. She had cleaned the superficial part of the wound to the best of her abilities, but she had not been able to follow it down to its limits.

Not that Surt was any sort of physician. It was merely that she was the only one of us who had picked up a few dismal scraps of healing lore and who knew her way around the common potions to be found on a ship. But she struggled to read the names of medicines, let alone the instructions that went with them, and she had no experience with surgery. We'd already done the best we could for Strambli. Surt changed the dressing and cleaned around the stitches once a day, and since none of us were likely to do a better job it was agreed that Surt should be relieved of some of her external duties, until such time as Strambli was stronger.

Looking at that little scratch, as I had done, it was hard to see how it could have set her back so badly. But I reminded myself that it been a Ghostie edge that slipped into her, not just any old blade. There was a wrongness about every aspect of the Ghostie stuff, from the way it looked to the way it felt when you were wearing the armour or using the weapons. And that same insidious, treacherous wrongness obviously extended to the effect it had on one of its victims, even if the wounding had been accidental.

Strambli was stable for those first days, drowsy when she was awake, complaining of discomfort some of the time, adamant in her lucid moments that she had committed no error. But the wound refused to settle down, the skin around it turning red and swollen, and worsening by the watch.

On the day before our rendezvous with the swallower, Strambli started running a fever.

"I cleaned it," Surt maintained, as if we doubted her, when we were discussing Strambli's predicament over bread and ale while Fura was off in her cabin, refining the elements of our plan with Paladin.

"Without you and Tindouf she'd be a lot worse off," I said, meeting her eyes and making sure she understood that I was serious.

"There are surgical tools in that room," Prozor said.

"And none of us has a clue what to do with them," I replied. "We can't go opening her up and just hope for the best. All we can do is keep her comfortable and hope that she can fight off that infection on her own."

"And if she don't?" Surt asked.

"We could take out the stitches, open the wound and flush it out again," Prozor said.

"No," I said. "Surt was thorough the first time. It'll only risk more infection. We keep on as we are. Strambli's strong and she has a good crew around her."

"Can't get to this wheelworld soon enough for my tastes," Surt said, rejecting a large chunk of green-mottled bread. "Swallowers or no swallowers."

"I know we have a few things on our plates," Prozor said. "But there's a detail or two we oughtn't to overlook. I know we ain't rounded the swallower yet, but if we don't start wrappin' our noggins around the other stuff, we won't be shipshape."

"The other stuff?" I asked.

"The name and history of this pile of rivets, girlie. We'll need to call ourselves somethin' besides *Revenger,* and it's no use Fura struttin' around callin' herself Fura Ness, neither. Be too easy to draw a line back to Bosa, and that won't do any of our necks any good, not until we've had a chance to sit down and explain ourselves, and I'd sooner do that at my leisure, not when some cove's got a blade against my gullet. What I'm sayin' is we need a story that'll tide us over until we're good and ready to put things straight. Any one of us that goes ashore is goin' to need a fresh name and a made-up past that stands a bit of scrutiny. Includin' you, Adrana."

"I thought we'd worry about that when we're a little nearer."

"No. Time to fret is now. No good some cove asking us for our name, registry and port of origin, and us saying, stand by, we'll get back to you in an hour, just as soon as we've got our stories straight."

"That's another kind of work we need to get busy with, then," I said, feeling as if there was no end to it.

"You told me you always did like makin' up stories and plays," Prozor told me. "Now's your chance to shine."

*

We could not operate the sweeper in advance, nor strike sail, but there was still the question of the coil-guns. They had been tested singly after we took the ship, using the remains of Trusko's vessel as a target, and there was no reason to doubt that they would function just as harmoniously in unison. Yet we had never discharged a simultaneous broadside, nor sustained a continuous rate of fire to the limit of the guns' ability to cool themselves.

The enemy's sail-shot must have been launched to us by chasing armaments, arranged to fire along the long axis of a ship, and if we had reciprocated with our stern-cannons, especially with a sustained discharge, there was an excellent chance that we would have exposed our position by dint of a thermal signature.

I'd never set out to become well-versed in the workings of armaments, but Bosa had had her own ideas for me. Once she identified me as her most likely protégée, she had been very keen to instil a comprehensive working knowledge of weaponry, including our own and the various kinds that might be used against us. Coil-guns were one of the commonest—and most effective—sorts of shipboard defence.

They worked on the principle of magnetic inductance, using a pulsed field to accelerate an inert slug to damaging speed. The repeated cycling of those inductance coils generated heat that couldn't be easily dissipated, and sooner or later that heat would find its way into the guidance rails of the gun, causing them to buckle or tighten, leading first to a degradation of accuracy and then to a loss of penetrating efficiency, and finally to a complete seizure of the entire weapon. The remedy for that was to allow the guns to rest, giving them time to cool down and regain their full effectiveness, but under sustained fire they could be cooked beyond the point of recovery, and in the very worst instance—so Prozor informed me—a ship might be incapacitated, or even destroyed, by the unexpected and damaging recoil of a cooked coil-gun. Long before that, though, the hapless ship would have given itself away by the heat of its overloaded guns.

Bosa's cannons were fine pieces, well-maintained. She had shown them off to me, proud as if they were her own murderous kin. They had double-stiffened guidance rails, triple-wound solenoids, and devilish ranks of bladed cooling fins resembling saw-teeth. They could be fed from the ship's water for additional refrigeration. Each gun was also capable of being fired manually from outside the hull, semi-automatically from within, or entirely under the captain's discretion. The guns were connected to a pair of duplicated aiming consoles, one in the main control room and the other in the captain's quarters.

This latter arrangement was now under Paladin's direction, and it was he who would be trusted with the disabling salvo as we passed the swallower. Only Paladin would be able to compute and aim quickly enough.

But first we had to be sure we could rely on the coil-guns.

"Until we turn, they have no direct view of our flanks,"

Paladin said. "A short test-salvo ought therefore to run a very low risk of detection, and I will be sure not to allow any of the guns to run warm."

By common agreement ships always fired away from the Old Sun during test exercises, with the hope of preventing any stray shots from wandering into the orbits of the Congregation, where they might strike a world or a vessel. We followed the same courtesy, aiming at a blank point in the sky and testing the guns singly and then in unison.

We were all ready for it, but it had been months since those test shots against Trusko's hulk, and the noise and fury of the weapons caught us as fully unawares as if we had never seen battle. First, a series of hard clangs running in rhythmic sequence from bow to stern, as if some ogre were striking a giant metal mallet against the hull, and with each of those clangs a twitch of unabsorbed recoil, as if the ship itself were startled. *Dong, dong, dong, dong,* gun after gun, until the last discharge.

Then the roaring simultaneous broadside, not a twitch now but a shudder that seemed fit to loosen every hull-plate, and the sound of it less a noise than a gut-punch.

"Again," Fura said eagerly, the glowy brightening with her anticipation of revenge.

Paladin fired another broadside, and another, and when we were done with the port coil-guns we repeated the exercise with the starboard batteries, as well as the dorsal and ventral guns, just in case we had need of supplementary fire. Then we returned to the port guns, and kept at it until Paladin said they needed to cool. Then it was time to reload the slug chambers, which could be done from inside the ship, and we all did our share, even Fura.

"I'll go and reassure Strambli that the world isn't falling in," Surt said, pulling a pair of padded stoppers from her ears, and making me wish I had thought to take the same precaution.

"We're not quite done," Fura said.

"Paladin says the batteries performed just as they were meant to," I answered.

"I'm sure they did, but all we were shooting at was empty space, and I'd like a little more reassurance that the targeting is precise. I have an idea, sister. I think it will suit both of us. Besides, it's more than time that we put that last body of hers to good use. I never thought that she deserved the common decency of a burial, but this will serve very well indeed."

It took me a moment to understand her meaning.

Bosa had left twenty-four of her own bodies on this ship. There was the final body she had been inhabiting at the time of her death, the shell that had once belonged to Illyria Rackamore, before she was taken and turned. We had kept that body alive long enough for Bosa to give up some of her secrets—teasingly, for the most part. I do not think she told us anything against her own wishes, even at the end—but we had not rid ourselves of it, nor, initially, of the twenty-three bodies we found in glass bottles, suspended in preservative fluid. They were dead, but some attachment or vanity had kept Bosa from disposing of them.

They had proven useful to us. I will not dwell on what Fura did to those bodies, suffice to say that she could not have completed *The True and Accurate Testimony* without them, and she had found a similar utility in the final corpse. We had thrown the other twenty-three into space, along with the bottles that hosted them, and the empty bottles that Bosa had kept for the bodies still to come—a lineage in which I might have come to take my eventual place. But we still carried the last iteration of Bosa Sennen, and now I grasped Fura's intention.

"We spoke of returning her to Rackamore's family," I said. "To his home, to her place of birth. We agreed that we owed her memory at least that much."

"We aren't touching Illyria Rackamore's memory. She died somewhere in the kindness room, under Bosa's treatment. It stopped being her body around the same time."

I do not know if I was persuaded that this course of action was either necessary or dignified, but there were occasions when it was easier to go along with Fura and it seemed this was one of them. So while we waited for the guns to cool, my sister and I went aft to the room where we kept the one remaining bottle, and in which we had stored the severely injured and mutilated remains of Bosa Sennen, who had once been the beloved daughter of Pol Rackamore. We persuaded her grey-green corpse out of that fluid, wrinkled our noses at the pickled stench of her, and then conveyed those remains to the nearest lock.

"I'd wish you a peaceful eternity," Fura said, taking the head between her hands and forcing the sightless face to meet her own. "If I wasn't sure you'd come back like a ghoul. You had your moment, Bosa. You had your ship and your crew, and you left your mark. But it's ours now. I took it, and I took you, and in a century or two no one will remember either of us. Ain't that sweet?" She leaned in and kissed Bosa on the forehead. "Now get the hell off my ship."

We sealed the door and charged the lock with lungstuff so that it would blow out when the outer door was opened. It was a little wasteful but we had more than enough in reserve, as well as ample lightvine to keep the lungstuff fresh.

Then we went back to the control room, and Fura told Paladin to open the lock. It gave a pop, nothing to compare with the guns, but we felt it all the same.

"Track her to out to one league," Fura said. "Then concentrate the guns. We'll be watching from the port galley window."

*

Not being privy to the inner workings of my sister's mind, I cannot say for certain what she expected from that moment. Perhaps she thought there would be jubilation among the crew; that the final, decisive extinguishing of Bosa Sennen—the complete destruction of her last mortal remains—would be the act that fully cemented Fura as our natural leader. She had, after all, been the one who ended Bosa's reign; what better ceremony to mark her own coronation? But when the guns turned Bosa to a grey cloud, a nebula made of ash and dust, already turning black at its heart as it thinned out and dissipated, the reaction was—I believe—a degree more muted than she would have desired. There was some clapping and cheering, but it was restrained, and the faces turned from the window with an unseemly haste, as if a thing had been done—a necessary thing—but not one that any of us cared to dwell on for a moment longer, once the deed itself had been completed. We felt like leering spectators at a hanging, witnessing a sort of justice but also demeaning it by the act of onlooking. Demeaning the act, and tainting ourselves with it as well.

"Rejoice," Fura said, lifting her arms as if to encourage applause. "This is what we've been waiting for, coves. This moment. We've scrubbed out the last stain of her. I feel better already—like there's one less stink aboard this ship. Should've done it the moment we took over!"

"It was just a corpse," I said. "If you'd come later—if you'd come too late—it would be me that you'd have had to kill."

"No," Fura declared, in the full hearing of the others. "You'd have been long gone, Adrana. And I'd have done whatever needed to be done."

"I don't doubt it," I said quietly.

I despised what had happened to Illyria Rackamore. I hated what had happened to the innocents before her, all the way back down that vile lineage. Perhaps greed had brought some of them to that state of being, but I did not doubt that some—most, perhaps—had been free of obvious blame or miscalculation. Certainly, I had done nothing that warranted my capture, besides wishing for some adventure and a modest amount of independent capital. And yet, in the months that I had been Bosa's understudy, I had seen something of the future that awaited me, if and when I was deemed worthy of her name and the captaincy of the *Nightjammer.* A ship without equal, and a command without complications. A crew that either loved me or perished, because Bosa Sennen permitted no intermediate condition. A name that made the twenty thousand worlds of the Congregation shrivel into themselves.

Although I wished to crush such thoughts, I cannot deny that they had their attractions. And while that future might have been closed to me, part of it still had a hold on my imagination.

I think I was the last one to turn from the window. By then there was no trace of Bosa Sennen left at all.

Outside, at least.

*

Nervousness was like a restless bird, moving from one perch to another. It had been settled on Strambli for long enough that I thought it might have found a home, content to remain with her even though she was incapacitated. But now that Strambli was ill, Surt was the one who had started getting the jitters. She was always stopping me to ask if I'd picked up anything new on the bones, and when she wasn't on shift she seemed to find it hard to tear her eyes away from the sweeper, just in case she was the one who spotted a blip that the rest of us missed. Surt's business was fixing things, hooking them together, persuading alien gubbins to speak to monkey gubbins, and vice versa. She was always sucking on a broken nail or blistered finger, because she spent half her life taking things apart or forcing them back together again, and when that was the entirety of her business she was very content. But she had done all that she could inside the ship, and being outside was much less comfortable to her, and besides which it made it impossible not to think of the other ship, since most of what there was to look at out there was space and emptiness, leagues of silky darkness in which something was trying to hide itself while inching closer to us.

She caught me between shifts, clawing at my arm as I tried to squeeze past on my way from the bones.

"Did you get a sniff of anything, Adrana?"

My patience was starting to wear thin. I had told her several times that if I had something to report, the crew would be the first to know. "No, Surt," I said, smiling through my exasperation. "Nothing this time, or the last time, or the one before that."

"Maybe they ain't there after all, do you think?" she asked, with a rising childlike hopefulness.

"No, I believe they're still behind us, much as I wish it were otherwise. But this...gambit of Fura's, that will give 'em cause to reconsider the pursuit. They'll understand that this is all just a big misunderstanding..."

"I was thinking about that. I know what Proz says, and Fura, but would we really be doing ourselves so much harm if we just...explained ourselves? I mean, we *is* innocent, ain't we? I'm not forgetting that part?"

I smiled, genuinely this time, because I shared her sense that it was growing harder and harder to remind ourselves that we had not chosen this path for ourselves. We might have set a trap for Bosa, one that she had fallen into, but we had broken no laws in that regard, nor in taking a hostile ship as prize. "No—we is...we *are*...innocent, and don't let that slip your mind, not for a second. And you're right. This is just a misunderstanding. But a knotty one, all the same, that we have to take great care in unravelling. And we will, Surt, I'm sure of it."

"Our story ain't too complicated," she said. "If we just laid it out, without goin' into all the details—the Fang and the Ghosties, and all that—they'd believe us, wouldn't they?"

"Yes, and that's what we'll do, if and when the moment is right."

She glanced aside, dropping her voice. "We could just do it now, Adrana—you and me. Get on the squawk, and..."

I cannot account for what happened to me next.

Or rather, I *can* account for it, very easily, but I would much rather not do so.

An image flashed into my mind, sharp and grainy in the same moment, as if I'd seen it on newsprint or a flickerbox. It was Surt, bending low to the main squawk console, the light from its dials and buttons outlining her face, which was averted slightly from the console, turned to a furtive angle so that she might detect the approach of one or more of us, and be done with her business. She had the handset raised to her mouth, and she was whispering into it, speaking into the void, arguing our case to the nearest ship with the capability of intercepting our signal. Pleading with them to abandon the pursuit and the ranging fire, because we were innocents...

I saw the image as a warning, or presentiment, of what Surt would do, or was considering doing, regardless of my cooperation in the matter. And it was intolerable to me. An anger swelled in me like nothing I'd known before, except perhaps in the full state of possession in which I had pressed a knife to Fura. But that had been months ago, when Bosa was still alive—when her psychological influence on me had been at its strongest.

I had thought myself rid of her—or nearly rid.

It was not so.

I grabbed Surt by the scruff of her neck, my movement savage enough, and fast enough, that I might very easily have snapped her spine. The action was autonomous, driven by that rising rage, and while it originated from a foreign part of me, it also flowed through and out of me just as naturally as any self-generated impulse. I pinched a ridge of skin and dug my nails into it so forcefully that Surt yelped, and that yelp, I think, was the merciful intrusion that broke the spell, puncturing Bosa's hold on me. I released her with a gasp of shock and shame, and the horror that showed itself in Surt's eyes must have been fully reflected in my own.

"I didn't mean..." I said, nearly stammering. "I didn't. I'm sorry. I just..."

I withdrew my hand and arm. I was repulsed. "It was just the ship. I thought you were going to...that you were thinking of endangering us, and..."

Surt was breathing heavily. She said nothing for a few moments, then reached up and rubbed at the back of her neck, where the skin I had pinched still showed the impression of my fingers, bloodless crescent depressions where I had dug in, nearly drawing blood.

"It's all right, Adrana."

"No, it isn't. I should never have..."

"It's all right. Because it weren't you, not really." She continued to regard me, as one might regard a snake that might be playing dead, and still contained a debilitating quantity of venom. "It was her, wasn't it? We blew up her body, but that was never going to be end of her, no matter what Fura reckons. There'll be a bit of her stuck inside you until the Old Sun swells up."

"She's gone," I asserted, as much to persuade myself as Surt. "I just...lost control."

"Maybe you did," Surt said, lowering her hand, her breathing starting to normalise. "But then the question is, are you sure it won't happen again? Because if that was just a glimpse of her, I'm in no hurry to have her back for good."

*

Surt made no further mention of my behaviour, for which I was keenly grateful. I had scared her, but just as crucially I had scared myself. That spasm of rage was the equal of anything I had seen in Fura, if not more shocking by virtue of the suddenness with which it had erupted from me. I had seen something of the hold the glowy had on my sister; the way it shaped her temper. There was no denying that it frightened me and made me apprehensive about its future progression. Yet the glowy was only an accomplice in the changes that Fura had willingly brought upon herself, abetting that hardening of her character that had commenced from the moment she had to save herself on the *Monetta's Mourn*. I believed that the glowy amplified her moods, and that it made their highs and lows more vertiginous, but I do not think that the glowy was itself the primary instigator of those changes. Rather, it responded to the natural patterns of her temperament; distorting and disfiguring in the process, most certainly, but never itself becoming the sole causal agent.

That was not what had happened to me, in the instant I seized Surt. My mood had been one of comradely concern, tempered only by a distant intimation that Surt might do something unwise if she permitted her own fears to swell and magnify.

But in a flash that concern had transmuted to a singular, all-consuming imperative, a totality of thought and action that excluded any introspective consideration. All that mattered was the preservation of the ship; in that instant Surt had become nothing more than a faulty component that needed to be eliminated, replaced.

I thanked the worlds that she had yelped, for without that intervention I think it very plausible that I might have killed her there and then. The rage had subsided, a tide of bitter regret taking its place, but I did not doubt for an instant that the originating seed was still within me.

That much was settled; beyond dispute. The only question remaining was how effectively I could deal with the residue of Bosa that I carried. Now that I knew she was there, now that I knew her ferocity, might I have the advantage of self-awareness of my condition? If I could sense the occasions when she might rise, and steel myself against her, might I be able to keep her at bay?

I didn't know; I could not know. It would depend, I supposed, on how thoroughly our coming circumstances put us to the test. It would depend on my strength, as well as hers.

And the degree to which Fura gave me cause to doubt our partnership.

*

I was glad to have the matter of our fictional histories to tear my thoughts away from Bosa Sennen. Prozor had crewed on more vessels than any of us, over a much longer period, and she had an inkling of the gaps where one could begin to spin a yarn, without getting too tangled up in the affairs of real lives and real ships. Without her I would have had no hope of coming up with an invented identity for our vessel and its hands.

So, when our eyes were not glued tight with tiredness, and our fingers not too raw to hold a pen, Prozor and I sat together and tried to cook up a story that would hold together at the first examination. It had to feel real and solid—but not so interesting as to invite further discussion. Like the cleansing of Strambli's wound, there was a limit as to how deep we could go.

"If a cove asks more'n two questions straight," Prozor said, "it means they've already got their suspicions. In which case more talk and lies ain't goin' to dig us out of *that* hole."

"If anyone takes that close an interest in us," I said, chewing on the end of the pen, "I hope we'll be ready to make a run for the launch."

"Keep our noses clean, not give anyone a reason to snoop around, we should be golden. Would help if I'd seen a little more of this place we're headed to."

"Are you certain you never went there?"

"Old Proz forgets a thing or two, especially since Bosa put a fresh dent in her skull. But not the places she's seen. Or the coves she's met."

"There isn't much in the *Book of Worlds.* It's a pity we're not going somewhere else, because then all we'd have to do is say we're from Wheel Strizzardy, and no one would be able to prove us wrong."

"So we need somewhere that's just as out-of-the-way. But not in the same processional, or one that's easy sailin' distance." The dawning of an idea lifted her features. "Here. Pass me the book."

I did, and she leafed through it with an obvious directed interest.

"What're you thinking?"

"Indragol," Prozor said, turning the relevant page to my eyes, so I could see how scant the entry was. "Laceworld, thirty-third processional, not so far out from the centre of things to be interestin', but not too close to anywhere glamorous or prosperous. I went there once, so I know the shape of the place, a few of the local customs. We'll say that's our port of origin, the place that built and crewed this ship first of all."

"Doesn't exactly roll off the tongue. Can't we have somewhere that sounds more like Mazarile?"

"If it did, you'd say Mazarile by mistake. Indragol's just the start of it, though. We won't all be from that world, but enough of us to fit the story. I'll work on that. You can give our ship a name, and decide how her ladyship wishes to be known henceforth."

"You're assuming she'll be acting out the role of captain, then."

"I'd say it's a foregone conclusion, girlie. Unless you know otherwise."

"If it keeps her happy, she can play at being captain." I felt my face tighten, wishing I could share my suspicions with Prozor. She had been our saviour, as well as a friend and confidante, and it aggrieved me to keep a secret from her. But if word of Fura's duplicity got out, there was no telling how far it would go or what the consequences would be for our fragile little crew.

I felt a rage beginning to stir inside me. I forced a torrent of placid thoughts upon myself; a succession of pleasing images, dwelling in particular on the many kindnesses Fura had done for me when we were younger.

"Somethin' troublin' you?"

I smiled quickly. "Just wondering how we're going to get through this, if we don't keep our story straight."

"I wouldn't worry about it too much." She was giving me a doubtful look, making me think she'd seen how forced my smile was. "Half the business of crews is lyin' about their pasts, coverin' up mistakes and makin' their successes seem bigger than they really were. Even a good cove like Rackamore wasn't above the odd bit of embroiderin', if it helped us along."

"We're doing a bit more than embroidering, Proz."

"We'll be all right. It's not like we have any complicated dealings do we? Some recruitin', if need be. Stockin' up on stores. Fixing Strambli, if she doesn't snap out of that fever on her own. That's normal business. Nothin' for any cove to raise an eyebrow over."

"We'd best hope not."

"If there's somethin' else about this place that has you bothered, girlie, I hope you'd share it with me rather'n let it fester."

"No...I..." I tried to fasten on a more convincing smile than my previous attempt. "I suppose it's just that we've been out here so long, skulking around, that it's going to feel a bit odd going back to civilisation."

"I know what you mean," she said, surprising me a bit with her agreement. "But you didn't sign up with the *Monetta's Mourn* to run away from your old lives forever, did you? None of us really does, no matter what we might say. We just want to see a bit more of the worlds, earn a quoin or two. Even old Proz had thoughts of settlin' down, until that bank run turned her savings to slush. Civilisation ain't a thing to run from, girlie. It's the reason we're out here riskin' our necks with baubles. But just now and then we need remindin' of that."

*

Fura and I were in the sighting room. She had her eye to one of the larger scopes, puckering her lips with tremendous concentration as she made a tiny alteration to one of the pointing dials. When she drew in breath to speak, it was as if she had not been breathing for at least a minute.

"There. I have it. Momentarily, at least. Our position's shifting and it won't hold for long." She squeezed aside, giving me room to lean over and squint through the same eyepiece.

Stars, a smattering of worlds. More worlds than a few weeks ago, and some of them showing flecks of colour. Glimmers of purple and red. The nearest worlds were still many tens of thousands of leagues away but with the best instruments it would have been feasible to identify them, picking out noteworthy features.

That was not our business today.

"I don't see it," I said.

"Watch the bright star in the middle. It's a true star, not a world. The swallower is exactly between us."

The star twinkled—swelling and fading in brightness—in a way that I had never associated with the lights of the fixed firmament, far beyond the jostle of the Congregation. The star regained its stability for a few seconds, then sparkled again, and for an instant it seemed to smear into a sort of crescent.

"Then it's real. Bosa's swallower."

"I never doubted it for an instant. The ephemeris was a little off, but not enough to upset our plan. Paladin's revising the schedule as we speak."

"How did you find it, if it wasn't where it should have been?"

"It was very close. Otherwise it would have been quite impossible. A tiny, dark thing like that—barely showing itself unless it happens to trick the light of another object, like a lens. I wonder how many ships have been lost, running into naked swallowers? Perhaps some of those thought lost to Bosa."

"There can't be many of these things floating around."

"We might hope."

"You said they only escaped when worlds were destroyed. We know there's a little dust and debris surrounding the Congregation, but there are still fifty million worlds that haven't been smashed up. There can't have been that many lost over the years, or we'd be swimming in dust."

"Doesn't it trouble you that it happened at all?" she asked.

"Of course it troubles me. If there's anything dependable in this Congregation of ours, it's the worlds we're born on. They've outlasted us and they'll outlast our descendants. If I'm on such a place, I'd sooner sleep in my bed knowing the world will still be there in the morning. Wouldn't you?"

"If I meant to spend much more time on worlds, I suppose I might." She paused, while I eased my eye away from the scope, now that the star had settled down again. "I don't like the idea of worlds being destroyed, of course. But it's the greater fate of the Congregation that concerns me more. Our Occupation, and how it will end. I thought it silly of Rackamore to be troubled by such a distant concern, but I find it much harder to dismiss his fears now. What is the point of any deed, good or otherwise, if this little window of civilisation of ours will soon have its end?"

"We don't know that it will."

"True. Perhaps we will be the fortunate ones. The lucky Thirteenth. If indeed we can truly call this the Thirteenth Occupation."

"Back to that, are we? I was hoping that shooting her body to smithereens would have purged you of Bosa's obsessions."

Purged you, if not me, I added silently to myself.

"Then you thought incorrectly." But she ameliorated her tone. "I'm glad to be rid of that body. But those obsessions of hers, as you call them, are questions that any sensible person would be drawn to." She gestured beyond the glass of the sighting room. "Think of all those worlds, Adrana—all the millions of lives going on in the Congregation. All the petty distractions of our so-called civilisation. The things we used to think mattered, like a proper education and 'getting on' in life. Moving in the right circles, and having enough money to be comfortable. Prestige and ambition. Finding the right man or woman. Being dressed properly for the season. Knowing when to speak, and when not to. Having opinions, but never too many of 'em. And all of it built on thin ice. A system of commerce, run by aliens for their own convenience. Occupations that end as soon as they begin, as if ours will be any different. A host of Shadow Occupations that were stillborn before they had—"

"I don't believe it," I said curtly. "I looked at those scribblings, and I see that they fit, and I still don't believe it. As far as I'm concerned, it's just scraps of madness that Bosa left behind, to pollute our minds and make us doubt things we never needed to doubt. And I include the quoins in that, in case you were wondering. We're done with her crew, done with her body, and in case it's escaped your attention we've very nearly transformed her ship. She's loosening her hold on us by the day, and yet you cling to these fancies of hers as if you owe her some sort of loyalty." I pointed a finger at my chest. "I am the one she meant to take her place. And I reject her, wholly and without compunction. She's dead and gone. We turned her body to splinters. Now let us both be finished with everything she stood for."

"You really feel you're rid of her?"

"Yes," I answered. "Beyond any doubt."

I think she might have been formulating a response—something barbed, no doubt—when Paladin buzzed across the intercom.

"Begging your pardon, Miss Arafura, Miss Adrana, I have the new calculations for our approach. We should begin striking sail in twelve hours, and in twenty-four we round the swallower."

# 10

I reached under the galley table, where I had bundled up six pieces of paper, of the same leathery constitution as the sheets Fura used in her *True and Accurate Testimony.* Each sheet had paragraphs of writing on, in my tolerably neat hand, which was the false history Prozor and I had come up with, beginning on Indragol, where our ship had first been commissioned and named.

There was a name at the top of each sheet. I passed them around, starting with Tindouf, continuing with Prozor and Surt, taking one for myself and leaving Fura to last. She hesitated for a second, then clasped her tin fingers around the sheet, nearly ripping it from my grip.

"What's this?" she asked.

"Your favourite thing in the world," I said. "Homework. Something to take our minds off the swallower. It's the history Proz and I cobbled together for this ship. But since each of us is supposed to have found our way onto the crew by different means, each sheet is a little different. It's got your name, the world you came from, any ships you crewed on before this one, the baubles you've cracked and so on. Anything pertinent—but not so much that it'll bog us down."

"The *Grey Lady,* under Captain Tessily Marance," Surt said, reading carefully, her lips moving as she formed the words. "And which of us is Tessily Marance, exactly?"

"Fura," I said.

"I don't remember the part where we agreed to that," Surt replied, meeting my eyes, twisting her head just enough that the weals on her skin showed above her collar, as if I required a reminder of what had transpired between us.

"It's a cover story, nothing more," I answered, brazening out her look. "One of us has to be captain, and Fura looks the part."

Surt nodded slowly. "So you'd be her sister, would you?"

"No," I said. "I'm Tragen Imbery—Trage to her crewmates. No relation to good Cap'n Tessily, although many's the cove who's remarked on our distant likeness."

"Distant likeness my—" Surt began.

"We'll wear our hair differently when we're ashore, and no one'll jump to the assumption that we must be sisters."

"In fairness," Prozor said, "you don't look half as alike as when you first showed up."

Surt was still reading. "Liz-zil. Lizzil Taine. Am I sayin' that right?"

"Perfectly," I said.

"I'd sooner be called somethin' else."

"So would we all, but those are your names. You're an Integrator, of course—we all stick to our given professions. Originally from Imanderil, which is a tubeworld in the eighteenth processional."

"What if I start bumping gums with a cove from Imanderil?"

"It's unlikely, but if you do there's enough on that sheet to throw most people off the scent. You crewed on the *Whispering Witch*, under Captain Mundry, then after a run of bad strikes you switched to the *Grey Lady*, hoping a change of ship would improve your luck. You've never run into Bosa Sennen, and truth be told you don't really think she exists. Those ships that have been lost, you're more inclined to put it down to mistakes and accidents."

"'Cept that's not how I feel."

"Not how any of us feel," Prozor said. "But we're a hardened crew who don't have time for fairytales and rumours. We don't mention Bosa Sennen unless we're drawn into it, and even then we're not that interested."

I tapped my own sheet. "Learning these identities will take some work. But that's only half of it. We've also got to know each other's stories, at least as well as if we'd been crewing together for a few months. It's going to be very important that we don't make a slip." I turned to look at Fura. "Are you agreed with that, Cap'n Tessily?"

"Cap'n Marance fits better," she said after a moment's consideration, her metal fingernails scraping against the paper. "Tessily would be the name I reserved for friends, wouldn't it? And I don't think this Cap'n Marance would be the sort to have too many of *those*."

*

It was an act of faith that the other ship was still behind us, but after the shot that hurt Strambli there had been no further sign of it. We had not been swept, there had been no sail-flash and nothing but routine traffic on the squawk. Fura and I had been to the skull, but beyond that first encounter I had nothing to prove that the Sympathetic in the other bone room was sending, much less showing an interest in us. But I believed that they were real, nonetheless. I had not imagined that distinct connection when the name *Nightjammer* ghosted between us like a curse, nor the sharp sense of withdrawal when the other mind sensed my own.

We would have proof of their presence soon enough.

As the hour drew upon us, the atmosphere on *Revenger* grew tenser, with the jokes and banter falling gradually away, leaving only clipped exchanges and muttered observations. We had tested the guns, we had prepared the sweeper, we had rehearsed the striking of sail a thousand times in our heads. Paladin had continued to refine the details of our approach to the swallower, taking us damnably close but not so close as to be suicidal. The ship would moan and groan when the strains hit it, so when we were not busy with control gear or vacuum suit checks, we were testing every bulkhead or hull-plate that had ever given cause for doubt, checking circuits and tightening the lagging on every pipe that might burst under pressure. Gauges and compasses were tapped until their dials and needles moved freely, and each of us verified that supplies of lungstuff were exactly where they were meant to be stowed, and in the intended quantities.

We were ready. We could not be more ready.

"It's not an act of aggression," I said aloud, even when I was alone. "It's reasonable self-defence. If we cripple their sails, and stop at that, they'll know we're not operating under Bosa's rules. They'll have all the evidence they need to decide that we're an innocent party."

Meanwhile, Strambli worsened.

Her fever deepened and the inflammation around the Ghostie wound became hot and swollen. When Surt changed the dressing we all waited for good news, but it only took one glance at her expression to set our minds straight.

"The sooner we're at that wheel, the better."

Strambli had been spending more time unconscious than awake, and if she was not sleeping she writhed and mumbled, making us shudder to think of the carnival of spectres haunting her dreams. We tried to take turns being with her, to ease her suffering with cold towels on her forehead, but she was having to get used to being on her own.

I felt bad, but I was never sorry to be out of the kindness room. All my arguments against the life Bosa had meant for me softened if I spent too long in that place. I would start thinking that perhaps I was not so grateful to have been rescued after all; that Fura had denied me my own future just as it was opening, demanding that I play a secondary role in her own ascendance instead. I knew it was wrong of me; that these thoughts were merely the delayed consequences of Bosa's conditioning, but that did not lessen them or their sting.

*

"If she has to lose the leg," Fura said, as we prepared to strike sail, "there're worse things. I went to the Limb Broker, didn't I?" She gave an admiring look at her forearm and hand. "Reckon I'm better off now than I was before. You saw how I knew when that ball was coming, in the Rumbler."

"It's a pretty arm," I said. "But you were able to trade in the old one without a scratch on it. Strambli's not likely to be so fortunate." I decided to test her resolve a little. "I'm concerned that she'll slip into delirium and start spouting stuff when we're in company. She could be a liability."

"What are you suggesting—that we throw her away like we did Bosa?"

"I'm just trying to anticipate a problem."

"Then I'll set your mind at ease. As long as we stick to our stories—your very excellent stories—we'll have no cause for trouble. You said it yourself. She'll be delirious. No one pays the slightest heed to delirious people, especially doctors. They hear enough craziness to last a lifetime. By the way, I rather approve of the role you've made for me. Captain Marance...there's a certain ring to it, wouldn't you agree?"

"It's time to haul-in," I said.

I should have liked it if Tindouf were the one to remain inside the ship while Fura joined us in the rigging. But Tindouf had gained too much secondary knowledge of the sails to be wasted on house-keeping, and since Surt, Prozor and I were also needed outside, it fell to Fura to keep vigil with Paladin.

It was hard on the nerves to be outside, knowing that a salvo of sail-shot could come in at any moment, harder still to think of the swallower being so close, and yet completely invisible to our natural faculties. Was it better to know of its position, I wondered, or was I happier in my former ignorance? I wondered if I would ever again view any piece of empty space with anything but apprehension, knowing the traps it might contain.

It was not even a large swallower. At the centre of the Swirly, so the old books taught us, especially the kind we'd gobbled up in childhood, with lots of pictures and diagrams and pages that folded out twice, was a swallower made up of the crushed corpses of a million Old Suns—maybe more. Even single stars, when they died, might leave behind swallowers that were at least as massive as our own progenitor. The naked swallower, if it followed the same rules as those inside the worlds of the Congregation, would be very much smaller. When they took apart the Earth, so it was said, there was enough material to make a hundred thousand swallowers, and if all the eight worlds were taken into account there was easily enough to make many millions of swallowers and still have enough rubble left over for all the new worlds and baubles.

You might think a swallower made up of a hundred thousandth part of one of the old worlds would be no small thing, perhaps the size of a little mountain or a big mansion, or at least as big as the ball that nearly killed us in the Rumbler. But the mathematics of swallowers was exceedingly slippery. I thought back to those books again, the coloured plates and charts, comparing the sizes of swallowers to various things such as railway stations, whales, horses, dogs, canaries, beetles, grains of rice and so on. Although we had seen the light of a distant star smeared and contorted by it, it was the space around the swallower that was acting like a lens, not the entity itself. The swallower was a black speck, tinier than the tiniest drop of ink on a page. I would have needed a magnifying glass to see it.

But if I had been within four leagues of that swallower, I'd have felt myself pulled to it with exactly the same force as if I were walking around on Mazarile. That was how close Paladin meant to take us; necessary if we were going to use the swallower to our advantage, and yet the slightest error in our course would be calamitous. A league nearer, and the swallower's pull on us would nearly double, and the strain on the ship would be proportionately greater the deeper we slid into that gravity well. Even if Paladin put us on the optimum course, the difference in pull from one sail to the next would be more than they were made to withstand, and even a slight error would make it uncomfortable inside the hull.

A thousand things could have gone wrong from the moment we jammed on our helmets and went outside. The queer thing is that for the most part they did not. The hauling-in went very quickly, and if a line snagged or a sail tangled on itself, it was nothing we were not prepared to fix. Paladin worked the winches, Tindouf kept an eye on the strain-gauges, and the rest of us—which was three, to be precise—jumped to his orders.

Still there was no sign of that wicked swallower. But we were close now, and when I wriggled out of my suit and went to the control room, Fura was bent over the drawings, while Paladin buzzed updates through the intercom.

"We're starting to turn," she said, grinning with wild enthusiasm. "Not a touch from the sails or ions, just the pull of the swallower, brushing us off our old trajectory. Paladin: you'll tell me the instant we're swept, won't you?"

"Of course, Miss Arafura."

She turned to me with a comradely smile. "They won't have cause to sweep us just yet, so I'm not expecting anything. They'll still think we're on our old heading."

Prozor, Surt and Tindouf arrived in quick succession. Prozor was rubbing the spikes back into her hair, Surt was nursing a broken fingernail, and Tindouf was examining a waxy deposit on the end of his thumb, which I think he had just dug out of his ear.

"Port coil-guns loaded, water-primed, and ready to be run out," Prozor said.

"Good," Fura said, in a low, serious voice. "We'll sweep at the moment we're past the point of closest approach to the swallower. Paladin says one hard pulse should suffice for pointing accuracy, but I'll chance a second if there's any doubt. He'll compute the firing solution, and we'll send them a rapid broadside, say ten slugs a piece. That'll put some recoil on us, difficult to predict ahead of time, but we'll consult the compasses and star-finders and recompute for a second salvo."

"Remember we mean to disable them, not destroy them," I said, as if there was a danger that this small distinction had slipped Fura's mind.

"Paladin will apply an offset to the targeting solution, as soon as we have a ranging fix," Fura answered. "We'll err on the side of caution. I would sooner miss their rigging completely than risk an accidental strike against the hull." She gave me a quizzical look. "Did you doubt my intentions? I am willing to murder when I have been deliberately wronged, and especially when I know my adversary. This is different."

"I am very glad to hear it," I said.

"Afterwards, if there is damage, I should be very surprised if they do not use their squawk or bone room. We'll maintain heightened watches until we arrive at port."

"Good," I said, finding little to disagree with, on this point at least. "I'll go and see that Strambli's comfortable, shall I, before we make our close approach?"

Fura looked down at the chart, knotty with scribbled annotations. "You have thirty minutes. Then I would like us all at action stations. Give my regards to Strambli."

*

It was a blessing of sorts that Strambli was unconscious. I made sure she was properly secured to her bed, sponged the sweat from her face and brow, and generally made her as comfortable as I could. She never stirred, and I thought it likely she would remain in this stupor throughout the coming engagement, even with the clamour of those broadsides.

We had pulled in all but the last thousand spans of rigging

and sail, so that *Revenger* resembled a flower with a crown of dark, attenuated petals, and that was as far as it was prudent to reduce matters, since we would need to restore our full spread once we were clear of the swallower. It was already tugging at us, though, its differential pull drawing a litany of groans and complaints from the ship's fabric as it was stretched and pressed in ways it had seldom been accustomed to. I say seldom rather than never, as it seemed very likely to me that Bosa must have used this swallower—and others like it—to effect similar course changes, furthering the myth that her ship had supernatural capabilities of pursuit and evasion.

We felt it in the galley, too. Under sail or ions, the ship was never truly weightless, but there was always a regularity to its movements, one that we had absorbed into our bones until we scarcely noticed it. Our habits adapted to that slow acceleration or deceleration and became second nature. Now all the rules had been suspended, for the forces acting on us were coming in laterally, and as my inner ear registered that critical difference, so my stomach remembered the nausea I had long considered a thing of the past. It was like learning to be in space all over again, and the sole consolation was that none of us were immune, not even Prozor.

The groans and complaints intensified. Despite our best preparations, some pipes and valves burst under the buckling strain, and we had to scamper around sealing water and pressure leaks. Paladin, meanwhile, called out our decreasing distance from the swallower, first in thousands of leagues, then hundreds, and now in a continuous, quickening report.

"Seventy. Sixty... fifty..."

The sounds of distress from the ship had shifted from low moans to high, wailing shrieks, like some prisoner being tortured to confess on a tightening rack. Tindouf eyed the strain-gauges with a mad intensity. Even with our hauled-in state, elements of rigging and sail-control gear tore loose.

"... thirty... twenty, ten..."

There was a point of maximum distress, a death-scream of sorts, and then by some miracle we were through and Paladin was counting upward instead. The ship had held. Whatever damage had been incurred, we had not lost hull integrity, nor the basic operation of electrical navigation and sensor systems. Even in that moment, knowing the worst was behind us, I felt my nausea start to abate.

There was, of course, still the small matter of retaliation.

"One hundred leagues," Paladin reported. "Clear for ranging pulse at your command, Miss Arafura."

Fura at least did us the credit of searching our faces before returning her answer.

"Send it, Paladin."

"Sweeper active. Ranging pulse sent and returned. I have a hard fix on the pursuing ship. She lies one thousand, four hundred leagues astern of us."

"Close," I said, speaking for all of us. Much closer than I had guessed.

"Targeting solution computed, and offset applied."

"Should we risk a second pulse, to be doubly sure?" I asked.

"Paladin says the fix is definite," Fura answered.

"Return sweep detected," he said, an instant later.

That was enough for Fura. They had detected our ranging pulse, sent back one of their own, and although they would initially be confused by our changed position, that state of bewilderment would not last indefinitely. Sooner or later, even with doubt in their minds, they would put another salvo our way.

"Fire all coil-guns," Fura said. "Ten slug salvo."

After the noisy protestation of the ship as we rounded the swallower, the report of the broadside seemed softer than before, and because it was a familiar sound there was a strange lulling reassurance in it, for it meant the ship could not have been hurt too badly.

The guns sounded again. There was an interval of a second between each shot, just enough to stop the guns from over-heating too quickly. The water pumps were surging now. Within a minute the pipes were scalding to the touch, and before long we had another series of leaks and shattered pressure gauges to attend to, this time with the added attraction of high-pressure water spraying into our faces.

The salvo—ten slugs apiece—ended, and Paladin began to rework his calculations for the second wave, allowing for our recoil displacement, and the deflection of the slugs' trajectories by the swallower's field.

"Our first salvo should now be arriving," he said. "And I have a second ranging pulse, which may be in direct response to our slugs."

"Give me that second broadside," Fura said.

"Recomputing, Miss Arafura... just a moment. There is some disagreement between our gyroscopes and star-trackers. I should like to confirm our pointing with a second ranging pulse of our own."

"If you have the slightest doubt about our orientation, those guns don't fire," I said.

Fura shot me a look of pure indignation, but even she must have recognised that we could not launch an attack with indiscriminate disregard. "Why are the readings not in agreement?"

"A consequence of our passage around the swallower," Paladin said. "There may be water contamination on some of the circuits. It should clear with time, but for the moment we must depend on a second sweeper pulse for pointing accuracy."

Fura gritted her teeth, fist clenched.

"Then do it. Hard and fast. Make it count."

Paladin sent out a second sweeper pulse, then reported that two more ranging pulses had swept us. Followed, almost immediately, by a report of muzzle flash.

"They're still using chasers," Prozor said.

"Solution re-computed," Paladin announced. "I am ready to... I am troubled, Miss Arafura. There is a curious pattern to the return pulse, an asymmetry about the central target."

"We got lucky, is all," Fura said. "Took out a few hundred acres of sail, I'll bet. There's your bloodying, Surt—we got 'em squarely where we meant to."

"Then we don't need a second salvo," I said, making my suggestion in a low, cautionary tone.

"We'll leave 'em in no doubt that we had the means to take them out," Fura said. "One salvo might have been a lucky miss, but when they see that we did it deliberately, they'll know we could have done a lot worse. Fire, Paladin."

The coil-guns sounded again, ten times, then fell quiet. This time the pipes and gauges held, and the silence that followed was broken only by creaks and bumps as the ship gradually relaxed. The swallower was thousands of leagues behind us now, and the heat generated by the broadsides was slowly dissipating.

"Run the short-range sweep, minimum power," Fura said. "I want to know if those chaser shots come anywhere near us. Tindouf, make ready with ions and stand by to run out all sail once we know we're clear of their grape-shot. I think they got the message."

Fura moved to the galley's sweeper console, bracing her hands either side of the screen like someone peering into a wishing-well. It had taken a minute for the first of our broadsides to begin arriving at the enemy; now the second wave was about to reach its mark.

Prozor, Surt, Tindouf and I squeezed around the console as best we could. A fan of lines scratched across it for an instant, then faded.

"Did you pick that up, Paladin?"

"Heavy return fire, Miss Arafura—chasing shot, with a high kinetic load. But well astray of our position."

"Polite of 'em not to hit us," Fura said.

The screen went bright, filling with yellow light, almost as if it had malfunctioned. I was starting to think that it must have been a powerful return sweep dazzling our own instrument, when the brightness faded save for a cluster of speckles near the scope's middle. I stared at them, not really understanding, as they faded and then were picked up again as the sweep returned.

"We're on the short-range setting," I said. "Aren't we?"

"Paladin?" Fura snapped.

"We are on the short-range setting. We should not be seeing a return pulse at this strength, unless there is a great deal of reflecting material."

The speckles were diffusing, but also moving slowly away from each other.

"Talk to me, Paladin," I said. "We're seeing something very odd on the sweeper. That ship's lit up like a beacon."

Prozor pointed a finger at the centre of the screen. "It ain't so simple, Adrana. Those crosshairs were lined up with the enemy, based on Paladin's last fix. But the bright stuff's spreading out from a slightly different point."

"It's still close," Surt said.

"But not that close." I looked around at my comrades, at my sister. "I don't think we hit them at all—certainly not close enough to the hull to do any damage."

"We sure as chaff hit *something*," Prozor answered.

"There was another ship," I said, hearing my own voice, but almost as if I were a bystander, listening to myself and marvelling at how cool and calm I sounded. "It's the only explanation. We aimed off-centre and hit a ship *we didn't even know was there*. There was never just the one, all this time."

"There's some other explanation," Fura said.

"You wish there were," Prozor said. "So do I. But that return looks just like a ship spillin' its guts into space after it took a direct hit. We must've caught a fuel tank, I think—blown them wide open."

Fura gave a shiver. "We didn't mean for this. We fired defensively. We couldn't have known there was a second ship."

I shook my head. "It's not what we meant to do that matters. It's how it'll look from the outside, and we already know this isn't good. Paladin: is there anything on the squawk?"

"Not yet, Miss Adrana, although I am monitoring as many channels as I can."

"Do you think the other ship took any damage?" I asked.

"Hard to say," Prozor replied. "We might've clipped their rigging, maybe worse, but if we'd opened 'em up as well I think we'd see it."

Fura hammered the side of the console. "Paladin: another hard sweep. I want to know what we did, and what's left behind. Damn it all: why didn't we see two ships when we ran that ranging pulse?"

"Paladin saw something unusual the second time," I reminded her. "The first time, their sails may have masked the echo from the other ship, especially if the one we shot is running astern of the first."

"We weren't expectin' to see two, so we didn't," Prozor said.

The sweeper flared and filled with the spreading, smearing debris of what we presumed was the second ship. It was like watching a firework burst in very slow motion, or dropping a spot of bright ink into dark water. Where the crosshairs met, though, was a harder return—the clear and distinct signature of another ship, with a symmetrical spread of sail.

Tindouf rubbed at his jaw. "They looks all right."

"They could be gaggin' on their last gasp of lungstuff for all we know," Prozor said.

"Should we... signal them?" Surt asked. "They ain't shot back yet, have they?"

Fura directed a withering look in her direction. "What, and say we're sorry we just blew up your friend, good luck rescuing the survivors? I'll remind you: they shot at us first, not the other way around. Strambli was hurt long before we fired back." She straightened up, pushing back from the console. "Nothing changes. We sail on, because we still have an injured party. But Paladin will keep monitoring the squawk, and Adrana and I will take a turn on the bones for the next watch. The rest of you..."

"What would you like us to do?" Surt said, with a dangerous sarcastic undertone.

"Nothing," Fura answered. "Not for another watch. Sleep and rest. Then we run out the sails again."

*

Fura spun the locking wheel behind us while I took the neural bridges from their rack.

"It's getting harder to chase a signal," I said, as we plugged in at different ends of the skull. "Quite a sharp drop-off compared to a few weeks ago. I wonder if we'll soon be in the market for a new one."

"I noticed it as well," Fura said, her hands still shaking as she adjusted the neural bridge. "I think it's the skull, but we can never be too sure it isn't our faculties tapering off."

"If we're like Cazaray, we'll have a few years left. Anyway, I'd be the first to feel it, wouldn't I?"

"Not always. Relative age plays a factor, so I'm informed, but so does the number of skulls you've plugged into, and the intensity of the exposure."

We were gabbling, because it took our minds off the immediate horror of what had just happened. We had acted in self-defence. But once we had rounded that swallower, we could easily have lost them anyway. They would have needed to sweep us to relocate our position, and without the cover of a solar storm that might have been a greater risk than they were prepared to take.

"How many skulls for you now?"

"Six, counting the two skulls on the *Iron Courtesan*, and the one aboard the passenger ship, when Vidin Quindar took me back to Mazarile. Otherwise this would be the fourth."

"Four isn't too many," I said.

"Not for us, perhaps. But then there are Bone Readers who never touch more than three skulls in their whole career, and some fewer than that."

"I don't doubt it. But then we're not most Bone Readers, are we? We're the Ness sisters."

"Yes," Fura said. "And look where it's brought us." She paused, eyes closed. "There's just noise on this input. Are you having any success with yours?"

"No, dead as a doornail."

"Move along."

We unplugged, plugged in, eyed each other, exchanged wordless nods and shakes of the head. This continued for several fruitless minutes. Then, just as we were ready to abandon the skull, some faint presence pushed through. We were connecting on nearby inputs and felt it at the same time. A whispering wind from which soundless voices emerged.

*...for pity's sake send help... lungstuff... suits...*

*...how many survivors...*

*...I don't know... beyond this room... if anyone...*

*...how did she slip from us so easily?*

*...For mercy's sake send what you can...*

There was no doubt in my mind that we were picking up desperate communication between the two ships, or more accurately between the wreck of one and the vessel that we considered spared. There could not be much left of the former, I thought. But bone rooms were often the best-protected part of any ship, and would hold pressure even after the rest of the hull was a splintered ruin. Not out of any consideration for the welfare of such talents as us, but a simple consequence of the protection afforded the skull, which was often the most valuable, temperamental and delicate of any ship's possessions.

Fura and I looked at each other, not needing to articulate our mutual discomfort. The voices that came through the bones were usually robbed of inflection, as cold as newsprint. It was very rare to pick up emotions, and still rarer for something to come through as clearly as the terror and distress of the first voice. It was true that we had been through our share of that as well, but far from hardening our feelings, our experiences had only made us more acutely aware of the cruel things that could happen to a person when they were alone on a wounded ship. Fura was lifting her bridge from her head, and I felt the same helpless impulse. We had not invited this trouble upon ourselves, but that did not mean we were immune from sympathy. A ship was made up of many sorts of people and I doubted that all of those distant crews could be held fully accountable for what had happened to Strambli.

Just as Fura was about to lift off the bridge, though, I allowed a word to drift across my consciousness.

*Lagganvor.*

Perhaps she heard me anyway, or sensed the shape of that unvoiced name. It was as if I had pricked the edge of her storm-cloud, making it twitch away from me. Recognition, I wondered, or puzzlement, the significance of the name lost on her?

I watched her eyes, as she watched me and wondered if I saw the tiniest lift of her brow, signifying curiosity or some cold amusement that I had penetrated her secrets. At the same time I felt her own scrutiny lying hard on me and our minds engaged in a kind of bloodless, passionless duel, stabbing and parrying, neither bettering the other.

*If you are holding something from me, now would be the time to confess.*

It was my inner voice and it was also Fura's, the statement equally applicable to both of us.

*Nothing you need worry about. Nothing you need worry about at all.*

Simultaneously, as if we were two dolls in a puppet theatre, being worked by the same strings, our hands moved to the input sockets. We disconnected in the same moment. That alien wind chased itself out of my head, leaving a ringing emptiness that only slowly filled with normal thoughts.

Fura finally removed her neural bridge, then took mine from my head as well, as gently and sisterly as you please. She spooled the contact wires back into their housings and put the bridges back on their hooks.

"I'm sorry for what they're going through. If I could send them lungstuff I would. But if they think they've seen the sharp side of me, they've a lot to learn."

"So have we all," I answered, low enough that I could not be sure she heard me.

# 11

A large, blurred object swam into view and I overshot before adjusting the sighting dials to bring it back into alignment, centring it against the illuminated crosshairs. I turned the focus screw just enough to snap the fuzzy shape into sharpness. It was a four-spoked cog, bristly and corroded-looking, like some metal ornament that had been left underwater for too long.

Wheel Strizzardy. Ten thousand leagues out, but we would be there soon enough now. It could be our salvation or our undoing, I thought, or more likely some murky business in between. I was starting to see that matters were rarely as clear-cut as those stories we used to read in the nursery, where ever-afters were always either happy or tragic, where the virtuous were rewarded and the bad punished.

In fact, I was starting to think that quite a lot hinged on one's point of view.

*

The grille crackled. A male voice buzzed out of it.

"This is the Port Authority of Wheel Strizzardy, calling the sunjammer at eight hundred leagues, approaching from the outer processionals. Identify your vessel, your point of origin and your intentions by immediate return of squawk."

Fura took the hand-held microphone and held it to her lips as Prozor and I watched.

"Good day, Port Authority. This is Captain Marance of the privateer *Grey Lady* out of Indragol. We've been scouring baubles on the Emptyside since '98—nearly two years since we made port. Our stores are low and we'd like permission to run our launch over and conduct free trade, as your terms dictate."

"Not a name known to us, Captain Marance." The speaker had a slow, phlegmatic manner of talking, as if he had all day to deal with us. "Yours or your ship's. Why would you wish to trade with us, with the rest of the Congregation at your disposal?"

"I wish the rest of the Congregation *were* at our disposal, sir," Fura said, putting on a hard-done-by tone. "The honest truth is that we're not exactly spoilt for choice, with an injured party aboard. We wouldn't make the thirty-fifth processional, let alone the Sunwards. We've done well with our baubles, but a holdful of quoins is no consolation when you're down to your last few drops of medicine." Fura paused, and I could almost see her counting out seconds before she continued, playing a part just as surely as if she had a script before her. "If the photon winds are kind, we might just be able to limp to Kathromil, and I know they're receptive to free trade—"

"No need, Captain Marance. We would, of course, wish to be of assistance in a medical matter... provided there is no danger of contagion?"

Fura smiled at us.

"It's nothing like that, sir—just a shipboard injury that we don't have the means to heal. The rest of us are quite hale and hearty, I assure you."

"How many shore permits would you require?"

"Five sir, including one for the wounded party."

"You'll squawk over the names and particulars. They'll be cross-checked, so make sure everything's in order. If there are no irregularities, you'll be given docking permission. Expect to be boarded and inspected prior to disembarkation, Captain Marance."

"I'd expect nothing less, sir, and I'll have my second-in-command squawk you those names immediately. Thank you for your cooperation. I can tell it's going to be a pleasure doing business."

I winced, thinking her sarcasm would get that door slammed in our faces just as it was opening. But the detection of sarcasm demands a certain wit on the part of the recipient, and I do not think that faculty was present.

"Hello, sir," I said, taking the microphone. "This is Tragen Imbery, Bone Reader on the *Grey Lady.* I have those particulars for you, sir, starting with Captain Tessily Marance…"

*

By the time we were ready to load her into the launch, Strambli was semi-delirious, her brow boiling with fever and her wound so hot and swollen that it hurt to look at it, even when it was bandaged. I'd done my best to school her on her invented history, and on some level I knew she understood something of the situation, and how careful we had to be not to hint at a link to Bosa Sennen, or for that matter any of our true pasts. But it had been several watches since Strambli was properly lucid, and lately her babblings were becoming more florid, spilling out of her at all hours, not just when she was in the obvious throes of nightmare. So Surt injected her with additional sedatives from the medicine store, and when she was so insensate that we could move her, we got her onto a stretcher and transported her to the launch.

"How longs will you be stayings?" Tindouf asked, as we made ready for departure.

"At least day or so, to start with," Fura said. "Time to get Greben sorted—" she nodded at the woman on the stretcher "—and to pick up some supplies, at least enough to justify the fuel we'll burn just coming and going. Glue yourself to the sweeper and the squawk, Tindouf—if you hear so much as a squeak about that ship, I want to know it. We'll check in regularly, but don't be too alarmed if you don't hear from us for a few hours. We've all got errands to run."

"Aye, Cap'n... Marance," Tindouf said, stroking his chin. "I do hopes you gets help for Stram, I means Greben." He cocked his head, regarding her fondly, and I thought of how much I liked Tindouf, and how little esteem I'd had for him in the early days, and felt a little prickle of self-recrimination.

We were all suited, save for our helmets, and once Strambli was lashed down for the trip we cast off, popping out of the mouth of *Revenger* like a bad-tasting minnow. Fura swung our nose around to face Wheel Strizzardy and poured on the rockets like fuel was going out of fashion.

I gave our ship a farewell glance as we sped away, trying to look at it with fresh eyes and judge if we'd done a handsome enough job of disguising her nature. To me she still looked like a wolf in sheep's clothing, and not very convincingly attired at that. But I knew too much of her history to be reliable judge. At least we'd made her lines a little less belligerent, and thrown out enough square leagues of normal sail to trick the gaze into not noticing the catchcloth. You might say that the prudent thing would have been to haul in all the sails completely, just as if we were in tight orbit around a heavy world, but to do that around a wheelworld would have invited questions and suspicions all of their own, so we wisely kept some sails deployed. We were all happier with that arrangement as it meant a quicker getaway if we had cause to run.

The crossing to Wheel Strizzardy only took an hour, which was just time to settle into our new characters. We talked as much as we could, only addressing each other by our fictitious names, knowing our act would soon be put to the test.

"I hope there's an infirmary, Cap'n Marance."

"Why wouldn't there be an infirmary, Taine?"

"I was just thinkin' it looks as if the place has seen better days. Don't you agree, Trage?"

"Oh, I do. But I'm sure there are worse places than this, and even they'll have infirmaries. Won't they, Lodran?"

"Even the worst dumps have infirmaries," Prozor confirmed. "They're the ones that have the most need of 'em, what with all the scrappin' and stabbin'. And morgues, too."

"I ain't... Fang. Not going near it. Tell Trusko I ain't! Not for no Ghostie gubbins..."

I moved to Strambli's stretcher and applied a cold towel to her forehead. "Easy," I whispered. "Soon be in good hands." And try not to blab about Captain Trusko, I added to myself.

Then a second, harder voice superimposed itself over my own inner thoughts.

*No, try not to blab, dear Strambli, or I might have to press something against your mouth...*

I willed her away, trying to make her shrivel and diminish. And, to a degree, succeeded. The rage had approached; I had felt its nearness, but it had not managed to consume me. Perhaps even Bosa Sennen understood that there was a right and a wrong time for her deeds.

I took a deep breath, then I returned to the view, comparing it against the distant image I'd seen through the telescope. I can't say I was greatly cheered by what I saw. Clarity and proximity only made our destination look less promising, but we'd made our selection and now we had to live with it.

The wheel was four-spoked, with a hub at the middle, but there were only lights showing from the rim, and then only in patches. The rim was circular in cross-section, and other than those lights there were no large windows or areas of skyshell. Pushing up from the rim toward the middle were forests of buildings, almost like spokes that had started growing and then given up before they finished, and there was a similar sort of growth projecting down from the rim's underside into open space, but again not all of these buildings were lit or clearly inhabited. Since the wheel was six leagues across, even the largest ships were tiny against it, hardly to be seen at all except as dots against those up-and-down pointing structures, which evidently served as docking facilities. They were launches like ours, for the most part, since it would be much too hazardous for a sunjammer to attempt direct docking with the moving rim. But there were a handful of sail-rigged vessels standing off in open space, only a league or two beyond the rim, with the sparks of rocket-propelled craft shuttling to and fro.

One of these sparks grew larger and brighter, putting a fat blob on our sweeper, until it became apparent that we were its intended destination.

"Hold your nerve, coves," Fura said. "Ain't no reason for them to think queerly of us, just yet. We stick to our yarns. Don't embroider 'em more'n we have to, and we'll be golden."

I glanced up, smiling with a sincere sisterly admiration, for she could very well have been Prozor speaking those words, so effortlessly did they now spring from her mouth.

As it drew nearer, we saw that the approaching vessel was another rocket launch, about the same size as our own, but conspicuously armed. It had flanking coil-guns on swivel-mounts, an energy cannon, harpoon and net-flinger batteries, and probably six or seven other kinds of nastiness we hadn't recognised. Our launch didn't even have a sharp tongue to its name.

"No, Drozna, I ain't agreein' to it," Strambli murmured.

The other ship pulled alongside, its nearside coil-gun tracking us. One shot would have taken care of us from that range, and we didn't even have our helmets on. After a minute a lock opened and a pair of fully-suited coves floated out and crossed over to us. Boots clanged against cladding and metal fists hammered on the outside of our hull.

"I s'pose they wouldn't mind bein' let in," Prozor said.

While Fura remained at the control console, I floated over to the lock controls and allowed the boarding party to come through. Just before the inner door opened I looked around at our small number, on the cusp of offering a final word of encouragement concerning our made-up identities, then wisely thinking better of it. If we didn't know our parts well by now, nothing I said was going to make any difference. All the same, I did mouth a silent prayer in the direct of Strambli, and hoped her mutterings didn't turn too colourful.

Considering they were officials, our two visitors didn't cut a very official-looking appearance. Their suits were made of mismatched parts, with the words "Port Authority" painted onto their chests, shoulders and helmets, done through a stencil that had left the letters a bit smudged and lopsided. They were fearsome enough, with armour and weapons, but they looked more like thugs that had been pressed into service than the servants of a respectable institution. This impression wasn't improved when they flipped up their visors. Now, none of us smelled like roses, not after months on the ship. But when these coves gave us the benefit of their fragrances it was enough to make the eyes water. They smelled like sweat and vinegar and blocked sewers, and those were just the aromas I could put a name to.

They had big, ugly faces, filling their helmets like bread that had been too long in the oven. Their mouths were wide, and when they grinned they showed a variety of gaps where there ought to be teeth. Their noses were flat, or rather flattened, because it was obvious neither had ended up that shape by the quirks of parentage alone. One had eyes too close together, the other too far apart. Both had eyebrows that went right across their foreheads, like single black caterpillars, and both had hairlines that started only a finger's width above the eyebrows.

"Which of you is the cap'n?" asked the one with eyes too close together.

"I have that pleasure," Fura said, turning from her controls. "Captain Marance. And you'd be?"

"Never you mind who we are," said the one with eyes too far apart. "How'd you come by the tin arm, Cap'n Marance?"

"I lost the original."

Eyes-too-close looked at his companion. "Sounds careless to me."

"It was," Fura said. "But I've grown accustomed to this replacement."

"Got a touch of the glowy about you, too," said eyes-too-far.

"More'n a touch," said eyes-too-close. "Any more glowy coming off her, we'd need sun-visors."

"Fortunately for all of us," Fura said, "it isn't infectious."

"How'd you come by it?" asked eyes-too-far.

"I had to eat lightvine to stay alive."

"No one's meant to nosh on the stuff," eyes-too-close said, with a smirk.

"If I hadn't *noshed* on it," Fura answered levelly, "I'd be dead. But if I can find a treatment to flush out the glowy, I'll gladly take it. Plus some urgent medical assistance for our friend over there."

"What's 'er problem?" asked eyes-too-far.

"An accident while repairing our rigging. Greben slipped with a yardknife, and it went clean through her. We'd hoped to treat the wound ourselves, but infection's set in."

"Just an accident, then?" asked eyes-too-close.

"What else would it be?" Fura asked, frowning so hard a notch appeared between her eyes.

"You've come in from the Emptyside," eyes-too-far said. "All sorts of trouble can fall on a ship in the Emptyside. Claim-jumping, piracy. Things worse than piracy."

"I can assure you we haven't been doing any sort of pirating," Fura said with an earnest indignation, as if the very foundations of her moral character had been challenged.

"And did you run into any ships or personages you'd rather have avoided?"

"No," she said firmly. "We just got about our business. A nice string of baubles—a run of luck, for once. Now we have some items to shift and I'd sooner not tramp around with them clogging up our hold for too long." She directed a look at Strambli, who'd been thankfully silent since the men had come aboard. "And if we have to pay for her care, then we've the means. May we approach, gentlemen?"

"You have a refined way of speaking," eyes-too-close said. "Suggests you're from one of the better worlds. There's speak of a pair of sisters who ran away from Mazarile, and one of them's s'posed to be down an arm and up a dose of the glowy."

"I had a brother," Fura said. "I'm reasonably sure I'd remember if there'd been a sister." She paused. "My full name is Tessily Marance. I was born on Indragol, not Mazarile, and if you think Indragol is one of the better worlds, you clearly haven't been there. My father was Darjan Marance, first owner and captain of the *Grey Lady*. Ask around and you'll hear his reputation. He funded her, and I inherited the ship from him in '93."

"You'd have barely been out of nappies," eyes-too-far said.

"Well I didn't have much choice in the matter. I was eighteen years old. I had the legal entitlement to own and command the ship, which is exactly what I did."

That would have made Fura twenty-five years old now, which would be a stretch were it not for the glowy and the hardness that had taken up residence in her face. Anyway, she said it with such brazen assurance that the men didn't blink.

"Well, if you do hear about a pair of sisters, you'll be sure to mention it, won't you?" said eyes-too-close. Then his attention shifted onto me, and some glimmer of interest or suspicion troubled the singular line of his brow. "And you'd be?"

"Tragen Imbery. Bone Reader. Why're you taking an interest in those two sisters?"

"Word is they got themselves tangled up with Bosa Sennen," said eyes-too-far.

"Ah," I said. "And you believe in fairies too, do you? Bosa Sennen's just a story. The time we've spent in the Empty, we'd know if it weren't. Unless you know differently?"

"We used her skin for paper," Strambli said, piping up unexpectedly. "We jumped her and cut her up with Ghostie gubbins. We had to pull her off the spike of her own ship. Went through her like a skewer, but still she lived."

There was a silence. The two Port Authority men looked at each other, and I think in that moment our fates stood on a knife-edge, with the worlds taking a breath in their orbits. Then their too-wide mouths cracked into grins again, missing teeth standing out like square sails of blackest catchcloth.

"She's got an imagination on her, that one," eyes-too-close said.

"Used her skin for paper!" echoed eyes-too-far. "Look at the state of these women. All scrag and bones, the lot of them. Jumped her! Perhaps they have been out in the Emptyside too long."

"We have," I said, seizing the moment. "And I know we don't look like much, and it's true we wouldn't be much use in a fight, but we do have valuables to trade. You'll have to forgive Greben. She's the only one of us who ever put much stock in those old sailors' tales about Bosa Sennen, and since that yardknife went through her she's been mixing up her own predicament and some of the stories."

"I've been doing what I can for her," said Surt. "But I'm not a physician. You'll let us through, won't you? I'm Taine, by the way—Integrator on the *Grey Lady*." She looked in Prozor's direction, while rubbing at the back of her neck. "This is Lodran—our Bauble Reader."

"Got a tongue in her own head, hasn't she?" eyes-too-far said.

"If you wanted to ask me something," Prozor said, folding her arms across her chest, "you had your chance. Now, do we get to spend our quoins around your flea-pit of a world, or would you sooner we carried on to Kathromil, or Metherick?"

"Give 'em credit," eyes-too-close said, speaking in a loud whisper. "They're not trying to win us over with nice words and flattery."

Fura coughed. "You'll forgive us, gentlemen. Things have been tough on the *Grey Lady* lately, and we're all running on empty bellies. Mainly, though, we're concerned about our friend. You'll have to excuse us if our manners are a little on the frayed side."

Eyes-too-far gave a slow nod. "Who are we to turn down honest trade? Your credentials were in order, and we won't turn you away, not with such an urgent case as your companion. But doing business with the wheel is a privilege, not a right. Before we let you dock, we'll need to see the colour of your quoins. The Port Authority levy is a thousand bars, payable immediately. Can you stretch to that?"

"Is that a refundable bond?" Fura asked hopefully.

"No," eyes-too-close answered.

"I suspected it mightn't be." Fura snapped a finger in my direction. "Trage. Oblige these gentlemen with a thousand-bar quoin, if you may."

"If you'd see your way to splitting that levy into, say, two five-hundred bar quoins, that would be a great convenience," eyes-too-far said.

Fura nodded slowly. "I understand you perfectly, and that'll be no trouble at all."

I went to the bag where we kept a small number of quoins for exactly this sort of petty transaction. In my time away from Mazarile I'd gained some ability to read the patterns of the bars, and my fingers quickly alighted on two five-hundred bar quoins. I dragged them out of the bag without hesitating, knowing this transaction had only put a scratch in our fortunes. It was odd to be so lackadaisical about quantities of money that would have transformed our lives only a year earlier, lifting Father out of his debt and perhaps easing the strain that had eventually sent him to his grave. Now it was just something we burned like fuel.

"You'll follow us in," eyes-too-close said, taking the proffered quoins and slipping them into a buckled pouch on his belt. "And dock under the rim, where we'll show you. Keep a light touch on your jets, Cap'n Marance, because it's no place to make a mistake."

"I'll be sure not to," Fura said.

"We'll squawk ahead to have the infirmary meet you at the rimside dock. Not a day too soon, by the smell of things."

They left us, and when the lock cleared and the men crossed over to their own launch, each of us except Strambli breathed out and grinned, as if we'd got through a dress rehearsal without so much as a fluffed line.

Fura soon put her serious mask back on, though. "That was just a warm-up for what's ahead, so let's not get over-confident. I don't care for the way they started talking about the Ness sisters."

I blinked, finding it queer that she was talking about us as if we were two other coves entirely.

"Do you think we threw them off the scent? One of them seemed almost certain we were sisters."

"You came back at them well, though," Fura said, and despite myself I felt a flush of pride that she was impressed by my performance.

"A thousand bars had better be worth the price of entry," Surt said.

"I doubt the official levy was more than five hundred," Fura replied. "Why else were they so keen to have it paid in two amounts?"

"Do you really think they checked our credentials?" Surt asked.

"I hope not," Prozor said, "because if they did, they'd find they were paper-thin. But I know how these backwater fleapits operate. They haven't got the time or the desire to be squawkin' other worlds to corroborate claims and documents, not when they're in a rush to see the colour of your quoins. Eventually, if we stayed long enough, someone might get around to checkin' the history of the *Grey Lady* and her crew, filin' an information request with the central registry down in the Sunwards, and then they might find a few things that don't tally. But we won't be stickin' around that long, will we?"

"Not if I can help it," Fura said.

# 12

We followed the Port Authority launch all the way in. As we neared, it veered off to one of the spiny, tapering structures jutting down from the rim in a radial direction. There must have been at least fifty of these docking towers around the circumference of the wheel, but no two of them were alike, and more than half were clearly in an abandoned or derelict state, judging by the absence of ships berthed on them. The tower we'd been assigned was half a league from the rim to its outermost extremity, and it was mostly skeletal, with numerous ledges bracketed off it at different levels, each of which was large enough to take a launch or similar-sized vessel. It reminded me of the spike-shaped dock at Hadramaw, except that one pushed up from the face of a world, rather than dangling down from beneath.

I could see now why landing needed to be approached with care. Since we had to match the rotation of Wheel Strizzardy to be able to dock at its rim, we'd gone from near-weightlessness to having a strong—indeed stomach-churning—sense of up and down. If our jets failed for any reason, our little ship would carry on in a straight line, which would feel just like falling away from the rim. Fine if we were in open space, with room to play with, but not so clever if we were just about to settle onto one of those precarious-looking ledges. If a ship dropped off one of the higher ledges, it would be lucky not to crash through several more on its way down.

We were assigned a mid-level ledge (the Port Authority ship shone its lamps onto the empty slot, then rocketed away) which was the best, or worst, of both worlds, depending on your point of view. There were ships stacked above us on the higher ledges, closer to the rim—and over-hanging us by degrees, since the docking spike grew wider as it went up—but there were also plenty under us, too, looking like little toy gaming pieces far below. Every now and then I made out the shiny stump where a ledge had broken away completely, no doubt to the miserable misfortune of some poor crew.

Fura set us down on the grilled platform of the ledge, easing off on the belly jets ever so gently, until she was sure the structure was taking our weight. Our bones protested as we got up, and we took very ginger steps as we moved around and completed suiting-up, as if one hard footfall might be more than the ledge could stand. It was necessary to take a short stroll in vacuum to get into the wheel, and of course there was no hope of getting Strambli into a suit the way she was.

Fura had already taken that into consideration, though. She had packed a pressure-tight cargo chest, long enough to take a body, and we loaded Strambli and her stretcher into it, stuffing some of our own clothes and belongings in as well.

"Will she be all right in that thing?" I asked.

Fura was hands-deep in the chest, moving things around and making sure Strambli was nicely restrained. Slowly she closed the lid, which had a pressure seal around its rim.

"It'll hold. Helps that she's unconscious, so she's only drawing shallow breaths."

"There's always an upside," I said.

The chest had handles on either end, so four of us managed it with moderate ease. We also had additional bags strapped to our suits, carrying money, short-range squawk sets, some small tradeable items, and additional changes of clothes. We carried her off of the launch like that, across that short distance of vacuum, and then through a pressure lock that allowed access to the elevators. They were powerful cargo elevators, easily large enough for a whole crew.

Once we were inside and ascending, we took off our helmets, got our breath back and then Fura lifted the lid on Strambli's casket. I had to bite down a gag reflex. She had only been boxed into that chest for a few minutes and already there was a putrid smell building up. I was very glad we would soon be at the infirmary.

"I wouldn't trust those auguries," Strambli said to us, looking up from the stretcher laid out in the box. "Wouldn't trust 'em to a Crawly. I promise you, we'll be better off out of this bauble..."

I touched my gauntleted hand to her brow, wishing I had a cold towel. "Easy."

Fura closed the lid again, curtailing Strambli's ramblings.

The elevator climbed to the top of the docking structure, went through a short interval of solid material (the outer crust of the rim, a hundred spans or so) and then burst out into the wheel's tubular interior. Our point of emergence was a rimside dock, which was about as unattractive and unwelcoming place as I had ever conceived. There were many elevator doors, all facing into the middle of a circular concourse, with tall, dark buildings looming over us, and only a few windows lit up in any of them. Above everything was the continuous ceiling of the world's inner rim. At some distant time, it must have been covered in illuminated panels, but only a few of them now remained, projecting a feeble sort of twilight onto the buildings and streets below. Those panels that did still work were blue with white dappling, which I knew from old books and pictures was the way the sky had looked before the Sundering, when the Earth was mantled in a skin of atmosphere that went on and on for dozens of leagues, hard as that is to conceive. In other worlds where such arrangements held, the sky might be the butterscotch of Mars, the gold of Titan or the sword-bright silver of Venus. It was said (long after the fact, of course) that after the dismantling of the old worlds, even though that act had been fully agreed upon, and only executed after a great and solemn deliberation lasting one hundred thousand years, and even though the fifty million new worlds offered abundant space and freedom, there was still a vast, aching sadness for what had been sacrificed, a sort of buyer's remorse that echoed through all the numberless centuries down to the present age.

Between those few extant panels were either their dead brethren or a grid of pipes and cables exposed by the falling away of other panels. In places a mist of water was leaking out of the pipes, transmuting into an oily rain by the time it found its way to the ground. It was hard to say whether that rain originated by design or neglect, but the consequence was that the streets had become slick black mirrors, and with treacherous deep puddles and sloping drainage channels situated—it seemed to me—exactly where they were most likely to surprise or trip the unwary, as if by some malicious intentionality.

I was forming a rapid impression of our long-promised destination, and it was not tending to the favourable.

"Have you got any weapons?"

"No, thank you," I answered, addressing the street vendor who had called out to us.

"Do you want any?"

In the middle of this concourse was a sort of dreary bazaar or market, hemmed in by braziers and piles of rubbish. Only a few desultory merchants were doing any sort of business and there were even fewer customers. Not that the wares inspired any sort of confidence. There were spacesuit parts that were fit only for smelting, bits of old broken robot, smashed-up navigational devices, junk tools, and damp, threadbare garments. The merchants coughed behind veils of smoke and airborne grease, and the customers slouched around, chiefly dressed in hoods and raincoats, picking their way between the water channels. There was a lot of picking up and examining things, a lot of shaking of heads.

"To think we paid a thousand bars for this," Surt muttered.

"Perhaps it gets better further along," I said, kicking a pile of rubbish out of my way. As it rolled away the rubbish flung out a pair of segmented arms and began to drag itself in to a damp corner.

"Captain Marance's party?"

Three figures were approaching us from the edge of the concourse. Two of them were bent over, pushing a wheeled trolley with a rain-sheet draped over a rib-like framework.

The third—the speaker—was a short but wide man who walked with a swaggering, side-to-side gait. He had a squat upper body, his head and neck almost sunken into his torso, somewhat like a cake that had melted into its own base, with the lower part of his head hidden by the upraised collar of his brown raincoat. What was visible of his face was long-nosed and weasel-like, with rows of hair plastered back from a flattened forehead.

"That's us," Fura said, not without hesitation. "I'm Captain Marance of the sunjammer *Grey Lady*. This is my crew—Tragen, Lodran and Lizzil—and this is our injured crewmate, Greben."

"Yes, we got wind of your poorly chum," said the short, wide man. "Don't you worry your pretty heads over her, now. You've come to the best possible place. Doctor Eddralder's cleared all the decks, sharpened his best knives and given everything a twice-over scrub, extra special. He'll smoke out what's wrong with your pal in no time, and if he can't fix it no one can."

"And you are?" I asked.

"Begging your pardon, forgot my manners, my dear." Our speaker touched a hand to the end of his nose. "I'm Mister Sneed. Old Sneed, or Sneedy, or Lasper Sneed if you're formally inclinated, or even Mister S." He grinned, exposing crumbling, gap-filled ranks of brown teeth. "Tragen, wasn't it?"

"Tragen Imbery, Bone Reader. Do you work for the doctor?"

Sneed considered my point as if it was of intense philosophical interest. "In a manner, I suppose I do, and in another he works for me, so to speak, and at the end of the day you could say that we both answer to Mister Glimmery, which is what matters."

"And what has Mister Glimmery to do with helping our friend?" Fura asked.

"Ah, I see you're not intimately acquainted with the present situation."

"Ought we to be?" I asked.

"I expect you will be, soon—Mister Glimmery wants only the best for his guests, you see, and since he has few guests of consequence at present, he'll insist on lavishing all his attention on you. That means telling Eddralder to pull out all the stops, even if he has to neglect some of his other patients, which won't sit well with him. But needs must, and the doc won't mind once he sees how prestidigious you are, and he wouldn't want to let Mister Glimmery down by not being an excellent and reliable doctor."

"We don't want to put anyone out," I said.

"Oh, you wouldn't, not at all, my dear. We'll be at the infirmary in two shakes." He nodded at the trolley-pushers. "Help 'em load their chum, boys, and be gentle with it."

Fura stood aside while Prozor, Surt and I assisted the trolley-pushers. Accustomed as they were to the wheel's gravity, they made Strambli's cargo chest seem much less burdensome. They slid her onto the trolley, peeling aside the ribbed rain-sheet and then drawing it back over the chest. Sneed then showed us a shelf under the main part of the trolley where we could store our helmets and any other parts of our suits we preferred not to carry. We unshipped lungstuff bottles, pressure bellows and portable squawk boxes, setting them carefully onto the shelf, and then off we trundled, Sneed leading the way, Fura and I flanking him, the trolley, trolley boys and the rest of our crew following.

"I don't know how it works with your hospital," Fura said, "but we'll meet any costs, within reason."

"Flush, are you? That makes a change from the usual crews. Most them couldn't rub two quoins together."

"We just want the best for her. This infirmary you mentioned—is it the best?"

"Oh, yes," Sneed said. "The very best, no question about that at all."

*

We moved through what I supposed had once been the civic gardens, but which was now a treeless wasteland of rubbish, fires, and gangs of loitering figures, with broken statues and fountains lying crumbled or toppled all around. Further off, the walls of the rim curved up on either side of us, streets and buildings clinging to the steepening sides almost until the sides were vertical and the buildings were fixed onto precarious ledges and protrusions. There were two principal avenues, as near as I could tell, one on either side of us, and they stretched away along the main curve of the rim, gradually climbing out of sight. Spidering away from these two avenues were smaller streets and alleys, but it was only close to the avenues that there were real signs of life, with electric and neon lights clustering around squares and main intersections. Elsewhere it was so dark that the buildings and roads were lost in the black, with only an occasional light or fire to show that there was any habitation at all. I realised that since we were between the two avenues, in the lowest part of the rim, we were trudging through a similar sort of darkness, broken only by more braziers and piles of burning rubbish.

Every now and then there was a road or walkway crossing the width of the rim from one side to the other, providing a sort of short-cut between those two main avenues. We were just going under one when there was a shout from a huddle of individuals above us, and a bottle came hurtling down. It shattered on the ground, giving off a sudden rank stink.

Sneed drew out a weapon, a small blunt-barrelled pistol, and fired a warning shot.

"Watch your step, coves!"

"Sneedy?" called back a voice.

"Yes, and these good people are under the special protection of Far-Gone. Get on the wrong side of me and you're on the wrong side of him, too, and you wouldn't want that, would you?" By way of emphasis he let off another shot, but the party on the bridge was already dispersing, having got the intended message.

"Who were those people?" I asked.

"Ne'er do wells," Mister Sneed answered, pocketing the weapon in the sure knowledge that he had made his point. "These are trying times, with all sorts of thievery and common lawlessness abroad. Mister Glimmery's doing his best to stamp some sort of authority on the gaff, but it's an uphill struggle, what with the hand he's been dealt."

"You mentioned Far-Gone," Fura said. "Who or what is Far-Gone, exactly?"

"A mere indiscresence that slipped my lips." Sneed rubbed at the tip of his nose, where there was a little pendant of mucus hanging down like the hook on the end of a cantilevered construction crane. "Think nothing of it, and please don't mention it again in any sort of company we might soon be enjoying."

We made our way out of the ruins of the civic gardens, through a bad-smelling pedestrian tunnel, crunched through tiles that had fallen from the roof, up a slope, skirted around another sort of market, a bit livelier than the last, and then up a sloping alley that took us closer to one of the avenues, although still a street or two from the electric and neon lights.

The infirmary was built onto a rectangle of level ground projecting out from the side. Or, I ought to say, it had been built that way. In truth it was an exceedingly odd kind of structure. It was hanging down from the ceiling like a grotesque chandelier, hardly any part of it in contact with the ground, except for some ladders, rope-bridges, chains, hoses and pipes. The top parts were suspended by hundreds of cables, some going up vertically and others reaching off at angles. It made me a little sick and giddy just to be looking at it, and even more so to think it was our destination, and Strambli's best hope.

The building had clearly started off with foundations, entrances and so on, but for some reason the bottom five or six stories had been blasted away, leaving a ragged stump of rubble, girders and masonry, suspended above a waterlogged crater in the rectangle of ground. The only way in or out was up those ladders and rope-bridges, which fed up from the street to what would have been the sixth, seventh and eighth levels, as near as I could estimate. Whatever catastrophe had befallen the original structure, either gradual or sudden, it was only those guylines holding it up now.

There was power, at least. Lights were on in the upper parts of the building, and not all of the windows in the lower levels were dark.

"It's a good joke they play on visitors, Trage," Fura said, shielding the rain from her brow with her hand, as she craned back to take in the suspended building. "Showing them this stupid ruin and letting them think it's the infirmary."

"I wish it were a prank, Cap'n Marance, sincerely I do. But the sorry truth is this is what we've been reduced to. I didn't lie, though—there's no better infirmary anywhere in the wheel."

Sneed led us to the base of one of the rope-bridges. Not the steepest of them—that would have been impossible to navigate, with the trolley—but it was adequately steep, and certainly long enough to put a lump in my throat.

"Now, before we go up, there's a little formality we need to put behind us. Some crews get the wrong idea, you see, and bring guns and such unpleasant things with 'em, and we can't be having that in our lovely hospital, can we?"

"We're not armed," Fura said.

"You'd be surprised how often I've heard that, Cap'n—no offence intended."

Fura stepped back and stretched her arms. "Search us, if you're not ready to take our word."

"Give 'em the once-over, boys, and be gentle about it. Mister Glimmery won't want his guests rough-handled."

They did search us, and since I knew myself to be unarmed I felt under no obligation to submit to this indignity with good grace. Prozor and I were declared to be unarmed, but they found a dull blade on Fura, fixed under her chest-pack by magnetic means, and Surt turned out to be carrying a miniature crossbow-pistol in the stores pouch on her boot. Sneed took the little weapon, regarding it more with pity than objection. "That the best you got? Expecting to run into a dangerous kitten or puppy, was you?"

"I forgot I had it," Surt said with a scowl. "It was from our last bauble run."

Fura stuck out her jaw. "If you think it's harmless, you can give it back to her."

"I'll confesticate it for now," Sneed said, slipping it into the pocket where he had also placed Fura's short-handled blade. "I suppose you do have to take precautions, going into baubles. I'm just happy you never needed to depend on any of 'em, or I don't think we'd be having this conversation."

"Aren't you going to inspect the chest?" Fura asked, planting her hands on her hips. "She was on our last bauble run as well, and I can't vouch for what she's still got fixed onto her suit."

Sneed considered her point and nodded. "Open her up, boys—we may as well take a squint. Who knows what she's got in there? Could be a fusion lance for all we know."

They leaned under the rain-sheet, opened the vacuum seal and inched up the lid. The men flinched back almost immediately, one of them raising a hand to his mouth, the other fanning away the bad airs.

"Be thorough about it, boys!" Sneed snapped.

"There's a stink on her like she hasn't washed since the Third Occupation," protested one of his men.

"Smells rotten. Like something going all maggoty," said the other.

"No," contradicted the first. "It's more like a sewer, or a toilet what's not been emptied."

"Maggots," replied the other. "Rotten meat, that's what it is. Not sewery at all. How you could say that's sewery I don't know."

Sneed pushed them aside and directed the tip of his nose into the opening under the lid. His shoulders moved as he rummaged around Strambli, picking at the belongings we had stuffed around her body like funerary goods. "I'm not sure which part smells worse, the cove or her laundry. Something's definitely *off*, though." He backed away, lowering the lid. "What did you say was up with your pal, Cap'n?"

"A leg wound that isn't healing properly," Fura answered coldly. "It hasn't been smelling very good for a few days. That's why we'd like her seen to as soon as possible."

"Speed is very definitely of the effervescence," Sneed said, moving to a chain hanging down from the infirmary and giving it a very sharp tug, just as if he were emptying a cistern.

He swivelled his eyes up and leaned back, even as his face stayed jammed into his collar like a plug hammered into a hole. Nothing happened for a minute or so, then a steel arm swung out of a window high up on the side above us, and a hook came lowering down with a basket under it. The basket was wire-framed, and about as large as a bath-tub.

"I ain't going in that," Surt said.

"No one's asking you to," Sneed said. "But if you put your helmets and assorted gubbins in the basket, that'll take a strain off the rope-bridge. You can collect them again when you get to the top."

"I don't like it," Fura murmured, loud enough for the rest of us to hear.

"He's right about not over-loading the trolley," I said. "We'll have less weight to push, as well."

We could have debated it for hours, but with a grunt of annoyance Fura reached under the trolley and began transferring suit parts into the basket. The rest of us followed, clanking our motley goods into the basket. We took off a few more bits for good measure, but there was no time to strip out of our suits completely.

Sneed waved a hand up to the window, and the hook and basket began to rise. Just before it ascended out of reach, Fura snatched back two of the squawk boxes. They were exactly small enough to be easily pilfered, unlike the heavier helmets and lungstuff systems.

Now the basket wobbled higher and higher.

"We'll meet it at the top," Sneed said, gesturing to his assistants. "Put your backs into it, boys. It can't start rolling down, or we'll never stop the blighter."

We all joined in, with the exception of Sneed, until there was no more room for another pair of hands. It reminded me of shoving the fuel tank up the sloping shaft in the Rumbler, only there was a friend's life at stake now, not just a bottle full of rocket fuel. So we shoved and shoved, and as the ground fell away and the angle of the bridge got steeper, and the sway of it got more pronounced, and the planks under us were occasionally rotted or missing completely, so that the trolley wheels nearly went through, I reminded myself that I was having an adventure, and that adventures were exceedingly fine things to look back on.

"What're they doing?" Fura asked, for the basket had stopped in its ascent, still far above us, but nowhere near the window where the winch had been swung out.

"Something's jammed," Sneed said, as if this was a very common and unremarkable occurrence. "No need to fret—they'll get it going again."

"If one of those suit parts gets a scratch on it..." Fura said.

Two figures leaned out the window, fussing with the winch. It seemed thoroughly stuck.

We carried on, forcing our minds off the trouble above. The bridge steepened and steepened, swaying from side to side in an alarming and lively manner. By some miracle we got the trolley all the way to the top without it toppling or rolling back, and as we neared the underside of the infirmary, where the bridge vanished into that stumpy tangle of girders and plumbing and masonry, two infirmary staff came out and helped persuade our cargo up the final incline, into the safety of the building. That was an irony all of its own, I thought, that I now considered this suspended rubble-heap to be in any way "safe." But it was certainly more pleasant than being on the rope-bridge.

"Show me where that winch is," Fura said.

"It's still a bit above us," Sneed said. "But it's on our way to the examining bay, in any case."

We had come out into what would have been one of the intermediate levels of the original building, but we were still a dozen stories under the lit parts I'd seen from below. This part of the building was a shell, with its windows blown out and nothing but floors and ceilings left behind, supported by bare metal pillars.

Sneed led us closer to the middle, where there had evidently once been a courtyard or atrium, with four inner walls surrounding it. Other rope-bridges spanned this gap, crisscrossing directly or stretching at severe inclines between different floors. We were spared those, thankfully. Instead, Sneed's boys wheeled the trolley into an elevator with trellis doors, with just enough room for Fura to get in as well. The rest of us were told to wait until the elevator came back down again.

I watched the elevator grind its way up to the higher floors, heard a distant racket of trellis doors, a rumble of wheels, then the whine of its slow descent back down to us. Sneed snorted and wiped his sleeve across the tip of his nose, making a little rope-bridge of slime all of his own.

"What's gone on here, Mister Sneed?" I asked. "I know this world is past its best days, but it looks like we've arrived in the middle of a war."

He sniffed, making a phlegmy rattle in the back of his throat. "Now, that's a tricky one, Trage. Not a war, exactly, but a bit of a readjustment. Things got a bit out of kilter here, you see, what with the declinating trade, last year's bank run, and a general breakdown in law and order, all most regrettable. But luckily Mister Glimmery had all the right connections to start putting things right again. The right man at the right time. Sometimes an opportunity opens, especially when things aren't going like clockwork, and it takes a man like Mister Glimmery to step up and do what needs doing."

"Sounds like a power grab to me," Prozor said.

"You're not one to mince your words, are you? Lodran, wasn't it? You look older than these others, you don't mind my saying."

"Older, uglier and wiser."

"I don't know about that, but you've definitely been around the Old Sun a few more times. How long've you been knocking around with Cap'n Marance's crew, Lod?"

"Long enough to know that's my business and no one else's," Prozor answered.

I cared little for Sneed on first impressions, but we were on delicate ground and I had no wish to get off on a bad footing with him or his supposed master.

I forced an obliging smile and said: "You'll have to excuse us, Mister Sneed. We're used to keeping tight-lipped about our operation. It's the only way to keep any sort of an edge on the other crews, but it makes us a bit suspicious of questions, and of help being volunteered when we haven't come begging for it. But we don't mean ill of it, and we're grateful for any help when Greben's concerned."

"Crews can be a bit tacitatious, I s'pose," Sneed said. "That Cap'n of yours doesn't look like one for idle chit-chat, either, Trage. I've only seen one case of the glowy more further along than hers. How'd she end up with the tin arm?"

"She's never said," I answered, which was the story we'd all agreed on. "Some bad business, that's all."

"That's a pretty arm, all the same. I could get a good price for that piece, if she's thinking of selling up."

"I'm sure the captain will take that under advisement," I answered.

The elevator had come back. We rode the cabin up the inner wall of the atrium, with two streams of brown water racing down either side of us, splashing into the waterlogged crater below. Eventually we reached the lit and inhabited levels of the infirmary. It was an improvement, certainly, on the wind-blown emptiness of the lower levels. But only in the most marginal sense.

It smelled bad. Not as bad as Strambli's cargo chest, but at least we could close the lid on Strambli, whereas the infirmary's smell was unavoidably present. The worst part of it, I think, was that someone had tried to smother the sickness smells with chemicals, which were potent enough to tickle the nose and make the eyes sting, and yet still not sufficient to fully mask the decay and sickness.

"It ain't so bad, once you're acclimatisated," Sneed said. "Spewed up a bucketload, I did, the first time. Now it doesn't bother me at all, which proves how bad your pal stinks! I'll go and rustle up Doctor Eddralder, shall I?"

"I'll save you the effort, Mister Sneed," said a man with an exceedingly deep voice, coming over to us by the elevator, an umbrella in one hand, held up and open, even though we were indoors, and a set of loosely-bound papers in the other. "I am Eddralder. Which one of you is the injured party?"

"The one on the trolley," I said, pointing to the cart. "Greben's in that cargo chest. We had to get her across a stretch of vacuum, and she wasn't in any condition to wear a suit."

"I see. And you'd be the captain I was told about—Marance, wasn't it?"

"No, that's—" I was about to say "my sister" but caught myself. "I'm Tragen. Captain Marance came up the elevator ahead of us. Where is she, Mister Sneed?"

"She couldn't wait to get to that winch, Trage. Pop along if you're concerned. It's beyond those blue curtains, all the way to end of the corridor."

"I'll fetch her," Prozor said.

"See you in a minute, Lod," Sneed said, raising a hand to his face as if he were saluting a war-bound friend.

Doctor Eddralder placed his papers down on the reception desk next to the elevator and fished a little lamp from his pocket. The examining area was just part of a much larger ward—or collection of wards, I supposed—that must have taken up a good part of this whole floor. It was a similar arrangement to below, with metal pillars rising up to the ceiling. But there was glass in the windows here, and sheeting over the missing bits, and electrical lights strung across the ceiling, as well as curtains and partitions to offer a scrap of privacy to both doctors and patients. There were beds and trolleys and various items of medical equipment, including a battery of powerful lamps that could be wheeled around.

"I do not know how much Sneed told you about our circumstances here, Tragen. Clearly I will do the best that I can for your friend. But I must ask you not to entertain unrealistic expectations."

"Sneed told us there was a man called Mister Glimmery taking an interest in our welfare," I said.

"Yes, I was informed that our... benefactor... has taken an interest." There had been a strain in his voice for an instant, but I wondered if it was no more than fatigue, the doctor struggling to find his words after a long day of ministrations. "We will do what we can. As we always do."

"We appreciate any help you can give us," I said.

Doctor Eddralder was a very tall man, one of the tallest I had seen, and he was also long and thin in his features, like an ordinary cove walking in front of a distorting mirror. He had a faded, colourless complexion, with bruiselike shadows beneath his pebble-pale eyes. His mouth and eyes were a long way apart, as if there was too much nose between them. He had a heavy jaw, a doubtful set to his lips, and black hair combed apart in two equal waves from his scalp. He wore a pale blue surgical gown that covered every part of him from the shoulders to the tips of his shoes, and he had a way of moving around that made me think of a gaming piece being slid from one square to the next, his legs hardly moving.

"Is there anything I ought to know about the nature of the injury, Tragen?"

"What did they tell you?"

"Very little." He was still holding up his umbrella, which had purple and white segments on it, and I noticed now that there was a steady dripping coming from the ceiling. "A wound caused by a sharp edge, in space. That covers a multitude of possibilities, from a simple accident to violent action."

"It was a slip," I said. "That's all. Luckily it didn't go all the way through. We tried to clean the wound, but it seems we didn't do a good enough job. We only had a small surgical bay, though. If you had to operate to remove the infection, could you do that?"

"There is always a way." He gave the umbrella a snap, partly closing it and then opening it again, so that the accumulated raindrops were flung away from its fabric. "Especially as—as appears to be the case—Mister Glimmery has made it clear the patient is to be given all available care."

With faint intimations of unease I studied the activity taking place. Over in one corner, not quite hidden from view, some kind of operation was going on. They had tanks of gas and a kind of cabinet with bellows in it, and a patient stretched out under green blankets. A robot was bent over the patient, with its two arms vanishing into a gap in the blankets. Standing on a crate behind it was a small woman in a surgical gown and mask, and she was pushing her own two arms into a flap in the back of the robot. The robot itself must have been all but dead, except for some locomotor functions that the woman was commanding. One of the other staff, monitoring the bellows machine, caught my roving eye and I looked away sharply, feeling that that I had been caught gazing at something that was none of my business.

"We don't expect to be treated any better than these other people, Doctor Eddralder."

"The choice may not be yours to make, Tragen." Then, to both of us: "Sit yourselves down. I will examine your friend and make an initial assessment. Then we may discuss a treatment plan."

Surt and I sat as elegantly as was possible while still wearing our vacuum suits. The chairs creaked under our weight but held. I was glad when Sneed showed no intention of joining us. He was still hanging around, eyeing us in a way that made me uneasy. He was brazen about it, too, not even bothering to pretend otherwise. I'd catch him staring in our direction and he would just wipe his nose and carry on.

"I don't care for that stumpy cove," Surt mumbled, as she eased her right gauntlet off, finally able to stretch her fingers. "Or the smell of this place."

"He's got a certain way about him, I'll admit." I sunk down into my neck ring as far as I could, preferring a dose of my own sweat and body odour to the smells of the ward.

It was noisy as well as bad-smelling. There was a drumming of rain on the roof somewhere above us, a hiss of it racing down the outside of the building, a constant dripping of it into buckets on the floor, a drone of generators, a continuous buzzing and clicking of machines, footsteps coming and going all the while, a low murmur of doctors and staff discussing patients, the crying and moaning of the sick, and always that smell, like a yellow haze fighting its way into your sinuses.

"Do you think the lanky one's to be trusted?" Surt asked.

"Doctor Eddralder? He seems all right, I suppose. Right now, though, I wouldn't trust my own left arm without written references. There's something odd about this whole set-up."

"I know what you mean about not trusting your arm," Surt said.

A swish of blue curtains drew my attention to the end of the room. Prozor came through, with a grim set to her face, the usual angles even more acute. Fura was just behind her, and neither of them was carrying any of our equipment.

Prozor marched on up to us while Fura veered off and headed for Doctor Eddralder, who was just wheeling Strambli's trolley and cargo chest into a curtained area.

I made to rise from my chair.

"What happened?"

Prozor held up her hand, encouraging me to stay seated. "We lost it all, Tragen. All our helmets and breathin' gear and anythin' else that was in that basket. I watched it fall all the way down to that crater under us, the one full of brown water, and if you fancy swimmin' through that on a treasure hunt, good luck to you."

"No," I said, astonished and dumbfounded. "We can't have lost it all, not like that."

"I'm tellin' you what I saw. It was jammed and two of Snot-face's coves were leanin' out tryin' to fix something in the winch. I think they almost had it loose, and then Fura...I mean, Cap'n Marance..." She glanced hastily to one side. "She shoves 'em out of the way, like she's got the strength of two of 'em, and tries to fix it herself. Only it's no good. The line breaks and down goes the basket, dreamy as you please, with our blessed loot in it."

"Wait!" I called, seeing Fura starting to remonstrate with Doctor Eddralder, raising her voice and practically bowling him over, not touching him exactly, but flinging her arms out and jamming her face under his, a wild madness shining through, as if the glowy had taken a new hold.

"They told us it'd be safe!" she was shouting. "They took everything, and now look what's happened!"

Doctor Eddralder still had his examining lamp. He stepped back from the trolley, holding up that light as if it were his only line of defence. Fura kept on advancing on him, her alloy hand opening and closing with a crazed whirr. Still in her suit from the neck down, she could have done the stick-like doctor an injury just by toppling over him.

I came behind her. "Captain!" I said, almost yelling myself, but still trying to preserve some sense of our imagined roles. "It isn't Doctor Eddralder's fault!"

She snapped around and for an instant all that anger was on me. She made a fist and I think she had some brief, brutal intention of using it.

"Don't you be tellin' me my business, Tragen."

I dropped my voice to hiss. "We have quoins. We have more quoins than we know what to do with. We can buy it all again. Better the second time around. Greben is what matters here—not a load of old suit parts we can easily replace."

Her nostrils flared, a tumult of rage and calculation going on behind her eyes. There was a rage in me as well, like a bottle full of fire. I fought to keep it from uncorking itself, and wondered if Fura detected my struggle as readily as I sensed the devious workings of her mind.

"It won't go well if you keep challenging me," she said, in little more than a whisper.

"No," I said, in a similar tone, and with the same brooding conviction. "It most certainly won't."

"She's still in you."

"She's in both of us," I hissed back. "The difference is I don't welcome her. The difference is I'm trying not to become her."

At last something in her eased and she dropped her arms. The anger was still there, but she recognised that there was too much to be risked if we broke through our invented personas.

In a normal tone she replied: "It'll delay us."

"So be it. It's just more one set of things to add to the shopping list."

Doctor Eddralder lowered his lamp, straightening up now Fura was no longer in his face. "Are we done?" he asked mildly.

# 13

Fura insisted on a moment alone with Strambli before the doctor vanished into the curtained area. When she came back she dropped her voice and said: "I just wanted to make sure she wasn't in a babbling frame of mind."

"And if she had been?" I asked.

"It's all right. She's out colder than the arse-end of Trevenza Reach." Fura tossed a bag to me, and then did the same for Surt and Prozor. "Your belongings. They'll whiff a bit, after being in that box with her, but I've a feeling we'll stop noticing after a few days."

"And if we're really lucky, we'll be on our way even sooner than that," I said.

"Well, let's not jump to conclusions. No telling how long it's going to take to get Strambli square, is it? If that leg turns gammy, she'll need it off, and then we'll have to fit her up with a tin one, and I wouldn't want her to be in quite the rush I was. Cheer up, s—I mean, Tragen. We might have some shopping to do."

"I thought you hated shopping."

"Depends on the shopping."

"We need provisions—even more than when we started out, after losing those suit parts. But I'm not in any rush to stay here longer than necessary. I don't like it. We weren't made to feel very welcome when we wanted to dock, and now I'm starting to feel as if we're too welcome."

"I've never been one to complain about being made too welcome," Fura said.

I turned to Prozor. "Is there a chance they've worked out our true identities?"

"Ordinarily I wouldn't say so. Even an information request ought to take days to work its way back out here. But something's wrong, and it makes me wonder what they know, or think they know. I ain't certain. That business with the two ships..."

"Could they have seen the attack?"

"Not unless they had scopes pointed in exactly the right direction at the right moment. It all happened too far away, even the explosion, and Paladin didn't pick up any squawk chatter that might have given away the game, did he?"

"No one could expect us here," I said, trying to reassure myself. "Ships come and go from places like this often enough, and it can't be too uncommon for a captain and her Boney to be a little similar-looking. Perhaps we're just being too jumpy."

"We are," Fura said, looking down at her arm. "And that's the worst thing we could be, because we don't want to look like coves who've got anything to hide." She lowered her voice further still. "I don't care for this place any more than the rest of you. But it's *her* only chance so we see it through. Meanwhile, we'll be as quick as we can about our other errands." She dredged up a dark, humourless laugh. "I don't suppose jumpin' ships is on anyone's immediate agenda, is it?"

Presently Doctor Eddralder came over to our row of chairs, still holding his umbrella.

"I've made an initial examination," he declared in his extremely deep voice, which didn't quite seem to match the rest of him. "We've given her some drugs to make her more comfortable and give her body a better chance at fighting the infection. When one of the robots is available I will conduct a thorough cleansing of the wound, chasing the infection as far as I may. I will do my utmost to save the limb, but nothing is guaranteed. An accident with a blade, you say?"

"A yardknife," Fura said. "What we use for cutting snagged

rigging, squaring-off sails and suchlike. A yardknife will go through just about anything."

"I should like to see the edge in question. If it's as sharp as appears from the injury, it would make a most efficacious surgical instrument."

"It was our best yardknife," Fura said. "Uncommonly sharp. Sadly she let go of it during the accident."

"How unfortunate," Doctor Eddralder said.

Mister Sneed swaggered over to our gathering. He wiped his nose on the back of his palm, then smeared the residue under his chin. "Having a little gossip with the clients, is it, doc?"

"Merely illuminating them on matters clinical, Mister Sneed."

Sneed worked his jaw, pushing his tongue from side to side in his mouth so that it bulged from one cheek and then the other. "So long as that's all it is. That *was* all it was, wasn't it?"

"He was just telling us about Greben," I said.

"Good. And the prognosteration is...?"

"She'll need surgery," Eddralder said. "If all is well, I'll operate within the next six hours. She'll be under my personal care while she is here—my *personal* care." He was looking at Sneed, giving his words a particular threatening emphasis. "And I'll make sure she is suitably undisturbed. You and your party may remain here if you wish, Captain Marance, but I presume you have affairs to attend to?"

"Actually, doc," Sneed said, "they've been invited upstairs. A personal audience with the man himself. Mister Glimmery wants to make sure they're getting everything they need. See, they're getting *his* personal attention too."

"I am very glad for them," Doctor Eddralder said, giving his umbrella a sharp snap.

*

Surt insisted that she wanted to stay with Strambli, so it fell to Prozor, Fura and I to represent the crew during our audience. We were not in the least bit enthusiastic about any part of that, but equally we understood that the quality of Strambli's care depended on the continued cooperation and sufferance of our hosts, and there was no agreeable way of getting out of the engagement.

Sneed took us up a flight of stairs onto the rain-sodden roof of the infirmary, leading us through a forest of cables that came down from the ceiling, taut as rigging, each being anchored into the roof with a great iron eyelet. He walked us to one crumbling edge, and then reached for a chain coming all the way down from the ceiling. He tugged six times, clearly a sort of code, since the tugs had distinct and deliberate intervals between them, and after a delay a metal walkway began to hinge down from above.

I had noticed the grid of pipes and cables where the sky panels had fallen away, leaking water and belching steam, but there was something else directly above the infirmary: a sort of localised plaque or growth of disreputable-looking structures built in, around and above the pipework, with more lights on than any of the buildings below. The walkway was angling down from one of these elevated structures.

Fura had left Surt in charge of our changes of clothes, and we still had our suits on below the neck. I trusted that walkway more than the rope-bridge, though, and other than the fact of my bones and muscles still aching, I had no trouble going all the way to the top, with Sneed bringing up the rear. Halfway up the rattling stairway, I paused to take in the dismal view, with all its queasy curves and bending perspectives. There was the clinic right under us, and the waterlogged hole beneath it, and stretching away beyond it the dark sprawl of Port Endless, hazed in steam and rain where it was visible at all, with many of its streets and buildings lost in gloom and only spots of fitful, flickering illumination where there was any sort of light. I spotted a few colourful signs and advertisements, and the blue flash of a tram's electricity pole laid a street corner stark for an instant, picking out stooping, stick-figure pedestrians as if frozen in a chalk sketch.

"Move yourselves, ladies—Mister Glimmery's got a packed schedule, you know."

"So good of him to fit us in," I said, certain Sneed would not hear.

At the top of the walkway was a doorway, and flanking it were Sneed's two accomplices from before, or perhaps two coves who were so like the others as to be indistinguishable. We were taken into an ante-chamber and examined again, at least as thoroughly as at the infirmary, but since Fura and Surt had already been divested of their weapons once, there was nothing to be found.

Satisfied that we were no threat to our host, Mister Sneed took us along a red-carpeted corridor which opened out into a large room that was misty with sweet-smelling steam. Enormous pipes criss-crossed above our heads. The walls were gold: gold-painted, or gold-hammered panels, wherever we looked, and the floor was gold as well, made of many glazed tiles. There were no windows in the walls, but here and there the floor had been cut away to allow a view down into the city below, glazed with what I trusted was suitably resilient material. Around the perimeter of the room were gold-lacquered partition screens, and at least a dozen barefoot, black-gowned attendants stood around with towels on their arms or buckets at their feet. They had a servile look to them, female and male both, but there was also something thuggish and muscular.

The central feature of the room—and the reason for that sweet-smelling steam—was not the pipes, but rather a circular bath which took up a large part of the floor, sunk down into it so that the floor was level with the rim.

Sneed walked to the edge of the bath.

"Your guests are here, Mister Glimmery," he said, genuflecting a little as he made his statement. "Captain Marance, and two of her associates from the *Grey Lady*. The other two are downstairs—one of 'em poorly, and one of 'em keeping vigil."

Mister Glimmery was up to his neck in the bath. Hot, white liquid lapped at the rim. It smelled like hot milk, seasoned with spices. We could only see his head, and that indistinctly, because of the steam lifting off the surface. The head was hairless and he had his face turned away from us, but the impression was of some raw pink thing being slowly boiled. Three attendants were stationed around the pool, while a fourth was just bringing a fresh pail of steaming milk, pausing only to add a generous fistful of what I thought might be cinnamon or nutmeg.

"Fetch my robe," the head in the bath said in a low and liquid tone, as if the speaker's mouth were partly submerged.

"You heard the man," Sneed said, snapping his fingers.

Two of the attendants departed.

Mister Glimmery began to rise from the white bath, keeping his back to us but spreading his arms as they emerged from the surface. The milk sluiced off him in thick white rivulets, tracing the muscled contours of very powerful shoulders and a broad, tapering back. His neck was as thick and wide as the base of an extremely old tree, one that had set down prodigious roots. I was not often intimidated by strong men, finding them laughable rather than impressive. Most such men, in my experience, had made themselves that way because their powers of reason and persuasion were lacking, and the abundance of muscle and bulk was a sort of unwitting advertisement for those deficiencies. But I had to admit that Mister Glimmery blunted my usual contempt. I could not say why, but something in his size and presence convinced me that he had always been this way; that it was the outcome of nature rather than some compensatory impulse, and that I could draw no safe conclusions from it about his reasoning faculties.

His size was not the most noteworthy thing about him, either—but it was the canvas on which the main matter depended. Mister Glimmery was a victim of the glowy. Those branching, entwining filaments of glowing skin covered his arms, shoulders and back, and now that there was less steam to obscure the view, I even made out fine filigreed projections curling up the back of his head.

He rose a little further, the base of his spine coming into view, then the upper parts of his buttocks, the glowy marking every part of him—but at that moment the two attendants stepped into the pool on either side and swept a gold cloak around him, Mister Glimmery only lowering his arms when they were safely sleeved. He did up the front of the cloak itself, and then slowly turned around to view us, stepping out of the pool by means of hidden stairs.

I suppressed an outward exclamation. The glowy had taken a much more dominant hold of Mister Glimmery's face. It shone like some crudely-daubed paint, shimmering with yellow-green light, and it was in his eyes as well, scintillating like embedded flecks of precious metal. The coverage of his skin was not uniform, but confined to stripes and curlicues, serving to exaggerate the lines and angles of his natural features, and also to cloud them, like a form of disruptive camouflage. Beneath his robe, his great chest swelled and deflated with each inhalation, and I would swear that the brightness of the glowy swelled and ebbed in sympathy.

"You'd be Captain Marance," he said, addressing Fura in the same low, liquid voice he had used when he was still in the milk. "Fresh in from the Emptyside, by all accounts. Did they say your ship is the *Grey Lady*?"

"That's what we call her," Fura said.

Mister Glimmery walked over to us, leaving huge milky footprints on the marbled floor, which his attendants were quick to mop away. He was breathing slowly in and out as he towered over Fura and I, that chest of his at the level of my nose, his head looking down at me like a boulder about to roll off a hill.

"I'm surprised you didn't haul-in closer. You must be standing off a hundred leagues or more. Makes coming and going very time-consuming."

"Hopefully we won't be doing much coming and going," I said.

"Not much business to be done, then?" He turned his gaze slightly onto me, the flecks in his eyes twinkling with a vivid and dangerous curiosity. "And you'd be…?"

"Tragen. Principal Bone Reader."

He looked back to Fura. "Like to keep such things in the family, do we, Captain?"

Fura looked puzzled. "Mister Glimmery?"

"There's an uncommon likeness to the two of you, is all. You might be mistaken for sisters."

A male attendant brought a small platter, upon which stood a single slim-stemmed glass containing a viscous, straw-coloured fluid. Mister Glimmery took the stem between the tips of his exceptionally thick fingers and lifted the glass to his lips, drinking it dry. He set down the glass and the attendant was dismissed.

"It would be a mistake if we were," Fura said, referring to his remark. "We're not related, and this is the first time we've crewed together." Her gaze sharpened. "Do you normally take such a personal interest in newly arrived crews, Mister Glimmery? It can't be very practical."

"You forget that we have very few visitors, Captain Marance. So few that it would be rather odd of me *not* to take an interest. A little discourteous, even. Which reminds me—I have forgotten my manners already." He extended a sleeved arm. "Please, take a seat. Would you like some wine? Bring wine! You will excuse me while I...attire myself. Of course, if you should care to cleanse yourselves in my milk bath, I could have it prepared to your requirements."

"It's all right," Fura said. "We washed fairly recently. Certainly within the last couple of days."

"The offer stands. In the meantime, there is a certain gentleman who would value a conversation, I am sure. If you would oblige, I'm sure he'll be most grateful. I won't detain you."

While Mister Glimmery went off to get dressed, we were helped to a corner of the room that had been screened-off with the gold partitions. Chairs and settees were positioned around a low table set with drinks and a miniature gasworks of glassware and pipes and bubbling retorts. That was when I had my second surprise, just as I was getting over Mister Glimmery's affliction. A Crawly was seated in its own specially upholstered chair, bending down over the table and inhaling from a hosed mouthpiece.

"Good day to you sir," I said diffidently, when neither Fura nor Prozor had uttered a word, and the silence was beginning to weigh. "I'm Tragen. This is Captain Marance, and this is Lodran."

The Crawly made a rustly sound that reminded me of old leaves crunching underfoot, or papers being shuffled. It took an effort of concentration to understand those noises as language, but I had heard Crawlies speaking before, and was therefore tolerably prepared.

"Good day to you all. I am... Mister Cuttle."

I'd seen a fair number of them during my life, but seldom at such proximity. Most of the alien was hidden under a hooded cloak, covering its head, body and the limbs it used to shuffle along with. The cloak had a slit at the front for its forelimbs, and two of these hooked appendages were taking care of the bubbling apparatus and mouthpiece. No part of its actual face was visible, except for a set of whiskers, antennae and mouthparts jutting out like a sheath of twigs, and moving all the while.

Fura, Prozor and I sat down with the alien to our right. For a moment none of us touched the drinks, although they appeared innocent enough, and nothing like milk or the straw-coloured concoction Mister Glimmery had just imbibed.

"Are you a friend of Mister Glimmery's, Mister Cuttle?" I asked, a little put-out that it was falling on me to make the conversation.

"An... acquaintance. I was called here on... urgent family business." Mister Cuttle set down his smoking apparatus, leaving the mouthpiece in a forked holder. "What brings you to Wheel Strizzardy, Captain... Marance?"

"The warm welcome and the valuable trading opportunities," Fura said.

"In which case," Mister Cuttle replied, "you have an unusual taste in such... matters."

"Well, they've been nice enough," I said, feeling that there could be well be ears pressed to the other sides of the partitions, and that one of us ought to say something charitable. "That doctor's been very helpful with our colleague, and Mister Glimmery seems keen to make us feel appreciated. I know this isn't the most prosperous world we could've sailed to, but it's not so bad, is it?"

"No," Mister Cuttle answered. "There are much worse."

"Have you seen many of our worlds?" I asked pleasantly.

"Quite a number, and of all dispositions. Wheelworlds and laceworlds, sphereworlds and tubeworlds, from the Sunward processionals to the edge of the Emptyside, to the Frost Margins... and beyond."

"Banker, are you?" Prozor asked, in a tone that was more inquisitorial than friendly. "'Cos that's the line most of you's in, isn't it? Sneakin' around, grubbin' up quoins..."

"We serve at the pleasure of your boards of directors. All the significant banking concerns remain under the control of... indigenous majority parties, do they not?"

"That being us monkeys," Prozor said, jabbing an elbow into Fura. "Indigenous majority parties. I've rarely felt so elevated."

"Have you ever been in a bauble, Mister Cuttle?" Fura asked, in not quite so needling a manner, but still with a directness that was less than cordial.

"No, to my regret I have never seen a bauble, either inside... or outside."

"And yet, you being so well-travelled... wouldn't you have liked to tick a bauble off your list?" Fura asked.

"It is not so simple, Captain Marance."

Fura looked doubtful. "Don't tell me you haven't got the readies for it, Mister Cuttle."

"No, funds are not the... primary issue."

Fura settled back a little. "Now that I think about it, I've never heard any mention of any Crawly ever going near a bauble. Or any other alien, for that matter. Not a Clacker, not a Hardshell. That's a bit rum, isn't it? Unless there's some reason, beyond funds, that hampers you. But I can't think what it might be."

"You are very good at your work," Mister Cuttle said. "People, I mean. You have a natural aptitude for the dangerous work of baubles." He was loosening up, I sensed, getting into the voluble swing of producing our language sounds, as if he had been a little stiff until we arrived. "The flow of relics and artefacts is of benefit to your great economy, is it not? It provides employment to thousands of crews, and those crews and their ships in turn depend on a great interconnected web of businesses, from the sailmakers and chandlers at the docks, the brokers and recruiting agents, but far beyond that, to your markets and chambers of commerce. Even if my kind were able to compete on favourable terms in the opening of baubles, which we could not, lacking your resilience and fortitude, what good would be served by such a division of interests?"

"Still," Fura said, "and I'm speaking hypothetically here, so no offence intended, if you had a liking for quoins, and you couldn't winkle 'em out of baubles yourselves—for whatever reason—the present arrangement wouldn't be too shabby, would it? We do the hard work, you grease our banks to keep the funds flowing, the ships being launched and the crews paid, and after a lot of shufflin' around, those quoins magically end up in your coffers."

"Quoins are a cumbersome sort of currency," Mister Cuttle replied. "If every man and woman had to look after their own fortune, inter-world commerce would be prohibitively slow and burdensome. If a quoin is worth less than the cost of the fuel it would take to move it from one gravity well to another, then the quoin may be said to be worse than valueless. Besides, by vesting quoins in the major banks, fortunes may be allowed to appreciate."

"Or, in some cases, depreciate," Prozor said.

Mister Cuttle swivelled his hood to look at her. "Have you been the victim of such a turn?"

"No, I'm slummin' it here because I like the scenery and being pissed on day and night. What do you think?"

"I am sorry for your bad luck. I know that a number of savings accounts faltered during the crash of ninety-nine, and perhaps yours was one of them. But this is a new century, and we may hope for better times." Mister Cuttle picked up his mouthpiece again and inhaled from the gurgling contraption. "But if I may speak boldly, I would think of other places to remedy your losses, than your present location."

"Is that a threat?" I asked, my mood turning like a compass in a solar gale.

Mister Glimmery chose that moment to step into the partitioned area. He had dressed properly now, at least compared to a man wearing only a gown. He had gold trousers and shoes on, and several gold layers on his torso, made of finely stitched and embroidered materials that gave off the light in differing ways, but his arms and shoulders were completely unclothed, and so was a good part of his chest, so that—even without the evidence in his face and eyes—there would have been no possibility of forgetting that he was a victim of the glowy, nor of the extent of its hold on him. I picked up a smell from him, too, but it was sweet and honey-like rather than unpleasant, and by a certain lustre to his skin I wondered if a perfumed balm had been rubbed into him after the milk bath.

"Where is the wine?" he asked, twisting his head so that the muscles and nerves in his neck stood out like details in an anatomical drawing, so exact you could have labelled them there and then.

The wine came a moment later. Mister Glimmery lowered his frame into a vacant chair, setting his arms on the rests and yet still looming over the rest of us. He had stationed himself opposite the four of us, and directly facing the Crawly. "There, Mister Cuttle," he said obligingly. "I told you I'd bring some company, didn't I? Mister Cuttle does so appreciate some new faces, and there's precious little to keep him stimulated lately." He poured the wine into glasses, not neglecting his own measure. "Did you ask them how they came to be in the Emptyside, Mister Cuttle?"

The alien inhaled before answering. "We had hardly begun to get to know each other."

"Well, there'll be time enough for all the questions in the

world," Mister Glimmery said, setting a small gold container down on the table before him. It had an expensive look, decorated with flowers and vines, and it was about long and wide enough to contain the handle of a skipping rope. "Their friend is very unwell, you see, and Doctor Eddralder won't be held to a timescale where her recovery is concerned, assuming there's any sort of positive outcome."

"There'd better be," Fura said.

"Help yourself to wine, Captain Marance. It will take the edge off your nerves." Before Fura had a chance to reply, Mister Glimmery said: "I hardly dare ask how you came by the glowy yourself. It feels impertinent to raise the subject, but we can't very well let it go unmentioned, given that we have the condition in common. It would be odd if we did not trade reminiscences."

I could feel Fura debating her answer, but after a pause she decided and took a modest sip of the wine, quite becoming and ladylike by her standards, and just enough not to be uncivil.

I did likewise, realising with a degree of amazement how thirsty I was.

"I had to eat lightvine," Fura said. "It was that or die. Isn't that how most people end up with the glowy?"

Mister Glimmery nodded, not without some interest or sympathy. "Yes—by all accounts. Lightvine isn't harmful in and of itself, and the genetic engineers who created it must have foreseen that it might need to provide temporary sustenance, to crews in distress. But there are correct ways to prepare lightvine, and incorrect ways. I suppose you had no means of cooking it?"

"I had to eat it raw," Fura said.

"Does it trouble you?"

"I'm managing fine enough, Mister Glimmery."

"And you've sought medical opinion, from a dependable source? Someone who really understands the condition, not just some quack willing to tell you anything you'll want, so long as it lightens your pockets?"

"I've seen who I need to see."

"Then let me blunt, just in case the quality of that medical opinion left something wanting. The glowy is caused by the accumulation of viable microbial spores in the circulatory, lymphatic and peripheral nervous systems. In its early stages there is no harm done, and the infection is easily treated. If left unchecked, though—over weeks or months—the glowy takes a more insidious hold. It becomes harder to eradicate—although there are still treatments, albeit of a harsher kind. Left longer still, the course becomes more uncertain. The glowy may stabilise, even retreat, or it may penetrate the central nervous system, lodging itself in the brain, the spine, the optic nerves and so on. Then it is much more intractable. Cases are rare enough to be anecdotal, but there is speak of changes in character and intellect—of the failure of the checks and balances of a well-tempered mind. Impetuousness, borderline sociopathy, the emergence of cruel desires and a vain disregard for the needs of others. Feverish, single-minded obsessions. And torments, in the worst cases. Terrible dreams by night and wrenching agonies by day."

"No one told me it was going to be a stroll in the park," Fura said. "But I didn't choose to end up this way, and just because I've got it in me doesn't mean I've got the funds to clear it up. You seem to have both time and money, though, and yet you're a sadder case than me." She set down her glass, mostly undrunk. "How'd you come by it, seeing as we're chin-wagging?"

"By mistake," he said candidly. "But not the same mistake as your own. In some instances, the glowy can stay within a host without any outward manifestation. The host themselves may not even be aware that they carry a significant microbial load."

"That was you, was it?" I asked.

"No, that was the man I ate." Mister Glimmery waited a heartbeat before smiling, the smile pushing apart the stripes and curlicues of his glowy, the flecks in his eyes seeming to glitter in flagrant self-amusement. "I had an accident, and needed a transfusion of blood at short notice. There were spores in the blood, unfortunately, quite a high density, and I went from clean to highly infected in one unfortunate stroke. It was a mistake of screening, a serious one, but I cannot be too ungrateful. I should be dead were it not for that transfusion. Were you informed of my nickname, Far-Gone Glimmery, or sometimes just Far-Gone? It started off as Too-Far-Gone, and then they shortened it, losing something of the sense in the process."

"Could you not take the treatments?"

"No... Tragen, was it? No, too far gone for the common therapies, and the stronger remedies were in woeful short supply at the time. Now, like your good captain, I must accept what I have become... what I am becoming."

"Has it got into your grey?" Fura asked.

"It has, and deeply. There are external signs, but also neurological manifestations, some of them obvious to me, and some of them requiring the patient detection of a physician's art. Occasionally, I am..." Mister Glimmery hesitated, his face clenching quite suddenly, as if with that line of thinking had come a spasm or the acute recollection of one. "Perturbed," he continued, loosening. "But the milk baths have a soothing effect on the peripheral nerves, and there are preparations that hold the glowy's most severe attacks at bay."

"Attacks?" Fura enquired.

"The torments and agonies I mentioned." He gave her a sympathetic look. "I see you are not yet fully acquainted with the likely progression of the ailment. I mean to cause you no distress, Captain. With luck, there is still time for you." While he was speaking, his fingers had wandered to the lacquered box, toying with the latch that held down its lid, almost as if by a will of their own. Slowly, though, he withdrew his fingers and left the box where it was, unopened. "And speaking of matters medical, I did not wish to give the wrong impression about your colleague, the one you call...?"

"Greben," I said.

"Greben, yes. Well, she is in most capable hands, I assure you. I know Doctor Eddralder very well—he has been my personal physician—and we could not hope for a kinder, more skilled practitioner. Of course the work of the infirmary weighs heavily on him, but he will never turn away a deserving case."

"It is very good of him to find time for Greben," I said decorously.

"We would have it no other way, Tragen. Our guests are few enough that we may lavish particular care on those who come. On that matter, will you not consider hauling-in a little nearer?" He directed this last enquiry at our supposed captain. "Not to be blunt about it, but our agents have questioned the condition of your sails."

"What concern is that of yours?" Fura asked.

"None, except that we would be remiss if we did not help where we may. We have a great surplus of good sail and yardage in our docks, according to the merchants. It is sitting there unused, a wasted and unprofitable investment. I am informed that the merchants would be very glad to see the back of it at a favourable rate to yourselves—much better than any offer you'll get in the lower processionals, where the market sides with the seller."

"Our sails are satisfactory, thank you," Fura said. Then, scraping up some morsel of politeness, added: "But it is considerate of you to make the offer."

"Nonetheless, the invitation to haul-in closer still stands. Consider it, because it will make your affairs here much more tractable, and there need be no suspicion that you are standing off at such a distance for any particular reason."

My sister could not contain herself from glaring. "What sort of reason did you have in mind?"

"For myself, none at all. It is..." He paused, stiffening in his chair, and a twitch dimpled the cheeks on either side of his mouth. "Excuse me for a moment," he said, forcing out the words between gritted teeth. "The affliction chooses its moments well." With a strain of effort he twisted in his chair and called out: "Bring the remedy."

One of the black-gowned attendants arrived. It was a woman, carrying a small, lidded golden tray balanced on her upspread fingers. She removed the lid and offered the tray to Mister Glimmery. It contained two gold syringes.

"Are these the last of them?"

The woman leaned in and said: "Doctor Eddralder will bring a fresh supply tomorrow, sir, as arranged."

"Very well." Mister Glimmery's fingers moved from one syringe to the other, as if undecided which to use. "Bring Merrix, will you?"

"Are you certain, sir? There are just these two."

"Bring Merrix."

The attendant placed the tray on the table before him, and Mister Glimmery opened the gold box with slightly fumbling fingers. He took out what struck me as a very unremarkable object. It looked like a piece of wood, perhaps the end of a broomstick, wound from end to end with string.

"You will accept my offer of accommodation, I trust?" he asked, forcing some sort of normality into his voice, even though his continuing discomfort was obvious. "I have private rooms that are very well appointed, much cleaner and warmer than anything you will find down in the city, and very much more usefully situated with regards to the clinic. You would be able to come and go at a moment's notice, and you would avoid any sort of disturbance or unpleasantness."

"That's very kind of you, Mister Glimmery," I said, trusting that I spoke for the others. "But we have a lot of procurement to do, and I think we would find it easier if we were down in the city, close to the docks and the boutiques."

He tried to sound agreeable, but I had slighted his offer and the fleeting coldness of his expression made his feelings abundantly plain.

"Suit yourselves. You won't be very far away, no matter where you lodge."

The attendant came back. She had a girl with her this time, dressed in the same kind of black gown, but with a dazed, somnambulant look to her. I thought she might be thirteen or fourteen years old, although it was hard to be certain. She regarded us with a dull absence, as if we were no more than patterns on wallpaper that her eyes had seen a thousand times before. She was long boned, her eyes pale.

"Extend your arm, Merrix," Mister Glimmery said, not without a surprising kindness, which almost encouraged me to see him in a slightly different light. "It isn't pleasant for either of us, but you know full well this is easiest in the long term."

The girl offered her sleeve, barely glancing at him. She swayed with a certain slow rhythm, and her lips moved softly as if a song were playing in her mind. Mister Glimmery's hand dithered between the syringes before making a selection. Then, without rising, he administered one of the syringes into the girl, observed her carefully, saying nothing even as she gave a sudden convulsion and needed to be kept upright by the attendant. Mister Glimmery placed the syringe back on the tray, took the other, and injected it into his own forearm. He set it down with the first syringe, his fingers still trembling, and reached for the wooden object. Leaning back into the chair, bracing himself as if for some coming acceleration, he opened his mouth and bit onto the wooden thing.

His own convulsion hit very hard, much more fiercely than the girl's, his eyes rolling and his facial muscles going into spasm. He groaned through the self-imposed gag, his teeth digging into the string-bound stick. Both his hands were on the rests of his chair, and his whole upper torso twisted and thrashed.

It was such an odd thing to see in our host, especially as he had been making genteel conversation only a few moments earlier, that I do not think any of us had a clear sense of how long the spectacle lasted. Certainly it continued for a greater span of time than was comfortable, even as the girl was taken away and a fine bubbling froth emerged from Mister Glimmery's mouth, forcing its lavalike passage around the string-bound stick. But then an easing came upon him, and—relaxing—he removed the saliva-sodden stick and returned it to the gold box.

"You will forgive me," he said, using his sleeve to dab the froth from his lips and the sweat from his brow. "It seldom gives warning, and I felt I would be doing Captain Marance a disservice if she did not witness the full severity of the attack. They come at more frequent intervals lately, although never with any predictability. I trust you were not distressed?" He rubbed at the spot on his arm where he had injected himself. "I myself am now completely at ease, I assure you. The remedy may not be a cure, but it is effective in the short-term."

"What about the girl?" Fura asked.

"Merrix? A deserving case. Not a glowy infection, but a congenital neurological disorder that responds to some of the same treatments. It has been very difficult to settle on a treatment regime for Merrix, so in the absence of better data we each receive our treatments at the same time."

"That's a very odd way of doing it," I said.

"It's a very odd condition."

The attendant came back and removed the gold box, suggesting that there was little chance of a repeat performance for a few hours. Seemingly restored, Mister Glimmery pushed his giant frame up from his chair, the muscles in his arms bulging like bladders.

"There are a number of hotels near the infirmary," he said. "Mister S will be happy to show you to one of the more reputable establishments. In the meantime, I wish you the best of news concerning your colleague. I expect we will speak soon enough."

"We'd be happy to find our own lodgings—" Prozor started.

"I insist." He was about to take his leave from us when some faint afterthought or recollection furrowed his brow. "I meant to ask. You informed our Port Authority officials that you'd come in from the Emptyside, where you'd been working a string of baubles. I've no reason to doubt that story..." He paused, smiling very slightly. "But it made me wonder if you'd heard anything about trouble in the near Emptyside? About ten days ago, some altercation between a privateer and a pair of ships operating under the recent bounty?"

"There was nothing on the squawk," Fura said. "Nor on the

bones. And I hold my crew to a hard schedule in the sighting room."

"Ah," Mister Glimmery said. "We've had a request for assistance, you see—from the survivor of the supposed incident. They'd like to haul-in in a few days and I considered their story so unlikely I thought I'd run it by you first."

"I think we'd have heard," I said.

"Yes, that was my thought as well. How could you *not* know of such a thing, if it had happened?"

Finished with us for now, he directed a significant glance at the Crawly. Taking the cue, the obedient Mister Cuttle took a final inhalation, then placed the mouthpiece back in its holder next to the apparatus, extracted his gowned and hooded form from his personal chair, leaving us to goggle—distractedly, I admit, in light of that recent intelligence—at the curious supports and voids which were necessary to accommodate a Crawly's nether-regions.

Then the alien and the man with the glowy left us alone, and we sat there for a few moments with only the bubbling of the apparatus to break the silence.

Until Prozor said: "What'd he mean by 'bounty'?"

# 14

Sneed insisted on showing us to our lodgings. We left Surt at the infirmary, where she said she would wait until there was more news about Strambli, and followed our swaggering guide through a warren of dark streets and passages, taking a generally steepening course toward the main avenue.

Gradually there were more signs of life. Windows lit in one building, a smell of cooking from another. Shouts and laughter from a cellar door. A cove nursing a bleeding nose in a back alley, another sniffing into a bottle before tossing it aside. Mutts fighting over scraps. A robot going round and round in circles, one of his wheels jammed in a gutter, his head just a little glowing orb like a light-bulb. We climbed some more. The larger streets, running all the way around the rim, were built on the level, with ledges and terraces cut into the steepening ground. The connecting streets and alleys were all steep, eventually needing to zig-zag back on themselves. There were sheer walls with staircases going up the side of them, some rickety and some carved out of massive stone blocks and looking as if they had been that way for a thousand years, and there were buildings rising from ledges, or with their foundations jutting out into space, only a bit less precarious-looking than the infirmary.

With Sneed in our company there had been scant chance to discuss recent developments, much less the unwelcome news about the damaged ship. We would all have been happier finding our own hotel, but as Prozor reminded me in a quiet moment, it was very likely that Mister Glimmery had his own contacts in such establishments, so our whereabouts and activities would not have remained private for very long.

My legs were turning weary by the time we climbed up the last zig-zag and stumbled out into Shine Street, the name of the main avenue on this side of the wheel. At long last we had arrived at something like civilisation. We almost had to blink at the colour and brightness of it. The rainlit pavements were busy with people coming and going or clotting together by tram stops or outside the shops, bars, boutiques and hotels. The tall, narrow-fronted buildings were jumbled together like books in a badly organised library, with a slovenly disregard for content. There might be a hotel, then a sail-merchant's emporium, then a coffee house, then a tattoo parlour, then a red-windowed house of ill-repute, then perhaps a Bone Merchants or a Limb Broker.

There was a choice of possible lodgings and Sneed seemed content to allow us the final decision in this matter. Prozor selected a tall hotel with a crumbling, many-balconied facade called The Happy Return. It did not look happy to us, nor the sort of place to which one might wish to return, but Prozor had a discerning eye for such things, and she was adamant that this was the type of place most likely to do business with visiting crews, and therefore our best chance for a sort of anonymity. There was also a bar across the street, and a good selection of shops and boutiques suitable for our immediate needs.

We dismissed Sneed, assuring him that we were quite capable of minding ourselves from this point on, and then went through the revolving door into the grand lobby. It was cold and draughty and almost completely lacking in furniture or ornamentation, save for a few dead-looking plants in pots, and a couple of sturdy chairs backed into a corner. A concierge desk stood at the back of the lobby, with elevators and stairs tucked around one side. The lone clerk was turned away from us, watching the bright rectangle of a small, grubby flickerbox perched on the left side of the desk. He could hardly have missed the clatter of our boots on the lobby tiles, but he still took no notice of us until Fura was leaning on the desk, tapping her metal fingers against the zinc surface.

"We'd like some rooms."

The clerk turned off the flickerbox, then swivelled his chair to greet us. He was a small, slump-shouldered man with a very wide and flat-featured face, almost like a circular doorknob.

"How many?"

"Two. Two beds apiece, adjoining. Four rooms if you only do single occupancy."

"How many nights?"

"As many as we need."

He turned around to look at the ranks of keys and mail pigeonholes behind his desk, scratching at his chin as if we were asking him for some very difficult and unprecedented thing. He had bits of paper stuck to his jaw, with tiny specks of blood in the middle of each piece, and he gave off a strong, astringent smell.

"I can do you two rooms on the eighth floor—that's the top. Lift only goes as far as the sixth, then you have to walk. Minimum stay is three nights. You'll pay up-front."

"Is there a strong-box in the rooms?"

"No."

"Then we'll need a lock-up for our belongings, exclusive use of my party."

"That'll cost you the same as a third room."

"Add it to the bill."

After some minor haggling—instigated by Prozor, who had a nose for what was a fair arrangement, as well as a sense of honour that forbade her from being unreasonably swindled—a deposit was agreed upon and a quantity of quoins changed hands. We took the single elevator up to the sixth floor, which chimed upon its arrival, doors grinding open, then from the sixth floor landing ascended creaking stairs to the eighth, where our rooms were halfway down a long, shabby, stain-marked landing.

Prozor and I took one of the rooms, with Fura taking the other, having it all to herself for now. We agreed to see each other in thirty minutes.

It was not as bad as I feared. The taps grumbled and the pipes rattled, but the room was clean and warm enough, and there was hot and cold running water. Prozor and I stripped out of our suits and gladly rinsed off the worst of our grime. We were under proper gravity for the first time in months, not counting the bauble, and some of that dirt had been caked onto me like freckles. You never really got clean on a ship, no matter how hard you tried.

We put on our shipboard clothes, pinching our noses at the smell still clinging to them from their time in Strambli's chest. I was starting to think that the odour in that box had been a lot worse than could be explained by any sort of bodily process, and that Fura must have stuffed some spoiled goods in there as well.

Prozor went to the window and looked out through the shutters on the eighth floor balcony. I picked up on her pensiveness and knew she was meaning to say something, but needed to find the words.

"There's somethin' we ought to talk about," she said eventually.

"I didn't like the sound of that 'bounty' part either."

"We'll need to get to the bottom of that sooner or later. It sounds as if some coves have decided to put up some money to finish us off. But that's not what I meant."

"Mister Cuttle, then?"

"I was troubled by him, to start with, I won't deny. He reminded me of Clinker, another Crawly I met, and I think Fura had the same thought. I don't think he was Clinker, though there's somethin' fishy about him, beyond a doubt—I'd like to know what his business is with Glimmery, to start with—but that ain't it, either." A tram slid past, blue light flashing off its cable, picking out Prozor's form like a shock-haired statue at midnight. "This is a rum one, Adrana. I don't hardly know where to begin. But it's about your sister, and what happened in the infirmary."

"What?"

She stood silent before answering.

"I wish I was sure enough to say." The pipework rattled again. It made such a racket that I guessed that Fura was running hot water in her room. In any case it did a good job of masking our conversation. "When they winched up our stuff, those coves had that basket under control. Until Fura barged in, shoved Sneed's men aside and…"

"And what?"

"I saw something 'tween her fingers. Like a bit of glass that wanted me to forget it. And she flicked it out right through the cable holding up that basket."

"You're saying she cut it deliberately." I paused, hearing what she was saying, knowing on some level it must be true, but part of me wanting to find a flaw in it. "She was wearing most of a suit, just like the rest of us. How did she hide a Ghostie blade?"

"You don't need to hide a Ghostie blade, it does the hidin' for you." Prozor turned from the window, frowning with concentration. "I think she must've had it stuck on her tin arm, somehow, where it wouldn't show up. She had it in her flesh fingers—in her suit glove, I mean, not her other hand. If she had it hidden on her left arm somewheres, she'd have reached for it with her right hand, wouldn't she?"

"But they took a knife from her already."

"I think that was the one she meant for 'em to find. To put 'em off the scent, so to speak."

I thought of how easy it would have been for Fura to fix a Ghostie blade onto her left arm, all of us long past the point where we paid that limb any attention. Prozor was right, as well. A Ghostie weapon could be lying in practically plain sight and your eyes would slide off it like a worn boot heel on black ice.

"Why would she do such a thing? She was furious about it."

The plumbing continued to rattle away, but Prozor still directed a guarded look at the adjoining wall. "I can only think of one reason. She knew those parts weren't worth much to us, and easily replaced. But it keeps us from leaving too soon."

"We'll leave when Strambli's well, and not a moment sooner."

"You'd say that, and so would I. But if Strambli took a turn... and you know what I mean by that... if there wasn't a *reason* for us to remain, why wouldn't we leave as soon as we were able?"

The plumbing gave a rattling shiver and then stopped making its din. Through the walls I heard Fura stomping around on loose floorboards.

"Why would she want us to stay here any longer than necessary?" I asked, entirely innocently of course, since I already had a shrewd idea of the answer and it began and ended with the name Lagganvor.

"She's got her reasons—she just hasn't got around to sharin' 'em with the rest of us. When Snot-nose showed up and it became clear things had gone from bad to worse in this place, I reckon she started worryin' we'd all get the jitters and want to clear out."

"But it makes no sense. Why would she be the one who's keen to remain? I know she was secretly hoping we'd fall in with her choice, and go to Kathromil. But we took the vote."

Prozor nodded slowly. "We think we did. But she's got a good case of the glowy in her now, and it turns coves sly, as well as makin' 'em latch onto things that aren't quite real."

She closed the shutters fully and moved from the window. I sat down on my bed, trying to put on a creditable act of being thoroughly shocked and discomfited by these speculations of hers.

"I know it's been getting worse," I said. "I can see that in her and it's been troubling me. But the more it takes its hold on her, the less she's going to want to see reason about getting it flushed out of her." My mind flashed back to the man in the gold room, convulsing in his chair, the string-wound stick jammed into his mouth. "I don't want her ending up like Glimmery."

Prozor faced me on her own bed, tucking her hands into her lap. I remembered how spiky and forbidding she had been when we first met her, how unimpressed by us she was, how unlikely it had been that I might feel warm thoughts toward her. Now she felt like a second sister to me, and closer than the one with whom I shared my blood.

"You'd tell me, wouldn't you, if you'd seen anything else about her?"

I skated the edge of telling her everything I knew, about the translated journals and the man she sought. We would be square then, but I would still have to explain to Prozor, this good and loyal friend, why I had not trusted her with this information until now.

Perhaps I even drew in a breath, ready to blurt it all out. Whatever Prozor had to say to me, I knew I would feel better in myself once the secret was shared.

But I could not.

The silence weighed. Presently Prozor pushed herself to her feet. "I'll go and see how her ladyship's feelin', shall I?"

*

Fura knocked on my door. She was dressed to go out, in a blouse, waistcoat, long skirt and boots. She had rummaged through her hair, tangling it to her evident satisfaction, so that it formed an unruly black halo around her head and shoulders.

"Where's Prozor?" I asked, realising she was alone.

"Gone ahead to scout out a table for us. If our luck's in she'll get the first round of drinks, too. Here." She threw me a laundry bag, which I caught automatically, just as if we were playing a game of ball in the long upstairs hallway of our old house. "Little present for you."

I opened the drawstring, and was immediately assaulted by the odour.

"It smells terrible—even worse than the other bags. I thought it was Strambli's wound, making that chest stink as badly as it did."

"Strambli didn't make it any fresher, no, but I helped it along a bit, just to deter those coves from taking too close an interest in the contents. Worked, didn't it?" She grinned, supremely pleased with herself. "I had to snatch a moment alone with her, when Eddralder wasn't with her, but that was enough."

"What are you talking about?"

"Open the bag."

I let her in, pushing the door ajar behind her, and tipped out the bag's contents onto my bed. There were a few nondescript items of underwear inside it, just off-colour enough to deter close examination, but these were merely padding or camouflage for the main items. There were two. One was small black pouch, about the size of a deck of cards, with a translucent block jutting from one end. The other was a compact grey box, which in some other life might have sufficed to contain a quantity of jewellery or make-up but which I fancied now served some darker purpose. I examined the small black pouch first, sliding out the translucent substance.

I recognised it instantly.

There was not enough of it to make anyone's fortune, but it was handsome piece nonetheless, and better than the rough item that had come with Fura from Trusko's ship. It was lookstone: one of the oldest relics known to crews, found in all baubles and believed to originate from the Second Occupation.

Squeezing it gently, I raised it to the level of my eyes, which were facing the blank wall between our rooms. The lookstone, frosted until then, gained a greasy transparency. Within the bounds of that little rectangle, the wall melted away. I could see into Fura's room, just as if there was a neat hole drilled into the wall, a hole which moved obligingly if I shifted the angle of the lookstone.

I squeezed a little harder, and the lookstone peered right through into the room beyond the adjoining one, and then further still, until I was staring down a sort of tunnel that went all the way out of the hotel, into the hot, dark night over Port Endless. Further still, and the lookstone offered a glimpse of the space beyond Wheel Strizzardy, out through the swarm of ships hauled close by, each vessel becoming glassy as my vision swept through it, so that for a moment I saw a blueprint-like fascination of ribs and spars, of struts and decks and divisions, of machines and tanks, of crews of tiny living skeletons busy with their chores.

"I brought it to trade with," Fura said, "if we get into a fix and run out of quoins, but mainly to keep ourselves safe. We can spy on each other very easily, so we'll always know if the other one's in trouble. Keep it with you from now on. I'll always have my piece on me."

"Did you think it likely they'd have confiscated something as harmless as lookstone?"

"No, although I wouldn't have put common pilfering past them, and I saw no good reason to throw 'em our prize takings like doggie biscuits. Take a gander at the other item, though. It's a prettier piece by far, and *not* what you'd call harmless."

I opened the box's hinged lid. Inside was a padding of purple silk, in which lay embedded a semi-transparent object that, under other circumstances, I might have taken for a toy pistol, or perhaps some novelty ornamentation to be worn with an evening gown. It was dainty, with jewelled ornamentation and a scarlet blush to its mostly transparent body.

"Where did you find this?"

"Among Bosa's effects. Kept under her desk, which I took to mean it was one of her favoured trinkets."

"It's not Ghostie," I said carefully, studying her expression.

"No, but just as rare—or nearly enough. It's a volition pistol. Eighth or ninth Occupation, so I believe. I'll be straight with you—I was planning on keeping it as my own."

"Why don't you?"

"Because I'm left-handed, and it turns out that a volition pistol needs flesh and blood to work properly. It's much better that you have it, considering."

"That's very sweet of you."

"It's an energy blaster, with a self-renewing power core. Variable intensity settings, from a nasty sting all the way up to high lethality. We'll test it later. I want to know it can disable a cove, without killing them."

"Lost your taste for killing?"

"Lost my taste for complications. For now. Take it out of the box. Get a feel for it, like I never could."

I took out the little weapon. I had small hands, but even so I could barely curl two fingers around the grip.

"Why is it called a volition pistol?"

Fura smiled. "Just be careful who you point it at."

*

The bar across the road was a flight of steps down from street level, a warren dug a long way back into the bedrock, with rooms, passages and snugs connected together in a geometry that was puzzling enough when sober, which I very nearly was despite Mister Glimmery's wine, and would have been downright perplexing otherwise.

There were no windows, just a few electric lights and some sickly lightvine that had been encouraged to fester over the ceiling and walls. Flickerboxes were on in a couple of corners, and a robot or two was bustling around clearing tables. There were clients of every sort, from coves in vacuum suits, some quite well-heeled types, all the way down to slouching or comatose drunkards. Even a few aliens were there, either keeping to themselves—reading newspapers or suchlike—or engaged in some sort of shifty business with their monkey companions. They had their own concoctions, drinks that shone vivid green or blue.

Prozor had found a snug for us, and already done the honours with regard to our drinks. Fura and I squeezed in next to her. Fura had a coat on over her blouse and waistcoat, but she shrugged out of it now that it was warm in the bar, and set her forearms onto the table, the metal one clacking against the wood. Pressed against Prozor, I felt the bulge of the volition pistol against my chest, where I had squeezed it into an interior pocket of my own jacket.

"I squawked Surt, and then I squawked the ship," Fura said. "There's no news on Strambli yet—but then I wasn't really expecting any, not for a few hours."

Prozor took the head off her beer with a swipe of her hand, then licked at her palm with an unhurried catlike attentiveness. "What did Tindouf have to say?"

"I only spoke to Paladin. Told him to maintain squawk and sweeper watch, and keep Tindouf on his toes."

"Did you mention the ship that might be dropping by?" I asked.

"The one Glimmery asked us about? It's probably nothing."

"The way Glimmery put it," I said, "it sounds like it could be the survivor of the two ships that were on our stern."

"Speculation, until we have something more concrete." Fura sipped at her own beer. "We can't go jumping at every shadow. Ships trade shots with each other all the time, especially in the Emptyside. We gave 'em the slip around the swallower, anyway. There's no reason for them to follow us all the way to Wheel Strizzardy, especially after we showed 'em our fangs."

"Unless they have injured coves, and damage, and this is the nearest port of call," I said. "Then they might limp here for entirely practical reasons. We should determine their plans, and whether or not Glimmery means to offer them safe haven. Then we ought to find out how far out they are—whether it's days or weeks, depending on how badly we got them. And then we should take every care to make sure we are long gone before they catch sight of our sails, and start piecing together what we are."

"If they ain't already smoked us," Prozor said.

"We'll concern ourselves with that ship... if it even exists...

when we have confirmation of it," Fura said. "Paladin will be the first to inform us. He can use his sweep with impunity now, so we'll have ample warning."

I understood her meaning. We were docked close to a world that was already employing powerful sweepers of its own, to monitor nearby space traffic, so there was no loss of concealment or surprise in using our own.

"In the meantime," I said, "one of us should check on Surt. She'll need to know her way to the hotel, and I don't like the idea of Sneed showing her the way."

"We've shopping to do first," Fura said. "All of us. And it'll be easier and quicker if we take on separate items. The suit parts are our first priority. You and Proz can sniff out a bargain or two, can't you?"

"And you?" I asked.

"I'm mindful of the condition of our skull. While it's still sending, we ought to be prepared for the worst. I'm going to scout out some of the local wares, and see if anything fits our needs." That decided—to her satisfaction, at least—she set down her drink and pushed up from her chair. "We'll meet here in a couple of hours? Stay sharp, and if you feel that Sneed or his men are shadowing you, give 'em the slip as best you're able."

Without any great ceremony, we left the bar and went our agreed ways. Fura crossed the road, and I soon lost her in the passing of pedestrians and trams.

It was still raining. Prozor and I backed under an awning for a few seconds.

"I was wondering if you were going to bring up the accident with the basket," I said. "Then I was more than a little glad you didn't."

Across the street, under an awning similar to our own, a man was trying to light a match. He kept taking one out, striking it, then discarding it when the match failed to light—but he persisted, taking out those matches with a strange and dogged regularity, until on the twelfth or thirteenth occasion the flame took.

"I thought we'd be better off seeing what she's up to," Prozor said, stepping aside as the awning billowed and discharged half its cargo of built-up water. "We need a new skull eventually, that's plain, but it's not half as important as the provisions or the suit parts. Mainly I think the good cap'n just wanted an excuse to send us off on an errand, so she could get on with her own—whatever that happens to be."

I was about to answer her when a pair of trams crossed in front of us, and when my view was clear again, instead of the man with the match what caught my eye was Fura, doubling back the way she had come, crossing over to our side of the street (unseen by Prozor, since I blocked her sight-line) and eventually vanishing back into the entrance to the bar we had all just left.

That familiar anger burned in me again. I was being lied to, by my own sister, and lies were a risk to us all. I felt a tingling in my fingers, a rawness under my nails, and realised it was the memory of digging my claws into Surt, for a crime she had not even committed.

Now I imagined a different neck under my grasp.

I slowed my breathing, forcing the anger to diminish, becoming as cool and faint as one of the oldest stars in the Swirly, those stars that were here before monkeys and would be here long after us; red-gold stars for whom our frantic little adventuring of worlds and Occupations and Sunderings was but a moment between vast slow inhalations.

When I was certain there was no chance of her coming back out again, I extended a hand beyond the awning.

"I think the rain's easing off a little."

# 15

I need not labour the shopping expedition. We had an inventory of the parts that needed replacing, no shortage of quoins, and also no shortage of places that sold the sort of wares in which we had an interest. We had to be a little scrupulous, though, not to throw our money around as if it had no value to us. Hard bargains had to be driven, false economies weeded out, dishonest merchants given the full and merciless lash of Prozor's opinion. Which they were.

When we were done we had accumulated four replacement helmets of tolerable integrity, as well as sufficient hoses, valves, regulators, filters and lungstuff recirculators to cobble together four life-support systems. It was a mongrel assortment, but then so were the original items, and none of it would look out of place next to our remaining suit parts. We carried the new items in heavy clanking pannier bags, for which there was a refundable deposit.

I will not say that we were pleased with our success, because our heads were filled with entirely too many qualms for that—Fura's behaviour, the question of the damaged ship, the troubling interest of Mister Glimmery—but nor were we displeased, and I felt a quiet satisfaction that we had already scuppered Fura's delaying tactics, at least in this one regard. She must have thought it would take more than one shopping expedition to meet our needs, perhaps several days of it, but she had not allowed for Prozor's tenacity and quick wits.

We were a few minutes early, so before we returned to the bar we went back to the hotel. Prozor needed to use the toilet, so she hurried back to our room while I lugged the bags up two flights of stairs to our landing, and then along the corridor to the lock-up. Halfway through that process I was perspiring so much that I took off my jacket and opened our door just wide enough to toss it onto my bed. I went back down to the sixth floor, collected the remaining panniers and sweated them to the lock-up.

I was just starting back down the corridor when something caught my eye at the far end, near the top landing. It was hard to make out, since there was only a single light at the top of the stairs, but I was certain I saw a shadowy form creeping down to the seventh floor.

I had about a second to choose whether I knocked on our door to summon Prozor, or just went after the shadowy figure on my own. I decided on the latter. It was just a shadow, but some suspicious corner of my mind was alert for a furtive, rather than legitimate, movement and it was telling me that this cove was trying to sneak down those stairs without being seen. I hurried to the end of the hallway, then out onto the landing, where the stairs came up through a square lightwell that went all the way back down to the lobby. I peered down, leaning cautiously over the bannister.

"You!" I called, catching a glimpse of the descending figure as it rounded one corner of the staircase. There was a cloak, and a hood, and the form moved with a shuffling locomotion that spoke of only one possibility. "Mister Cuttle!"

The descending form paused, its hood twitching my way, and for an instant some twiglike sensor or appendage projected from the hood. Then the Crawly redoubled his descent, one of his forelimbs skimming against the bannister. I set off after him, skipping down two stairs at a time, even as my bones protested.

"Cuttle!" I called again. "Whatever Glimmery sent you for, you have no business snooping on us!"

I caught another glimpse of the alien as he skirted a corner, sensing that he was moving with a new urgency. I redoubled my own descent, and I had taken a gamble on skipping three steps when my ankle gave way and I went tumbling onto the seventh floor landing. I lay there for an instant, quite winded by the impact, my cheek and jaw pressed into hairy, threadbare carpet that might as well have been sandpaper for all the cushioning it offered. Then I gathered myself up, winced as I placed weight on my foot, and hobbled on. My ankle ached, but since nothing had snapped or torn, I thought it a minor sprain not any lasting injury.

I did not intend to hurt Mister Cuttle—Bosa's anger was not roused by this intruder, strangely—but had I not discarded the jacket I might have been tempted to sting him with the volition pistol, provided I could have found the lowest setting. Cursing myself for throwing the jacket and pistol onto the bed, I continued my pursuit, thinking that at the very least I could grab the alien and pin him against a wall. Why did I not wish the equivalent of his neck under my fingers? Because he had not lied to me, I supposed, and his actions—puzzling though they were—were more a mystery to be solved, than a clear and direct threat to the security of our ship and crew. Bosa's anger, I was starting to sense, was not an indiscriminate thing. It had purpose and capabilities of curious restraint.

That, or I was learning to wield it, as one would a weapon.

I was halfway down the flight of stairs between the seventh and sixth floors when I heard the chime of the elevator. "Cuttle!" I shouted, knowing I would lose him if he made it into the elevator ahead of me. "You can't get away!"

Which was, of course, rather contrary to the truth, but I hoped the confident certainty of my declaration might give him pause for some tiny but decisive interval.

I heard the grind of the elevator doors, a shuffle of footsteps, and a moment or two later the sound of the doors closing again. Then the whine of the elevator's motor as the car began to descend back down to the lobby level.

"No!" I called out, despite the self-evident futility of it.

There was only the one elevator and if I waited for the car to return, Mister Cuttle would be out of the hotel and into the night long before I made it to street level. But I could not hobble down the stairs fast enough to catch him.

Still wincing, I made it to the sixth floor landing and hammered the elevator button, as if by some magic I might short-circuit the mechanism and freeze the car between floors. That was when I heard a patter of light, rapid footsteps on one of the floors above mine, and I looked back up the stairwell to the eighth floor landing, where Prozor had just appeared, leaning recklessly far over the bannister.

"It was Cuttle," I said breathlessly. "Him or one just like him. Sneaking down from our floor. He's on his way down to the lobby."

But Prozor looked past me and down and said: "He ain't on his way down, girlie. He's already there."

Her meaning eluded me since the elevator was still in motion, and I knew Mister Cuttle could not possibly have made it down six sets of winding stairs in the time since I had last glimpsed him. I followed the direction of her stare in any case, and then understood only too well.

I was still six floors above the lobby, so it formed a small square of black and white tiles, like a pattern at the end of a rectangular kaleidoscope. A dark form lay smeared across a portion of those tiles. I knew instantly what it was, of course, but to begin with I resisted the recognition, not wishing to accept the fact of it, as if by the act of that acceptance I might concretise something which had not yet slipped into full and definite certitude. There was a hood, a gown, a spray of broken limbs and appendages, like a sack of twigs that had ripped open, and a dark green stickiness encroaching further and further into the regularity of the tiles.

Prozor was coming down the stairs from the eighth floor landing and I wanted her by my side very badly. My feelings toward Mister Cuttle had been neutral in the company of Mister Glimmery, although I had strived to be cordial. When I had detected his presence here, my sentiments had shifted to a hard suspicion, and yet even then I had wished to corner and interrogate him, not see him broken and ruptured six floors under me.

I realised then that I was being observed.

There was a watcher, precisely level with me. It was in the space between me and the opposite side of the stairwell, floating in mid-air. It was an eye, or more properly an eyeball, very accurate in its size and details, from the white of its globe to the fine veins on that globe, to the pupil and iris regarding me with an immense, unblinking intensity. I stared at it and the eye stared back, and although I was the more shocked party—how could it be otherwise?—the eye could not help but appear startled, simply because it was an eyeball, absent of eyelids, absent the context of a face, and incapable of evoking any expression but a sort of continuous fearful astonishment.

Prozor was just rounding the last set of stairs, onto the landing. I turned to her to declare that there was an eye watching me and demand her immediate confirmation of it, but I was paralysed into speechlessness and all I could do was make a stupid guttural clicking sound.

"What is it, Adrana?"

Perhaps she sensed that there was more to my stupefaction than the mere fact of Mister Cuttle's demise. I turned back, just in time to see the eyeball drop away, much faster than if it had been simply obeying the pull of gravity, or the centripetal illusion that passed for gravity in Wheel Strizzardy. And then it was gone.

Prozor joined me at the bannister.

"He might have stumbled, I suppose."

"There was something looking at me. A few seconds ago." I swallowed before I finished what I had to say. "An eye. Just hovering out there."

I expected her to question or refute my observation, but all it seemed to do was put a new severity in her face, as if all our troubles had only been a rehearsal until this point.

"We'd better go and see Mister Cuttle. Have you got a strong stomach for this sort of thing?"

"I'm learning."

It would have taken me as long to make my way down the six remaining flights as it did to wait for the elevator again, but Prozor wanted to get to the lobby sooner than that so she rushed ahead and was kneeling next to the broken Crawly when I came out.

"I can't be sure he's the same one," she said, lifting back his hood very delicately, so that more of his face was visible. "But I'd stake quoins on it if I were pushed. Cuttle must have been sent here as soon as Sneed reported back to Glimmery about our hotel."

It was a very bad thing to have happened. Unlike a monkey, Mister Cuttle was hard on the outside and mostly soft within. The fall had crushed and shattered the outermost parts of him, so that a stew or soup of brackish green had been free to spill and ooze out onto the floor. It was still oozing, and Prozor had to shuffle back in her kneeling position as the vile tide threatened to lap against her shoes. One of Mister Cuttle's longer appendages, a sort of forearm, had come off completely, and the single hooked digit on the end of that limb was still twitching, tapping against the floor.

I was struck by two powerful, conflicting emotions. One was the sense of awe that came from being in the presence of a profoundly alien individual, whose life process were entirely distinct from our own. The second was a wrenching sense of empathy, a conviction that no creature deserved a death like this.

"You were careless," I said, noting where Prozor had planted a footprint in the middle of the green spillage.

"It weren't me," she answered, standing up, and exhibiting a clean pair of soles.

We were just around the corner from the concierge desk and it struck me as rather odd that no notice had been taken of recent developments. I moved around into sight of the desk, with its still-glowing flickerbox and the keys and mail pigeonholes behind it. The round-featured clerk was still there, but slumped face-down on a newspaper.

I went to him and lifted his head slightly. There was drool blotting the newspaper, and some faint animation stirred in the slits of his eyes.

"Out like a light," I said to Prozor. "Knocked out by something."

A cold draught kissed the back of my neck. I turned around. It was the revolving door, wafting some of the night's damp into the lobby. Fura was coming through.

"I thought we agreed to meet at the bar?"

"We did," I said, with a terse disregard for her feelings. "Then we ran into the small matter of a dead Crawly."

"What?"

"Mister Cuttle came down from Glimmery's palace. We think it's him, anyway. He was sneaking around upstairs when I surprised him. Then…this." I nodded over to the corpse, which she would have noticed for herself soon enough, since it was in plain sight.

She stared, the glowy brightening around her eyes and nose as if it were freshly daubed warpaint.

"What in chaff did you to do him?"

"She didn't do anythin'," Prozor said. "The cove fell, or was pushed, but it weren't anything Adrana did. Someone else was here, too. Knocked out the knob-faced cove on the front desk, too. Did you see anyone comin' out, as you were approachin'?"

"No."

Fura joined us at the fallen Crawly. By now two or three other guests had been drawn from their rooms and were looking down from the next landing over the lobby, but it only took a sharp look from Fura to convince them that this was not their problem.

She examined Cuttle with what I believed was the same commingling of revulsion and pity I had felt. There was a toughness about my sister, and an increasing estrangement, but she was not so far removed from her former self as to be devoid of the kinder sensibilities.

"This is a very bad business," she said, in a tone of low, slow reverence. "I like to pick my enemies in my own good time. I wanted to know what they were about, but that doesn't mean I was in any rush to get on the bad side of the Crawlies."

"If he was here on Glimmery's business," I said, "then who killed him?"

"That footprint might be a clue," Prozor said.

"The elevator sounded as Mister Cuttle was coming down. I thought it was him, calling it up from the lobby, but now I wonder if it was someone else coming up." I glanced at Prozor, then back to Fura. "Something else, too, and I'm not sure how it fits. Just after Mister Cuttle fell, there was an eye."

"An eye," Fura echoed.

"Just floating there, looking at me. And then it went. I've never seen or heard of anything like that. Have you?"

"No... nothing like that."

It was either a lie, or a scarcely credible error of recollection. But we must both have seen the entry in Bosa's private journal where she spoke of giving Lagganvor the gift of an eye, and wishing for it back. I had never heard of an eye such as this, one that could float around on its own, but it seemed unlikely that the two eyes were unrelated.

My anger swelled, my palms turning slick with sweat and anticipation. Confront her now, I thought, and be done with it. All the lies, all the evasion, out in the open—and let Prozor be the arbitrator. But a shrewder part of me encouraged the anger to dampen down again, and to my quiet satisfaction it obeyed.

I wished to see how her scheme was going to adapt.

Fura retraced her steps from the revolving door. Then she

knelt down and prodded a patch of stickiness on a white tile. "Whoever stepped in him is long gone. We can guess it was the same person that tipped him off the stairs, if that's how it happened." And then, with a firmer emphasis: "I didn't see anyone. I crossed over between two trams, and came straight in. I was minding where I stepped, not who was coming and going from this flea-pit."

"I believe you," I said. "It's not as if you'd have anything to cover up, is there?"

Fura eyed me, but an answer she might have been considering was snatched from her lips by the renewed movement of the revolving door. We all turned, doubtless forming a host of individual theories as to the likely identity of the incoming party. I doubt if any among us imagined that the door was about to divulge two Crawlies, though. They came through via separate partitions, shuffling in their hunch-shouldered fashion, hoods low over the mysteries of their faces.

"Remain," said a Crawly's rustling voice, like a parcel of sticks being rubbed together.

"We didn't do this," I said.

"Remain. Do not attempt evasion."

Something metallic glinted out of a fold in the first Crawly's hood, clutched in a birdlike talon. The second produced a similar item. I did not need to recognise a weapon to know a weapon, and I raised my hands in slow, unthreatening fashion.

"Why did you kill Mister Cuttle?"

"We did not kill him," I answered, trying to sound firm but rather undermining my efforts with the nervous quaver in my voice. "He came here for some reason, probably on the authority of Mister Glimmery. I was trying to speak to him when he ended up down here."

"You are party to a crime against our kind. There will be very serious repercussions."

"She didn't do it," Prozor said, sighing slightly. "Look at the mess someone left after they stepped in your friend. Someone came here, tripped Cuttle over the bannister, and scarpered fast. You can look at our shoes if you like. You'll see that the sole patterns don't match."

"The man at the desk is out cold," I said. "Maybe he saw something before they put him under."

"Move away from Mister Cuttle."

"Gladly," Fura mouthed. We stepped aside, backing against the wall with the chairs and the potted plants. The two aliens moved to either side of their fallen associate.

"A third party was here," said the second Crawly, bending over the remains of Cuttle, but keeping the hem of its cloak clear of his broken parts and the dark green margin of his inner ichor. "It is likely that the third party was the culpable agent."

"But these are not absolved."

"No, they are not absolved. But the unconscious one may prove a material witness."

They were speaking our language until that point, a queer sort of courtesy, but then they broke into a much more rapid exchange of rustling and snapping sounds, like a bonfire just getting started. It was futile to try and guess which Crawly was speaking and which listening, and if they had been monkeys it would have been a case of each talking rudely over the other, but their faculties of language and comprehension were as different from our own as speech is from the quacking of ducks.

Something rum happened then, and it disturbs me even now. The Crawlies began flicking something over the corpse of Mister Cuttle, scattering tiny saltlike grains from somewhere within their gowns. I was touched by it, initially, thinking we were witnessing some tender rite or observance of the dead. Perhaps we were. I have heard it said that birds will scatter flowers on their own deceased, and I am sure there are stranger ceremonies among the many sentient species. But this was like nothing in my narrow experience.

Mister Cuttle began to give off smoke. It started in two or three places then took a more fervent hold, and within ten or fifteen seconds that smoke was coming out of every part of his corpse, even the pieces that I would testify had never been touched by the saltlike grains. It consumed him totally, and yet there was no smell, no sound, nor any sense of the smoke lingering in the higher spaces of the lobby. It seemed, instead, to disperse into invisibility once it had lifted free of his corpse, and when the smoking was done there was nothing left of the corpse, not even an ashen outline. The black and white floor tiles were exactly as grubby as they had before, neither more nor less, and if there had been a remnant trace of Mister Cuttle's former existence I do not think it lay within the reach of our forensic science, nor that of any Occupation.

The first Crawly directed the darkness of its hood in my direction.

"What is your involvement with Mister Cuttle?"

"I..." I stammered, finding it hard to think—let alone speak—given what I had just seen. "I only met him today. We all only met him today. He was with Mister Glimmery, up in his gold palace above the infirmary."

The second Crawly said: "What is your involvement with Mister Glimmery?"

"Nothing we chose," Fura said, snarling out her answer. "We docked. One of our friends is sick, and she needed treatment at the hospital. Glimmery...chaff it, why am I the one being asked? What's *your* involvement, exactly, coves?"

"Our interest is mercantile."

"Your arrival has been noted," said the other. "You came from the Emptyside, with questionable credentials."

"I think you'll find that this world is under monkey jurisdiction," I said. "Our papers were accepted by the authorities. If you've got a problem, take it up with them. We had nothing to do with the death of your friend."

"Who would have left the imprint on the floor?"

"How are we to know?" Fura asked, squaring up to the Crawly with her hands on her hips. "We've only just arrived. We didn't ask to be looked after by Glimmery, or get dragged into whatever connects you to him."

"We have common interests. But we also have points of difference."

"Mister Cuttle looked like he was pretty tight with Glimmery," Prozor said.

The aliens turned slowly around, making me think of the wooden figurines that come out of mechanical clocks when the hour strikes. The revolving door was working again. Sneed's two men came into the lobby, each carrying a pistol. One of them went directly to the slumped clerk, lifting up his head and allowing it to thump back down onto the newspaper. The clerk gave a groan and then came to startled life, throwing out an arm so suddenly that he knocked the flickerbox onto the floor, where it shattered very impressively. The other man addressed the assembled gathering, monkeys and Crawlies alike.

"Mister Scrabble and Mister Fiddle. How many times do you need to be told that you don't have dispensation to go poking around willy-nilly? You ought to know better by now. Clear off and leave these good people unmolested. They're the personal guests of Mister Glimmery, don't you know?"

"Mister Cuttle is no longer animate. His embodiment was on the floor, having fallen from above. Mister Cuttle would not have fallen by accident. There must be a culpable party."

"He oughtn't have been here in the first place, not without Mister Glimmery's say-so. You know how it works, coves. Mister Glimmery's very happy to have you nosin' around in Wheel Strizzardy, but it has to be on his terms. The trouble with you devils is you take a league when you're offered a span." He made a waving motion with his pistol. "Now scuttle off!"

"What do you want with us?" I asked, as the Crawlies made their departure, seemingly persuaded by Sneed's man.

"Mister Glimmery wanted your presence. He tried telephoning, but there was no answer from the lobby, so he thought it best to send us around just in case there was trouble."

"You got here very promptly," I said.

"We did, yes. Always got your best interests in mind, we have. Now will you come with us? Mister Glimmery's tram is waiting outside."

*

He was taking his milk bath when we arrived at the gold-walled palace above the infirmary. It was only a matter of hours since our last audience with him, so I wondered how great his need for that soothing immersion had become, and how much it must have discomfited Fura to see her own future laid out for her so starkly, like a fortune teller's card predicting only a catalogue of sorrows.

Doctor Eddralder was there as well, kneeling very awkwardly at the edge of the milk bath, while Mister Glimmery offered an arm so that the doctor might take a skin scraping. Eddralder had a black medical case opened next to him, with a selection of devices and potions already laid out on the gold tiles. He was still wearing the same full-length surgical gown, and one of the attendants held his umbrella.

"You've done enough for now, doctor," Mister Glimmery said, withdrawing the arm. "I expect our guests will be anxious for news of their colleague."

Eddralder packed away his things, then rose from his kneeling position, doing so in a single smooth oiled motion. He collected the black bag, reached for his umbrella—which was presented to him horizontally and double-handed, as if it were some ancient, venerated sword—and then nodded at Fura, Prozor and I.

"I spoke to Lizzil Taine earlier, but I believe she had trouble reaching any of you on her squawk equipment." He meant Surt, and after an instant's hesitation we all nodded as if the name was perfectly familiar to us. "I was able to procure a robot and operate on Greben. It went quite well, and I think I was able to cleanse the infectious site reasonably thoroughly."

"Reasonably?" Fura asked.

"You must make allowances for the state of our equipment, and the fact that some of our medicines are in short supply."

"The doctor is seldom satisfied," said Mister Glimmery in his liquid voice, before submerging his head beneath the milk.

"I have done what could be done, to the best of our abilities," Eddralder said. "The next couple of days will be crucial. The wound will be monitored, and if all is well she will be spared the loss of her limb. But I stress that there can be no guarantees."

"I'm sure you've done all you can," I said, looking to my colleagues for affirmation. "Might I ask something, Doctor?"

Mister Glimmery was still beneath the milk.

"By all means."

"The other patient—the girl. Merrix, wasn't it?"

I observed something tighten in his face. "What of her, Tragen?"

"I just wondered if there was a…likeness, that's all. To yourself, I mean. Mister Glimmery said she had a neurological condition, an illness that responded to a similar treatment regimen as the glowy…"

Mister Glimmery was resurfacing. The milk was cascading off the crown of his head as it emerged into view. He came out slowly, his eyes closed, and an impassive set to his features.

"There's no likeness," Eddralder said, in such manner as made it plain that there was to be no further enquiry along those lines.

"Likeness to what?" asked Sneed, stepping into the room from between two of the gold partition screens.

"Nothing, Mister Sneed," Eddralder said. "We were discussing the weather."

Sneed swaggered over to us. He still had his big brown coat on, his face sunk down into the collar, merely his nose and eyes showing above the rim. He pinched at his nostrils and wiped the resulting offending substance onto his sleeve.

"You really should have taken Mister Glimmery up on his offer of accommodation, Cap'n Marance. I hear there was a terrible goings-on at the hotel."

"Is that something stuck to your shoe, Mister Sneed?" Fura asked.

Sneed frowned, lifted up his right foot, and picked at a gluey green mass that had adhered to the sole. "Right you are, Cap'n, and very considerate of you to point it out. I must've trod in something unspeakable on my way here."

Mister Glimmery came out of the milk bath, two of his attendants presenting him with his gold gown.

"Show our guests to the private area, Mister Sneed. I will be there directly. Doctor Eddralder: you are free to return to the infirmary. You have been very helpful."

Eddralder turned to us, snapping open his umbrella in readiness for the stroll down the connecting walkway to the infirmary. "I will endeavour to keep you informed about your friend. Is there a message you'd like me to pass to Lizzil?"

"Tell her we'll be along shortly," Fura answered.

"I hope that is the case," Eddralder said, and his eyes locked onto mine with what I took to be some wordless imprecation, one that felt to me very much like a warning, offered sincerely. More a plea, perhaps, than a threat.

We were in danger in Glimmery's company. I had sensed it from the moment we met him, but until now I had not quite triangulated Eddralder's place in things. Now I had a better sense of it. I believed that Merrix was his daughter, and that Eddralder was under some degree of coercive control. He had refuted the likeness, but in the paleness of her eyes, and her long-boned looks, I believe I put the lie to his denial.

We were taken to the same enclosure where we had been introduced to the late Mister Cuttle. The wine was gone now, and so was the complex glass apparatus that had served the Crawly's requirements. Now there was just a tea urn and some small shot glasses.

"Sit yourselves," Sneed said. "There's news, coves, and it'll gladden your hearts, I'm sure."

"What would this news be?" Fura asked.

Sneed poured the tea before answering. "It's about that shadow hanging over you—that cloud of suspicion we alluded to."

"I don't recall any such allusion," I said.

"Well, never fret, because it's about to be dispersed in any case. That ship that squawked in, the one that was in need of help?"

"What of it?"

"You're all going to be extriculated from under this cloud I just mentioned. Exonerised. And in pretty short order, too."

Mister Glimmery joined us. He was just wearing his gold gown now, cinched loosely across his chest, and he still gave off a delicate milky smell, seasoned with rare spices. "I see Mister Sneed has begun to speak of the matter I felt was worth your attention. We have had renewed contact with the damaged vessel I mentioned—the one operating under the letter of marque of the recent bounty. With which you are amply familiar, I am sure."

"Amply," Prozor said.

"Let us be sure we are equally up to date." Mister Glimmery sipped at a measure of tea, the glass pinched delicately between his thumb and forefinger. "A few months ago, a consortium of banking and shipping concerns, spread across many worlds, agreed to do something about Bosa Sennen. Now, you may have your own opinions as to whether that name connotes some actual figure, or serves instead as a catch-all for all the miscreant elements who ply the high processionals and the low vaults of the Near Empty, making an easy living by bauble jumping and the reckless plundering of honest vessels. I myself have no fixed view on the matter. What I do know is that there *are* losses to shipping and profit, and criminality is almost certainly a factor."

"A terrible thing, criminality," Fura stated.

"Quite, Captain Marance. I am pleased that we are of one mind on the matter."

"The thing is," Sneed chipped in, "they've had enough of it."

"There was a spate of losses near the end of '99," Mister Glimmery said. "Rackamore, Trusko and others. Honest captains, honest crews lost, we presume, to violent action. The combines and privateer fleets have lost their patience, and who can blame them? Now there is a push to strike back. It begins in modest fashion. An incentive—a bounty, in plainer terms. A select number of privateer captains were invited to take up the hunt, within stipulated terms of action and engagement. They have been given good equipment and compensated for the loss of ordinary earnings while they sweep the hunting grounds most favoured by their illustrious quarry. Two of those captains were Restral and Chemaine. Old rivals turned friends, and in command of two excellent, swift sunjammers: the *White Widow* and the *Calenture*, operating out of Causterant, and lately plying within ten million leagues of our present location. It was the *Calenture* that met with recent misfortune, though—attacked without provocation. Not just a disabling shot as may be permitted within the terms of civil engagement, but hull-piercing slugs, and by the accounts transmitted she came to a gory end, with only a few survivors who have suffered greatly. Chemaine died. The *White Widow* was close by and was able to effect a partial rescue, but she did not escape undamaged, for the same attack took its eventual toll on Restral's craft as well, damaging rigging and sail-control gear, and he himself was very gravely injured."

"And you mention this... why, exactly?" I asked.

"The whole affair has Bosa's hallmark, you see," Mister Glimmery said. "Which is very unfortunate for any innocent ships that just happened to be operating in the same volume of space, as you yourselves evidently were. You saw and heard nothing, and who would doubt such a claim? Yet you can understand why there might be... let us call them reasonable grounds for suspicion, shall we? Now I, having enjoyed your company, am fully settled as to my own opinion of your innocence. But not everyone will have the luxury of hearing things from your own lips, and we must make allowances for those less fortunate. As Mister Sneed has likely intimated, though, the means to clear your names will shortly be at hand. Go ahead, Mister S."

"They've taken a right hammering, Restral's lot," Sneed said. "That ship'll limp in eventually, but she ain't anywhere speedy enough to help her injured parties. Just like you, with your poor chum, they need to use our excellent facilities, and not be too slow in getting here."

"Then," Fura said, "it would appear they have a problem."

"But one," Mister Glimmery said, raising a finger, "for which a partial solution lies within our reach. They have put their most severely injured personnel into a rocket launch and sent them on ahead. It has cost them their entire supply of fuel, and the launch will speed by us unless one of our own is sent out to intercept. But that we can arrange very easily. In thirty hours we hope to effect that rendezvous, and very shortly after that, Restral's party—the injured, and those deputised to care for them—will be here."

Fura nodded slowly. "I'm very happy for them."

"As are we all, Captain Marance. But for you especially this is welcome news, is it not? So much nuance is lost over the squawk. When Restral's party arrives, we will at last have a coherent account of what happened to those two ships. I am in no doubt that Captain Restral's crew, once they have spoken to you, and clarified the position and course of your own ship at the time in question...and perhaps satisfied themselves with a visual inspection of the *Grey Lady*...why then they will be more than willing to clear you of any possible involvement."

"You'd like that, wouldn't you?" Sneed asked.

"I did not realise I was required to prove my innocence," Fura said.

"You are not, Captain, and let no one cast any unwarranted aspersions." Mister Glimmery took the opportunity to recharge his shot glass. "But tongues will be tongues, and a lingering... rumour...could be disadvantageous to fair commerce. Restral is a respected authority, and once he has underscored your honest credentials, and those of your ship and crew, you will have the tacit blessing of all the concerns united behind that letter of incentive. Credit will flow your way. The banks and ports will rush to your assistance, secure in the knowledge that you operate a ship of excellent reputation."

Fura considered this, took a sip of her tea, then said: "It sounds very reasonable, Mister Glimmery. I have nothing to conceal, so no cause to be concerned. Indeed, I would offer all practical assistance in the matter of Captain Restral's party, were our own fuel reserves not also depleted."

"Generous of you to even consider it," Glimmery said. "But rest assured that all is in hand. Now, setting aside the unfortunate incident with Mister Cuttle—which I trust you will put behind you—is all to your satisfaction? The doctor confided in me that he would like your colleague to remain under close supervision for a number of days, but if my reading of his mood was correct, Eddralder was quietly satisfied with the outcome of the operation."

"I'm glad to hear it," Fura said. "You've had a long working relationship with Eddralder, then, to know him so well?"

"It is fair to say that our acquaintance has grown closer over time. Speaking for myself, I find his services quite invaluable."

"He seems to know more about the glowy than most."

"It is a particular interest of his, yes. Did he discuss your own situation?"

"No, it didn't come up."

"You still have time. I doubt you were infected more than a year ago? With the right therapies...an aggressive course of flushing agents..." Mister Glimmery halted, and a curious disaffection showed in his face, as if he had been struck by a sudden toothache. "You have much further to go than me. Might we...move..."

"I'll fetch it," Sneed said. "Do you want the remedy? We've got fresh shots."

"No...not necessary. But bring the biting stick."

Sneed stood up, poked his nose beyond the partitioned area, and called for one of the attendants.

"I was just saying..." Mister Glimmery said, shoulder muscles moving powerfully under the gold of his gown, "that we might move onto a more...commodious..."

"Did you send that eye?" I asked.

Sneed was handed Mister Glimmery's lacquered box, which he set down on the table before the larger man, opening the lid but not going so far as to remove the string-wound stick.

"Eye, Tragen?"

"There was an eye looking at me, just after Mister Cuttle fell. I saw it shoot off, and I wondered if someone had sent it."

"I did send it, yes," Mister Glimmery said, after gritting his teeth through a momentary spasm. "A remote security device. Think no more of it. I just wished to know that my...guests... were..." He jerked, stiffening in his chair and arching his spine, the muscles and sinews in his neck writhing like a nest of worms, and even as his own eyes rolled to the ceiling he reached for the biting stick and clutched it as tight as a relay baton. He did not place it in his mouth, this time, but the fact of holding it appeared to offer sufficient solace, enabling him to pass through the eye of this storm. He relaxed by degrees, let out a sigh—more of relief than contentment—and allowed himself to return the stick to its container. "A minor squall," he said, with a half-smile. "I assure you that it was nowhere near as severe as the attack I embarrassed you with before."

"You didn't need the injection this time?" I asked, thinking of Merrix, on whom he had tested the dosage.

"The cure is sometimes worse than the attack, Tragen. If I sense that I have the fortitude to do without it, then I will do my utmost to do so. The efficacy of the remedy decreases with time, meaning that I must steel myself against the day when it does not work at all. Now, will you accept my apologies for this late audience? You must all be very tired, especially after your encounter with Mister Cuttle, but I was most insistent that you be notified about Captain Restral's party."

"I'm very sorry about your friend," I said.

"Mister Cuttle? Yes, we had some enlightening discussions.

But you can never speak of friendship where the Crawlies are concerned. They are useful to us, and we are useful to them, and sometimes that dictates a closeness, even a confidence, that might be mistaken for warm familiarity. But it was not friendship. There is a void between our two species as wide as the Empty—wider, in fact, than the gap between the Old Sun and any of the fixed stars. We cannot know them, and deep down they can never, truly, know us." He paused, studied his still-trembling hands, a certain fond remembrance lingering on his features, as one might reflect upon a lost pet or some kindly but passing acquaintance. "There are always other Crawlies, Tragen—we must ration our mourning to those who deserve it."

# 16

We had to insist on not being taken straight back to the hotel, but after some persuasion we were able to visit Surt, who was still keeping vigil in Doctor Eddralder's infirmary. Or was intending to, at least. She was in one of the chairs near the reception desk, lolling face-down with her arms drooping either side of her. Prozor gave her a gentle shove, just enough to rouse her.

"You look bushed, cove. You've done your stint here."

"What time is it?" Surt asked, peeling apart gummed-up eyes with her fingertips.

"Three in the morning, and we've had a rum old night of it. First they took us to see Glimmery upstairs, then we had a run-in with a Crawly back at the hotel, and he ended up dead. Now Glimmery says there's a crew of survivors on their way to us."

"Survivors of what?" Surt asked, but then some delayed process of comprehension furnished her with the answer. "Oh. I see. That ain't good, is it?"

"Not greatly," I said.

"I think the cove upstairs is trying to smoke out what we are," Prozor said, looking around to make sure we had our conversation to ourselves. "He thinks he knows, but he ain't certain. That's why he mentioned that launch coming in, when he didn't need to. Why he made a point of draggin' us all the way to his bath, just so we could be told somethin' we'd find out anyway in thirty hours."

"What's he hoping to achieve?" I asked.

"Hopin' to spook us, girlie," Prozor said. "Rattlin' our chains just enough to get us doin' something rash, like attemptin' to make a dash for it, while we still can. Then he'll know what we are."

"If he thinks we're..." I dropped my voice. "If he thinks we're anything to do with Bosa Sennen, why doesn't he just have us rounded up right now?"

"'Cause he can't be sure how many of us are left on the ship. That's the main prize, and he won't want it slippin' out of his grasp. Which it could easily do if he started clappin' the rest of us in irons and so forth. He can't even be sure if one of us is Bosa. No, he's got to play his cards very cleverly, and tellin' us about that launch was part of his gambit, and now he's got his eyes on us more than ever."

"Literally, in the case of that eye he sent to the hotel," I said.

"That wasn't him," Prozor said bluntly.

"He confessed!" Fura said.

"That's why it wasn't him. Anyway, I watched him carefully and he wasn't sure what Adrana was on about. But I think he's the sort of cove who can't stand the thought of anything going on that isn't his responsibility, so he said it was his eye even when it weren't."

"Then whose...?" Fura started.

"Someone else with an eye, I suppose," I put in.

Doctor Eddralder came over. He looked very tired, the elongation of his face more pronounced, and the shading under his own pebble-pale eyes enhanced to a bruiselike purple.

"You should get some rest, Lizzil," he said, nodding at Surt. "You've been very loyal, but there's nothing more you can do for her for the time being. Strambli needs rest, and a large portion of good luck."

"Her name is Greben," I said.

"Yes—that's what I was told. But after the operation she returned to consciousness, albeit briefly, and not with great lucidity. She was confused, and distressed, and I attempted to reassure her that she was in safe hands and her friends were not very far away. I would have called you, Lizzil, except you were exhausted, and I felt you needed rest just as surely as your friend." He paused, shaking water from his umbrella, which if anything seemed to sag along its spines more than it had before, as if it shared some of its owner's fatigue. "Anyway, she denied that her name was Greben—insisted, instead, that it was Strambli. She also mentioned other names that were unfamiliar to me—Surt, Prozor, and so on. I…did not contradict her. I find in these instances that the patient is generally more content if their falsehoods are indulged. Is *it* a falsehood, I trust? It was a slip of my tongue to mention her preferred name…"

"I was right about your daughter, wasn't I?" I asked.

If he had dismissed my assertion before, now his hesitation offered all the confirmation I sought.

"None of us choose the paths we walk, Tragen. Or should I say…Adrana?" Then, to my sister: "You would be Arafura. She was very particular about that. Said that you had led them all into trouble, but that she loved you for it. And when I asked about Captain Marance she seemed bewildered and troubled."

"I knew those names wouldn't stick," Prozor said, which would have been a damaging confession were it not abundantly plain that Doctor Eddralder had already settled his mind about our true natures.

"What you have discussed," Eddralder said, "remains between us. I do not know who you are, nor why you should wish to travel under false names. I can guess well enough, though. You are either the crew who are being sought, or you think there is a chance of your being mistaken for them. Either way, you must distance yourselves from your true identities. That is no concern of mine."

"I am very glad to hear it," Fura said.

"But you should be aware of the risks, Captain... shall we continue with the pretence?"

"Perhaps we should," she said.

"Very well, then—Captain Marance. I have ministered to Strambli... Greben... as well I can, but there are times when I will be called away and my staff may have to answer her questions. If she babbles in their presence, I am powerless to deflect their curiosity. Equally, I could do very little to stop word of her true name reaching Mister Glimmery. He has his suspicions, but as yet they are too uncertain to act upon. That may change when the launch arrives, and it would certainly change were he to pay heed to Greben. This places you in an extremely doubtful position. Would you like my advice?"

"Be my guest," Fura said.

"Leave while you are able. Abandon Greben. You have brought her here, and she would surely have died had you not. That fever would have taken her within a day, perhaps sooner. You have done what you could for her."

"You can vouch for her safety, can you?" I asked.

The bluntness of his reply surprised me. "No—not really. Nobody is safe here, as you will have likely gathered. But she will be much less safe if you are captured and interrogated, or worse, before Far-Gone claims his share of that incentive money. Need I speak for his cruelty? You may have heard him joke about how he acquired the glowy. It's true. He did kill and eat one of his enemies, and that is how he acquired the glowy."

"We do not leave," Fura said, after an interval of consideration. She was shocked, and we were all shocked, and although none of us were under the illusion that Mister Glimmery was any sort of paragon, I do not think we were quite ready to accept that he had declared his appetites so brazenly. "Not until she's ready to be moved."

"You are taking a great risk."

"It would be just as bad if we ran now. That's what he's expecting—hoping. I'm not going to give him that satisfaction."

"In which case... I admire your fortitude, and the depth of your loyalty to your injured friend."

I smiled tightly, for much as I might have wished to applaud these sentiments, I knew that Fura had ulterior reasons for not seeking an early departure. Yet, because I still wished to see good in my sister, I chose to believe that the question of Strambli's welfare was not fully absent from her thoughts.

"You are his doctor," I said quietly. "You are the one who treats him, injects him and so on. If he is the monster you claim him to be, why do you not find a way to end him?"

"Because I am his doctor," he answered, in the same soft tone. "And even if I lapsed in my... duties. Even if I could bring myself to turn my hand against him, even if I felt that some greater good would be served by that treason... there is always one complicating factor."

"Whatever you do to him," I said, understanding, "must also be done to Merrix."

*

It was closer to four in the morning by the time we got back to the hotel, and by then I was as ready for sleep as at any point in my existence. I had all sorts of doubts and qualms that ought to have kept me awake and fretting, siding with Fura in one thought and taking against her the next, but that tiredness, the accumulation of many days of worry and unrest, would not be held back any longer, and I slipped into deep, dreamless oblivion about a second after my head hit the pillow.

I was alone. Prozor had said she would take over Surt's vigil, and now Surt was sharing Fura's room next door. Just before we said goodnight, Fura had agreed to squawk Paladin, alert him to the fact of the launch, and promised that she would wake me when there was any news. I told her I did not wish to sleep for more than four hours.

In the end it was closer to six when at last she knocked on

my door, and another thirty minutes before I had washed and dressed. My foot still ached from my tumble, and there was a nice swelling around the ankle, which hampered me somewhat. I opened the bedroom shutters a little warily, not quite sure that I wished to be reminded of our situation. But by some quiet miracle the world was still there, and so were we.

It was late morning in Port Endless—well into what passed for day in this gloomy place. Perhaps one or two more sky facets had been turned on, or their brightness increased, so that the prevailing illumination was a fraction less sepulchral than the night before. The rains, too, had decreased. Parts of the sky were still emitting steam, but the former torrents were being held in moderate check. The streets below were still wet, though, and the puddles and drainage channels and sluices remained waterlogged, embedded in roads and alleys like little chips and slivers of highly reflective material. Blocky grey buildings stood out a little more distinctly than the night before, and more of the city's geometry presented itself to me. It was still dim enough that the street lights remained on, and the few windows that had been illuminated before were still lit, but in this improved light it struck me as not so terrible a place after all. A world that might have been tolerable, or even pleasant, prior to its recent troubles. I thought of Mister Glimmery's taste for gold, of the lavishness of his surroundings and his many fastidious attendants, and when I recalled the doctor's words about the glowy and how it had come to be inside Glimmery, I discovered a new shade of loathing within myself. I needed no biography or newspaper clipping to envisage the course of Glimmery's career. A strong, dangerous man who had moved from criminality to effective control of a whole world, and who now ruled by fear and blackmail. Doubtless he had been on his way to power when the last banking crisis had come, but that downturn—the same one that had cost Prozor her earnings—would only have hastened his ascent. Sneed had killed Mister Cuttle, I was sure, and since Sneed was operating under Glimmery's instructions, I had seen first-hand the workings of a man capable of easy murder. I wished him gone, but more than that I wished us a way to slip free of his entanglements.

A thought crossed my mind: it would be so much simpler if Strambli were to die. So very much...cleaner. I flinched, recognising it as Bosa's way of thinking, a reminder of the abiding presence of her. The anger was one thing; this was an alteration in the pattern of my reasoning. This was what she had been trying to make me in the kindness room—a colder, sharper version of myself. I crushed it immediately, as one might mash an insect. But obliterating a thought was not the same as eradicating its point of origin; or as not having it in the first place, as well I knew.

"The important thing," Fura was saying as we went down in the elevator, "is to keep on just as we were yesterday. Shopping and suchlike. Let Glimmery keep his spies on us. He'll see nothing to suggest we're in any way perturbed."

"That launch will be here in less than a day. Do you still intend to be here by tomorrow morning?"

"Fleeing will give our game away, so it's the last thing we'll do."

"Do you think they'll let us walk out of here, when we're ready?" Surt asked.

"Even Glimmery can't detain us without consequences. There's a saying in the worlds: cross one honest crew, and you cross 'em all."

"Except we're not quite an honest crew," I said, feeling obligated to point this out. "Did you speak to Paladin?"

"Yes, and to Tindouf as well. They've nothing untoward to report at their end. Paladin has a sweeper fix on that launch, which matches Glimmery's account. It's coming in very quickly, and there's a sunjammer a few hundred thousand leagues astern of it which is likely to be the *White Widow*. Paladin says the sweeper profile is similar to the phantom that shadowed us from the Rumbler." She gave Surt a chastened look. "I'm minded to apologise, after all this time. I should have given more credence to your observation of sail-flash."

"You weren't to know what a thorn they'd turn into," Surt said, scratching at the back of her neck.

"I have to be circumspect with Paladin," Fura went on. "Our squawk transmissions are vulnerable to interception, so I can only phrase my queries in innocent terms. But I hope I have made it clear that we may need all sail and ions at rather abrupt notice."

"You needn't beat around that bush," I said. "No sane captain would want to spend an hour longer in Mister Glimmery's company than was strictly necessary."

When the elevator disgorged us into the lobby I was unsurprised to see a different clerk manning the desk. It was the day shift now, and in any case our flat-faced friend had looked very groggy and unwell when we returned in the small hours. We had tried to get some sense out of him regarding the cause of his unconsciousness, but he claimed to have no recollection of the circumstances leading up to Mister Cuttle's fall. As skeptical and distrustful as I was inclining to be, I believed him. Prozor had told me that some neural weapons left the victim with a memory scrubbed of all recent events.

"I know you've been told to report to Glimmery," Fura said to the new clerk, leaning on the desk. "But that don't preclude you reporting to me as well. Cuttle was snooping around on some business that we don't fully understand, and I'd be surprised if he's the last to pay us a visit. I want to know who comes and goes. Any questions, any odd types, you let me know. If I'm satisfied with the gen, there'll be a quoin in it for you—and not some low-mark piece, neither."

The day clerk was a blob of a boy with a cowlick and a nervous restlessness to his eyes, always looking to one side or the other. I had an inkling he was aware of some of the trouble that had happened the previous night and wanted as little to do with it as possible.

"I can't promise anything, Captain Marance. And I'm not always at my desk. The hotel doesn't run itself, you know. There's the laundry delivery, the night kitchen..."

"What you're saying is, you know when to turn a blind eye," Fura replied. "Which is a very sensible survival ploy, I don't doubt. But I don't like snoopers, and I especially don't like alien snoopers. Mister...what were their names, Tragen? Gabble and Rachit, or something like that. Any Crawly interest, I want to know about it." By way of emphasis she slipped him a ten-bar quoin. "That's a down payment on your cooperation. Don't make me reclaim it."

The lad pocketed the quoin under his waistcoat, glancing shiftily to either side as he made the item disappear. "If someone asks after you, what should I tell 'em?"

"That they'll need to make an appointment," Fura said.

*

It was hard to set our minds to such mundane matters as the procurement of food supplies, fresh water, new lightvine cultivars, surplus yardage, spare hull material and so on, but our practical needs had not vanished simply because of our entanglements with Glimmery. Part of me was rather keen on the idea of insisting on the three of us going shopping together, partly on the grounds of safety, and partly in the interests of denying Fura the chance to go off on any clandestine errands. Yet a colder consideration suggested to me that letting Fura go off on her own was not such a bad thing. While we still had a chance, and supposing Strambli was well enough, I thought it would be wise to leave this world as quickly as possible. Fura would find impediments to that, though, until such time as she had located Lagganvor, or proven to her private satisfaction that he was no longer here. If I forced her to go shopping, I might keep watch on her. But I would also hamper her mission, and that might be to our greater detriment.

So after due consideration I suggested that I take over visiting the bone emporiums, searching for a possible replacement for our failing skull, while she and Surt attended to the other matters as they saw fit. She agreed. Perhaps she sensed that there was some calculation behind my proposal, but since it was to her immediate benefit she did not quibble, and after taking coffee in the downstairs bar, I went off on my own.

I had been truthful, at least. I meant only to visit the skull shops, and that is what I did. Fura had given me a list of the places she had already been, with some remarks about the skulls she had tested and their likely suitability, but there were a dozen other establishments within a tram stop of the hotel and I was of a mind to begin afresh. Walking into each shop, all of which were dusty, dark and forbidding to various degrees because bone sellers did not need to rely on passing custom, my thoughts flashed back to Neural Alley—leading Fura into Madame Granity's boutique; pretending that it was my first visit when, in fact, I had already been tested and found to have the basic faculties of a Sympathetic, and believed that my sister was likely to share the same talent.

I had been correct, and if my adaptation to the skull had been quicker than Fura's at the outset, she had soon made up the ground. I had come to accept that, while we were both gifted, her innate aptitude was stronger and more sensitive than my own. Soon enough, though, both our capabilities would fade. The likelihood was that the degradation would set in with me first, as the older sibling, but such things were by no means predictable. The only certainty was that the gift would leave us, as it did all Bone Readers. It might, in exceptional cases, remain in some attenuated form until one was thirty years of age. Such outliers were uncommon, though, and it was much more likely to vanish somewhere in the early twenties. I had been eighteen when we ran away from home; now my twentieth birthday was only half a year away and Fura had turned eighteen. I had detected no loss of sharpness in my own abilities, quite the contrary, but our skull was dying and the absence of a stable baseline made it very difficult to assess my own decline.

Young women and young men were the natural customers of

bone merchants, so I drew only cautious glances as I went into each shop. I might be a hopeful case, wanting to be tested, with dreams of a new career. Or I might be an experienced hand, looking to test and procure a new skull on behalf of a proven crew. Either way, my being there was not a strangeness, and I had to be taken seriously. I damped down my Mazarile accent as best I could.

Wheel Strizzardy had one advantage over our own home-world when it came to the matter of skulls: skulls never worked close to swallowers. They never worked well close to civilisation, either, but there was less of that here, what with the power cuts and the general smallness of this world, and under optimum circumstances some signal transmission was still feasible. That meant there was a chance of an exceptionally good skull, with no significant flaws or marks of repair, stuffed with twinkly that still twinkled vigorously, a skull that had not been drilled into too often, nor been exposed to too many clumsy Sympathetics, and which was housed in insulated surroundings, and came equipped with excellent, well-calibrated neural bridges. Only a handful of the shops ran to anything like that, but I made sure I visited all that did, and insisted on trying their skulls. In most cases this required a non-refundable down payment, in case of damage. Sometimes that was almost enough to buy a low-grade skull off the shelves, but since I was flush with quoins I made only meek protestations and then—after the obligatory haggling, because I did not want to seem as if I were *too* flush—I coughed up.

It felt odd to be alone with those bones, and to place unfamiliar neural bridges on my head. Nothing felt quite right, especially after my long adaptation to the skull on *Revenger*. But I had studied my trade well and I also knew exactly how to chase down a signal, even in a skull whose attributes and quirks were entirely foreign.

Even a viable skull may not always perform, and even if it does, there may not always be anyone else sending, at least within the limits of the mutual sensitivity of both the skull and the reader. So whenever I settled those neural bridges onto my head, and started plugging in, I did so with no strong expectation of success. Even so, I felt I might be able to reject certain skulls as being unsuitable for our needs.

But on the third occasion, in the third such boutique that allowed me to test their wares, something came through, and much more strongly than I was expecting.

*It's you.*

The mind was known to me. It had come through a skull once before, when it let slip a word that betrayed its immediate interest in us. "*Nightjammer.*" And no sooner was it in my own head then by some reciprocal slippage it was in the skull, speeding away from me, into the mind of the Bone Reader who had just recognised my presence from that earlier union.

I chased my own thought with a hasty qualification.

*We were never the* Nightjammer.

A pause in the silent, voiceless exchange.

*You claim some other identity?*

*We are an innocent vessel. You pursued us from the Empty. We saw your sail-flash and tried to make good our escape. But you came and came, harried us into near-Congregational space, and eventually wounded one of our own with your sail-shot.*

*And your wounded party?*

I tried to squeeze the thought from my mind. But an image of Wheel Strizzardy flashed across my mind before I could suppress it. My inner discipline was not as rigorous as it was in our own bone room.

*Yes, we thought you had made it to port. You needn't chastise yourself for that slip. Conventional channels of intelligence had already exposed your nature and location. I wished only to see if you were aboard the larger vessel: you had been maintaining Bone Silence for some time, and my captain would be very glad to learn of your present disposition with regards to crew. Or he would be, if he were not suffering abominably from his injuries. Have you heard about our wounded?*

I remembered the desperate exchanges we had picked up over their squawk, in the aftermath of the attack. The terror and the desperation of people who were either dying or fully certain they were about to, and the knowledge that we had done that to them.

*It was an accident. We aimed at what we thought was empty space. We could not have known there was a second ship. Believe me, we had no desire to wound any of you.*

*You inflicted much more than a wounding on us. Your accuracy, penetration and rate of fire were very creditable. Water-cooled coil-guns, our armourer said—exactly the kind employed on the ship we had been licensed to hunt.*

*It isn't us. You must understand. We engaged you, yes, but with the intention of disabling your rigging, handicapping your pursuit—no more.*

*Tell me your name. If you wish to protest your innocence, why would you keep it secret?*

*You do not need to know my name. We are both Bone Readers, are we not? Confidentiality is the essence of our trade.*

*I think you are a woman. I might be mistaken—very probably I am—but it would tally with our intelligence. Two sisters were drawn into her web, and at least one of them had a useful faculty with the bones.*

*I am not... her.*

*Adrana Ness, Arafura Ness—you are one or the other.*

*No...*

But I had allowed too much of myself to show, and the lapse could not be undone.

*I think you are Adrana. I should like to meet you, one day. I would find it very instructive to see one of the minds behind that deed. Or do you deny your culpability?*

*I told you we acted in error.*

*You have a will. You did not have to choose this life.*

*It chose me. And we're not what you think. We killed her. We killed Bosa Sennen.*

*A frank admission. At least there is no denying your connection now.*

*I don't deny it. But I promise we never meant to hurt you, not the way it happened.*

*Do you know something, Adrana Ness? I almost believe you. I have been reading the bones long enough to learn some of the subtler aspects of this peculiar trade of ours. And I think, in some small way, I have learned to sense the character behind these voiceless words. You seem strongly persuaded of your own innocence… almost enough to have me doubting the certainty of our own position. Yes, I almost believe you.*

*I am sending you the truth as I know it. We used a swallower to gain the element of surprise, and we meant to disable your outer sails. If we had known of the other ship, I swear we would have avoided it.*

*There. That insidious conviction. You do believe it. Perhaps you were lied to. Is that possible?*

*No. I know what happened, the exact circumstances. And I am sorry—truly sorry. I have lost friends in action, and I know something of how bad it can be. You must believe me that we would never have wished to visit those horrors on another crew.*

*Not even in vengeance for your own wounded?*

*No, not even for that. Tell me—what is your name? I have as good as confessed my own. At least do me the kindness of sharing yours.*

*Kindness, Adrana Ness? How could any of your crew ever hope to know of that? I shall tell you my name, yes. But only because the information is valueless to you since I have nothing to hide, and I would think it rather fine if my name was one of those ringing through your head when they put you to the firing squad, or however they mean to execute your party. I am Chasco, Bone Reader to Captain Restral on the sunjammer* White Widow, *and I hope your end will be as slow as you deserve.*

His words—his voiceless words—cut me to the marrow. I had to fight not to unplug from the skull at that moment, and sit in a shivering huddle, wishing that my life had brought me to any point in time and space but this precise juncture, knowing how it felt to be the focus of a hate that was both deserved and entirely without any shred of personal animus.

But I remained connected to the skull.

*I am sorry, Chasco. Believe me or not. We never meant to do this.*

*

Even after I'd unplugged, it was as if his voice was still inside me, the words of his judgement sounding over and over, the tone of their deliverance as empty of sentiment as any verdict ever given in a court of law.

I knew I ought to be thinking about the skull's worth to us, being satisfied with its condition and suitability for our existing facilities, and knowing that its cost was well within our means. But I couldn't bring myself to attend to anything so pragmatic as the purchase of a skull, especially as our old one was still functional. I felt cored out, reduced to a thin, brittle shell of myself. From Chasco's standpoint, I thought, and knowing only the things that he knew, I would have no great difficulty in despising myself.

That is a state of self-reflection that I would wish on few other people. It is easy to accept that one is hated, provided one has the assurance that the other party has come to that judgement on deficient grounds, either because of some baseless grudge or an error of reasoning. It is much harder—singularly harder—to review the evidence against oneself and conclude that, yes, on that dispassionate basis, the hatred is not without foundation.

I left the shop, retaining just enough mental composure to add an additional deposit on the skull, so it might be held for a day or two, and then concluded that I had lost any desire to go after the other items on the list. I retraced my course back in the direction of Shine Street, hardly minding not to step in puddles, and then, confident of my navigation, took what I thought was a clever short-cut through some of the narrower streets backing onto the main avenue. They were gloomier, even in daylight, and as the grey buildings loomed over me, seeming to close tighter and tighter, like the jaws of a vice, I became aware that I was being followed. It was just a pair of footsteps, but they had been creeping up on my own for a few turns, and it took only a couple more for me to satisfy myself that this was no coincidence.

I turned a corner into a tight passage, took a few steps and then spun around, preparing to face my pursuer. With my free hand I delved into my jacket pocket, felt the pistol and drew it out, levelling it in preparation.

A figure came into view, halting before me. It was Mister Sneed, of course, and I suppose I ought not to have been surprised. His right hand was tucked deep into a pocket. With his left he reached up and plucked at the wobbling gemstone of mucus dangling from the tip of his nose, dragging it away between his fingers and making a snorting sound as he did so. His fingers silvered with his own slime—it formed a sort of horrible webbing between them—he jammed the offending hand back into his pocket.

It was a form of distraction, and I should have been wise to it. With the other hand he extracted a weapon from his right pocket. It was a pistol, larger and clumsier-looking than my own, and he aimed right at my chest.

"That's a pretty little stinger you've got there. Just the ticket for a stroll through these less salubrious quarters. Where'd you come by such a dainty piece, girlie?"

The volition pistol was in my hand, but it was only aimed at him in a vague sense. I meant only to demonstrate that I had the means to defend myself. Then a sudden and severe change of mood came upon me. I decided that I hated Mister Sneed and wished to do him considerable and irrevocable ill. This hatred flowed into me with a sudden enlightening force. It was Bosa's influence, and that was troubling enough, even as I grew more accustomed to the fact of her episodic holds on me. But now that residue of her had gained an additional means of expression.

With a quick jerking action, my hand and arm moved until the volition pistol had its point of aim exactly on Mister Sneed's forehead. Then it felt as if something locked in my bones and muscles, holding the aim as steadily as if my whole body were an expertly engineered artillery platform.

Mister Sneed should have fired by then, but I think the suddenness and precision of that snapping action was more than he expected, and it startled him just long enough to lose the edge. He took a precautionary step backward, and a little to his right, beginning to lower his own weapon, and the volition pistol held its lock on his forehead just as surely as if invisible arms were guiding and supporting my own.

"What do you want with me, Sneed?" I asked, with an arrogant authority.

"Mister S was just watchin' out for you, is all. No harm meant by it."

"By creeping after me with a gun?"

"In case you were accosted, or waylaid, or suchlike." He was speaking faster now, flashing his ranks of bad brown teeth. "I came round this corner not really knowin' what I'd find, so it paid to be prepared, so to speak. I weren't stalkin' you, if that's what it seems."

My voice retained its commanding edge. "Why did you kill Mister Cuttle, Sneed? I thought he was working for you and Glimmery."

"Mister Cuttle had an unfortunate trip, is all." He took his other hand out of his pocket and waggled the fingers by way of nervous demonstration. "Stairs and scuttly aliens don't really go together. An accident waiting to happen."

"And then you accidentally stepped in him. You've made an enemy of the Crawlies, I think—Mister Scrabble and Mister Fiddle. Was that wise?"

"They know which side their bread's buttered. They won't be rocking any boats, not if they know what's good for 'em."

"They seemed very upset to me, Sneed. I think you might

just have overstepped your mark. But I still don't know why you killed Cuttle."

"They get ideas above their situations, Miss, and they needs to be brought down a peg or two. Happens all the time. Not that I'm admitting any culpabilitation."

My finger itched, starting to squeeze the trigger. I had become a trinity, my free will divided between the pistol, Bosa and what remained of my own self-possession. I understood very well that the two silent partners in this mismatched union were complicit, encouraging me to complete the act that had been initiated when I drew out the weapon.

"I'd get back," I said warningly, trying to flex my finger off the trigger, while at the same time trying to unsnap my arm. By some great force of will I jerked the aim away from his head, but only just before my finger heeded the weapon's will.

An energy pulse flashed from the muzzle, a sort of pink-white spitball that lashed against a drainpipe and severed it cleanly, scorching the wall beyond it.

Then the pistol regained its authority over my arm, snapping back onto Mister Sneed, but by then I believe he had been sufficiently persuaded of my seriousness. Raising both hands, his own weapon dangling by a thumb, he made a stumbling rearward retreat. His eyes were as wide and pleading and pitiful as those of a whipped dog.

I strove to do as I done before, to contain Bosa by a supreme assertion of calm and placidity. I filled my head with pleasant conceits. I thought of pretty tunes, lovely fabrics, daily acts of sweetness and charity. I tried to ram my skull with such an overabundance of sickening pleasantness that there was no room left in it for thoughts of retribution or cruelty.

By some miracle I felt her influence diminish; a large hateful presence becoming smaller and smaller, as if seen through the optics of a sighting tube being pulled back from maximum focal length. Diminishing but not disappearing.

A small distant voice said:

*Face it, you wouldn't want to get rid me of completely, would you? Not when you've seen how useful I can be to you.*

"You're no part of me," I whispered. "You never will be."

My finger itched on the trigger again. But as Mister Sneed went round the corner it was as if the pistol relinquished its hold on me, my arm slackening and my finger no longer compelled to fire. I waited a few moments, listening for his footsteps as they moved away, slowly at first and then with evident haste.

When I was certain that I was safe from him, I slipped the volition pistol back into my pocket. I loathed and treasured it in the same breath—wished to crush it underfoot and press it to my breast like a gift from a lover.

I stood still for a few moments, gathering what very little composure I could summon. I was shaking.

That was when I saw the figure watching me from the far end of the alley. Tall, thin and dark: not much more than a silhouette. The watcher was male, I believed, but I did not think he was one of Sneed's men, nor—even though his clothes were dark—was he one of those black-gowned attendants I had seen around Glimmery. He surveyed me for a moment longer, sufficient for me to establish that I was the particular object of his attention and that he had been monitoring the entire exchange with Sneed.

"Lagganvor."

I had called out the name with no assurance that this was him. If I was in error, then it was likely that the name would mean nothing to this stranger. If I was correct, as intuition persuaded me I was, then he must already know of our interest in him. Either way, no lasting harm would be done.

Perhaps there was a hesitation as he heard me call out the name—an instant when he might have been about to turn, but delayed the action. The light shifted and I caught a trace of his features, partly obscured by a curtain of hair that hung to his collar. A young man's face, not unhandsome, and one that triggered in me some faint, imprecise sense of familiarity. I felt that I knew him, or had seen him before, impossible as that was.

"Lagganvor," I said again, quieter this time, for my benefit, not his.

He lingered for a few heartbeats, then snapped his gaze from me. He turned, standing in profile for a moment, then passed out of my line of sight.

# 17

I was nearly back at the hotel when I swerved on my heels and took off for the infirmary instead, gripped by an impulse to speak to Doctor Eddralder. I took a roundabout route, not wanting to be followed, or at least not make it too easy for anyone, and spent a minute or two skulking under the cover of the surrounding buildings, before finally making a dash to the muddy, cratered ground over which the infirmary was suspended like a piece of scraggy gristle.

There was no one to greet me, no one to speak to, and the rope-bridges and ladders had been drawn up off the ground.

Glancing over my shoulder so often it must have looked as if I had a twitch in my neck, I finally summoned the nerve to ring one of the chains hanging from above, yanking it down and putting all my weight into the act until it budged enough to send a signal.

I had to do it three or four times before a wooden shutter popped open far above and a round, scrawny-necked head projected out like a lollipop on a stick. The cove searched the surroundings before appearing to notice my presence.

"This ain't visiting hours," he called down gruffly.

"What if I was sick?" I called back.

"Then you wouldn't have been able to ring the bell. If you can't ring the bell, you're sick. If you can ring the bell, you ain't."

I digested this logic, deciding it was the sort that was best not challenged.

"And what if I had someone sick with me?"

"Have you?"

I looked around.

"No."

"Then buzz off until visiting hours."

"And when are they?"

"Whenever you ain't around, precious. Go away and make some trouble elsewhere."

"I'm not going anywhere. I want to speak to Eddralder." Realising that this alone would not get me an audience with the doctor, I added: "It's to do with Mister Glimmery, a very important medical matter. You wouldn't want to be the one who delayed it, would you?"

"You want a chat with Mister Glimmery, come up and see the man himself."

"It's more a matter for his physician." I dug a heel into the mud, looking up with my hands on my hips. "I bet Mister Glimmery's had his share of hopes dashed, about treatments and cures. I wouldn't want to add to that... but Doctor Eddralder will know what has and hasn't been attempted, and he'll be able to spare Mister Glimmery any unnecessary disappointment."

"Got some quack potion you want to peddle, is it?"

"I can't be the judge of that, sir—but Doctor Eddralder can."

I jumped as a hand settled on my shoulder. I'd let my attention linger on the man above me, but I had still been alert, and there had been no sign of anyone approaching me. The volition pistol was still in my pocket. It might as well have been back in the hotel for all the use it was going to be now.

But a voice that I knew said: "I can be the judge of what, exactly?"

I turned around slowly, recalculating my assumptions. I had thought it might be Sneed, or one of Sneed's men, or perhaps Lagganvor, sneaking up on me. But it was Doctor Eddralder himself, looming over me with his umbrella held high and turning slowly, like a wheelworld spinning on its axis.

"I thought you'd be in the infirmary," I said.

Eddralder set down the heavy medical bag he had been carrying. It was already covered in muddy stains so I suppose a few more made no difference. "There are needy cases beyond our walls, Tragen, and when my schedule permits, I attend to them as best I can."

I studied the lines of weariness etched into his face. If anything they were deeper and longer than the last time, so precisely vertical it was as if the rain had eroded them.

"I take it there's not much you can do?"

He blinked away my question. "When there is news on your friend, I will be sure to let you know. That *was* your business here, I take it?" His eyes were hard on me, and I wondered if he saw something of the state of mind that the volition pistol had left me in. I had glimpsed the true face of free will and found that it was a paper-thin mask, easily shredded. Beneath it was a steely autonomy, a mechanism of desires and impulses over which I had much less control than I'd hitherto believed.

"Can we talk, Doctor Eddralder?"

He cocked back his umbrella to shout at the man above. "It's all right—her business is legitimate. Send down my box."

"You certain, doc?" called the man.

A cold insistence entered his voice. "Yes—quite certain."

The face retreated, shutters clacking shut. After an interval a larger door opened and a gallows-like crane swung out from a hidden recess. On the hook of the crane was an upright container, like a coffin tipped on its end. It began to lower down to us.

"You were saying, Tragen?" Eddralder prompted.

"You have to find a way out of this mess you're in, sir. For your sake, and for Merrix as well."

"Did I not already explain my predicament, Tragen?"

I watched as the box continued its descent. It was only large enough for one person so it was plain to me that our conversation was not going to be a long one. "You did, sir, and I understand. And I know you feel a duty of care to that man, no matter what a monster he is. But there's got to be a way."

"To condemn both myself and Merrix, you mean?"

"Maybe you've had the means already," I said. "But not any way of getting away from him in safety. Wheel Strizzardy's too small a place for you to be able to hide, and he controls most of it anyway. Even if you brought yourself to kill him, there'd be his associates to worry about. But it's different now. There's a ship that could take you away." I nodded at the bag he had deposited in the mud. "You're a good man, a good doctor."

"You hardly know me."

"I don't need to. I know you're in an impossible situation and I think we can help. Besides, there's a bit of self-interest. We've got a good sick-bay on our ship, but none of us is really able to use it. If you'd been with us from the outset, you could've fixed up our friend without us ever needing to come to this place."

"If half the rumours about your crew are true, Tragen, then I would be condemning myself to a fugitive existence."

"But a free one, and with Merrix away from that man. You'd have our protection and our gratitude."

"And your leader—Captain Marance?" He spoke her name with an exaggerated care, as if emphasising its falsehood. "She is in concordance with this proposal?"

"Yes," I lied. "Totally."

His box landed hard next to us. It really was a like a coffin, with the same wedge-shape, flaring wider near the top. The only difference was that there was a little window in the door. He opened the box, which contained nothing except space for the doctor and his bag, the latter item being heaved inside, along with a generous skirting of mud. "Then I thank you for the kind offer, Tragen—and please express my gratitude to Captain Marance. But there remains a stumbling block. He is still my patient."

"With all the drugs you've got, sir…"

"Each of which he insists is tested first on Merrix. There is no possibility of deception, Tragen. Nor would my conscience permit it, even if I saw a way." He snapped shut the umbrella, which was too large to have fitted into the box when open, then stepped within, nodding a temporary farewell to me before drawing the door tight. For a moment his long, lined face loomed behind the window, and I wondered if I saw something in his eyes, some sudden calculation, but then he was being pulled aloft, up into the infirmary.

*

I returned to the hotel, but I could abide the emptiness of our room for no more than a minute before deciding I would prefer the bustle and warmth of the bar. I bought a drink for myself, sufficient to settle my nerves but not dull them, and was on my way to find a private corner when a pudgy hand grabbed at my sleeve. I was about to slap it away when a mouth pressed itself up to my ear and said: "The one you're after ain't around right now, but he agreed to your suggestion and says he'll see you across the road."

I snapped round, dislodging the hand with a flick. The woman who had spoken to me was one of the staff, for I had seen her beating one of the cleaning robots with a broomstick when it became stuck in a decision-action loop. She wore a grubby apron, and had a gap in the front of her teeth and a scar up the side of her lip. Her eyes were set so widely in her face that I fancied she could see right around me.

"Begging my pardon, miss," she said, pulling away. "I thought you were someone else. I should have paid more heed."

More heed to my arm, I thought, for it was plain that she had mistaken me for Fura, which was not so unforgivable in the low light of the bar, especially as my hair was unruly from the neural bridges.

"It's all right," I said, smiling despite my general discontentment. "Captain Marance sent me to make sure all was in hand.

We are talking about the same person, aren't we? Tall and thin?" I motioned across my face, suggesting a sweep of hair such as I thought I had seen on Lagganvor.

"You can say his name, girlie—it ain't any kind of secret." She narrowed her eyes at me. "You *do* mean Mister Cull, don't you? Trabzon Cull?"

Thankfully my wits were still present, and I do not think the confusion showed in my face long enough to register. "Yes—Mister Cull." Because of course Lagganvor would not be using the name by which Bosa Sennen had known him.

"Is that how it normally works with your captain and her crew?" she asked, and I realised that she must think some assignation had been arranged between Fura and this man, and that I was at the very least a willing intermediary.

"So long as she finds us the quoins," I said, moving to distance myself, "she can do what she likes in port."

I reached my desired corner and sat brooding over my drink, my mind a furious mill of calculation and speculation. There was almost too much going on in it, like some infernal machine whose governer had failed and which was now intent on turning itself into a pile of hot wreckage. First the Bone Reader from the *White Widow*, then the encounter with Sneed, and then meeting the man I now held to be Lagganvor. And then—this. Proof, if any were needed, that Fura had already used her time here most profitably. I knew she had stolen back into the bar during our first shopping expedition, and I guessed that she had been making enquiries after her quarry. Very delicately phrased enquiries, I did not doubt, but then she was adept at that sort of thing. She would never have come out with it and asked for Lagganvor directly. But she would have been sure to mention that she was in the recruiting game and particularly interested in any talented person who might have come to the wheel in recent times, who might be in want of employment. Names and habits would have been presented to her, for no one, not even a fugitive, could arrive in a place like this without making waves. Fura would have quickly homed in on the individual most likely to be Lagganvor, and then she would have begun setting her trap.

I finished my drink. We had started from the hotel late and my shopping had taken up most of the afternoon. It was early evening now, and Port Endless was slipping back into its more habitual state of illumination, after the temporary respite of day. The lit windows of the hotel stood out like playing cards, laid out in the interrupted ranks and rows of some vast round of Solitaire. Against one of them, on the eighth floor, stiff as a marionette, a figure stood watching. She had her left arm at her side, her right at her waist. She must have been looking down into Shine Street, perhaps thinking of the coming assignation. I do not think she saw me, but after a long moment she pivoted from the window and closed the shutters.

A few minutes later I went to my room for long enough to take off my jacket and comb my hair. I slipped the volition pistol into my blouse pocket, closed the door and knocked on the adjoining room.

Fura was alone. Surt had gone back to the infirmary to get a first-hand account of Strambli's condition from Doctor Eddralder. I wondered how close our paths had come to crossing, and if Eddralder might now mention something to Surt about my own conversation with him, and the offer I'd dangled.

"Do you think Surt will be all right?"

"I didn't want her going off on her own, but she wouldn't hear anything else," Fura said. "I asked her to pass a message to Prozor, asking her to come back here and collect a few items on the way. I'll explain when she arrives. Anyway, you're back sooner than I expected. Did you chase up a skull?"

"I found one that I think might fit our requirements," I said, not without a certain brusqueness. "We can afford it, and I think it can be installed without any complications. We can collect it tomorrow, if you wish. With the other items we already have, it wouldn't hurt to make a return trip with the launch. I don't trust the lock-up here very much, and it would be a terrible inconvenience if we lost everything again, and had to further delay our departure."

"If all goes well—with Strambli, I mean—there'll be no need to delay at all. I'm thinking we might even cast off tomorrow."

"Good," I said decisively. "I'll squawk Tindouf to make immediate preparations."

"No—not just yet. Squawk only when we have a firm intention, or we'll only confuse the poor fellow. Besides, I have something in mind. Do you have the volition pistol?"

"Yes, and I already tested it against Sneed."

She looked at me with fear and wonder and not a little admiration. "I'm sorry, you did what?"

"Sneed was shadowing me. I took out the pistol and let off a shot. Don't worry, though, I didn't hit him." I unpocketed the weapon and regarded it. "You should have told me what it would do. I might have thought twice about aiming it anywhere near Sneed."

Fura took the pistol from me and made a careful adjustment to a ring-shaped dial situated behind the grip. "It was a low setting, mercifully—if it hadn't been, you'd have blown a hole right through to space. Slight exaggeration, perhaps, but you could still have done a lot of damage."

"Are you making it stronger?"

"Exactly the opposite, dear heart. I'm putting it at the lowest setting." She handed the weapon back to me. "You probably felt as if the pistol had a will of its own."

I thought back to the encounter with Sneed, and the way Bosa had almost usurped my control over the weapon.

"It did."

"It's an illusion. The only mind operating it is your own. What it does is cut through inhibitions and doubt, silencing qualms and second-guessing. It compels you to shoot the person you would most like to shoot, without any higher reasoning getting in the way. Think of it as a weapon that by-passes your frontal lobe. If you'd prefer something cruder...?"

"No," I answered. "If I wanted crude, I'd have brought something like a Ghostie blade with me."

Her smile was guarded.

"What a curious remark."

Fura had a telephone directory on her bedside table. She picked it up, walked to the room's limit and held it outstretched in her alloy fingers.

I looked at her and shrugged.

"What would you like me to do?"

"I would have thought it was obvious. Shoot at the directory. These walls are paper-thin, so if a shot penetrates the directory there's a good chance it will go through the wall as well."

"And this is of interest to you...why, precisely?"

"Shoot at the directory."

I squeezed the jewelled trigger. The weapon gave a little twitch in my hand and a spark of pink-white light leapt from the muzzle to the telephone book, boring a crude, lopsided hole near its edge, and projecting a dark, hyphenated scorch mark against the wall beyond it.

"Good. Now take it a little higher. The setting dial is that bevelled circle you saw me adjust. One notch at a time. Delicately."

"I am being delicate."

"Try again."

I fired. The kick was stronger, but I was ready for it and my aim was truer, concentrating the pistol's fire on the middle of the book. The same snap of light, but this time the hole was narrower, more neatly formed, and a spark of flame danced on the wallpaper for an instant.

"A notch higher. The wall will absorb more of the energy, when you shoot through it."

I did it, punching a thicker hole through the book, and creating a fist-sized scorch beyond it. Flames licked the edge, but did not take. The wallpaper was too damp to be truly combustible, I decided.

"Good. I think we're close."

"We could just shoot through the wall and eliminate the guesswork."

"I don't wish to damage the wall. Later tonight I expect a

visitor. He may try to get the better of me, and I can't be seen to have a visible defence. Prozor will help, when she brings the items I asked her to collect. But you will also be watching from your own room with that piece of lookstone I gave you, ready to fire a disabling shot."

"Let's hope it works better than the last disabling shot we tried."

Fura swapped the telephone book from one hand to the other, so that she had it in her flesh fingers. "One more time."

"Please don't do that."

She was holding her metal hand beyond the telephone book, in the path of the energy pulse.

"It won't do me any harm. Fire again."

"Fura, please."

"Just do it. Or damn it, I'll find a way to do it myself. I have to know that the blast will be debilitating, but not lethal."

"And this is how you propose to find out?"

My hand wavered, feeling as if it were being nudged to one side by a subliminal pressure, and the muzzle of the volition pistol drifted onto Fura's head. I had no doubt that a shot at this range, without the muffling influence of the telephone book, would suffice to drop her dead. Fura seemed to realise it as well. Her eyes met mine, some silent understanding passing between us, and with a distinct force of will—as if my arm would much rather be aiming the muzzle at her head—I swivelled the pistol back onto its proper alignment.

"I meant nothing by that," I said.

"Of course you didn't. Fire, please. I must know that we have the correct settings."

I maintained my aim. But some wild, wicked impulse overcame me. I had been waiting for the decisive moment, half convinced it would never come, and here it was, me with a pistol pointed at my sister's hand. There was anger in me, and indignation, but for once I did not hold Bosa entirely accountable.

"This visitor. Do you know who he is?"

"That's what I'm hoping to find out."

"Then I'll help you along a bit. Around here he calls himself Trabzon Cull. But his real name is Lagganvor."

To her credit, she controlled her reaction well. Just the merest lift of her eyebrows, the slightest curl of suspicion and doubt on her lips.

"And how would you know that?"

"It wasn't difficult. In fact I've known about him for quite a while." I watched her face take on a steadily more troubled aspect, as my words hit home. "Since before we rounded the swallower, in fact. You found his name in Bosa's private journals and realised he could be useful to you, if only you could track him down."

"This is...not what I expected of you. More like what I expected of *her*."

"She's gone from me. She tried to get into my head and I wouldn't let her. But you? It's almost like you want to live up to something."

"How can you stand there and say that?"

"Very easily. I'm not the one who duped her own crew, and lied and cheated, for the sake of a piece of information."

If she felt that I had gone a little far in accusing her of outright treachery, she let it pass for now.

"And what information would that be?"

"The location of Bosa's cache of quoins. Somewhere out there in the Emptyside, most probably, but not easily found from her records. But a man like Lagganvor, her go-between, might know the whereabouts. Or have enough knowledge to break a coded entry in her navigational documents, or the ship's own memory registers. Something even Paladin can't get at. Either way, you won't rest until you have him. Which is why you schemed to bring us here, making it seem as if we were going against your intentions, when in fact we were stuck on them like a tram following its rails down Jauncery Road."

"I didn't..."

"Shut up," I said. "Not one more lying word, sister, or so help me I'll turn the yield up as far as it goes. We're finished with untruths, you and me. Total honesty from now on, or we're done."

"I came for you."

"Yes, and the decent thing might be to stop reminding me of it every five minutes. You have my gratitude. You've had my gratitude for every waking instant since you rescued me. But that doesn't excuse your duplicity. I could almost stand the thought of you lying to the rest of them, even Prozor, but that you'd do it to me, to my face, after all we've been through." I shook my head, trusting that my disgust and disappointment needed no clarification. "I thought better of you. But you've changed. Whether it's the glowy, or some of *her* seeping into you, there's something in you that I neither understand nor care for. I want you back, Fura—the sister I ran away with. I know you're still in there. But I'm worried that you're slipping away."

She was still holding the telephone directory, I was still holding the energy pistol. What an odd tableau we would have made, had anyone crashed through the door at the moment: two sisters, standing in stiff opposition, more alike than either of us cared to admit but with a widening gulf between us, opening like the space between two worlds moving on different processionals.

"I shouldn't have done it," Fura said, sounding as if she had pricked her own rage. "Not the way I did. I see that now. I ought to have trusted you—all of you—to see what I saw."

"Why the sudden change of heart?" I asked, unconvinced by this show of contrition, which I had seen a few too many times in our long association. "Don't you see the danger you've led us into?"

"Our every waking breath is a risk, Adrana. We must have those quoins, don't you see?"

"We can barely spend what we already have. What use is more of it?"

"Not to make us richer. I'm not so callow, and neither are you. Of course a little more leverage wouldn't hurt, but that's not the main reason for locating the cache. There are questions that need answering, truths we need to uncover, and those quoins are the key to it." A pleading look entered her eyes. "Admit it, Adrana. You're drawn to it yourself. The riddle I showed you, of those intervals... the Shadow Occupations... don't tell me that hasn't played on your mind. It's all interconnected."

"Don't drag me into this," I said.

"But you're in it already," she insisted. "Tantalised and troubled, just as I am. The glowy's got nothing to do with that."

"Are you really so sure of that, after seeing what it's done to Glimmery?"

"Oh, I know it has its way with me on occasion, and perhaps I've allowed it to run too far. But what's driving me is the same yearning that drove us to run away in the first place. You feel it too. Maybe it burns a bit less brightly for you but you can't deny it."

"I would never have lied."

"It was a mistake. But for the sake of the cohesion of the crew..."

I finished off her thought. "You want me to join you in your duplicity."

"What's done is done. Lagganvor is nearly ours. He'll be here this evening."

"I know. I was told that he meant to keep his assignation. I presume at some point you meant to tell me what my role in all of this would be?"

"Tonight. Of course tonight. Look—surely you can agree that no harm has come by any of this?"

"Tell that to Strambli."

"Blame me for anything, Adrana, but not that. No matter which world we sailed to, we'd have needed to disguise the ship."

"Things might have played out differently," I said.

But it was unkind of me to blame Fura for that misfortune, and I felt one of us had to rise above such pettiness.

"Just make sure the lies end here," I said.

"You can't tell the others. Not now, just when we're getting somewhere. Say you'll keep this between us. There'll be no more secrets."

"Pray there aren't."

She swallowed. "Once we've got Lagganvor, the crew will see how we needed him. I'll... make it seem that we found him by good luck, not design."

"Yes, and you'll need equal good luck with the consequences of letting one of Bosa's own anywhere near the ship."

"What would you suggest I do?"

"Stir his bowels with a yardknife, and take your sweet time doing it."

"And you say I'm the hard one," she said, her quiet admiration shaming me. "He escaped from her, just as you did. Who's to say how he first fell into her employment? He might have had as little say in the matter as you did." Her jaw tensed. "Enough of this. Do we understand each other or not? You've no desire to set the rest of the crew on me, and I've no desire to deepen your evident disappointment in me."

"I shouldn't give you this last chance."

"But you will, for the sake of where we've been, and what we've been through. Just as I would, if our places were swapped." She flicked her eyes to the energy pistol, which was growing heavy in my hand. "Be done with it. Shoot me."

"If you insist," I said, and squeezed the trigger.

The weapon had the desired effect. It blasted through the telephone book, adding a dark-lined hole to the ones already present, and what was left of the energy pulse—still some considerable part—lashed against Fura's metal hand.

She let out a gasp of suppressed pain, something close to delight in her eyes, and although she was holding it with her other hand, the shock was enough that she dropped the book. She rubbed the forearm and wrist of her artificial limb.

"Did it sting?" I asked, with cold indifference.

She was breathless for a moment. But she gathered herself, inspecting the arm—it appeared undamaged, at least to my eyes—and answered: "The cove in Mazarile told me my nervous system would eventually bind to the arm's sensory mechanisms, so I'd feel heat and cold, the texture of things, and also pain. He was right, too. Especially about the pain."

"Was it sufficient?"

Fura knelt down and gathered the sorry-looking telephone book. "I think so."

"Good," I said, levelling the pistol again. "But we had best be sure, hadn't we?"

*

Prozor came by the hotel about half an hour later. She had the items Surt had told her to buy, and she had found them easily and without any great expenditure, although she had no idea why they were needed.

"A tin arm from the cheapest Limb Broker within a square league of here, and a filthy wig I wouldn't embarrass a dog with." She dropped the offending items onto Fura's bed. "I hope you've got a sensible reason for sending me after these, girlie, when I could've been pickin' scraps out of the gutter."

"I'll explain," Fura said. "Over a drink. Did you speak to Eddralder?"

"Yes, and he's still not makin" any promises. He wants the best for us, strangely, which means he's ever so keen that we should leave before that launch comes in. But he won't let Strambli out of his sight until he knows he's got the infection beaten, and that could take days or weeks, for all he's prepared to commit. Meanwhile, that launch will be here by about six in the morning.

"Less than twelve hours," I said. "Assuming it's still on course."

"Paladin says it is," Prozor said. "I squawked him and got the latest sweeper fix. Comin' in a little faster than planned, if anything. They must have squeezed a few more drops of fuel from their tanks. It's a fine old launch, too—much bigger than our little tub."

"Big enough to contain a skull, do you think?" I asked.

"I've heard of such things," Prozor said, stroking the hard

angle of her chin as she reflected on this point. "Ain't ideal. Lot of noise in a launch, and you'd have to damp the rockets if you wanted to tune in. But if you've already got a bone room on your main ship, and you can afford the space and room on a launch, there's no handicap. Why?"

"I just wondered."

"Do you think the doctor's happy in his present employment?" Fura asked, directing her question at the two of us.

"I imagine his happiness has very little bearing on the matter," I answered, glad not to be pushed on the question of the bone room. "He is chained to Glimmery by Merrix. So long as Glimmery has Merrix, Eddralder cannot cross him. Besides, he has his infirmary. He may slave under a monster, but I think he shows kindness to his patients, and wishes he could do more."

"Where are you goin' with the line of speculation?" Prozor asked Fura.

"Nowhere, other than to consider how much easier it would have been if we'd had the services of a physician on the ship. Still, as you say: speculation." She glanced at her timepiece, flicking open its jewelled cover. "There isn't much that needs to be discussed, but I promised you a drink and I doubt you'll refuse. Adrana already knows her part. Yours won't take very long to explain."

# 18

I felt the lookstone's rough edge between my fingers. I held it up to my eyes and squeezed gently, activating the mysterious and invisible machinery embedded in the relic.

The adjoining room was as dark as our own, with only a few slants of coloured light spilling in through the shutters, flickering and changing according to the illuminated signs and hoardings outside. That was sufficient, though, because my eyes were well-adjusted to the gloom. I made out the form on the bed, lying on her back, black hair spilling onto her pillow, face averted, one flesh arm tucked under the sheets, the mechanical one resting above them, metal fingers and sleeve catching the light's play so that the alloy gleamed ruby one moment, lilac the next, bronze green the moment after that.

Footsteps passed in the hall, then halted. After a silence I heard the sound of a doorknob being tested, then a click as it worked, and a louder, more protracted creak as the door was pushed open. The hall's brown light fanned into the room, quenching the colours, until the door was pushed shut again.

A figure moved to the bedside, moving in a stealthy but confident manner, lowering down to kneel at the level of the sleeper, reaching out with one hand to brush aside the tousled hair.

A soft voice, not without education or refinement, muffled

further by the intervening wall. "Wake up, Captain Marance. Have you forgotten our appointment?"

Something gleamed in his other hand, held lightly but with unmistakable purpose.

The sleeping form murmured a response. The man swept the curls fully away from the face and some doubt or apprehension touched his expression, the first intimation of a dawning wrongness. The hair must have felt too loose in his fingers. He tugged at it again and the entire body of hair shifted, spilling onto the pillow as one mass. The hair beneath was shorter by far, and paler, consisting of matted and tousled spikes.

Lagganvor pivoted, still kneeling. Tentatively, weapon still in his other hand, he made to touch the artificial hand and sleeve. It rolled to one side, too loose to be anchored to any anatomical part. Now he began to sense the grave depths of his error and made to rise, jerking the weapon into the corners of the room while always keeping an eye on the sleeping form.

I judged my moment as carefully as my point of aim. The volition pistol discharged, most of its yield exhausted in the process of blasting through the wall, leaving only a stinging, scalding charge to strike Lagganvor. I had aimed for his weapon hand, and the shock of it made him yelp and drop his pistol. It clattered onto floorboards, and that was Fura's signal. Before Lagganvor had a chance to scrabble around and retrieve the weapon, she was out of the cupboard and onto the man, catching him from behind.

"Don't struggle," she said, very loudly and firmly. "This coldness you feel against your throat is a Ghostie blade which will go through you so cleanly you won't feel a tickle until your head thuds against the floor."

Now that Lagganvor was preoccupied, Prozor rose from the bed. She left the wig and the false arm behind, moved to the wall and switched on the main light. Under that unsympathetic glare the artefacts of our trickery, the wig and the arm, looked incapable of fooling a child. The wig was nothing like Fura's real hair, being far too curly and far too black, almost like catchcloth, but shot through with shimmery purple highlights, and the artificial arm, while comparable in size and function to Fura's own, was much more crudely manufactured, and decorated in a garish and tawdry fashion.

Pocketing the lookstone—it had served its purpose—I left our room and went outside to the hallway. The other doors were dark, and if our commotion had drawn any of the other guests from sleep they were sensible enough to limit their curiosity. Perhaps they had already learned their lesson from the death of Mister Cuttle.

I entered Fura's room, the door not quite latched. By then Prozor had retrieved Lagganvor's energy pistol, so there were two of us covering him, as well as Fura with her Ghostie knife.

In the light it made a sort of stiletto-like mirage, dancing out from between her fingers. If I looked at it directly it squirmed from my attention, making it seem as if Fura was playing a foolish game of make-believe. But if I averted my gaze slightly, the Ghostie blade snapped back into smoky reality.

"I only wanted—"

"Shut up," Fura said. She had her left hand to his throat with the knife, and the other dragging his right arm behind his back. "You speak when I tell you to speak." Then, directing a nod at Prozor: "Between us I don't think he'll be much more bother. If you think you ought to go back to Surt and Strambli, please do so."

"What should I tell 'em?"

"Get the straight story from Eddralder about Strambli's chances of being moved. It might be sooner rather than later. Be coy about it—no mention of any of this. We don't want Glimmery thinking we're about to leave. Oh, and Proz? You did very well."

"Much obliged, Cap'n. And when you feel like tellin' me how all this came together, I won't complain."

"This man tried to break into my room earlier, according

to the concierge. When I know who he is, you'll be the first to hear."

Prozor held the energy pistol out to Fura. "I'd watch 'im if I were you. Looks the slippery kind." Then she lifted up the fringe of Lagganvor's hair, studying his face with a doubtful squint. "Have we met before, cove?"

"I suspect I would recall."

I cuffed him silent. He could ask all the question he wished, and we likewise, but only when Prozor was out of the room.

"I don't need the weapon," Fura said. "You hang onto it, and be very careful on your way. I'll squawk when I have some news, but in the meantime just go about your business as if nothing's out of the ordinary."

"It ain't been close to ordinary since we arrived," Prozor said. "But I'll do my best. You sure you can manage him?"

"Between Adrana and I? I think we have the advantage, thank you very much."

I nodded at Prozor as she left, thinking that I was now fully complicit in this act of dishonesty, whereas before I had been only a peripheral accessory to the crime. It made me feel more than a little repulsed by myself.

I listened carefully for her steps going down the stairs at the end of the landing, then—just as telling—the chime as the elevator arrived.

"I didn't enjoy that at all," I said.

"Nor did I," Lagganvor said. "It's almost as if you want to keep something from her. Does she know who I am? As you so evidently do? You've been asking around freely enough, after all—you at least, Captain Marance. If that's your name, which I think doubtful."

Fura kept the knife on him. "Who do you think I am, exactly?"

A strain showed on his face, and once again I felt that it was both familiar and unfamiliar, in a sense that I found very hard to analyse. "You arrived here in a dark ship, curiously rigged, having sailed from the Emptyside where there's lately been some trouble. I think that ship used to belong to someone else, and that you are very understandably anxious that no one should mistake you for its former custodian." He risked a smile, the strain making it a death-mask rictus. "I think I know that ship. I also think I know its former captain. There's a similar wildness in your eyes, but you're not the same woman. If you were, that knife would have opened me up already."

"You'd know Bosa Sennen, would you?" I asked, dropping her name like an oath, a dangerous flirtation given how shallowly she lay under my skin.

"Of course," he answered placidly. "I served under her. Knew her ship inside-out."

"Why did you turn from her?" I asked.

"Because I could. Because she was insane and I knew it was only a matter of time before I said or did something that drew her spite. It's a long story. Do you really wish to sit and discuss it with a knife against my throat?"

"Where would you rather?" Fura asked.

"Any place but here. I'll be frank with you. It's not safe for me in Wheel Strizzardy. The thought of Bosa coming after me was bad enough, but even believing her to be dead doesn't change my predicament. You are aware of the bounty?"

I said: "What of it?"

"It's only the beginning. First they grant licences to well-equipped ships—privateer sunjammers like the *Calenture* and the *White Widow*, with which you are doubtless acquainted. Yes, I gathered there had been action. I don't blame you, either. What could you do but act in self-defence? Still, it won't end here. They will send more ships, and encourage their captains to use increasingly ruthless and unscrupulous methods. There is speak of putting together an organised squadron—an actual fleet, under military command, with better ships and weapons than anything those two captains could muster. In the meantime, the banks and combines have been using all the intelligence-gathering tools at their disposal, including informants and advance agents, to chase down any lead on Bosa Sennen, including the identities of her former associates."

"Such as you," Fura said.

"When they learn my name, and if I were taken," Lagganvor said, "I would either be killed, or captured for interrogation—and I am not sure the latter would be any sort of improvement on the former. When you arrived and started making such bold enquiries…I thought the net was closing in. But you could be my salvation, as much as my nemesis."

Fura relaxed the knife very slightly, although it was still only a nail's thickness from his flesh. "Think you'll be welcomed back aboard the *Nightjammer*, do you?"

"No," he answered carefully, as if a single slip or ill-judged phrase could still be the end of him. "But you are not her, and you are not the agents pursuing her. Lock me in irons if you will, but get me off this world and you will have my gratitude."

"We're not cut from Bosa's cloth," Fura said, after favouring me with a look and giving her answer long consideration. "We took her ship, but not her methods. And you don't have to be our prisoner. I'd like it if you came willingly, but I won't force you."

I looked at my sister, saying nothing, but thinking a lot. She had been plotting her way to this encounter for weeks, prepared to sacrifice friendship and bonds of trust for it. I found it rather unlikely that she would let Lagganvor go if he was not minded to accompany us.

"What are your terms, if I might be so bold?"

"Did anyone follow you here?" Fura asked, not answering him.

"I don't think so. Were you expecting someone to?"

Fura nodded. "Mister Glimmery's men."

"You'd have done yourselves a favour by not getting involved with that gentleman."

"We didn't have a lot of choice," I said. "You heard what we told our friend. A friend of ours was injured. We had to take her to the infirmary, and that's how we met Doctor Eddralder. But Glimmery was tracking us from the moment we approached. He wants a share of that incentive money, but he has to wait until the right moment to pounce or he risks losing the ship itself. Then there's Sneed, and the Crawly who was hanging around with Glimmery, Mister Cuttle, who Sneed killed, right here in this hotel."

Fura withdrew the knife a little more.

"Do you know these coves?"

"To a degree. I've met Eddralder once or twice. He's a decent man in an impossible position. You know about his daughter, of course. Glimmery is your average thug made good. A local crime boss who saw his moment and had the right connections in place—chains of bribery and blackmail—and who now runs all of Wheel Strizzardy. He's extremely dangerous, more unpredictable by the day, and he gathers bad people around him, like Lasper Sneed. It wouldn't be tolerated on any world further Sunwards, but things are a little more relaxed out here."

"We noticed," I said. "What about Cuttle?"

"Here I have something to confess. Would you mind holding that knife a little further away from my neck? I didn't kill the Crawly. That was Sneed's doing. But I did startle him."

Fura made to put the knife back against his neck, but I stilled her hand.

"Hear him out."

"I wanted to learn a little more about the crew that had taken an interest me, so I decided to pay a visit to the hotel, ahead of any planned assignation. Unfortunately I went at the same time as Mister Cuttle. I think he may have come to warn you against Sneed and Glimmery."

"But he was with Glimmery," I said.

"But no friend of his, I imagine. More than likely Glimmery had compromising material on Cuttle, something that would put him in poor standing with the other Crawlies. He was squeezing Cuttle for information, and doubtless wanted Cuttle to offer to investigate your identities. Crawlies have their own intelligence networks, you see, and Bosa Sennen is just as much a problem for them as for us. Instead, Cuttle tried to reach you. He knew it was risky, and there was a chance Sneed would get to him first. When he sensed my presence on the eighth floor, he panicked and fled—he must have thought I was Sneed, or one of his associates. Only Sneed was behind him. There was nothing I could do about it."

"You were in the hotel when all that happened?" I asked.

"I lay low on the seventh floor, and left when it was safe."

"We saw each other, I think," I said, thinking of that floating eye in the stairwell.

He nodded slowly. "The remote? I am sorry if that discomfited you. It was a gift from Bosa, after I suffered an accident in her service. I say 'gift,' but it was more a case of making sure I remained useful to her as an agent. I admit I have found it very handy since leaving her service." He gave me an appreciative smile. "I saw you dispensing with Sneed's attentions, as well. You showed admirable restraint in not dropping him on the spot."

"We don't like being snooped on," Fura said.

"Neither do I," Lagganvor answered. "So it seems we have that much in common."

Fura put the Ghostie knife down on the bedside table, next to the blasted telephone directory, where the knife seemed to lose focus, becoming not just harder to see, but harder to think about, harder to remember that it had ever been there in the first place.

"We sit tight, at least until there's news from Prozor," Fura said. "No rash moves, from any of us. We'll be leaving this world sooner or later, but on our terms. And I don't want to run foul of Glimmery in the process. We have weapons, but we also have a friend in that infirmary so we can't just shoot our way out of here, much as that would suit me."

"And do wonders for your reputation," Lagganvor said.

She met this remark with an equivocal look, but instead of rebuffing him she said: "I can't help our reputations, not any more. They've already made up their minds about us—as far as the worlds are concerned we're either Bosa or the remnants of her crew, still doing her bidding. We tried to act reasonably, in self-defence, and ended up destroying another ship—just as Bosa would have done. Now anything we do, for better or worse, will be viewed through that prism." Fura forced an ironic smile. "She's trapped us from beyond the grave. Freed us, or damned us, I don't know which—not just yet. But I refuse to become her, not while I've still got a choice. Would she have shown kindness or consideration for one of her own?"

"Only if that person was useful to her," Lagganvor answered coldly.

"Strambli's useful to the crew. But beyond that, she's one of us—our friend. We won't leave without her."

Deciding that my sister and Lagganvor could be trusted not to kill each other, at least for a few moments, I moved to the window and opened the shutters just enough to peer down into the street below. It was fully dark now and the sky had begun to emit its usual quantity of rain and steam. Figures moved from bar to bar, shop to shop, trams coming and going along Shine, the neon signs and advertisements providing splashes of colour against the tomb-grey buildings and the black-mirrored puddles and sluice channels. I thought again of the man I had seen trying to light a match, striking it over and over until the flame caught, and that in turn sent my thoughts drifting back to the journal and its speculation about the Shadow Occupations.

"Did Bosa ever speak to you of her private concerns, Lagganvor?"

"She had very little choice," he answered me, reaching up to push the hair from his eyes. "Anyone in my position had to know many of her operational secrets."

"The quoin cache?" Fura asked.

"Yes. She called it The Miser. It's a rock, with no field around it, so not really a true bauble. Perhaps it was a bauble once, until the field expired."

I glanced at my sister. This intelligence was much more

specific than I would expect were he making up a story on the spot.

"You're willing to tell us this much?" I asked.

"I've told you nothing. How many fieldless rocks do you think are out there? You could scour the Congregation for a thousand years and never stumble on The Miser."

"But you could find it again," I said.

"We visited it often enough. Bosa never wanted to carry quoins around for too long, so if she'd had a run of successes then we always swung by The Miser to off-load."

"Is it occupied?" Fura asked.

"No—but it does have a will of its own. A robot mind, enslaved to control its defences. I know the location. If you gave me access to charts and an Armillary, I could plot you a course to it immediately. If I am not mistaken we're presently on the same side of the Old Sun as The Miser, so your quarry should not lie too many weeks from the wheel."

"Will it recognise us?" I asked.

"Even if it did, it would still require an approach password."

"Which you will give to me now," Fura said.

"Or I could keep it back as a form of personal insurance. I will give you the password in good time, believe me. My own survival would depend on recalling it."

"You are quite sure it hasn't slipped your mind," Fura said.

"Little chance of that," Lagganvor said, not without a touch of pride. "I have always had a gift for such things. It was why she was so determined to come after me. Malice was part but not all of it. She wished also to protect her long-term interests. Kill me, and she would eliminate any possibility of her stores and hideouts being discovered."

"You and I," Fura said, "are going to have so *much* to talk about."

Lagganvor flashed a quick, nervous smile. "In which case I hope that I will provide sparkling company."

"Oh, I'm sure you won't disappoint," I said, trying not to sound rankled, but unable to avoid the feeling that my sister had just found herself a much more engaging conversational partner.

The squawk buzzed. I picked up the handset, thinking that it could only be Surt, since Prozor could not have reached the infirmary yet.

Yet it was Prozor.

"That you, girlie?"

"Yes," I answered, picking up on the tension in her voice, and knowing it did not bode well. "We're still here. We have things... under control."

"That's good. That's very good. I wish I had better news from my end, though. I'm with Glimmery's people. They jumped me on the way, and there wasn't nothin' I could do about it."

I had the handset set to speaker, so Fura was able to follow the exchange.

"Have they hurt you?" she asked.

"No, Cap'n—not so you'd notice. Roughed me up a little, but what's a little roughin' up between friends? Anyway, they're taking me to see Glimmery, and they wanted you to know."

"Is Sneed with you?" I asked.

"No—no snot-face, just a few of the other specimens that keep bobbin' up. Glimmery's decided to play his hand, though. He's got Strambli and Surt hostage, and it looks like I'll be joinin' 'em. He says he'd very much welcome your company."

"The launch hasn't even arrived yet," I said.

"He's decided not to wait, if he ever planned to. Look, I can't speak for Surt or Strambli, but don't get yourselves caught on my account. I've wriggled out of worse scrapes than this. Get to—"

There was a thud and a crackle, then a sort of fumbling sound as someone picked up Prozor's fallen handset.

"No scarperin', Cap'n Marance," said a thick, gravelly voice, which I took to be one of Sneed or Glimmery's enforcers. "Not you nor yer ringer, the one you claim ain't related, oh no, sir, not at all. You get yer skates on and come over and see your chum at the infirmary, where Mister Glimmery's very keen for a chin-wag."

"Why?" Fura asked, snatching the handset from me.

"Because he likes your easy-going company. Bring your new pal, as well—Mister Glimmery can't wait to be acquainted."

"Pass a message to Glimmery for me," Fura said. "Tell him I'm coming, and to be ready."

"You give in easier than I expected," said the voice.

"You mistake my meaning," she replied, ending the call. Then, to the two of us: "We'll need the suits. Go to the lock-up and cobble together what you can while I squawk Paladin. Take only what we need to get back to the launch."

"What about the other supplies?"

"We'll do without."

I still had the volition pistol and I was glad of it as I escorted Lagganvor to the end of the corridor. I opened the lock-up. "If you're coming with us, you'll need a suit. Put on as much as you can, then help me carry the rest."

"Thoughtful of you to think of me ahead of time."

"We didn't. One of us will have to make other arrangements. That may be the least of our concerns, though." I indicated for him to get into Surt's suit, which I judged would fit him better than Prozor's. He put on all the parts except for the helmet, with the easy familiarity of someone who had spent ample time on ships, quickly figuring out the connections and completing the pressure seals. For all my misgivings over Fura's duplicitous means of reaching him, I was starting to think that he might not make such a bad addition to our crew.

"Would you like me to hold that weapon, while you put on your suit?" he asked.

I looked at him with amused skepticism, that he could be so naive. "And shoot me where I stand?"

"I wouldn't dream of it. Our interests are very closely aligned, so I would only be shooting myself." His tone softened. "Adrana, wasn't it? That was what the woman on the squawk called you."

"Just a name," I said, putting on my suit one-handed, which made a difficult process virtually impossible.

"She *is* your sister, isn't she? Arafura Ness. Two respectable daughters of Mazarile, swept into Bosa's influence."

"You don't know us."

"But I know everything there is to know about Bosa. I've made it my hobby. If I am being chased down by intelligence forces following particular leads, it is in my very best interests to be one step ahead of them."

"Then those same people will know we're innocent."

"No—they know only that Adrana and Arafura Ness were documented victims of Bosa Sennen, and should therefore be considered turned to her side, as was her usual habit. One or both of them may even have supplanted the former Bosa."

"They're wrong," I said curtly. "She had me, it's true. But not long enough to turn me, the way she did Illyria Rackamore." I stepped into my boots, giving him a sharp look. "You'd know all about Illyria, I think. I imagine you were already in Bosa's service when she took Rackamore's daughter. Why didn't you *do* something?"

"I . . . did not condone what she did," he said, glancing away at the critical moment, as if I might read some weakness or regret in his eyes. "She was turned quickly, anyway. That was a mercy."

"Why didn't she turn you just as thoroughly, Lagganvor?"

He scooped up another helmet, some boots and a pressure suit. "Let's get these things to Arafura. I get the impression Mister Glimmery is in no mood to be kept waiting."

*

The elevator doors unlatched, Fura scissored them open, and we stepped out in silence. There were only two sources of light beyond the elevator itself. One was the puddle of yellow-brown illumination concentrated over the front desk, hardly enough to read by, and the other was a changing pattern of night-time lights and neon banners playing through the glass panes of the revolving door, spilling pastel colours across black and white tiles. There was no sound but gusts of drizzle on windows, hard footsteps on damp pavements, and the rattle of passing trams.

We walked toward the revolving door, which was still turning. That struck me as an oddness, because I knew how quickly it stopped after someone had come or gone.

The flat-faced desk clerk was slumped down over his newspaper again, just as he had been the previous evening. Fura shook her head. "I wasn't keen on him, Lagganvor, but you didn't have to knock him out just to pay us a visit, did you?"

She had her metal hand around Lagganvor's sleeve, clutching him like a hostage.

"It wasn't my doing," he said. "I waited until he was away from the desk, then came straight up to your floor."

I moved to the clerk, dug my fingers into the hair on the back of his scalp, and pulled his head up from the desk. It came away with a pudding-like slurp, leaving rather too much of him still imprinted on the newspaper. I held his head where it was, long enough to prove my point, then allowed him to return to his earlier restful posture.

"Are you sure about that?"

"It wasn't me," Lagganvor said, with a force that encouraged me to think he might not be lying. "I swear. He was a nuisance, and greedy as well, but he wasn't mixed up in this." He turned to both of us in turn. "What I did for Bosa was another life. Self-preservation is one thing—I'd have killed to protect myself from her, if I ever thought she'd come back—but I wasn't responsible for this."

"It's all right, coves," said a voice I felt I had known all my life, and would count myself blessed never to hear again. "It wasn't 'im. The boy was on the take from Mister Glimmery anyway, so it was high-time he was moved on."

Sneed had been in the lobby all along—watching us from a dingy corner between two potted plants, his brown-coated presence easily melting into the shadows. He had a weapon, the same gun he had pointed at me in the alley, and this time he was taking no chances. "A twitch from you, Miss, and I'll take both your arms off before you know what's happened."

"Mister Sneed," said Lagganvor. "You and I can do business. These women are your primary interest, not me. Let me go and I'll tell you everything, here and now."

Fura snarled and tightened her grip on him, fingers digging into the leathery fabric of Surt's suit. "You won't rat us out, you weasel."

"Let me help you along, Sneed," Lagganvor said, persisting in his attempted negotiation. "I even have a gift for you—a token of my goodwill."

He wrenched free of Fura—before either she or Sneed could react—and held out his right hand in a curious beseeching manner, with the palm raised to the ceiling. Then, with his left hand, he struck the back of his own head.

His right eye popped out onto his palm. It sat there, perfect and glassy, just as I had seen it hovering in the stairwell, with that peculiar look of fixed surprise about it. Even I, who had seen the thing once before, was unavoidably mesmerised. I hardly dared look at Lagganvor's face, but a glance confirmed all I had feared, which was that there was now a dark socket where the orb had been, and that the production of his eye had been no conjuring trick.

Sneed still had his weapon, which remained pointed directly at me, and I think some slow-geared part of his mind was registering a developing wrongness, a sense that he had been played.

Lagganvor threw the eye into the air.

The orb came off his palm in an arc, reached its apex and *stopped*.

It was hovering just under the ceiling, the pupil staring out horizontally.

Mister Sneed was torn. He twitched his weapon from me to the eye and then back to me again. Then the eye dropped down until it was level with his own two eyes and swept forward until it was no more than a span from his nose. Then it slowly began to narrow the distance.

Mister Sneed brought his aim back onto the eye, taking a step backward, then another, and the eye slid forward to neutralise his advantage. It was enough for me. I wanted him removed as a problem; wanted him dead. I drew the volition pistol, felt my arm lock onto him, the weapon both responding to my desire to eliminate Sneed and hardening that desire, concretising it as an obligatory act, something that must and would come to pass, and my finger itched and tingled until squeezing the trigger felt as natural and thoughtless as breathing. I shot him at close range.

The pink-white energy bolt lashed over him like the static fire that sometimes plays in the rigging of ships. Mister Sneed dropped his weapon and the rest of him followed, collapsing to the ground with no more than a single attenuated whimper.

I walked over, scooped the pistol from his lifeless fingers, and tossed it to Fura.

Lagganvor's eye was still in the air, turning on its axis like a miniature globe. I had a hundred questions about that eye, about its provenance and capabilities.

"It's likely he came with others," Lagganvor said. "They're most probably outside, covering any possible escape routes. I'll send the eye out ahead of us."

It swooped out through the revolving door. I looked down at the still form of Mister Sneed, thinking that my life had just divided itself into two parts, one in which I had not killed a person standing before me and one in which I had, and there was no undoing that separation. Fura and the others had killed before, of course, and we all shared in the unwitting butchery of the *Calenture*. Yet beyond the conscious acceptance of what I had done, all I felt was a sort of heavy solemnity, as if I had just put my name to a legal document that came with numerous ramifications and responsibilities, codicils and appendices that would likely shape the form of my life until my grave, but which had precisely no impact on the immediate minutes or even hours ahead of me.

*I am a murderess,* I thought. *I was not, and now I am.*

Lagganvor held up his hand, palm vertical this time, and the eye came back through the door and sped into his clutch. He pinched it between his fingers, raised the curtain of hair, and corked it back into its socket, just as if it were the most commonplace thing.

# 19

Glimmery's men were at the base of the rope-bridge, and were brazen with their weapons. There were a dozen of his thugs, more than I had seen in any one place before, and if they were expecting some trouble from Fura and me they had certainly left nothing to chance.

Fura and I were either side of Lagganvor. We walked slowly up to the men, Fura sticking out her jaw in her most defiant manner, even though all she had by way of persuasion was Sneed's pistol.

"Where is Mister S?" asked one of the men, who had the handset of a squawk box sticking out of his coat pocket, and whose greasy, gravelly voice reminded me of the man who had demanded our presence. He was a tall, frog-chinned man with a deep dent in his forehead.

"He's indisposed," I said, as we came to a halt about twenty paces from the rope-bridge, with only an expanse of muddy ground between us and them. The rain had become torrential since we left the hotel, and now it was coming down the side of the infirmary in continuous brown conveyor belts of filthy water. "Pass a message to Glimmery for us, will you? If he releases our friends and allows us free passage to the dock, there'll be no more trouble."

The man started laughing. It was a wet, guttural laugh, slow at first, but increasing in speed as he got into his stride. The bulge of his throat began to oscillate in sympathy. Picking up on his mood, some of the other men began to laugh along with him. But they remained hair-trigger tense, and I could not help but notice that the muzzles of their weapons were sweeping the shadows and corners beyond us, not just the three members of our assembled party.

"No more trouble, she says!" the man said, bending at the waist as if his self-inflicted mirth was more than he could reasonably bear. "You've got the wrong end of it, cove." He had to stop as his laughter overwhelmed again, although it was even more forced than it had been the first time. "The trouble's coming your way, not ours. Now put down those little toys of yours."

"If we don't?" Fura asked.

"There's two possibilities," the man said, wheezing a bit as he got his breath back. "Mister Glimmery wouldn't like it and, since he knows what's going on down here, he might decide to take it out on your friends. Or he might tell us to shoot you and be done with it."

Fura peered up at the infirmary. "Glimmery's watching, is he?"

"You can depend on it."

"Then I imagine he can hear us as well. Can you, Glimmery? I have something to tell you. You demanded an audience when we arrived. Now I demand mine."

*

We were allowed into his presence a final time. It was in the infirmary, not his gold palace, and after we had been searched, and disarmed, and roughed-up enough to know our place, we were allowed our audience.

Glimmery had made a little reception area for himself, with a table, chairs, some curtains for privacy, and a number of his attendants standing around ready to answer his immediate needs. There were drinks on the table, as well as his lacquered box, and the chair he was in was bulky enough to have been his own, brought down specially.

Prozor and Surt were alive, if battered, and we were permitted to examine Strambli and satisfy ourselves that she had come to no additional harm. Eddralder was there, as was Merrix, and he said Strambli was showing increasing signs of lucidity, between bouts of unconsciousness.

"Sit down, please," Glimmery said, beckoning us to the empty chairs. "There's much to discuss. You'll be pleased to hear that the launch has docked. The injured from the *White Widow* are being brought straight to the infirmary as we speak, as well as the walking wounded, and those deputised to care for them."

Fura scoffed, but she took her seat as commanded. "Did you think you'd spook us into leaving that easily?"

"I thought I would test the limits of your resolve, and that I seem to have done. Killing Sneed was an ill-considered act, born of desperation, which gives me every grounds to detain you. For which Captain Restral will be most grateful. When he is sufficiently recovered to consider such matters, I believe he will be more than willing to discuss splitting the incentive money."

"You're on borrowed time out here, Glimmery. Money won't help you. Sooner or later the same banks and combines that put up that incentive will decide they don't like the way you're running things." Fura lifted her chin. "They'll put up with a bit of lawlessness, especially in the aftermath of last year's banking crash. You're an irrelevance for the time being. But that won't last. Enjoy your milk baths, and all that gold you like to surround yourself with. A year from now you'll be lucky to be breathing."

Glimmery met this with a tolerant smile. "You're in a fine position to be making that sort of prediction. You have no weapons, and you barely have a crew. You'll be breathing in a year from now, I'm sure of it, but only because you'll be locked up in some Sunwards cell, kept alive while they sweat out every last drop of information about Bosa Sennen and the *Nightjammer*. Either way, I doubt it will go well for you. They'll either decide you were close to her but never privy to her innermost secrets, and you'll lose your usefulness as a living witness. Or they'll decide that you are, in fact, the current embodiment of her, immune to interrogation and torture as only the truly insane can be, and short of scooping the desired knowledge out of your brain with a fork there's no way you'll give anything up. At which point, it pains me to add, you'll also have exceeded your usefulness to them." Then, slowly, he turned his gaze onto me. "Of course, they'll be certain to extend the same courtesy to you. You might just as well be Bosa. They'll need to make certain, so there'll be no favours, no dispensations, no special treatment for either of you. I imagine you'll be locked up separately, on different worlds, to die separately and alone after a succession of miseries."

"You're wrong about one thing," Fura said. "I didn't come here without a weapon."

Glimmery chuckled. "You've been searched. Thoroughly this time. Your suits and equipment alike, and I told them to be specially watchful for Ghostie gubbins, since it's rumoured you have such things. I even had them run a piece of lookstone over that arm of yours, just in case there was something lodged inside it."

"The arm isn't the weapon."

"No?" he asked, with the air of one losing patience, even if the topic under consideration was of some minor interest. "Then you'd better enlighten us, because—"

Fura touched her face. "It's what's in me, Glimmery. Our mutual affliction. The glowy."

He looked sad and a little disappointed, as if he had been counting on something more imaginative.

"Then I regret to inform you that you are mistaken. I have studied the glowy in all its guises. Doctor Eddralder has been tireless in furnishing me with medical literature going back many centuries. The condition is rather well documented—as is its progression and the options for treating it, which in my case are now very greatly diminished. It *is* an affliction, as you will find out for yourself—or would, if you had the luxury of living with it long enough. But it is entirely harmless to the unaffected. It cannot be transmitted from host to host except by unusual means. And it has absolutely no utility as a weapon."

"You misunderstand me," Fura said. "I know what the glowy is, and what it can do. It makes me see things differently. Makes me think and act in a way that I wouldn't, if I didn't have the glowy, and that's no different to having a physical weapon."

"The glowy makes you a little madder, you mean, and therefore less predictable?"

She nodded with uncharacteristic meekness.

"If you want to put it that way."

"There might almost be something in that," Glimmery said, conceding her point. "The glowy certainly predisposes one to rash action. The circumvention of forethought and analytic thinking. But if that is the case, you have merely regained parity. It is no advantage, when I also have the glowy. We would be as mad and reckless as each other, and any such benefits would be completely..."

Glimmery stopped in mid-sentence. A huge, buttress-like muscle twitched near the base of his neck. He made to speak, then swallowed hard. With a tremendous and visible effort of will, much as if he were passing a large kidney stone, he contorted his features into a smile, directed solely at Fura.

"You do have a peculiar effect on me, though, Miss Ness. I have noticed it twice now. Just being around you seems to bring on my attacks."

"I noticed it too," Fura said. She touched her cheek. "I can feel it tingling a little under my skin."

"Just a tingle? How I envy you."

"You shouldn't envy me. It's going to get a lot worse, so you said."

"Yes, that is true. I do not wish to strike a pessimistic note, but you may already be beyond the more orthodox therapies." He shifted in his chair, spasms clearly shooting through his great frame. "Despite what I said about the glowy being useless as a weapon, I admit that there may be some influence between our two colonies of spores."

"They say lightvine glows more brightly in the presence of more lightvine," Fura said. "It could be psychosomatic, I suppose."

"Psychosomatic?" Glimmery twisted in the chair, the veins in the side of his head standing out like luminous worms, as bright, or perhaps even brighter than the surrounding traces of his lightvine infection. "No, I don't think so. Eddralder—if I might impose on your service. Bring Merrix, and the remedy."

Eddralder nodded to his clinical assistants, and then knelt by Glimmery, leaning in with great gentleness to assess the condition of his patient. "It seems bearable," he said, in a tone of hopeful encouragement. "The remedy is available, of course, but if you think you can—"

"I have too much to do. Give me the fix."

"Each dose hastens the next attack, and depletes our supply of medicine. I must remind you of that."

"No lectures, Doctor—not now."

Long vertical grooves formed in Eddralder's face, bracketing him from eye to chin. "Of course. But just this once... might we spare Merrix? If I had ever meant to—"

"Bring her."

Merrix was brought forward, and so were the two gold syringes on their little platter. They had puzzled me to begin with, but now I understood them to be identical, charged with the same drug. Glimmery would make the final choice as to which syringe was injected into him, and which into Merrix. Merrix was being slowly debilitated by these needless injections of the counter-glowy preparation, but the ritual ensured that there was no risk of Eddralder trying to poison his patient. It was no more than a secondary precaution. Even if by some means he had found a way to get poison into one of those syringes but not the other, or had abandoned Merrix to her fate, the doctor had no means of escape. This was a backwater world where Glimmery exercised an iron control over the entry and exit. Short of forcing Eddralder to inject the same drugs into himself—which would have quickly rendered him ineffective—it was the ideal means of coercion.

Glimmery snatched up one of the syringes without hesitation and jammed it into his forearm, the veins already standing out. As the drug hit he reached for the lacquered box containing his biting stick.

"Inject her, Doctor Eddralder," he said, grimacing as he forced out the words. "You may have the pleasure this time."

"Please don't make me," Eddralder said.

Glimmery ground his teeth together, barely able to speak now that the medicine was taking its effect. "Unless you would rather one of Sneed's men did it?"

"No," Eddralder said, resigned. He took Merrix's arm, which she offered without resistance, not even looking at him, not even flinching as he slid the needle in and depressed the plunger. He withdrew the needle. A second or two later, Merrix began to palsy, her eyes turning to blank whites as they rolled back in their sockets. Eddralder touched her wrist, whispered some plea for forgiveness, then turned back to Glimmery. Two of the attendants took Merrix away and lowered her quivering form into a nearby seat, one of them supporting her head.

"It will pass," Eddralder said to Glimmery.

Glimmery took the biting stick from the box, looked at Eddralder and nodded once, before ramming the stick between his teeth. His jaw clamped tight with reptilian swiftness, as if driven by some entirely primal reflex.

Eddralder reached into his surgical gown and drew out a black pouch. He set it down on the table and unrolled it from one end to the other. It contained six gold syringes.

The counter-glowy drug, as we had already witnessed, was as cruel as the malady itself. But these agonies of convulsion were temporary, and within perhaps ten or twenty seconds I sensed an easing in Glimmery, a sure indication that the worst was over, at least until the next attack, and the next dose.

But even as Glimmery became more subdued, a secondary wrongness became apparent. He was calmer, and yet his eyes were widening. He still had the stick firmly between his teeth.

Eddralder had his surgical gloves on now. With one hand he pinched down Glimmery's lower jaw, the action demanding considerable effort on his part, and with the other he extracted the stick and returned it to the box.

"No one should touch it without gloves, and even then the gloves should be disposed of very carefully." He snapped off his own gloves with practised effortlessness, never touching the fingers with his bare skin, then dropped them into the box. He closed the lid, did up the little clasp, and returned his attention to Glimmery. "I couldn't get poison into the syringe, not without endangering Merrix. But I was able to coat the string around your stick with a very potent toxin. It will induce a gradual paralysis, eventually extending to your heart." He indicated the six syringes. "There is, of course, a counter-agent. One of these injections will reverse the effects of the toxin, at least to the point where you are able to make a reasonable recovery. Then you will only have the glowy to concern yourself with. For that, I am afraid, you will need to seek the services of a different physician."

One of the gowned attendants sprung forward and held a pistol against Eddralder. One of those who was already with Merrix grabbed hold of a clump of her hair and wrenched it back, so savagely that even in the throes of her convulsions she gave a pained gasp.

But Glimmery twitched his head from side to side, his eyes still wide.

"He understands," Eddralder said, pushing the pistol away. "His life depends on one of those syringes. Here is my promise to you, Glimmery, as your doctor—however temporary that station may now prove. You have about six hours to administer the correct dose. Any longer than that, and you will either be dead or too far-gone for the counter-agent to have any useful effect. Too far-gone, Far-Gone. How do you like that?" Eddralder was standing now. "You will allow the Ness sisters, their companions, their injured friend, and Merrix and I, free and unobstructed passage to the port. You will assist them in any way they request, and we will depart. Once we are in clear space, I will tell you which syringe to use. You are, of course, free to take your chances at any point. Perhaps you will think the odds short enough to risk a random selection. That will be your choice. I will merely leave it to your imagination as to the effect any of the other five syringes would have on you."

Although the paralysing toxin was clearly taking its toll, Glimmery found the strength to speak, albeit only a single word.

"You..."

"I would save your energies if I were you," Eddralder said, not without a certain physicianly kindness. "You're going to need them. Now, in addition to my earlier stipulations, the following arrangements will be made without obstruction. I will remove a quantity of medicines from the infirmary—just enough for our immediate purposes. The Ness sisters will be given sufficient vacuum gear for the entire party, including Merrix and Strambli. There will be no trickery, and no duplicity. It is in your very best interests to ensure that we have a frictionless departure, because the sooner we are safe the sooner I can transmit the information your life depends on. Is that fully understood?"

By some heroic means Glimmery managed a nod.

"Very good," Eddralder said. "I think we have an understanding." Then, to Fura: "Do we still have an arrangement, Captain?"

His question must have taken Fura off her guard, but she held her composure very creditably. "Whatever... has been agreed, Doctor."

She directed a sharp questioning glance in my direction, but it was there and gone in a blink and I do not think any other soul noticed it.

"Good," Eddralder said. "Then let us begin. Mister Glimmery will thank us for not delaying a moment longer than necessary."

Mister Glimmery looked at us with wide and terrified eyes. Already I fancied that his lips were turning a little bluer, as he found it more of a struggle to breathe. I should imagine that there were a number of things he wished to say to us at that point.

"One in six," I said, nodding at the syringes. "If it were the other way around, I don't think I'd hesitate."

# 20

Glimmery's people were reluctantly cooperative. Doctor Eddralder was permitted to stock a small portable medicine chest, which he stuffed to the limits of its capacity, while Prozor and Fura made sure that we all had the necessary vacuum gear to make the short crossing to the launch. This was more easily achieved than I had expected, although it took a few minutes for the desired elements to be brought to the infirmary. Glimmery must have kept a supply of suit parts in his palace, just in case he and his associates had an urgent need to cross vacuum. Then we were left unmolested as we completed our preparations. Glimmery's thugs stood around us with pistols and blades, only a twitch away from using them, but Doctor Eddralder's gambit had dropped a curtain of invincibility around us that was as impervious as any bauble field. If hate could have been bottled, though, we could have set ourselves up with a lifetime's supply. I have rarely felt as loathed as in those final minutes.

Doctor Eddralder tried to give some comfort and reassurance to Merrix as she was put into a suit, and he was able to administer an injection that offset some of the effects of the previous dose, but she was still confused and somnambulant. There was a listless absence of focus in her eyes, as if her mind and body were greatly displaced from each other. I felt for her, and could hardly bear to imagine the torments she had been put through, but I reserved judgement as to how much of a soul remained behind that brow even as I vowed that we would do our level best for her. We could promise no comforts on *Revenger*, and no great prospect of continued security, but even the worst of our days would be an improvement on her life under Glimmery.

So I told myself, and in those moments I managed to believe it, too.

Then there was the matter of Strambli. She was conscious, but also confused, and there was clearly no prospect of getting her into a suit. Her wound was still heavily padded and bandaged, and she could not have walked in any case. So—after quick consultation with Eddralder—it was agreed that she would leave the same way she had arrived, in the cargo chest. I whispered a few words of comfort to her as we lowered her into the chest, leaving the lid off for the time being. I did not wish her to think she was being stashed in a coffin.

Lagganvor had Surt's suit on, and it was too much trouble to swap them now. So Surt and Prozor made do with the parts that came down from the palace, while Fura and I scrabbled around for helmets that would fit well enough to get us to the launch. Our last demand was to be given back our own weapons, as well as some extra ones by way of insurance. Glimmery, by then, was incapable of offering a verbal response, but he still had enough residual movement to signal his angered, impotent compliance. He was in a pitiable condition, and I wondered if that six-hour estimate had been overly optimistic. But I supposed there were many stations on the way to the final state, including deeper and deeper degrees of immobility and unconsciousness, and I assumed that Eddralder had taken each of those stages into full account. Glimmery did not need to be the one who injected himself, after all.

When we were set to leave, which could not have been more than thirty minutes after Glimmery had clamped his teeth onto the biting stick, Fura and I went back to him. He was still in his chair, almost jammed into it, his swelling muscles locking into rigidity. His underlings were fussing around him to the limit of their abilities. Short of taking pot-luck with the six syringes, though, there was nothing they could do to lessen his discomfort.

Fura brought her face level with his own.

"All we wanted to do was heal Strambli. Granted, I had some business of my own with Lagganvor, but that never needed to be *your* business. And now look at you."

Glimmery tried to speak, but all that came out of him was a hollow gurgling. Fura used the back of her glove to wipe the spittle from his lips, as sweetly as a mother tending an infant.

"Just think how much better it would have been," she went on, "if you'd let us come and go. There's lesson for you there, I think. You got on the wrong side of us; you over-reached yourself." Then she paused, pushing herself up, directing a glance at me. "We won't meet again, so let this be a parting. I am Arafura Ness. I took down Bosa Sennen, and I took her ship, but that does not mean that I have become the thing that she was. I never desired to take her name, or to adopt her ways. And I won't. I'm going to be much too busy for that." She smiled down at him. "Yet I must admit to a certain dark admiration for one of her traits. In the midst of her madness she was always prepared to take the necessary action. As am I, if my existence depends on it. You made a very grave error in presuming to think you could better us."

"Goodbye, Mister Glimmery," I said.

We wheeled Strambli to the elevator, Lagganvor and Eddralder helping Merrix, while Surt and Prozor deterred any advances against our party with vigorous jabs of their pistols and blades. The elevator took us down to the lowest level of the infirmary, from where we had a clear passage to the rope-bridge that led down to the fixed surface of Port Endless. We were never more exposed than in the long, difficult minutes it took to get Strambli to the base of that ladder. The same detachment of thugs waited at the bottom, and I wondered if we might have trouble from them. But word had clearly been sent down. They stood back, flanking our exit from the bridge, but not impeding it.

"Better pray he lasts until you're on that ship," said the

frog-chinned one. "'Cause if he dies, I wouldn't give any of you five seconds."

"He will make the six hours," Eddralder said, pausing to snap open his umbrella. "I am very rarely wrong in calculating my dosages, and I took particular pains in this instance. He can expect the necessary information as soon as Captain Ness deems us safe from any reprisal. Now, would you gentlemen be so kind as to escort us to the dock?"

"Move aside!" a voice called. "Wounded party coming through!"

They were coming up the muddy rise to the ground under the infirmary. It was a huddle of figures, some in vacuum suits and some not, some walking alone, some being assisted, and some leaning hard into trolleys bearing blanketed forms. The rain made glossy statues of their suits, curtaining off capes and hoods and the improvised protection they had rigged over the trolleys. The trolley-pushers were slipping on the greasy ground. Bringing up the rear, crouching into the steepening incline, were two hooded forms who moved with a familiar shuffling gait.

We slowed. Fura and I, who had been flanking Strambli's trolley, advanced across the treacherous ground until we had halved the distance to Captain Restral's group. I needed no confirmation that it was them.

"Halt where you are," said one of the walking wounded, speaking with a commanding but broken voice, as of some capable man who had been brought to his limits. "We know who you are. You'll surrender to us immediately."

He was at least as tall as Eddralder, and he wore a vacuum suit up to the neck, but no helmet. He was, I should estimate, sixty-five or seventy years old, with what had once been fine, aristocratic features, but which now looked sunken-cheeked and desperate, with a high mottled forehead and a wild white sweep of dishevelled hair. He had a long-barrelled pistol aimed at us in his right hand, and his left hand was not there at all, the sleeve of his suit ending in a crudely-welded stump, a lathering of metal that was too shiny and fresh to be anything but recent work.

"Captain Restral, I presume?" Fura asked. "I heard you were injured, sir."

"Surrender," the man said, his pistol wavering from one of us to the other. "Which of you is Adrana Ness? Which is the other?"

"I am Adrana," I said. "And I'm very sorry for your injury, Captain Restral. But we won't be surrendering." I cocked my head at the men at the base of the rope-bridge. "Tell them!"

Frog-chin cupped his hands to his mouth, bellowing above the sound of the rain. "They're under Mister Glimmery's protection. They're not to be delayed on their way to port. The tall one, Doc Eddralder, spiked some poison into Glimmery and if he don't make it to space, he won't say how we undo the poison."

The man listened to this, rain streaking down his face, gluing his hair to his scalp in ropy strands. He reached up with his silver-capped stump, as if he wished to wipe the rain from his eyes but had forgotten his deficit.

"Is this true, Doctor?"

"Yes, and I'll be true to my word. But we must have passage. I am sorry for your wounded—sorry also that I will not be able to attend to them. But they will be treated to the best of the infirmary's capabilities."

A much younger man stepped out of the party. He was uninjured, so far as I could judge, and had been assisting the others. He was a little shorter than me, and in place of a vacuum suit he wore ordinary shipboard clothes, trousers, tunic and lace-up boots, all now muddy and rain-sodden, as if he had slipped several times between here and the port.

"Adrana Ness?" he asked, meeting my gaze. "I am Chasco. I said I would be glad to make your acquaintance, and now I am glad to be able to address you face to face. I hope you and your sister burn for what you've done."

I could not say with confidence if he was younger or older than me, but I doubt very much that our ages differed by more than three years, for his face was unlined and boyish, even as I saw in it the evident strains of recent experience. I would not say that he was handsome, not by the common criteria, but there was some pleasing aspect to his features, a humility and openness that under other circumstances—any but these—might have made me think well of him, even as I chided myself for being taken in by such disarming superficiality.

"Chasco," I said, trying to project my entire being into my voice and expression. "We did not intend this. It was a mistake—an innocent error. You must believe me."

"I would like to," he said, looking into my face. "You almost seem to believe it yourself."

"I swear to you, we thought we were firing away from the *White Widow.* We only meant to take out your peripheral rigging. We never meant to strike the *Calenture.* We had no idea she was there."

"If you had struck with grape-shot, I might accept that. But those were hull-penetrating slugs. They have only one function, which is to mutilate and murder. It was a deliberate, cold-blooded retaliation—cruelly disproportionate to the minor damage we inflicted on you."

"I am sorry for Captain Restral," I said nodding at the taller man. "Truly I am, and for your other wounded. But an injury like that…" I stumbled on my words, not wanting to cause more offence than had already been committed. "Accidents happen in space, Chasco, even to the best of us."

"That is not Captain Restral," Chasco said mildly.

"I was told he had survived."

"He did. Shall I show you? This is Mister Trensler, our senior navigator and master of sail. He lost part of his arm, but as you say—accidents happen in space. Captain Restral is over here."

I should not have let him lead me to the trolley, but I did. There was an awning worked up over it, a sheet of canvas supported by four upright rods, and beneath the awning was a blanketed form, covered in its entirety. I had not given it more than a glancing consideration until that point, but now that it was the sole object of my attention I grasped that there was not enough beneath the blanket to be the whole of a man. There was too much missing, the blanket sagging to the platform of the trolley where it ought to have followed the contours of a body. And yet there was a body there, and by the care being given to it, it could not be a corpse.

"Show her," said a stocky, gruff-voiced man, who had a week's growth of beard and a bandage wrapped around his scalp.

"She's seen enough to understand," Chasco said.

"Show her anyway."

Chasco reached to the near end of the trolley and with immense care peeled the blanket away from the head of the form below it. Captain Restral was there, and by some terrible mercy he was unconscious. He had been burned, and what I saw was testament enough to the severity of his injuries. I was spared the worst of it, though, because a close-fitting mask covered the entire lower part of his face, from the nose down. By some quirk of preservation his eyes were undamaged, and with his eyelids closed I might almost have said that he looked restful.

"Whether you believe me or not, Chasco," I said. "Tell him that we are not the crew he sought, and that this was an accident."

"I will relay your statement," Chasco said, beginning to lower the blanket back down onto Captain Restral.

He was not quite fast enough, or I was not quite fast enough in averting my gaze. Restral opened his eyes. There was a moment in which he regarded me with a soft absence of concern, as in our first waking moments. He seemed neither to recognise nor hate me. Then his eyes narrowed, as if a troubling thought had made its first foray into his consciousness. His eyes widened again, and he tried to squirm, and beneath the mask I believe that he was screaming a soundless proclamation of fury and agony.

I pulled away. The ground was treacherous under me and I slipped into the mud, my pistol spilling out of my hand. My knees and palms hit the filth and the rain shocked the back of my neck. Chasco stepped forward and placed his heel on the volition pistol, squashing it into the mud. Then he reached down and wrenched me to my feet, my hand in his, my dirt adding to his already dirtied palm.

"If it was an error," he said quietly, "then I trust that the processes of justice will treat you fairly. But I would not count on clemency. I should run, and keep running, and not look back. Is that your intention now?"

"You have us wrong," I said, breathless after my fall. "You have *me* wrong, Chasco."

Eddralder came and sheltered me beneath his umbrella. He placed his free hand on my shoulder. "We should not detain these deserving cases a moment longer, Adrana."

"You side with them?" Chasco asked.

"My situation here was not one I wished to prolong."

"Then pray that they don't ask too many questions about your association with Glimmery," Chasco said. "I know, Doctor Eddralder. We had ample time to prepare for our arrival, and that included learning all about you."

His words troubled me, but I refused to be drawn into delaying gambits.

"We should go."

Chasco turned to watch as our party passed the much larger one from the *White Widow*, but there was nothing more to be said between us. Or rather, there were a thousand protestations I might have uttered, a thousand cases for our defence, a thousand pleas for understanding, but none of them would have made the slightest difference to Chasco, nor, I think, to any member of that party. Our reputations might as well have been carved into the rock of a bauble and sealed over with a field, for all that our actions mattered. Bosa was laughing at us, I thought, mocking our audacity and foolishness in thinking we could take her ship and that no other part of her would come in the same bargain. Whatever we said or did now, it would be regarded as just another of Bosa's stratagems, fully in keeping with her many lifetimes of subterfuge and trickery.

Then came a voice like dry twigs rustling: "Miss Arafura Ness, Miss Adrana Ness."

It was one of the Crawlies bringing up the rear of the group. They turned to us, rain puddling on their cloaks, only a hint of quick bristling mouthparts and sensory appendages moving within the cavelike darkness of their hoods.

"Mister Scrabble, Mister Fiddle," Fura said, for it was clear these were the same aliens who had tended the corpse of Mister Cuttle. "May we extend our sympathies on your loss, before we depart? You know that it was Mister Sneed's doing, not ours?"

"You are absolved of the crime itself," said the Crawly on the left. "But you were the instigators of the events which precipitated it."

"That's not true," I said. "We didn't ask Cuttle to turn against Glimmery."

"It would not have happened without your presence," said the other Crawly.

"I killed Sneed," I said, picking a strand of mud-smeared hair off my face. "You know that, don't you? I killed the man who killed your friend...associate...however you want to think of him. That makes us square."

"Sneed was an instrument," said the first one. "What of the man who directed him?"

Fura cocked her head. "He's up there. You can go and see him if you wish. Don't expect to get too much out of him right now, though."

"Wait," I said, with a sudden lurching intuition. "You can't kill him, if that's your plan. Not until we reach clear space."

"Arafura Ness. Adrana Ness."

"Yes?" Fura answered.

"This man with you. Lagganvor."

Lagganvor stepped forward. He had his helmet cradled in his arm, ready to drop it over the neck ring of his suit, but for now his head was uncovered, his long hair rain-plastered to his scalp.

"Let 'em go, Mister Scrabble," he said, directing his words at the first Crawly. "And don't lay a feeler on Glimmery until these folk have reached their sunjammer and started making headway."

"You have information," said Mister Fiddle. "Knowledge obtained by Bosa Sennen."

"Knowledge which could be highly detrimental to economic stability," Mister Scrabble said.

"Perhaps I do," Lagganvor said, the shoulders of his suit moving in an easy-going shrug. "I really don't know. She didn't tell me *everything*, you know. Maybe I know about some quoins, maybe I don't." He shot an apologetic look at Fura, which she met with a frown. "I know you'd like to silence me, coves. Shoot me down here, or however you'd do it. But you can't. Much as it grieves you, you still have to operate within the constraints of common law and order, even in a place like this, and especially in the presence of so many honest witnesses in Captain Restral's good people. So you'll have to let me go, just as you have to allow Fura and Adrana to go."

"If we might proceed..." Eddralder insisted.

"Captain Ness," Mister Scrabble said, directing his words very pointedly at Fura. "You may depart. But you will cease your investigations into The Miser. They will only bring you trouble."

Fura was silent, but after an interval she nodded and said: "There's been enough trouble, Mister Scrabble. I want no further part in it."

"Then we wish you good voyaging."

That was the last we saw of the aliens, or Captain Restral's party, or the infirmary. Eddralder hastened us on, and although I believed that he had calculated the toxin dose as accurately as was possible, I also believe he was anxious not to put those calculations to too stringent a test. As we were forced into a thicket of alleys, Lagganvor took out his eye and sent it scouting ahead of us, making sure there were no ill-advised ambushes. He knew those backstreets very well, leading us through with unerring confidence, as if he had plotted and memorised every possible escape route, identifying short-cuts, dead-ends and likely points of concealment. We had made several turns when he paused, held up his hand, and waited for the eye to spring back into his palm. He whispered another command and sent it on ahead of us, winging high over the dividing walls and rooftops of the alley. Once, I saw a hard blue flash and a dog went yelping away from us, its hide singed.

"Can it kill?" I asked him.

"Only if killing is warranted," Lagganvor said, turning back. "Most of the time it serves as a passive observer or tracker. It can see under most conditions, and transmit the information across at least half a league, even when underground or in a built-up area. Simply knowing what is ahead or behind me is often enough of a boon to render force unnecessary."

"I'm surprised Bosa let you have such a toy, if there was a chance of you turning it against her."

"She had no reason to question my loyalty. Besides, the eye was very useful to her. You can imagine how it helped us, during bauble raids—we could send it through any little mousehole, and it never stopped working."

I nodded, thinking of the advantage that eye should have given him when he entered Fura's room, or how he could so easily have turned the tables on us when I shot him through the wall. Perhaps he had not been expecting the ambush, and was taken by surprise before he had a chance to deploy the eye. With Fura pressing that Ghostie knife to his throat, I could understand any willingness not to take a chance.

All the same, there was a small, quiet doubt in my mind.

# 21

We reached the port without difficulty, and completed the crossing to our launch. Given more time, I suppose it might have crossed Glimmery's mind to sabotage it, or drain its fuel tanks, but he had been planning to take both us and *Revenger*, and any action against our launch, besides being clumsily provocative, might have caused the larger ship to slink away uncaptured. Glimmery was not to know that she was short-handed, or that Tindouf and Paladin would be hard-pushed to sail her without assistance.

Although we had one injured party, and no more fuel to splash around than when we had left the Rumbler, Fura was not sparing with the rockets. She poured them on hard, rivets and hull plates groaning under the strain and Wheel Strizzardy falling away behind us with indecent speed. For those of us accustomed to being thrown around in a metal coffin, it was testing enough. There was barely time to lash ourselves down, and we would all sport a fresh catalogue of bruises by morning. For Doctor Eddralder and Merrix, who were not seasoned space travellers, it was a special kind of discomfort. Even Lagganvor had been world-bound for long enough to have forgotten the questionable pleasures of rocket navigation, with bouts of hard thrust and stomach-loosening weightlessness juxtaposed like a perfect form of torture. Yet still, we were away from Glimmery, and I would have considered any sort of unpleasantness to be fair exchange for that freedom.

"Paladin," Fura said, flicking open the ship-to-ship squawk channel. "Do you have us on the sweep?"

The robot's deep voice came over the general speaker. "I have you, Captain Marance. Mister Tindouf has already been notified of your imminent return, and has taken this as an indication to make ready for all ions and sail. Is there anything else you wish me to tell him?"

"No, Paladin, that's good enough for the moment. You don't need to call me Captain Marance any longer, either. Captain Ness is all..." She paused, catching herself, and glancing around just enough to meet my eyes, before averting her own. "We'll return to the old arrangement, Paladin—for the time being."

"Very well, Miss Arafura."

I loosened my buckle so that I might lean closer to the console grille. "Paladin—this is Adrana. We don't expect to be pursued for a few hours, but I want to make sure that the *White Widow* doesn't get any silly ideas about coming after the *Dame*...I mean *Revenger*, once we're under sail." I gave a shudder, smiling at my error. "Just a slip."

"What else?" Fura asked.

"I have computed the possibilities, Miss Adrana," Paladin said, "and the situation is entirely in our favour. The other vessel is far too damaged to attempt pursuit. Even if that were not the case, and she had the full benefit of her sails and ions, she would have no hope of engaging us."

"Be sure that remains the case," I said. "And don't stop sweeping nearby space just in case any other foolhardy souls try for a piece of us."

"They won't," Lagganvor said, strapped in just behind me. "By now everyone within a thousand leagues of Wheel Strizzardy will know about the doctor's little ploy with those syringes."

"I should think there are plenty who wouldn't mind seeing Glimmery dead," I replied.

"No shortage, certainly. But Glimmery has an organisation

around him, and it won't simply collapse the moment he dies. The head of a snake can still deliver a venomous bite, even after it has been decapitated. His enemies will be mindful of the consequences of turning against him. Besides, he has a one-in-six chance of survival, which would not seem such terrible odds if he or his people knew there was no hope of hearing from Doctor Eddralder. It *was* very well done, Doctor. I congratulate you."

"I would have done it sooner, if I'd had a means of escape," Eddralder said, with a nod in my direction. "For Merrix, if not for myself. The toxin itself was not difficult to formulate, for a man in my position."

"It was a strange thing that man said, before we left Captain Restral's party," Lagganvor said.

"You mean Chasco, the Bone Reader?" I asked, contorting myself to face Lagganvor and Doctor Eddralder, who were sitting on opposite sides of the launch's aisle. "I wouldn't pay much heed to anything that came out of him. He was full of spite. You saw the way he made up his mind about me."

"And yet..." Lagganvor said, but then he shook his head, smiling as if he had something very concrete on his mind, but was content to let it go for now. "You are right, Adrana. We shouldn't read too much into baseless accusations."

At last Fura dampened the rockets, saving what little fuel remained in our tanks for the final docking with *Revenger*. "Thirty minutes," she said.

"We are safe now?" Eddralder asked.

Fura adjusted a gyroscope setting. "I wouldn't say we're safe until we've put about fifty million leagues between ourselves and this place."

"By my estimate ninety minutes have passed since Glimmery bit into the toxin. He still has a reasonable margin of error, but I should not like to put too much faith in that. With your permission, might I squawk the infirmary?"

"Not now."

"I must insist."

"You'll insist on nothing. Let him sweat a little longer, then you can send the word."

"I admire your resolve, Captain Ness. But please do not put me in the position of breaking my own promise. I will remind you of it shortly." Doctor Eddralder reached forward to place a consoling hand on his daughter. "It's all right, Merrix. It will be better now. We can help these people."

"Lagganvor," I said, drawing breath. "You never did tell us how you managed to slip out from under Bosa's influence. We have a little time now, so why don't you explain how you managed what no one else could achieve."

Fura gave me a sharp look, as if to say that by questioning some aspect of Lagganvor's account I was doubting some fundamental part of her own judgement as well.

"There's no mystery," Lagganvor said, after the briefest of intervals. "I'll gladly tell you the bones of it now. You'll have questions, too, and I expect them. What do you really know of me, after all?"

"Not much," I said.

"But more by the hour, I hope, until we have the basis of trust. I think it will come a lot more readily when we are on the ship. Then you will understand that my fingerprints are already all over it. I know the *Nightjammer* very well—better, I might warrant, than some of you. I was on it for years."

"Then how did you escape her?" Prozor called, from one of the aft seats.

"Because I could. Bosa had always depended on occasional business with the outlying worlds, much as she'd rather have done without them. There's only so much you can scrape from baubles and by plundering other ships. You know this already, I imagine."

"We manage," Surt said.

"Nonetheless, you operate under similar constraints. Bosa has—had—always depended on agents like myself to go where she could not, buying and selling according to her needs. She would rather not have relied on such arrangements, but she had no choice."

"She bent her crew to her will," I said. "How were you immune?"

"You're right about the crew. Truth is, they loved her as much as they feared her. But the methods she used were never applicable to the agents she had to send out into the worlds. We had to be more independent, more free-willed, or we couldn't do our work. It was a narrow line she had to walk. It was the same with her Sympathetics, but at least she could keep them on a close leash, inside the ship. Not so us. When she stuffed our pockets with quoins and sent us out, there was always a chance we'd turn against her."

"She'd never have put up with that," Prozor said.

"She had no option," Lagganvor snapped, almost losing his temper. "It was deal with the worlds or die, and we were her only tools. She kept us in line with the minimum of conditioning, some handsome rewards, and even more handsome punishments if we let her down."

"Rewards?" I asked.

"I was treated like a king on board that ship. My own quarters, a double share of the prize money, crew to boss around, and the close ear of the captain when she felt the need for advice. It was a good life, allowing for the fact that I was an outlaw, under the thumb of a tyrant with a very short fuse. Still, I didn't cross her—not once. Played my part well, and never gave her cause to doubt my attachment." He paused. "She had the use of a physician. Cowed and brow-beaten like the rest of them, but he'd made a mistake with one of his dosages, and killed the Master of Ions." He smiled at the physician. "Not as thorough with his calculations as Doctor Eddralder, you see."

Eddralder watched him wordlessly.

Lagganvor continued: "Bosa didn't know. But I did. I'd seen him being sloppy with his dosages before. So we came to an arrangement, this gentleman and I. I wouldn't inform on him to Bosa, and in return, he'd slip me a counter-agent. Just a little tincture, a drop a day, just enough to take another edge off her conditioning. Got me back a little more of my free will, enough to see that I didn't have any sort of future on that ship. Sooner or later I was bound to end up on the wrong side of her. Rather than wait for that, sitting on my useless fortune, I decided to jump ship."

"At Wheel Strizzardy?" I asked, thinking of what I knew from the private journals, and that I might catch him out.

"No," he said. "Ten worlds from here. I could never have lost her in a place like this. I chose my moment carefully, picking a time when she had to sail away urgently or risk being found, so didn't have the opportunity to come after me directly. I waited until it was safe to move, then bought passage. Skipped from world to world, always looking over my shoulder, always knowing she was out there somewhere, and that she wouldn't let such an indiscretion go unpunished. But it seems, at least for a while, that she had other distractions..."

"Why'd you stay here, so close to the Emptyside?" Surt asked.

"I was playing a game of stepping stones, and I hopped to a stone too far—a world from which there was no easy escape. Far fewer ships pass this way than I expected, and even fewer allow passage to the Sunwards, or anywhere near. You would think a man of means would have no difficulty in paying his way. But I was bound by the need for discretion. All this while, as the weeks turned into months, I had been greeting each day as if it might be my last, certain that Bosa had identified my whereabouts and was coming for me. Or, if not Bosa, then the agents of the banking concerns and the merchant combines, determined to hunt her down once and for all—the very men who sponsored poor Captain Restral and his companions. I watched the skies very carefully, and paid great heed to all incoming vessels... with particular interest in those of doubtful provenance, arriving from the Empty."

"You thought your last day had come," I said.

"It was a change of fortune," Lagganvor answered, casting a

sidelong glance at Doctor Eddralder. "For several of us. But tell me—how in all the sundered worlds did you ever take her?"

"It was easy," Fura said. "She took something of mine without asking, and I took it back—with interest."

Twenty further minutes brought us within easy visual range of *Revenger.* Fura fired the rockets again, slowing down our approach. Then she wheeled us around in readiness for docking tail-first. Lagganvor pressed his face to the porthole as the ship came into view, her dark hull pinned at the focus of many radial lines of rigging, invisible except where some trick of reflection and angle caused them to gleam back at us, like a pattern of fractures in the thin ice of space.

"Credit where it is due," Lagganvor said. "She might almost be a different ship."

"If you know her as well as you say," I answered, "you should be able to state the points of deviation."

"I can. Very easily. You have applied some stiff but thin material to soften her lines—canvas or tarred sail-cloth, I should imagine. Metal would be too heavy, and she certainly has no need for additional armour beyond her original specifications. You have cut away some of her crueller embellishments, including the corpses. I do not envy you that task."

"You oughtn't," Prozor said.

"You have disguised her true weapons complement. She has two rows of flanking coil-guns, with breech-loading capability and water-cooled solenoids for maximum rate of fire, as well as fore and aft chasing pieces. But you haven't gone so far as to make your ship appear toothless. That would look just as questionable as a fully-armed marauder. I must also remark on the disposition of your sails. The bulk of your manoeuvrability must still depend on the catchcloth, but you have spread enough acreage of conventional sail to deflect the uninformed eye, at least from a distance." He seemed done, but he was merely drawing breath. "She is four hundred and eight spans from bow to stern, although that may have altered since you made your amendments. The bone room is aft of the coil-gun batteries, with the kindness room just a little forward of it, under the batteries and tucked behind the main sail-control room, which in turn abuts the main airlock, although that saw very little use during my service, Bosa preferring that we came and went via the docking bay."

"A lot of ships are laid out on similar lines," I said.

"But not many have a kindness room," Fura said, working the steering jets with both her hands, so that we backed in to the red-lit maw of the open docking bay, like a little fish willingly sacrificing it to some gape-mouthed monster.

"It has been more than two hours," said Eddralder. "I should very much—"

"Not yet," Fura said.

We made contact, the jaws clamped shut, and a moment or two later Tindouf hammered on the outer lock. I was the first through, not needing my helmet since the connection to the rest of the ship was pressurised, and I clasped my gauntlet around Tindouf's big scarred hand, wondering how and where I ought to begin with the things he needed to know. "We have some guests, Tindouf," I said, feeling this was as good a start as any. "The tall one is Doctor Eddralder, and the girl with him is his daughter Merrix. The other man is Lagganvor. He used to serve on this ship under its former captain, but it appears we can trust him."

"Appearses?" Tindouf asked.

"He could be useful to us," I allowed. "We'll make him welcome, and treat him as one of our own—for now."

Lagganvor had come up behind me. He moved easily in weightlessness, and nothing about his manner suggested any degree of unease in these surroundings. His fingers found the handholds with ease, and he needed no assistance into *Revenger*.

"I understand your misgivings, Adrana," he said, his tone one of intimate confidence. "They are natural, and I would be surprised if you did not entertain a doubt or two. But I assure you there is nothing about my past to conceal."

Was it my imagination, or had he put the slightest stress on the "my" in that sentence, as if to contrast his own provenance with that of the physician?

"We'll learn soon enough," I said. Then, to Tindouf: "We'll need to find new rooms for them all. Doctor Eddralder can advise as to the best arrangements for Merrix."

"Why's is Strambli still in that box? I thoughts she was going to be fixed."

"She was," Fura declared. "But she still needs to recuperate. The kindness room is still the best place for her. Surt, why don't you show Doctor Eddralder there directly? He can square away his potions, and start thinking of the place as his own."

"That is very kind," Eddralder said. "But I cannot rest until I have set things right by Glimmery. I will serve you very well as a physician, but you must allow me to discharge my outstanding obligations."

"You'll never see the cove again," Fura said, shaking her head. "He'll be dead before long whatever happens. You were the one who poisoned him! Why would you give two squints for him now?"

"I was his doctor," Eddralder said. "And I would extend you the same courtesy."

She turned to Tindouf. "We have sail and ions?"

"Yes, Miss Ness. We's making headway very handsomely. I had Mister Paladin set us an anti-Sunward course, because I thoughts that what you would've done."

"You are right, Tindouf," she said, with a grand commanding wave. "Sail on. Lagganvor and I will discuss our next heading, but in the meantime it won't hurt if we put our backs to the worlds for a little longer."

"We have nothing," I said quietly. "No more fuel than when we left the Rumbler—less, after what we wasted here. The supplies we bought are still in the hotel. We don't even have a replacement skull for when ours finally cracks on us. I doubt that we have rations to make it through two months, let alone the time you doubtless have in mind." Now my voice began to rise, and I did nothing to counteract it. "We have escaped Glimmery, and by some miracle disentangled ourselves from the attentions of the Crawlies. But we are in no state to go chasing baubles again, or quoin caches, or whatever you would have us do. We are *finished,* Fura, and the sooner we submit ourselves to justice the less protracted and painful it will be."

I had thought my angered tone might provoke her to similar spirits, or even draw a reaction from the glowy. But she met me with a disarming equanimity.

"You are right, by the usual measures. But since we have been declared outlaws, and our protestations ignored, I see no great disadvantage in living up to the image they would insist is our true nature. I do not mean that we will slip into Bosa's habits—not at all. We will not murder, nor predate for the sake of profit alone. The Miser remains our chief objective, Crawlies or no Crawlies, and since those quoins were already stolen, we can hardly be accused of theft if we retake them. But in the service of that end, if there are ships out there that have the items we require..."

I stared at her with frank astonishment.

"You're saying that we... take them?"

"Why not? The worlds have delivered their verdict on us. Would you not agree, Lagganvor? That incentive is just the start, is it not?"

"I think worse will come," Lagganvor said. "The plan for a squadron raised against you will be expedited, now that Restral's party are free to offer their testimonies."

"We were already hunted," Fura said. "We shall be hunted. Our enemy was once Bosa Sennen. Now it may as well be every ship under the Old Sun." Her fingers worked, squeezing onto nothing. "We take what we need, but we do so with clemency and restraint. We will leave their ships operable, and their crews unbloodied—provided they offer no resistance. But we shall have our supplies, and our bones."

"I'm glad you've thought this through," I said, before adding, with a dark and intentional irony: "Captain Ness."

"It does pay to think ahead," Fura said, offering no contradiction of the title I had just bestowed on her, as if it were both fitting and timely.

*

Fura and I brought Lagganvor to the Glass Armillary. I watched his reaction carefully. It was a rare and delicate instrument, as I have intimated, and any ordinary spacefarer, even one who had seen and examined many precious items, might have expressed delight or admiration at the possession of such an exquisite piece. I doubted that Lagganvor would be quite so foolish as to act as if he had never seen the device before, if he had not in fact been part of this ship's crew, but it was possible that his mask might slip in the face of such beauty, even for an instant. It did not, however. He studied the Armillary for a few moments, impassive more than dazzled, then moved his hands to it, stroking an edge of glass here or a fine-threaded gear there, all with perfect and intimate familiarity.

"A less prudent captain would have broken it by now," he said, in a low respectful tone. "Especially one who had been through recent action. I congratulate you, both of you, on having the wits not to damage it through carelessness or inattention. You would struggle to replace it, even if you could move with impunity through any port of your choosing. Given her rages, it's a wonder it survived Bosa."

"Yes, it's a pretty bit of glass," Fura said, with her customary dismissiveness. "Fancy to have, but not essential, not when you've got charts and almanacs and a good robot to plot your crossings. What interests me is The Miser, and its whereabouts."

"Pardon my frankness. But if I divulge such intelligence, I am surrendering most of my usefulness to you."

"Some," I said. "Not all. You said you knew the access code, access passwords and so on."

"I do."

"Then get us off to a fine start and give Paladin something he can sail for," Fura said.

Lagganvor sighed, taking in the entirety of the Armillary with his hands planted on his hips.

"She never allowed me this close to it. There was no need: I was her negotiator, not her navigator. She dropped me on a world and sent me off on my business, but there was rarely any need for me to know how we sailed, or for how long."

"You'd better know *something*," Fura said.

"I do. Starting with this. These red marbles signify baubles, do they not?" His hand moved gently from one of the stalk-mounted marbles to the next. "Each is marked with a set of engraved ephemeris numbers—identifying the world by its orbit. You'll have cross-referenced them against the baubles in your books, I assume?"

"It was the first thing I did," Fura said. "And none of 'em is The Miser. Anyway, these baubles all have fields and auguries. You said The Miser had dropped its field long ago."

"If it ever had one. One of these baubles is an impostor, though. Or did you not look closely enough?"

"What should we have looked for?" I asked.

Lagganvor took one of the marbles from the Glass Armillary, unscrewing it from its stalk so he would know exactly where to replace it. "One of these has a double inscription. There's the obvious one, which is a false identity, and then a secondary inscription engraved on a deeper layer of the marble. Very hard to see, unless you know it's there, and even then you could easily mistake it for a blemish in the glass." He held the marble to his good eye, squinting hard. "Not this one. But it's here somewhere. It's just a question of examining them all, until you see that dual inscription. Disregard the outer numbers. The inner engraving contains the true ephemeris for The Miser."

"And you know this... how, exactly?" Fura asked.

"I said she didn't let me near the Armillary. I didn't say I wasn't privy to some of its secrets. There wasn't much the physician didn't know—there's not much people won't say under the influence of drugs." He replaced the marble and moved to another, unscrewing it with Fura's tacit permission. "Not this one either. Onto the next."

Fura looked at me, and then bent her face to the nearest speaking grille, flicking the switch next to it. "Tindouf. If you are satisfied with the set of our sails for the moment, you may come to the control room and show Lagganvor to some suitable accommodation."

After a silence Tindouf's voice crackled back through the grille. "On my ways, quicks as I can. Will you be wanting Doctor Eddralder? He's very consternated about something."

"He may wait a while longer," Fura said, before flicking off the speaker. Then, to Lagganvor: "Leave the Armillary. I'm quite capable of examining those baubles for myself."

"Are you done with me for the moment?"

"Almost. But since Tindouf has mentioned Doctor Eddralder, I thought I'd push a little harder for your opinion on him. In the hotel you said he was a decent man, working under intolerable conditions. That was before you knew you were likely to share a ship with him. Is there anything else you ought to add?"

"Should there be?"

"Adrana—the young man from the other ship, with the wounded party. What was his name, again?"

"Chasco," I answered, with a catch in my throat, for I could still feel the force of his judgement, a hard, cold slap against me.

"Yes. He said something about Doctor Eddralder, didn't he? How we shouldn't ask too many questions about his association with Glimmery." She switched her attention back onto Lagganvor. "Then *you* told Adrana that there was nothing about your own past which you wished to conceal, as if to contrast yourself with someone else. Did you have Eddralder in mind?"

Lagganvor seemed to debate with himself before answering. "I would not wish to pour fuel on rumour."

Fura flashed her teeth for a single fierce instant.

"I suggest you do."

"Wait," I said, raising a hand. "The situation is transparent. Doctor Eddralder was coerced into working for Glimmery. We saw the evidence of it—Glimmery had Merrix as a hostage and his patronage kept the infirmary running. That doesn't make the doctor a bad man—just one who did what was needed, to protect his patients and his daughter."

Lagganvor was silent for a few moments. But then something could not be held back.

"If only it were that simple, Adrana."

"In what way isn't it?" I asked.

"As I said, I don't wish to pour fuel—"

Fura clenched her fist. "Just answer her, you slippery piece of—"

"Doctor Eddralder is an excellent physician. Of that I have no doubts. I also believe he only ever acted in the best interests of Merrix and his patients. But his usefulness to Glimmery went far beyond the services you witnessed."

"Explain," Fura said.

"Glimmery had need of a man who could inflict pain, as well as relieve it. To enforce his reputation, and extract information, when it was needed. Who better than a surgeon, to turn torturer?"

"No," I said, in flat denial, for I still remembered the care and devotion he had shown to Strambli. "He isn't like that. We saw enough of him to know his kindness."

"I didn't say he wasn't capable of kindness," Lagganvor answered. "Just that there's more to him than that."

There was a knock on the bulkhead frame behind us. Tindouf had come to show our guest to his quarters and Fura waited until he had taken Lagganvor away, then invited me to the Glass Armillary.

One by one we began to search the marbles. I was on my dozenth when a tiny, sub-glacial blemish snagged the light, something I might have noticed a thousand times without ever once questioning its significance.

I held the marble closer to my eye. The blemish was a milky

patterning, floating just beneath the outermost inscription. It was composed of lines and angles, faintly formed but beyond any doubt writing.

"I think I have it," I said, marvelling that it had been so close to us all the while. "I think I have The Miser."

# 22

Fura closed the door, then moved to her desk, buckling herself into the chair, and setting her elbows on the leather surface, facing me with a knowing tilt to her head, a skeptical set to her jaw. Her glowy shone softly in the red light coming from Paladin's busily calculating globe.

"Eddralder first, then The Miser. I'm concerned about the doctor, Adrana. Who have we brought into our midst?"

"Don't tell me you believe a word of that."

"Lagganvor has no reason to lie."

"He has every reason, especially if there's some aspect of his own past he'd rather we didn't dig into too closely. What better way to deflect our attention, than to start making us think badly of Doctor Eddralder?"

"You were there when Chasco made a similar allusion."

"Allusion's all it was. Chasco wasn't from Wheel Strizzardy, so everything he picked up was hearsay. Of course Doctor Eddralder's had to do some things he'd rather he hadn't. But that's not the same as saying he's a torturing monster."

"We'll speak to him presently," Fura said. "And if there is a stain on his past, then we will act upon it as we see fit. Are you acquainted with the Inter-Congregational treaties on space law? Beyond the jurisdiction of a world or port, a captain may exercise a variety of punishments if the immediate well-being of her crew and ship have been jeopardised by someone trading under a false past. Up to and including abandonment or execution, if there are particularly pressing circumstances."

"Let's hope there are enough ropes to go around, then. Which one of us hasn't got something to keep quiet about?"

She pursed her lips ungenerously. "There are degrees of falsehood—our little lies hardly amount to anything as serious as torture in the service of a criminal." But some tiny trace of doubt creased her brow, as if she was not quite convinced by her own words. "In any case, my immediate concern is with Lagganvor."

"Good. So is mine."

"I mean, it lies in your evident distrust of him. After all this trouble, would you deny me the pleasure of finding the man I sought?"

"I'm not denying you anything. I want to believe his side of things just as much as you do. But it's not as if he came to us with glowing credentials, is it?"

"What did you expect? He was a fugitive from Bosa Sennen. She was hardly going to write him an enthusiastic reference for future employment." She looked down her nose at me, shaking her head very slowly. "I thought you might grasp the larger panorama here, sister. We do not have to like the man, or have a high opinion of his former career, to put him to good use." She tilted her gaze to the globe. "Anyway, we can already put part of his claim to the test. Can you read the secondary inscription on this marble, Paladin? Focus your beams a little under the outer layer of the glass."

A spray of red light danced over the red marble she had brought from the control room, still on the end of its stalk.

"It is legible, Captain Ness. The inscription is encoded, but in one of the encipherments we have already broken. It fits the established format for the orbital parameters of a body revolving around the Old Sun in an eccentric orbit, such as a bauble or a swallower."

"Can you match these numbers to any known object?"

"Not yet." His lights flashed a little more vigorously. "Orbits may have shifted between Occupations, of course, but...I do not yet have a match, even after expanding my search space."

"Then it's a bust," I said, feeling a queer sort of relief.

"Not necessarily," Fura said. "There are fifty million little rocks out there, and only a fraction of them have ever been properly entered into journals and almanacs. What Paladin's telling us is that it isn't a settled world or bauble, nor any place that anyone's ever bothered visiting long enough to stick a name on it. But that doesn't mean it isn't out there, still following its orbit. We know where to look for it, too. Bosa left it in the Glass Armillary, and these numbers should settle any remaining uncertainty."

"Where is it now?" I asked.

Paladin answered. "Thirteen million leagues beyond the thirty-seventh processional, near the Sunward extremity of its orbit, and eight million leagues from our present location."

"I expected it to be further out," Fura said.

"Too far out and she wouldn't have been able to visit it as often as Lagganvor says she did," I replied. "She had to compromise, if she didn't want to be lugging a hold full of heavy quoins around for years at a time. If it's just a rock, with no possibility of settlement, and no rumours of treasure, there's no great risk that anyone else would have stumbled on it while she was away. There's no doubt, sister. It has to be the one."

"The Miser," she said, smiling, as if the words alone carried a rare and seductive flavour.

"Do you wish me to enter this designation into the memory registers, Captain Ness?"

"Wait," I said, raising a hand. "She is *not* Captain Ness, so stop calling her that. Her name's Arafura, and she has no more claim on the command of this ship than I do."

"Tell her how she will be addressed henceforth, Paladin," Fura said.

"I am instructed to call you Captain Ness, Miss Adrana. I am also instructed to call Miss Arafura Captain Ness."

"What?" I asked, wrong-footed, and instinctively suspicious.

"Do not make more of it than is necessary," Fura said, sighing, as if she had presented a gift and been underwhelmed by its reception. "I just thought it would simplify matters. I know I have no natural claim on the command of this ship, and that even if I felt our welfare was best served under my authority, it would engender bad feelings. So..." she turned her metal hand so that the palm was facing away from the table. "Let it be joint authority. I have my strengths, and you have yours...as you have demonstrated...and it is foolish to deny it."

"The two of us seizing command is no better than one of us."

"But you will not argue against it quite so vehemently, I fancy." She favoured me with a smile, while her metal hand toyed with the magnetic paperweights on her desk. "It is not so very bad a solution, sister. And who else has shown the necessary fibre?"

"Prozor—" I began.

"Prozor," she said, gently interrupting, "has been a good and loyal friend, and we could not have managed without her. But do you think she would welcome the mantle of responsibility? As for the others...Surt is barely literate, Strambli is still invalided, and Tindouf's wits were scrambled years ago. And now we have three additional lives to consider. Make no mistake, Adrana. This is no easy station. But if the Ness sisters do not rise to the occasion then who shall?"

I should have denied her there and then. A great many things would have been avoided had I done so. Instead I brooded, and considered, and wondered if she did not make the tiniest grain of sense.

"You believe Lagganvor can get us into The Miser?"

"Yes..." she said, visibly relieved to be drawn away from matters of title. "He visited it, and knows enough about it. We won't steer for it immediately, though. We'll put some space between us and the wheel, enough that we drop off any sweepers, and run on dark sails before we make our turn. This is *my* prize, and I've no intention of leading anyone else to it."

"You don't even know how long we'd have to sail."

"Paladin? Calculate a crossing for The Miser, given the terms I have just stipulated."

"It is already done, Captain Ness. If we maintain a heading into the Empty, then turn once we are safely beyond deep sweeper range and have run out all catchcloth sails, we may approach The Miser in..." Paladin made a very human show of flickering his lights, even though I was certain he already had the desired figure. "Between forty-nine and fifty-one days."

"Seven weeks," Fura said, marvelling. "Seven weeks and it's ours. Can we get there a little sooner if we run out the ordinary sails again, Paladin, once we've made our turn and we know we've lost 'em?"

"The additional photon pressure may spare us a save us two or three days, depending on the solar weather, Captain."

"Then we'll chance it. If I could tear my other arm to get us there an hour sooner, I would. I have to know what I've found myself."

"What we have found," I corrected her.

"Yes—transparently." Then she shot me a penetrating, accusatory look. "Are you fully committed to this cause, sister? I need to know. There can't be any half measures... no doubts."

"Whatever it is."

"Are you with me, sister? I need to know before I commit myself to this. There can't be any half measures."

Before I could give her the answer she desired, there was a knock at the door and Surt jammed her head through the widening gap. She studied us for a second, a judgemental look on her face, as if some shrewd part of her had already deduced the essentials of our recent conversation. "Begging your pardon, *sisters*, but it's the doctor. He won't stop harping on about his chaffin' syringes."

"It must be three or four hours now," I said. "We're safe, aren't we?"

"Surt?" Fura said, beginning to unbuckle from her seat. "Bring Doctor Eddralder to the control room. I will see him by the squawk console."

"Are you going there directly?" I asked.

"Almost. I thought I would have a word with Lagganvor first, just to see if his tongue is starting to loosen up. See me in the control room, will you?"

"I'll be there in a moment," I said. "I'd like to talk to Paladin about our course, and whether we ought to chance another turn around that swallower, if it'll help us slip away a little faster, and throw 'em even further off our scent."

"Do," Fura said keenly. "After all, we have joint responsibility for these decisions now."

When she was out of the room, and knowing I had only a few minutes to myself, I moved the paperweights aside until I had free access to *The True and Accurate Testimony of Arafura Ness.*

For once it was not the thick papers that drew my attention, nor the dark red handwriting that Fura had filled them with, laying out her version of our story. It was the cover that the pages had been bound into: all that remained of Rackamore's personal copy of the 1384 edition of the *Book of Worlds*, the contents of which Bosa Sennen had gutted, before Fura liberated the remaining part from the wreck of the *Monetta's Mourn*. The cover was very old and very worn, and had been like that even before Bosa hacked it about.

What concerned me now was the faint ghost of something on the inside of that cover, where a few swatches of marbled paper were glued to the backing.

"Paladin," I said, very quietly. "There is an inscription here, I think. It has been effaced, but I think the pen might have dug into the paper enough to leave a trace. Do you think you can read what was written?"

"Present the book to me, Captain Ness."

I held the cover up to his globe, where I knew it would fall within reach of his scanning beams. "You don't have to call me that all the time," I told him. "Miss Adrana will do just as well."

"Do you wish me not to call you Captain Ness?"

"No," I answered, on a hesitant falling note. "You can call me that. I'm not ashamed that we've taken this step—it's the right thing; the only right thing." Even if, I reflected, shame was a very large component of the misgivings I now felt. "But don't overdo it, for the time being. Can you read the trace?"

"I think I can. It is easier than the inscription in the marble, and in quite a legible hand."

"Tell me what it says."

"I may show you, instead. Hold the book as steady as you are able, Miss Adrana."

A scratch of red light came out of him, and played across the cover. Then it concentrated in the area where I thought the inscription had been rubbed away, and a neat, handwritten dedication presented itself to my eyes, etched in trembling red fire.

It said:

*To Captain Pol Rackamore, on the achievement of his first command. With pride, admiration, and generous affection, from your brother.*

"Is there a name?"

"No name, Adrana."

I snapped tight the book, and returned it to its safe place under the paperweights.

"He never mentioned a brother," I said, speaking as much for my own benefit as my robot companion. "But then again, he never mentioned having cause to strike out a brother's dedication. That book meant a lot to him, and yet he could not bear to see his own brother's hand on the inside cover. Something very bad must have come between them, I suppose."

"Do you wish me to bring this inscription to the attention of your sister?"

"If she knew of it, you would not ask that question."

"You have not answered mine, Miss Adrana."

"Then . . . no. Not for the moment. There will come a time, I'm sure—but she has much too much on her mind at present." Too much, certainly, for her to be made aware of the faint unease that was beginning to form in my own mind, an unease that was as yet far too tenuous to count as a suspicion. "Unless she makes a direct enquiry, this will remain between us, Paladin.

No mention of that inscription, no mention of Rackamore's brother, no mention of me talking to you about any of this. Is that understood?"

"It is, Miss Adrana."

"I'm sorry to put you in this position. I'm not asking you to lie to her, though. Just...not mention things. That's not so hard, is it?"

"I will do my best."

"Then I'd better go to the control room. She'll be wondering where I am."

Surt, Doctor Eddralder and Fura were already gathered around the main squawk console when I arrived. The doctor had a sickly look to him, which I took to be the outward manifestation of a combination of worry, the recent strains, and his forced adaptation to near-weightlessness.

Fura had the handset clasped in her metal fist.

"Ah, Adrana—good of you to join us. We were just speaking of Glimmery's predicament. Doctor Eddralder is most particular that the identity of the correct syringe be transmitted back to the infirmary."

"That was the understanding," I said, sensing the developing edge of something ominous, yet not quite comprehending its form or extent. "He gave his word."

"He did, and I respect that."

"Then let him send the information."

"Doctor Eddralder," Fura said. "Might I ask you something, before we discharge your obligation? It concerns a couple of rumours. I just wanted to clear the air, so to speak."

"Whatever it is," Eddralder said, "might we discuss it later?"

"We could, I suppose. Or we could discuss it *now*, while you've an extra incentive to come clean with me." Her hand tightened on the handset, which emitted a creaking sound, as if under a developing strain. "Your terms of association with Glimmery, Doctor. Would you care to clarify them?"

"What needs to be clarified? You saw for yourself what he was doing to Merrix. He forced me to work for him. I needed him to keep the hospital running—if I'd denied him, he would have made things even harder for the other physicians and our patients."

"There's more to it than that, though," Fura said. "Isn't there?"

"I am not sure what more you expect me to say. Did it please me to serve under Glimmery? Not at all. I detested every minute in his presence. But it served a greater good."

"They say you were also his torturer," Fura said.

Doctor Eddralder met this remark with a curious stoicism. He was silent for a moment or two, then said, very calmly: "Might we discuss this after I have told them about the syringes?"

"Let him," I urged.

"There's no need. I absolve the doctor of any further responsibility in the matter. He *would* transmit the information, and that is all that needs to lie between him and his conscience." With that, Fura squeezed harder. Under the terrible press of her fingers the handset gave away and shattered into a hundred tiny pieces, falling away like the shards of some ruined world. "The fact that he cannot is an entirely separate matter, which casts no shadow on the doctor's good character. No additional shadow, I should say."

"No," I said, astonished, and not quite ready to believe what I had seen.

"You didn't need to do that," Surt said, in a low admonitory tone, as if she hardly dared raise her voice in criticism.

"I did," Fura said, quite without rancour. "It was necessary. Glimmery would have given us no quarter, and so he deserved none. I am very glad to think of him choking on his last breath."

But the one among us who ought to have been the most affronted was the least affected.

"You are wrong, Captain," Doctor Eddralder said, more in regret than sorrow. "You have sullied my word, but that is only a private concern. Doubtless you could repair the squawk, rig in a substitute, or use the one on the launch, if you were so inclined. That was little more than theatre. Glimmery will still be alive in two hours. He will still be alive in three, and four, and perhaps longer. That depends on his enemies, not on the syringes."

Fura loosened her fist and the remaining pieces of the squawk handset drifted free, following the slow arc of our feeble acceleration.

"No," she said firmly. "He needed to know."

"He did not," Eddralder said. "I made certain of it. All of those syringes contained the counter-agent. It did not matter which one he took."

Fura mouthed a nearly soundless: "Why?"

"Because it was always in my mind that I might die, or be prevented from calling back. That was unacceptable, Captain Ness. I had a duty to my patient until the very end."

"But if they don't know which one—" I started.

"They will use one eventually," Eddralder said. "That is basic nature, Adrana. When he is close to his last breath, as your sister puts it, he would see no harm in committing his fate to chance. He would have nothing left to lose, and the men around him know it."

"No," Fura said again, but it was less a denial than an abject curse, delivered against herself and the creature she knew she was becoming. She had wished to see Glimmery dead, I think, because killing Glimmery would let her stop dwelling on her own fate, and the progression of the glowy.

Yet he lived, and she could do nothing about it now.

"You are right about me," Eddralder said, letting out a sigh. "I did as he asked of me. All the things. Had I not done so, it would have been very much worse for Merrix, and for all those other people, as well. So I carried the knife for him, and used it as he ordered. I caused pain, and death, as well as preventing each. So, I was, as you say, his torturer. But you did not need to ask me that question, nor listen to the rumours. You should already have known."

"Known what?" Fura asked sharply, a fleck of spittle flying from between her teeth.

"I kept him alive, didn't I? He did far worse with his own hands than I ever did with mine. Where I cut with compassion, and speed, and skill, he hacked and butchered. Where I tried to make the pain as brief as possible, to bring death quickly, even at the risk of contradicting my orders, Glimmery sought to maximise and prolong those agonies. So that is my greater crime, Captain Ness. Not that I tortured for him, because I did, and I own that part of me, and I will carry it with me until I am dust; but because I allowed him to be what he was." Something eased in the long lines of his face, his lips forming a half-smile. "But you already knew that, I think. And you were prepared to overlook it because I was useful to you. As I still am." He turned from us. "You will find me in the kindness room. I still have a patient to attend to, and she is by no means out of danger."

*

An hour or two after that difficult exchange, with the mood on the ship still tense, Prozor and I were passing each other on our way to different rooms. I touched her elbow, arresting her motion in a gentle but insistent manner.

"Can you spare a moment, Proz?"

Her face was set with complications. "You got a troubled look about you, girlie. I'm startin' to think it's moved in for good."

"These haven't been an easy few days, for any of us. Just when I thought we could do one good and honest thing, to help Eddralder, it turns out that nothing's that simple. Now we've helped a torturer escape from justice!"

"I don't get the impression that torturin' was his life's ambition. More that he drifted into it, and got in a bit too deep. Can't be too hard on the cove, can we, if he was only lookin' after his daughter's interests?"

"You make it sound as if we should just forgive and forget."

"I've crewed on one or two more ships than you," Prozor said, which was a very kind way of putting it. "And if I've learned one thing in that time, besides never trustin' a bauble with my life, it's that there ain't one of us who doesn't have a blemish or two. The fact is, if we get too choosy about our shipmates, it ends up a very lonely life indeed." She flicked her eyes to the outer hull.

"Somewhere out there's a crew made up of coves who've never set a foot wrong, but I can safely say I ain't ever met such a crew, nor heard of one."

"Rackamore's was a good crew, wasn't it?"

"In comparison," she conceded. "But only in comparison. Did you ever ask Trysil about the stories behind her tattoos? I did, and got nightmares for weeks. And Mattice? Big, cheerful Mattice? Wouldn't hurt a fly Mattice? He killed a man once, in cold blood."

I had to fight to bring their faces to mind, these old crewmates of ours.

"He must have had a reason."

"Oh, he did—punishment for selling him contraband equipment. Cost us badly, when we were deep into a bauble, and Mattice's tools broke down on us. Mattice waited two years to see the man again, two years in which he hardly spoke a word about the whole affair. But he was plottin' and plannin' the whole while."

I nodded slowly, thinking of Prozor herself, and the biological weapon she had carried with her, the symbiont organism that had eventually wrought a terrible death on Gathing.

"Rackamore, though," I said, easing my way around to the topic I had meant to initiate from the outset. "He was free of blemishes, wasn't he? Besides what happened to Illyria...and that was hardly his fault...there wasn't any bad business in his past, was there?"

"Why'd you ask?"

I drew breath before answering. "You knew him better than Fura and I, Proz, and for much longer. Did he ever mention a brother to you?"

The angles of her face gained a hundred new acutenesses. It was as if Prozor were holding up a mask, embossed with a harder, sharper caricature of herself. "What makes you think there was ever a brother?"

I met her deflection with a firming of my own resolve. "Was there?"

After an interval Prozor said: "Once."

"What does that mean?"

"Something had happened, is what it means. Enough that they weren't brothers any more. Not to each other. Rackamore... Rack made us promise we'd never mention the other one. Not once. And although it hurt us, we loved Rack enough to do his bidding."

"Tell me what happened."

"Not now, Adrana." But then some calculation proceeded behind her brow and she regarded me with new and direct suspicion. "What've you found, that you're rakin' over this? What do you *think* you've found?"

"Rackamore's brother inscribed a message in a gift to him. It was obviously well-meant. Then Rackamore erased the message—almost as if he were erasing his own brother, his own flesh and blood. What happened between them that was so bad?"

Prozor glanced aside and I think for an instant she had decided to say no more on the matter, at least not until some suitable interval had passed. But I had uncorked something, if only momentarily, and she must have realised that it was better for the truth to flow now, however painful the process.

"Illyria. Illyria is what happened. She was Rackamore's daughter, but his brother loved her like she was his own. He'd spent a lot of time with her, when her own father was away from the worlds. Eventually, Rack decided to take her with him into space, so that he could spend more time with her. Brysca—his brother—disagreed. Said it was too dangerous. Argued and pleaded with Rack. But it wasn't to no avail. Rack's mind was made up. Brysca disowned him—cut him off cold. Hated him, and considered him reckless to the point of cruelty. They never spoke after that."

"And when Bosa took Illyria... I don't suppose that helped."

"Rack was broken, proper desolate. He reached back out to Brysca, but his letters came back unopened. It was much too hard for him to carry on as if his brother was still out there, so he just wrote him out of his own life, as if he'd never drawn a living breath."

I considered the depth of feeling that it would take to shut my own sibling out of my life to that extent. Fura had acted in ways that left me exasperated, perplexed and angry, but I had never come close to wishing her out of existence, and I doubted that such a capacity lay within me at all.

Or, reciprocally, in Fura herself.

"Did you ever meet Brysca?"

Her answer was blunt, inviting no further enquiry. "No."

"There'd be a likeness to Rackamore. Would you recognise him, do you think?"

"I ain't ever been one for faces, and even less so since they put several sheets of tin in my head."

But I wasn't done. "If Brysca's still alive, he'd have heard about what happened to his brother. It was all over the worlds, after Bosa's attack. That, and what she did to Captain Trusko, is the reason they've finally agreed to pool together and do something about her."

"He must've known," Prozor said, with evident reluctance. "And maybe that's softened his views on Rack."

"Brysca would have lost two loved ones to Bosa," I said. "First Illyria, who was almost his own daughter, and then his brother."

Her eyes narrowed. "What're you drivin' at, exactly?"

"Nothing very much," I said, unwilling to speculate further in case I did more harm than good, rubbing nerves—the collective nerves of our crew—that were already raw. "It's just...if Brysca *was* out there, and did know something of Rackamore's fate, that might make him very, very determined to put an end to Bosa once and for all."

Prozor nodded slowly, taking in my words even if she did not fully comprehend the thrust of reasoning behind them, or the intimation of disquiet that had instigated them in the first place. It was not properly a suspicion, for a suspicion required rather more in the way of secure foundations than a general unease about the legitimacy of a new crew member, or a faint fretfulness concerning an erased dedication that I ought never to have glimpsed in the first place.

"You're a puzzle, girlie, and no mistake," Prozor said.

*

Fura was in her quarters, consulting books, tables and scratchy journals, trying to evaluate our best chances for stalking a weak crew. "We'll operate as Bosa did," she said, throwing herself into this new enterprise with enthusiasm. "Pick 'em off near baubles, just as she tried to do with us. Except we'll be kinder, and only take what we absolutely need. Our reputation will precede us, at least to begin with, and for once it will work to our advantage. The first sight of our sails and they'll be opening their holds and flinging their treasure at us. Anything to avoid close action."

"No complications at all, then," I said.

"Only if we make them."

After a considerable silence, I replied: "I will cooperate in this venture. We will do what we need to do, and we will inspect this quoin cache, if indeed it exists, and we can do so without making further enemies of the Crawlies and their associates. I will do nothing to obstruct you, provided you do demonstrate that clemency you just mentioned."

"It matters to you that much, after all we have seen and done?"

I nodded earnestly. "I have come to accept that she left a part of herself in me, a part that I will never fully extinguish. There is something of Bosa in me by design, and there is something of Bosa in you, as a consequence of what you needed to become in order to face her. How you choose to live is yours to decide. But my own mind is settled. If I cannot extinguish her completely, I can at least resist her in a thousand small ways, starting with clemency." I nodded again, meeting her eyes and holding them. "That is my side of the arrangement. Yours is still be finalised."

Fura looked satisfied, but also a little puzzled.

"I think my position is plain enough, dear heart."

"No. There's something else." And I shoved aside her books and papers and paperweights until there was room to spread out the journal of the Shadow Occupations, which had been in her cabin since before our expedition to Wheel Strizzardy.

I opened the pages and turned to the careful, hand-drawn

diagram, with the timeline of the familiar Occupations and the translucent overlay which implied the existence of hundreds of others.

"I thought you had dismissed this as beneath your consideration."

"I had. Then I chanced upon a man striking a match repeatedly, down in the streets of Port Endless, and it set an idea in motion."

Fura surveyed me with a guarded, provisional interest, as if I were proposing the outline of a new parlour game. "Continue," she said.

"I asked myself if we might be looking at the problem in the wrong light. We have been fixating on those four hundred Shadow Occupations, and wondering why there is no trace of them in the historical record. I see the answer now, or at least I did when I watched that man. The question is wrongly framed. We ought instead to be asking why the thirteen Occupations caught fire, when four hundred others did not."

"I still don't—" Fura began.

I silenced her. "When I had a moment, I asked Paladin to consider that recurrence interval. Twenty-two thousand years, and a little more, if I remember rightly."

"Yes."

"I think there may be something out there, Fura. On a very long orbit—much, *much* longer than anything we are ordinarily accustomed to. A twenty-two thousand year orbit may be absurd, compared to anything in our common experience. But there is nothing in celestial mechanics to forbid it. It would only mean that there is a thing, an object, which spends the greatest part of its existence in the high Empty, far beyond the worlds of the Congregation. And yet, every twenty-two thousand years, it loops close to the Old Sun, and sometimes—sometimes—*something happens*. A civilisation begins. A bright sliver in the darkness. A new Occupation."

"And yet... mostly it does not."

"That is the conundrum," I said, agreeing with her. "There

is something else. We have already noted that the interval between the observed Occupations is lengthening. That can only mean that this…thing, whatever it may be, is becoming less successful in igniting these windows of civilisation. As if the man striking the matches is nearing the end of the box, and those remaining are increasingly soggy, and less prone to work."

"I am…glad," Fura said, "that you have found something of import in these old writings. And I admit, there is a fascination in it. You have me persuaded, or at least on the way to it." Her face fell into sympathy. "But there is one fatal drawback."

"Which is?"

"We could never hope to find such a thing. An orbit like that would place it impossibly far from the worlds, beyond any hope of detection. It must be, or we would know of it."

"You are right, in the sense that it will be difficult to find," I said. "But not as impossible as you make out. What is the present year, if I might be so bold?"

"You know it to be 1800."

"Recorded history never starts at the very onset of an Occupation—there is always a period of uncertainty before inter-world civilisation becomes sufficiently settled to permit an agreement about dates and calendars. But we can be confident that it is not more than three thousand years since the start of our Thirteenth, and probably less." I leaned in to reinforce my point. "It's out there, sister, and not even a sixth of the way into its orbit around the Old Sun. And I wish to find it. That will be your side of our agreement—your complete and unswerving cooperation in this matter. We will locate your quoins. Then we will locate my objective, even if that means sailing further out than any ship has ever gone."

"Suicidally further."

"We would find a way, no matter the cost."

She met my words with a look of dark admiration. "We sound as ruthless as each other."

"Perhaps we are. Does that trouble you?"

"No." Fura teased me with a half-smile. "In fact I rather like it. But there is the small matter that you don't have the first idea where to begin."

"No," I agreed. "But I do have time to think about it, and I have Paladin, and all these records which Lagganvor will eventually help us with. It was one of *her* concerns as well. This ship still has secrets to yield. How do we know she didn't get halfway to the answer?"

"You are mad to think of this," Fura said, but the look in her eyes was more admiration than pity, as if my madness brought us a little nearer, two sisters once again united by the fever of a shared enterprise, even if our individual goals were in only partial alignment.

"Perhaps I am. But no madder than you and your interest in those quoins. Ultimately, we are driven by a similar curiosity. You sense that the quoins have a significance beyond their transactional value; that they have a meaning beyond mere currency. A clue, perhaps, as to the concealed mechanism of our civilisation. That interests me as well; I shan't deny it. But I am also concerned to know something of the origins of our Occupation, as well as the factors that may govern its demise. If we were speaking of a clock, I would say that your interest lies in the complexity of its hidden workings, the mysteries of gears and ratchets. Whereas I would also like to know who made the clock. Your interest is functional; mine ontological."

"I am glad you know yourself," Fura said, "as well as you seem to know me."

That was when Paladin said: "I am sorry to inform you, Captains, that there is a ship approaching us. It is the rocket launch from the *White Widow*, closing quickly."

*

When it must have become clear that Glimmery's survival was not contingent on our own, the able members of Captain Restral's party had recovered their heavy launch, refuelled it, and set off in rapid pursuit. Between worlds, only a sunjammer could ever catch another sunjammer, and only then with expert handling and the favourable alignment of external factors. But a ship such as ours was intensely vulnerable in the vicinity of worlds, where it lay within the reach of rocket vessels like the launch. The launch had neither the fuel nor the endurance to pursue a sunjammer into deep space, and that disadvantage was one that captains could usually depend on.

Not now. We were being chased by a smaller but formidably quick and well-armoured craft, and while the launch might be technically out-gunned by *Revenger*, it would only need to deliver a single accurate shot to disable us, or worse. It was an engagement that ran counter to all the accepted norms of war and civility, and for which there were only questionable precedents. The common good relied on the extension of reciprocal courtesies, even in space, and this action was highly discourteous. Yet we had earned it, I thought, by failing to honour our promise to Glimmery.

With the main squawk out of commission, Fura went to our launch and tried to reason with our pursuers. There was an exchange of signals. The opposing craft, she reported, was under the command of the one-armed Mister Trensler, and it was equipped with a high-calibre chasing piece that could easily shatter our flanks, destroying our ion-emitter, or piercing the hull completely. *Revenger* was handsomely armoured in comparison to most ships, but all armour came at a cost of weight and bulk. Much of the *Nightjammer*'s former reputation had depended on stealth and ambush rather than impossible invulnerability.

Fura tried to dissuade them from continuing their approach. She warned them that she would strike if they came nearer, and that while she would strive to disable them, showing that excellent clemency she had promised me, it would be much harder to cripple a launch than a fully-rigged sunjammer, and should a shot of ours find its mark it would most likely destroy the launch completely.

This they understood. They could hardly fail to understand it, since a man such as Mister Trensler would have been perfectly acquainted with the realities of an asymmetric engagement.

And yet still they came.

So—because I could think of no other means of persuasion—I went to the bone room. There was a bone room on the launch, I knew, and while that was an unusual arrangement, it was feasible aboard a heavy, well-outfitted vessel. And I was certain that the *White Widow*'s Bone Reader would be aboard the launch.

I plugged in with all the haste of battle. I knew I did not have very long to argue them out of this course, and that Chasco was my only point of leverage.

By the cruellest of ironies, our skull worked the first time. It would have done me a lasting kindness not to have worked, or for Chasco not to be connected, but that was not how it was.

*Chasco?*

*Adrana Ness. I am surprised. I did not think you would have the nerve.*

*Then why were you connected?*

*We are coordinating resources, Adrana. Transmitting tactical intelligence. You will soon see the fruits of that. It was thought better not to use the squawk, even with encryption.*

*Do you know Mister Trensler well, Chasco?*

*Tolerably. I respect him. He is no Captain Restral, but then none of us are. Why do you ask?*

*With whatever influence you have, please convince him to give up this chase. It will come to no good. We will fire on you. Fura won't wait until you're close enough to use that stern-piece. Paladin's already computing the firing solution. We made a mistake when we hit the* Calenture, *but it was no fault of Paladin's.*

*He won't turn. I know the man too well. And I wouldn't permit him to change his mind, even if it were within my ability. Captain Restral did not last long in the infirmary, you should know. But Trensler was with him at the end. He vowed…*

I felt it then.

A single shot, a single discharge from our stern coil-gun. I imagined the slug streaking away from us, falling through space, destined for two possible fates. It would either miss the launch, or intercept it. There was no intermediate condition. I could only hope that the discharge had been a warning ploy, a calibrating shot, or that Paladin's aim had been in error. But I suppose a part of me knew that it would be none of these things.

I tried to close my mind to Chasco, to shield from him the knowledge of what was coming.

*It's no good, Adrana. Either I am too good at this game, or your mind is too bright.*

*Then you know.*

*Yes—and I suppose I ought to thank you for that final kindness, in not wishing me…*

There was a moment, a hiatus. The stream of rational thought had ceased. Yet his mind was still connected to mine through the skull. I tensed, half knowing what was coming, but no more capable of shielding myself from it than I'd been able to shield Chasco from the fact of his own certain demise.

Then his screams came through.

There are many ways to die in space, and some of them—by dint of painlessness or swiftness of effect—are almost merciful. But death on a dying ship, struck with hard and deliberate force, need not be merciful at all. What reached my mind through that ancient conduit of alien remains and unliving technology was a howling agony, beyond anything I had ever experienced in the bone room. I tried to pull the plug out of the skull, before that scream ripped my soul to ribbons, but I was not quite fast enough. Nor was I fast enough to drag the neural crown from my scalp, and fling it against the wall.

The scream grew and grew. Then, just as I felt that my world would contain nothing but that scream, that it would build and reverberate until there was no more room for sensible thought, no more room for my own sense of being, no more room to remember who I had once been, or what had brought me to this moment, our skull split open from end to end, fracturing into two halves, the twinkly dying within it like the last ebbing flickers of civilisation. And Chasco was gone.

# 23

Bone Silence.

That was what it meant not to have a skull any more. The bone room had gone from being the most valued place on the ship, the third eye by which it gleaned and transmitted intelligence that could make or break crews and their fortunes, to a wasteful hollow. A scooped-out windowless socket, a place I could barely stand to be near, let alone think of visiting.

When the skull ruptured, it felt as if some part of Chasco's dying mind had leaked through into the room itself, lingering there even now, with no living body to return to. Knowing that this was irrational did not make it any less forceful or persuasive. I could not go back there, not even to confirm that the skull really was as ruined as it appeared. Fortunately I did not need to. Fura took that task upon herself, and while I do not think she relished being in the bone room any more than I did, she was punctilious about trying all the input sockets, testing each in turn until she was certain that the skull was dead and useless.

We would have been well advised to run silently from that point on, but now we had no choice in the matter. We were blind. We still had the squawk in the launch, and could listen in on all the signals and transmissions from the Congregation's civilian and commercial senders, but nothing of direct relevance to our own predicament would ever be sent by those means. We had no means of signalling without giving away our position, and even to use the sweeper was a risk too far. So we ran, and ran. We turned at the swallower, as we had done before, but this time without a ship or two nipping at our heels, and by the time we had executed that change of course I felt sure that we had escaped any possibility of pursuit.

And so we had. We maintained a stringent watch in the sighting room, and there was never the slightest glimmer of sail-flash. That launch was really the only thing that could have stood a chance, anyway. We were fast and dark, and although there were still quoins and treasure in our holds, we turned easily.

We had sailed between worlds and baubles many times and, except for our new hands, we were all suitably accustomed to the strain of those long weeks with little to do. At least the time between the Rumbler and Wheel Strizzardy had been filled with the work of transforming the lines of our ship, but now that we had finished that task all we had left were the normal chores and duties. Sighting room. Gun practice. Cooking and washing. Sewing and darning. Navigation cross-checks. Teaching and reading. Suiting-up and suiting-down, over and over, until we could do it in our sleep. Eating and drinking and sleeping, telling stories and playing games, and trying not to get on each other's nerves more than was strictly necessary. And even with all that there were still too many hours left over.

Of course the first couple of weeks were a little novel, because of our newcomers. How they fitted in, whether we liked them, whether they liked us, whether they were ever going to be proper members of the crew, as opposed to temporary passengers, was a question each of us had to puzzle over for ourselves.

I kept thinking how much simpler it would have been if there were no nagging little doubts. Merrix was the least problematic, I decided, because there was no reason to think that any part of her story—as it had been relayed to us—was less than true. Her father was a different kettle. Doctor Eddralder had set up his affairs in the kindness room very thoroughly, organising medicines and wares and generally inhabiting the place as if he had a long and distinguished career ahead of him. And perhaps he did, because the one thing I did not doubt was that he was an excellent and scrupulous practitioner. He had brought Strambli back from the brink, and by the time we were two weeks out of Strizzardy she was up and about like the rest of us, albeit shakily, and starting to share in mealtimes and some very light duties. If I had slipped with a knife myself, or worse, I would have very gladly submitted to his ministrations. But there was that business with Glimmery, and I could not let it out of my mind. Would he ever have told us, I wondered? Or would he have hoped it never came to our attention?

None of us were pure in mind and deed. I knew that. We had all done things that we either regretted, or would much rather not have been obliged to do. I had put a knife to my own sister's throat and come close to shooting her with the volition pistol. In order to escape and rescue me, Fura had inflicted a terrible toll on Father, one that had hastened him to his grave. Worse than that, if I could be bothered enumerating her failings. But none of us had taken on cruelty as our occupation, accepting it as a continuous and permanent part of our personalities. I kept telling myself that Doctor Eddralder had only dispensed one type of cruelty to offset another, and that would settle my qualms for a shift or two, but never more than that.

Then there was Lagganvor, who was another sort of conundrum entirely. If I laid out the sequence of events in my head, it all made sense. Fura had gone looking for a man who had useful intelligence. She had found that man, and now he was with us, and starting to share that intelligence, and it was going to lead us to The Miser. His story was like a very simple sort of jigsaw, with the pieces cut from thick wood, which went together almost too readily. And all would have been well, except for the pieces left over. Fura had found him readily—almost too readily.

I know she had asked a few questions, perhaps with a lack of discretion, but there was a whole world for him to lose himself in, and yet he had flung himself into our hands almost as if he *wished* to be taken. And when we cornered him in the hotel, and looked as if we were on the point of murdering him, why had he not turned his pistol, or that eye against us, as a weapon? Surely there had been opportunities.

Why would a man who had run from Bosa Sennen want to have anything to do with her former ship? Even if he needed passage off Wheel Strizzardy, were we not the last crew in the Congregation or beyond that any sane man would choose?

There was, as well, the fact of his familiarity to me. We had never met; had never had the possibility of meeting. Lagganvor had already left the ship before I joined Bosa's crew.

And yet, when I put these nagging details to one side, I had to balance them with others—the details that did fit his story, and were hard to explain unless he was exactly what he seemed. His knowledge of the ship, from its lines and layout to the secrets of the Glass Armillary—how could anyone but Lagganvor ever know such matters?

When an answer to this riddle had presented itself to me, I had desired only to spit it out like a piece of poison.

But I could not.

*Only Lagganvor could have known the things Lagganvor knows.*

*But that does not prove that this man is Lagganvor.*

*It means only that he is someone very good at extracting knowledge from another man.*

*Extracting knowledge, perhaps on the point of death, learning it thoroughly, and going to extreme ends to adopt the guise of that other man.*

*Becoming Lagganvor.*

I hated myself for entertaining this notion, but once it was there I could not rid myself of it. All that remained—to make those left-over pieces fit—was to find an explanation for his presence among us. And once I had allowed the idea into my head that Lagganvor might be someone other than Lagganvor, the answer to that question flowed easily enough.

The only reason to become Lagganvor was to infiltrate our ship. To infiltrate us, report on our methods, and lead us to our capture or destruction.

To betray us, and take us.

And who would be better motivated to pursue such an end, than a man who had already suffered through the acts of Bosa Sennen?

It was a hypothesis, not a settled conclusion, and I knew that I had arrived at it via a process of questionable intuition, rather than irrefutable deduction. Intuition which, in no small part, felt like the sort of suspicious theorising that would have come naturally to a hardened survivor like Bosa Sennen. I could prove it to no one, not even to myself, and to act on such a doubtful grounds would have brought no benefit to any of us. And even as I marshalled my arguments, I could just as easily undo them by my own wits, let alone Fura's, who would always be ready with a sharp, sabotaging retort. Perhaps it suited the real Lagganvor to rejoin his old ship, now that Bosa Sennen no longer captained it. He had other enemies, after all, and we offered a sort of sanctuary, a ready means of escape from the effective dead-end of Wheel Strizzardy. That was why he had presented himself to us, and allowed himself to be taken without resistance—mere self-interest. And the quoins, too, might have factored into his thinking. He knew where they were, and that was a potential treasure that could not have slipped his mind. In us, he saw the means of claiming some fraction of it for himself. And for that he needed the ship, since without the Glass Armillary there was no means of locating The Miser.

Yes, that fitted as well—at least as tolerably as my own narrative, and it should have defused my qualms very satisfactorily. I knew that Fura would muster these counter-arguments, and others, and that they would undo my version much as scatter-shot undid rigging, tearing through it and leaving gaping holes. Worse, Lagganvor would say all that was required to undo my dark theory, and because of the time and effort she had invested in him, Fura would be inclined to value his account over mine.

No: no good would come of mentioning it. Worse than no good. It would re-open grievances and drive a division between Fura and I that I had hoped might be on the point of healing, especially in light of our joint captaincy.

I could only act, and continue to act, as if Lagganvor was the man he claimed to be. I would force myself to think of him in those terms. But I vowed to be alert to him, to watch and wait for the mistake I believed he would make, given time. The error that would expose his true nature, and provide evidence that not even Fura could ignore.

So we sailed, and I went about my days as if no doubts had ever penetrated my thoughts, and for a while that habit became so ingrained that I nearly forgot that I had ever had cause to question his story. Once we had turned at the swallower, the only treacherous part of our crossing, and the only one that demanded quick, coordinated action, and once we had run out the ordinary sails again, giving us a little more speed with the solar weather in our favour, the remaining part of the trip was one of supreme uneventfulness, but for two things that happened when we were almost within sighting range of The Miser.

Even at that point, the rock's existence remained hypothetical. Somewhere in the Congregation, forgotten in some dusty journal or time-worn log, there might be a record of a tiny dark body orbiting the Old Sun. No such entry lay anywhere in *Revenger,* though, beyond that inscription on the marble. Even if our ship had been taken—disarmed and boarded around Wheel Strizzardy, or on our passage to that world—there would have been no clue to The Miser's existence or whereabouts, beyond that faint blemish on an otherwise innocent-seeming marble. I did not doubt that Bosa had committed the relevant information to memory, and that she would have done so many bodies back, passing it from one vile incarnation of herself to the next, like an heirloom or a curse. Yet it was plain that, of all her operational secrets, this was the one she held the nearest to her heart.

I believed it was there. I wanted it to be otherwise, because the absence of The Miser might take the sting out of my sister's late-dawning obsession with quoins, but because I wished for that so fervently, I counted on the universe to provide the exact opposite of my desires. The Miser would prove real; I knew it with a soul-deep certainty.

When we were five weeks out from the wheel, and only two weeks from our supposed destination, Fura was minded to use the long-range sweeper at its highest power setting, snatching an echo of any little rock or obstacle that might lie ahead of us. Or, equally, the absence of an echo—how glad that would have made me. But wiser heads prevailed. The back-scatter from a powerful sweep might yet signal our location to any elements still interested in pursuit, and so Fura was persuaded to wait another week, until the rock might be detectable on a much lower sweeper setting.

That was the hardest week of our voyage—the one in which the hours stretched the longest, in which nerves were frayed to their ragged limits. I had never seen my sister so tense with expectation as in those days.

I slept badly, which did not help. I was having nightmares, and they were all to do with Chasco. I would be in the bone room again, and the skull would be present—damaged or undamaged, depending on the flexible logic of the subconscious—and I would be trying to persuade Chasco to abandon the pursuit. Sometimes I managed it, and thereby spared his existence, and accordingly suffered the deluded, temporary bliss of the dreamer, until roused and reacquainted with the harsh facts of the waking day. Half the time, though, I was chased and tormented by his agonies. I would snap out of my dream with a profound and lingering sense that he was still present, disembodied but cognisant, and I would know that further sleep was futile.

I would lie in stillness for a little while, well used to the ship's sounds by then, and if I had screamed in my nightmare I might hear one of the others mumbling or grumbling at the disturbance to their own rest. One night, though, when the dream of Chasco had been particularly vivid, I woke to the sound of someone else's discomfiture.

It was a sobbing, I realised, and it came from nearby.

I found my clothes and moved through the semi-gloom of the sleeping ship. Surt was on sighting watch, I believed, but the rest of us were following the same waking and sleeping shifts. But it was not Surt that I had heard. It was a man's sobbing, and it was coming from the kindness room.

"Doctor Eddralder," I said, in a low, soft tone, announcing my approach as I neared the door.

He was strapped into one of the chairs, bent low over his magnetic desk, his medicines and instruments—usually so carefully ordered—ranged before him in a mad and profligate disarray. We were under sail, so there was a little gravity, but I could easily believe that the contents of his cabinets and drawers had exploded out into weightlessness, such was the chaos. He had a syringe in his hand, the plunger retracted and a dark green fluid filling half the tube. The needle was already puncturing the skin on his left arm, and I believe he could only have been an instant away from depressing the plunger.

"Adrana," he said, with only mild surprise. "I did not mean to disturb you. I must apologise."

His face was nearly averted from me.

"What were you about to do, Doctor?"

He did not move. The syringe was still jabbing at his flesh, and his finger was still on the plunger. "She is blameless in all this. You understand that, don't you? None of this can be laid against Merrix."

I laid my hand over his, gently easing the syringe away from his arm. The needle had broken the skin, leaving a blood-spot where it withdrew.

"Why would you kill yourself now?"

He dwelled on my question before answering. I could see more of his face now, its long lines streaked with tears.

"I have discharged my immediate obligations. Your colleague... Strambli... will fully recover, I think. In any case, I've done what I can for her. There are limits to my ability. As for Merrix, I think she will do well among you. I sense already that she is escaping Glimmery's influence. Would that I were able to do the same."

"You can," I said, putting the syringe back in one of the drawers, so that it was at least out of his immediate reach. "You must. You were forced to do very bad things, Doctor Eddralder, things that can't be forgiven or wished away. You'll carry that with you forever. But I can't stand here and say you shouldn't have acted the way you did. Your only real sin was to care too much. You fell into the orbit of an evil man and he turned your kindness into a weapon. A lesser man would have sacrificed Merrix and turned his back on the patients in the infirmary. You did not."

"You don't understand what he made me do."

"I don't care to. Not now, not ever. Those deeds are between you and your nightmares. My judging you won't undo them, or lessen the cost of them. But I will say this. You are a good man, tainted by an unspeakable act. And we have need of you. All of us, aboard this ship."

He lifted his face to mine, as if my words might contain a trap, a cruelty, that he was about to wander into.

"I wish you meant that, Adrana. I wish it will all my heart."

"Stay with us, Doctor Eddralder. For the sake of Merrix, but not merely Merrix. There is... trouble, ahead. I am sure of that."

"And if I am the source of that trouble?"

"I do not think that will prove the case. You will be tested, though. Your services will not end with Strambli." I paused, glad—in a perverse way—to be thinking of something besides Chasco or Lagganvor. Glad to have this man's troubles before me, eclipsing my own. "If you wish to lessen that stain on your conscience, as I believe you do, then you must dedicate yourself to the betterment of this crew."

"They do not like me. Lagganvor never will."

"Is he your captain, Doctor Eddralder?"

"No," he reflected. "I do not suppose that he is."

"I am. I am Captain Adrana Ness, and you have my confidence. My confidence, and..." I paused, shaking my head ruefully. "I meant to say my friendship. But I do not think we are quite there yet."

*

We gathered in the galley. Surt was already there, a little bag on the table before her, clamped down by the magnetic attraction of whatever was inside it.

"Can't believe I'm the first to pick up on this," she said, looking at all of us, but in particular at Fura. "But then it seems I must be, or someone else would've mentioned it."

"Mentioned what?" I asked.

Surt undid the cinch at the neck of the bag and delved inside. There was a jangling sound, and she came out with a quoin, one of her own, which she set down on the table before us.

I studied the patterns of interlocking bars on its face. A hundred-bar quoin, by my reckoning. Not enough to call a fortune, but a nice piece to jam into your pocket all the same.

"And?" Strambli asked.

"Proz," Surt said. "Would you be so kind as to turn down that sweeper console, and the lights on that squawk box? I already closed the shutters on the Sunward window, but we could use a bit more gloom."

Prozor was always happy to comply when a request had been put in such companionable terms. She drifted over to the equipment consoles and flipped the master toggles that cut off their power. A hum went out of the room. Now that the instruments had been dimmed, the only other fixed source of light in the room was the lightvine, and that was only glowing very feebly, since the lightvine spreading into this part of the ship was a little past its best, succumbing to the speckling and fading characteristic of older cultivars, and rarely depended on since the equipment usually gave off more than enough illumination. There was also the matter of Fura's glowy, but it was only as effective as a small patch of lightvine, and made no significant difference to the room's brightness.

"There's a point to this, is there?" Fura asked.

"There is, Cap'n," Surt said. "And it's starin' you right in the noggin', if only you'd clamp your eyes on the table."

The quoin was also glowing. The visible face, and in particular the grid of bars, put out a yellowish cast. It was a colder, more sickly sort of hue than came out of the lightvine or Fura's flesh.

"I don't know when it began," Surt said. "But I'm thinkin' it can't be too many days ago. Maybe not even a day since. I think I'd have known otherwise—I count 'em often enough. It ain't just this quoin, either. All the ones in my bag—all the quoins I've got to my name. They're all lightin' up the same way. Take a gander, if you doubt me."

There was no need. That same emanation was coming out from the bag's neck, projecting a vague yellow smear onto the ceiling.

"We'd better check all our quoins," I said. "If there's something funny happening to Surt's—"

"No need," Fura said, with an easy indifference. "The effect is widespread. It applies to my quoins as well. I noticed it a couple of watches ago."

I kept my voice level.

"You ought to have said something."

"There was nothing to be said, nothing beyond the obvious inferences, which we are all capable of making. The quoins on *Revenger* are sensing the quoins in The Miser. That's correct, isn't it, Lagganvor?"

"It would be hard to argue otherwise."

"Why didn't you tell us this would happen?" I asked.

Something tightened in his face, as if his skin had shrunk tightly. "It's not an effect I've seen before. It's true we came here on several occasions under my period of employment. But the quoins were never left lying around. They were kept well away from the likes of us, boxed and crated in the holds, or kept in very heavy bags. This was Bosa Sennen's crew. None of us were paid a wage, or allowed to keep prize money in our cabins."

"You went on her errands," I said. "She gave you funds for that."

"Yes, when we were back in the Congregation, or near it. Never near The Miser."

"I s'pose it's possible," Prozor said.

"I'm as intrigued as any of you are by this phenomenon," Lagganvor said. "It's never been documented, to the best of my knowledge."

"The banks hold quoins in large quantities," I said.

"But apparently not in quantities to compare with the reserves in The Miser. You've got to remember that this is not just the work of one woman, over one lifetime. The iterations of Bosa have been busy for much longer than that; longer even than the institutional histories of some of our oldest banks. And rarely were they as single-minded or ruthless as Bosa Sennen." Lagganvor took the hundred-bar quoin and examined it with a scrupulous close attention, flipping its face over so that the yellow radiance spilled on and off his face, catching the dark gleam of his artificial eye. "I cannot tell you what this signifies," he said, clacking the quoin down onto the magnetic surface, and sliding it back to Surt before she got anxious. "But it never seemed to interfere with our business. We came, deposited our quoins, and left. This effect must fade once we leave, or else every quoin on the ship would be tainted, and useless for any transactions. Which they were not."

"I don't cares for it," said Tindouf. "Quoinses acting as if they knows there's other quoinses. T'aint proper, t'aint natural."

"Natural's not in it," I said, trying to reassure him. "None of this is proper or natural, not from the moment we took her ship. Bones aren't natural. Ghosties aren't natural. Swallowers aren't natural. Sailin' around in ships isn't natural. But we're here and this is what we have to work with. If all they do is light up a little... then I suppose it's good news for us, and even better news for Lagganvor. It means we can start believing that The Miser's real."

"I never had any doubts," Fura said.

# 24

The quoins brightened and brightened as we slipped nearer. It affected every quoin on the ship, regardless of denomination or where they were kept. Fura even took one into the bone room, which was as secure and private a place as anywhere, and by her testimony the quoin still shone. I took her word for it, since I could not bear to go near that useless, skull-cracked room after what had happened to Chasco.

But by then we had all become accustomed to that yellow glow, and while I would not go so far as to say any one of us was exactly comfortable with it, we did at least have Lagganvor's assurance that nothing untoward was likely to happen. There were already plenty of mysteries attached to quoins, I told myself, and it was not so queer to add another one to the list.

Our final approach, until we furled sail and sent out the launch, was perfectly uneventful. Such friction as there had been between different elements of our crew—between Lagganvor and Eddralder, Eddralder and Fura, even Fura and I, became less apparent. Lagganvor was doing nothing to rekindle my suspicions, causing me to wonder if they had indeed been baseless, while Eddralder was settling into his new role as our permanent physician, seeming to accept my assurances that his past was of no concern. Merrix was growing brighter and more confident by the day, now that she was no longer under Glimmery's leash, and showing a willing eagerness to muddle in with various shipboard chores. Strambli was rallying. Mainly, what helped with the collective mood was that we were all caught up in the mystery and excitement of what was ahead; what was indeed now very close at hand.

From the sighting room I had spied our objective across thousands of cold leagues, doubting that such an unprepossessing object could ever be the repository of such wealth. The Miser was indeed nothing to look at, but I suppose that was the point. Stripped of their fields, most baubles would be just as unexceptional to the eye. Millions of little wrinkled rocks orbited the Old Sun, and if some fraction of them had once been settled, it was so far back in the long history of the Congregation that no legible trace now remained of monkey presence. Such cities that might have once have adorned their surfaces had been scoured away millions of years ago, and any trace of living matter had long been reduced to dust. It was proposed by the scholars that a very great proportion of the fifty million worlds had been settled before or during the first and second Occupations, but that a war had come, a terrible world-burning conflagration, and no subsequent Occupation had approached those former glories, nor ever would.

In Bosa's case, the anonymity of this rock could not have been more capitally suited to her needs. A ship could sail within a thousand leagues and sniff nothing out of the ordinary. Even the most desperate of crews, run ragged after a string of bad baubles, would disdain such a pebble, knowing that the likelihood of finding even a single marketable trinket was vanishingly tiny; that they would be wasting fuel and lungstuff to no good purpose. So they would sail on, pinning their dwindling hopes on the next strike, and never guess how close they had come to the motherlode of all treasures.

We knew, though—or believed we did. The behaviour of the quoins added to our conviction. And because we had been warned that The Miser would protect its riches, we stationed *Revenger* at a thousand leagues, hauled in yardage, and ventured the rest of the way in the launch.

There were four of us aboard. Tindouf, Strambli, Surt, Eddralder and Merrix remained on the sunjammer, leaving Fura, Prozor, Lagganvor and myself to complete the expedition. It was a small party, but we had come to confirm a rumour, not to crack a bauble.

"You said there'd be a welcome," Fura said, turning from the controls to address Lagganvor when we had put a hundred leagues behind us. "Now might not be a bad time to put a bit of flesh on your story."

"There's a robot mind running the place. It will know that we're here, even with those dark sails of ours." Lagganvor was leaning hard into his seat restraints, only a row behind Fura. "But it won't act until we're about five hundred leagues from the rock."

"And the act would be?" I asked.

"Destruction. It has coil-guns all over it. You can't see them, because they're small calibre and well concealed, but you have my absolute assurance that they are present and under the command of the robot. They will target the launch first, and then concentrate a disabling spread on *Revenger.*"

"That's all very pretty," Prozor said. "But you told us there was a word that'd get 'em playin' nicely."

"There is."

"And the word is, what, precisely?" Fura asked.

Lagganvor smiled obligingly. "Not a word in the strict sense. What it is, I would rather not disclose it at this instant."

"You know, Lagganvor," my sister said, switching her attention back to the console for an instant. "I'm starting to think you and I are not getting on quite as well as I'd hoped."

"Maybe he doesn't even know this word what ain't a word," Prozor said. "Maybe he's been stringin' us along until the absolute last minute, knowin' how little he's worth to us otherwise."

"I assure you I know the procedure. As to my worth, would you have found this place otherwise?"

"Until we see a single quoin," I said, "this is just a speck of useless dirt."

"Tell 'em what it is," Prozor said.

"Not yet, if you don't mind. Bosa was very particular at this stage. She wouldn't transmit her credentials until she was very near the rock, and I don't think that was merely to avoid using a stronger signal, in case she was detected by some other party. There's more to it than that. The Miser will demand an answer when it is ready, and not a moment sooner, and if you transmit when we are too far out, that will be taken as uncharacteristic behaviour. You must be patient, Fura."

"To hell with patience. Give me the word."

"And risk you giving it immediately? No—I'll hold my tongue until we're ready. Is your squawk active? Turn the gain high and start sweeping the frequencies around the middle bands."

She scowled but complied, and the speaker grille erupted with snatches of voices and melodies as she adjusted the dial. We were lying beyond the Congregation, but by much less than the extent of the Congregation itself, and there was no difficulty in picking up transmissions from worlds on our side of the Old Sun, if not further out. There were news broadcasts, dramas, sports commentaries and musical recitals, as well as the pulses of code that kept the timekeeping and financial arrangements of the Congregation in harmony. It was all achingly familiar to Fura and I, for we had often sat with Father as he listened to similar transmissions, especially in the days before our household possessed a flickerbox. It made me think of the pleasures of home, the dependable routines and comforts of a family life, however narrow our means and expectations.

"What am I waiting for?" Fura asked.

"You'll know it when it comes. Slow our approach speed down a little, if you'd be so kind."

"Anything to oblige," she said, with excessive sarcasm.

We were just a whisker inside the five-hundred league threshold when the grille burst with three sharp similar tones. Judging by its clarity the signal had come in from very nearby.

As one, we looked at Lagganvor.

"That is the request to comply with approach clearance," he

said, relaxing a little, as if we had not been the only ones harbouring some doubts as to the accuracy of his intelligence. "The Miser puts it out on quite a wide frequency spread, but it's as well to be sure by shifting your dial around the central band. There are normally three such transmissions, varying in central frequency, and we are obliged to respond within a minute of the last of them. It's advisable to assume that you have missed at least one of the transmissions."

"Then . . . that password, if I may?"

"Activate your sweeper, and transmit six ranging pulses at The Miser. Six only, closely spaced. No less, and no more."

Fura flicked toggles and directed the launch's nose-mounted sweeper to direct a salvo of pulses at the rock. Six times we felt the slight jar as the sweeper's energising solenoids powered up and discharged.

Then nothing. We continued our approach. A minute passed, then two. Lagganvor was as on-edge as the rest of us. I do not think he took a single breath in those entire two minutes.

Two more pulses were picked up by the squawk.

"That is your approach authorisation. Continue at your discretion, Captain Ness. Do you see those three large craters, in a rough alignment? There is a landing point between the second and third, and you may already pick up indications of an entry point."

Fura applied retro-thrust. "It's pulling us in."

"There's a swallower. Be glad of it. It makes moving around in The Miser much more straightforward."

After our close approach to the naked swallower, the idea of one being bottled up safely inside a world—even a dead boulder like this one—filled me with no great trepidation. I realised now that there were layers of strangeness to our existence, and that the things I had once taken to be exotic or disquieting were in fact mundane, especially compared to the doubts and questions now at free liberty in my head.

We landed without being destroyed. If the coil-guns were present, as opposed to a figment of Lagganvor's mind, or phantoms of false intelligence, we never saw them. But by then none of us had significant cause to doubt his veracity. The quoins were glowing, The Miser had spoken to us, and there was indeed a landing point where he had stipulated.

If there was a swallower, it was not a prodigious one. The pull at the surface could only have been half that on Mazarile, and yet The Miser was only a quarter of the diameter of our homeworld. How must it have been, when every rock around the Old Sun (not so old then, either) was meant to have people on it? I could barely comprehend such a state of affairs. It was hard enough now, keeping track of twenty thousand settled bodies. I was not so sure I would have liked to live in those dawn times, when an entire world could be as anonymous as a single person. Mazarile might not have been the grandest or liveliest place in the Congregation but there was still a chance that people had heard of it, or thought they might have heard of it, or knew someone who had visited once. Better to live in the ruins of empire, I thought, and stand a hope of being remembered, than to be lost in those golden multitudes.

Once we had secured the launch, we completed our suit preparations and ventured outside. We carried some cutting and opening equipment with us, axes and torches and so on, distributed equally about our persons, but it was only in case we ran into difficulties.

Fura had brought a bag of quoins with her. They had been glowing yellow for days, but in these last hours their intensity had increased, so that some of their light was beginning to seep through the weave of the bag's fabric. That bag was never far from Fura's hand, and she made a habit of inspecting its contents with some regularity.

"Perkier than they've ever been," she said, her visored face underlit by the yellow light from the bag.

There was no lungstuff in The Miser, which made getting in and out of it far less irksome than if we'd had to go through locks and seals. If this was indeed Bosa's stockpile—and I was close to accepting that as truth—then it was plain that she had not made it into any sort of home or hideaway, treating it only as one might a hole in a wall, into which the family jewels might be entrusted. She came, deposited her gains, perhaps withdrew such negligible amounts as were occasionally needed for her business transactions, and she left again, spending as little time as possible in The Miser's grip. Our intentions, unless I misread my sister, were similar. We would confirm the nature of this place, deposit some quoins of our own, extract any supplies that might be of immediate utility, and depart. Fura's curiosity might or not be sated by such a visit, but whatever her degree of satisfaction I believed it would be months or longer before we chanced to return. It would be enough to know that it existed, that we had located it, and that it was now ours to visit as we pleased.

We walked down a sloping tunnel for about twenty paces, unlit save for the glow of our lamps and quoins, and then came out into a larger chamber, which was empty but for two items of note. The second of these items was a trolley, which I shall come to, but not before discussing the first.

It was a pedestal, thrusting out of a circular hole in the ground, with wires and cables festooned all over it like a particularly fecund growth of lightvine. These wires and cables went into the floor, from whence—it was reasonably surmised—they spread out to operate The Miser's sensors and defences. On the top of the pedestal, like an oversized paperweight, was a glass hemisphere containing a dull twinkling. It was a robot, plainly enough—or a robot's head, I ought to say. In that sense it was no better or worse than our own robot. But whereas Paladin had substituted his old body for the diaphonous limbs and far-seeing faculties of a sailing vessel, and thereby gained a new independence of movement and perception, this poor robot was stoppered into the rock like a cork in a bottle. The Miser could not move itself; it was destined to orbit according to the whims of celestial mechanics and no other influence. Nor could it communicate, except in the very limited sense of interrogating any ship that ventured within its threshold of action. And its only means of physical interaction, if we were to credit what we had been told, lay in the firing of coil-guns: a hypothetical measure that might never be needed in reality.

The time was when I would have looked on such an impoverished condition with scorn or indifference. What were robots to me but the stupid, clumsy relics of an earlier age? I had never respected Paladin when we were younger, and it was only with painful enlightenment that I had come to understand the error of my former prejudice. Robots were meant to be our allies, not our servants. And to enforce such a state of being as this upon a thinking machine—such a cruel, limited existence, with no prospect of relief or betterment was a horror at least as bad as any imprisonment, because even the lowliest captive may cling to the sweet promise of death, when all other hopes are extinguished.

Not so this poor robot. This meagre, watch-keeping existence was the sole extent of its life. It was like shutting a person in a dark room, chaining them to the floor, and giving them only one menial responsibility for the rest of eternity.

"Can you hear me?" I asked, on the general squawk. "I am Adrana, and this is Fura. These are two other friends of ours—Prozor and Lagganvor. Blink your lights if you can understand, machine. If we can help you, we will."

There was nothing. That dim twinkling continued. The lights in Paladin's head were much brighter and more active in comparison. I began to suspect that this robot had suffered a withering, or an attenuation, of its higher mentality. Perhaps, when it no longer had need of parts of its mind, like language, or the instruments of companionship and sociability, it had disconnected them, the one kindness it could bestow upon itself.

"Don't feel too sorry for it," Fura said. "We don't know how many crews saw the sharp end of its guns, just because they got a bit too close to this speck."

"It wasn't the robot's fault, what she made of it," I said.

Fura hooked her bag of quoins to her belt, then unhitched an axe. I tensed, expecting her to use it, but she passed it to me instead.

"You feel so bad about it, you know what to do."

The twinkling intensified. It was still nothing like Paladin, but more than what we had seen.

"I think it's sensing us," I said, touching a glove to the glass. "Can you really hear me, robot? Blink as hard as you can."

Now there was no doubt. On some level, the robot was responding. It had recognised our presence, and was able to understand my words.

"Can we help you? Blink twice for yes, once for no."

The lights blinked twice.

"Good," I said. "Very good. Back on our ship, there's a woman called Surt who can help you. There's also another robot, Paladin, who Surt has helped. We could take you from this place..."

The lights blinked once.

"You don't want that?"

There was no response this time. I suppose I had put my question in a way that would have made any answer ambiguous. Swallowing, I started again.

"Can we help you?"

Yes.

"By moving you?"

No.

"You wish to remain here?"

No.

"You don't want to move, and you also don't want to remain here. Is that what you mean?"

Yes.

I glanced back at my companions. "Then... are you saying that you wish to be destroyed?"

Yes.

Yes, yes, yes.

"I'm sorry," I said, separating my feelings from the action I was about to commit. "I'm sorry, but I understand. You mustn't blame yourself for anything she made you do, all right? You deserved none of this. And I hope that there will be some release for you..."

Gently, Lagganvor touched his hand to the axe, even as I made to swing it. "I think, perhaps...a period of reflection is warranted?"

The robot blinked: no, no, no.

"I made a promise."

Lagganvor's answered me gently, but with a calm and persuasive authority. "Actually, you didn't—I was listening. The main thing, though, is that we don't know quite what will happen if we disconnect this robot, and I'll warrant the robot hasn't much of a clue either. We can't take such a chance, not until we've disarmed those coil-guns. Surt would also need to examine it much more closely, and so would Paladin, just to be safe."

"The cove's not wrong," Prozor said. "Smashin' that tin-head might be a kindness, but it wouldn't necessarily be very kind to *us*, not with our ship turned to matchwood."

Lagganvor twisted the axe from my fingers and gave it back to Fura.

"I'm sorry," I repeated, but with a different intonation this time, apologising for my weakness, not my fortitude.

"It's the right thing," Fura murmured, as if I wanted or needed her validation. "Leave him...it...for now. We know what has to be done, just not yet, not right now." She hefted the quoin bag. "This is what matters, this is what we came for—not to put robots out of their misery."

There were rails in the tunnel, stretching away into the distance in the glare from our helmet lamps. At the near end, as I have already intimated, was a sort of trolley. It consisted of a large, flat platform, long and wide enough to take our entire party, with an upright metal stanchion at the end facing into the tunnel. The trolley had small wheels that rested on the rails, and the stanchion contained a set of levers that operated a winching apparatus, as well as a manual brake, like the kind I had seen on the trams on Mazarile.

We examined it for a minute or two, but such was the simplicity of the arrangement that there was no great mystery to the trolley's operation. The winch was for hauling it back up the slope of the tunnel, by means of a long cable, while the brake was to allow the trolley to free-wheel down the length of the tunnel, to its presumed destination.

"We shouldn't trust anythin' she left behind larger than an eyelash," Prozor was saying.

"There'll be no traps from this point in," Fura declared, with an imperious certainty. "This is purely a practical arrangement, for moving quoins in and out of The Miser. Mostly in, I suppose." She hopped onto the trolley and set her hands on the brake, ready to release it. "We take it, mates. We've come this far, so what else are we meant to do, besides gawp?"

"What if it won't bring us back up the tunnel?" I asked.

"Then we stroll back, just as if there'd never been a trolley in the first place." She fixed me with a doubtful look. "You ain't getting the shivers, are you?"

I smiled back through my glass, trying to push the robot out of my thoughts. "Why ever would I get the shivers, raiding the private treasure of a dead pirate queen?"

"Because you've still got a dose of sense, girlie," Prozor whispered, giving me an encouraging slap on the back.

# 25

We got on the trolley. With just the four of us there was no shortage of room, and there were rails around the outer edges to hold onto. The ceiling was a bit closer to our helmets now, but there was still room to stand up straight, provided the tunnel kept its dimensions all the way down. Without any further word, Fura let the brake off and the trolley started on its way, quite softly and smoothly at first. Of course there was no noise as such, but a vibration came up through the wheels and platform, into our boots and suits, and our minds—mine, at least—had no difficulty turning that vibration into a squeaking, squealing clamour, gathering in volume and shrillness as the trolley picked up momentum.

"Ease back on the brake," Prozor said.

"Not until we've got a bit of speed up. Don't want to be wasting half our reserves of lungstuff just getting to the motherlode, do we?"

We kept accelerating, and the rumble smoothed out. We were going faster than any tram now, the walls speeding past like the lining of some awful throat down which we were being swallowed. I wondered how effective that brake would prove if we suddenly found ourselves heading for a rocky dead end. Eventually even Fura bowed to caution and she worked the brake back and forth enough to damp some of our speed, while not sapping our momentum enough to stop us. Gradually, the tunnel levelled out, or so it seemed to me. We continued a little further, a thousand spans if that, and then our lamps picked out a change in the situation ahead. Fura jammed the brake on harder and we slowed to only a brisk walking pace, before coming to a smooth halt. The rails stopped only a trolley's length ahead of us, in the middle of a circular chamber. Had we continued, a wall would have met us.

We got off the trolley, stepping down onto a hard, level floor. The chamber was about thirty spans across and ten high, shaped like a pill-box.

Our rails had terminated, but there were seven other sets in the circular room. They started near the middle and ran off in radial directions, each vanishing into a doorway and sloping off down a smaller version of the tunnel we had come in along.

"There's no doubt," Fura said, opening the bag of quoins, the golden light spilling across her helmet and face, smothering—for a moment at least—the visible manifestation of the glowy. "They're brightening even more than before—starting to throb, too, if I'm not mistaken."

"Odd that you never mentioned any of this," Prozor remarked to Lagganvor.

He smiled back. "Odd that you never asked."

We walked around the perimeter of the room, shining our lamps down the other tunnels. There were no trolleys waiting for us this time, but there were fixed winches at the top of each tunnel, set back onto the level floor next to each set of rails. Sturdy metal cables stretched away into the tunnels from the winches, under evident tension.

"The quoins must be cached down those tunnels," Fura said. "Spread around, for some reason." She was circling the room with the sample of quoins open before her, examining them as if some fluctuation in their brightness might persuade us that one tunnel was more worthy of investigation than the others. "Anyone's guess. I don't think we need to go down them just yet, though. The trolleys she sent down last time must still be laden, judging by the tension on these winches. We just have to haul 'em up, one at a time."

"Why wouldn't she have unloaded them?" I asked.

"Sometimes we were in and out of here very quickly," Lagganvor said. "Those were drop-offs only, when she was in a hurry to be off on some other business—such as jumping a ship like the *Monetta's Mourn*. Other times, once a year or less, she'd spend a little more time here—counting and arranging her loot, I suppose. But Captain Ness is quite right: there's every chance those trolleys are still laden, and ready to be winched back up."

"One way to find out," Fura said, setting down her bag of quoins and bracing herself by the first winch, near the door that came first in clockwise order from our own tunnel. "Adrana, Proz, Lagganvor. Pick three others and start winching."

"Why the rush?" I asked.

"Because I need to know, and I need to know *now*. What's on these trolleys will only be a small part of her gains, I know. But I have to see it with my own eyes. Once we know we haven't been sold a dud, we can spend as long as we like wallowing in the rest of it." She bent herself to the winch, and with a grunt of effort strained at the handle. It must have been stiff to begin with, but it soon freed—it could not have been all that long since Bosa had been here, after all—and the line began to creep back through the winch's rollers, dragging the distant trolley back up the tunnel. It was slow going, perhaps a span a second, but I had no doubt that Fura would not slacken until she had her prize.

A strange and insidious competitiveness overcame me then. Rather than assisting with her plan out of a sense of sisterly obligation, I was determined to raise my trolley sooner than hers. I went to the third tunnel and began to work the winch. Submitting to the same impulse, or one closely aligned to it, Lagganvor and Prozor took the fifth and seventh tunnels respectively. Each of us gave an initial grunt as our winches loosened, and then we settled into the tedious but bearable labour of dragging our cargoes into the light.

How far down those tunnels went we had no notion, but I did not think it could be terribly far—certainly no more than a few hundred spans—or this manual arrangement would have been superseded by something faster and less labour intensive.

"Why'd she do it this way?" Prozor asked between breaths.

"Which way?" I asked back.

"Spreadin' out her gains like this, with these tunnels all branchin' off. This place is already knotty enough to find, let alone break into. Why make things tricky for herself, by splittin' up the quoins?"

I kept on working the winch as I spoke. "She had her reasons, I suppose. Maybe these tunnels were already laid out like this, and she just used what was available to her."

"Look at the bag," Lagganvor said.

The quoins had been glowing before, but now the throbbing yellow radiance was bright enough to spill right out of the bag, even though the neck was drawn.

"Is there anything you feel we ought to know, Lagganvor?" Fura asked.

"I was never this close to the quoins—not at this stage of the operation."

"The banks keep quoins in vaults," I said. "Wouldn't someone have noticed, if they glow like this?"

"Maybe the banks never kept enough quoins in one place to find out," Prozor answered. "Or the Crawlies and Clackers and so on never let 'em, breakin' up the deposits before they got too big."

Inside my helmet I nodded. "Because they knew what would happen?"

"Or no one was ever this rich," Fura said. Then, with a sudden excitement: "It's coming up the tunnel, coves. I can see the glow."

After a moment Lagganvor said: "Yes. I can see a yellow light too. We can't have very far to go now."

I saw it down my own tunnel then, and doubtless Prozor made the same observation. The same glowing yellow throb that was emanating from the bag, but magnified in power, and gaining in brightness with every crank of the winch handle.

Gradually our four trolleys came into view. We called out our observations to each other. The trolleys were smaller versions of the one we had ridden, riding narrower rails. They had railings around the sides, and each was piled with many bags. The same yellow radiance came out of the bags, leaking not just through their tops but pulsing and throbbing through their fabric. My trolley must have had fifty bags on it, easily sufficient to hold a thousand quoins, if not two thousand or more. Even without seeing a single quoin, even without knowing their individual denominations, I did not doubt that it was the greatest concentration of money I had ever seen in my life. And yet, I thought, this could only be a tiny part of Bosa's total wealth, for she must have loaded and unloaded these trolleys thousands of times over the dreadful course of her existence.

My muscles were starting to burn but the sight of the trolley encouraged a late burst of effort. Yet Fura was ahead of any of us, and it was her trolley that reached the top of its tunnel first, levelling out as it climbed over the threshold. The light from its bags flooded out to fill the entire chamber, bathing us all in its sickly phosphorescence. The trolley's contents looked less like an assemblage of items than a single molten mountain, bursting with some vast internal lava pressure.

As if rising to the challenge, the bag of quoins was now shining even brighter than before, and its throbbing seemed to be matching the rhythm of the larger haul.

My trolley was the next to surmount the rise, then Lagganvor's and Prozor's arrived nearly simultaneously. Some instinct, though, compelled them to stop winching when the trolleys were still on the sloping part of their track.

"This is enough," Prozor said. "Count a few bags, just to satisfy yourself, then put this lot back where it belongs. I'm startin' to believe there's a good reason she never brought all this money together at once."

Fura scooped one of the bags from her trolley. She uncinched the neck, and almost jerked back at the brightness she had unleashed. It was yellow shading to white now, and even the filtered emanation from the other bags was starting to become uncomfortably intense. I was beginning to feel as if we were in a furnace, growing hotter and brighter with each moment.

Then came the sound. Lagganvor was the first to notice it, I think. He reached up, quite unconcernedly, and tapped the side of his helmet, just as any of us would have done if our squawk boxes had started malfunctioning, giving off a buzz or static.

I heard it too. It was a whistle, not a buzz or a hiss. It was gaining in both intensity and frequency, and there was a cyclic rise-and-fall to it that exactly mirrored the throb from the quoins.

"They're singing," Fura said, raising her voice.

The whistling was growing louder. I reached up to turn down the gain on my squawk. Prozor and Lagganvor did likewise.

The whistling remained. It was inside our suits, perhaps inside our heads, but turning down the squawk had done nothing to dampen it. Now it was becoming unpleasant, pushing into the margins of pain.

"They ain't singin', girlie," Prozor said. "They're screamin'."

"Send them back!" I called out, immediately starting to reverse my winch. The trolley began to descend back down the tunnel, but barely any faster than it had ascended. It needed hardly any effort to work the handle now, not with the weight of the trolley working to my benefit, but some brake or governer in the winch was preventing the trolley from picking up any speed beyond its previous crawl.

The pitch and intensity of the whistle was still climbing. I had experienced curious and disturbing auditory phenomena while under the influence of the bones, but this was a different sort of noise. It was choral: not a single tone, but an assemblage of them, amplifying and resonating the total effect. And although I knew that it was being produced by a hoard of metal quoins, that there was nothing sentient or feeling about them, I could not dispute Prozor's observation. It did not feel like singing to me. It was a great and terrible lamentation, a collective expression of agony and misery and all the colours of sadness and regret and despair, and above all pain, more pain than the universe ought to have contained, and all of it concentrated in this one room, in these collections of quoins.

The whistle was too much to bear now. Lagganvor fell to his knees, his winch abandoned. Prozor was still trying to send her trolley back down the tunnel, but as with mine the trolley was only descending at a crawl, too slowly to undo the collective effect we had unleashed. Fura had begun to work at her winch as well, but her trolley appeared stuck on the level rails.

We had seconds, I thought, before the whistle squeezed consciousness from our minds. Seconds or less. Trying to block the pain and the despair filling my head, I plodded back to our tools and looked for something that might cut the cables. It was all I could think of doing: anything to get those quoins as far from each other as possible.

The tools were useless. I knew it instantly. A flame-cutter that needed a minute to be primed; diamond-headed jaws that ran off a hydraulic pump that was not yet connected; saws and blades that might sever a line but would need minutes of preparation and patient work to do the job. None of it anywhere near fast or dependable enough for what we needed.

"Fura!" I said, bellowing her name above the whistle. "Ghostie blade! Tell me you brought a Ghostie blade!"

She looked back at me, a dull incomprehension showing in her face. It was as if the idea I had mooted was both peculiar and foreign to her thinking. Something, be it the glowy, or the mental pressure of that whistle, was dulling her concentration.

"Ghostie!" I shouted.

At last she understood. She stepped back from the stuck trolley, and with a slow and deliberate motion reached to extract something from under the sleeve of her suit. It was no use to her, not there and then, so she dropped it to the floor and gave it a firm kick in my direction.

The Ghostie blade sped across the floor, spinning end to end. Of course, it was all but invisible unless I averted my eyes, and also my mental focus, as if to hold the idea of it in my head, the sharp and dangerous actuality of what it was, I was first obliged to forget that it existed at all.

I stepped out of its way. It spun to a halt, and—still looking anywhere but at the direct location of the blade—I reached out for its handle, or where I believed it to be. My fingers closed. Had I misjudged, and closed my mitt on the blade itself, I would have felt a cold clean absence snip the fingers from my knuckles.

I had not made an error. I squeezed the handle, took the blade with me, and leaned out beyond the winch to touch the edge to the still-taut line of the cable.

It severed instantly. Whatever braking mechanism had slowed the trolley until that moment, its effect was now negated. The trolley began to gather speed, carrying its glowing, shrill-singing cargo with it. The yellow glow dropped to a sepia emanation, then darkness ruled again—at least down the length of my tunnel.

I went to Lagganvor's trolley and severed his cable. He was still on the ground, writhing with his hands either side of his helmet. It was bad for me, but not so bad as it seemed to be for him, and I wondered if the neural mechanisms of his eye were enhancing the effect, giving the whistling an additional pathway into his brain. I watched until his trolley had also taken its glow with it. Then I went to Prozor and she took the Ghostie blade from me, motioning—because it was now impossible to speak—that I should go and assist Fura.

Her trolley was still stuck on the level part of its tracks. Fura leaned into it from behind, though, and so did I, and with the two of us applying all the force we could the trolley began to budge. Once it was moving, it was easier. We got it over the lip of the tunnel and then the cable snapped to tightness. Prozor had severed her own line by then, and came back to us with the Ghostie blade. She cut Fura's trolley, the last of the four, and we watched as it rumbled back down the tunnel.

The yellow glow had faded, but Fura's little bag of quoins was still ablaze, and I did not think the whistling had lost any of its intensity. Perhaps, in bringing the quoins into proximity, we had unbottled something that could not now be contained.

"See to..." Fura was trying to say, nodding at Lagganvor, who was still squirming.

I had made a step in his direction when the first impact came. It was a soundless crash, transmitted through the fabric of the chamber. A few seconds later came a second, then a third, and by then I understood that these impacts were due to the trolleys, running into the far ends of their shafts. The fourth and final one soon followed.

The whistling stopped. It did not fade away, or phase out of our range of hearing. It simply abated, as if a door had been slammed shut.

The quoins in Fura's bag went instantly dark.

I went to Lagganvor and helped him back to his feet, steadying him until he had found his balance.

"Are you all right?"

"Yes," he answered. "I think so. Do we know what happened?"

"Only that it stopped."

Fura stooped down to pick up her bag. Then she and Prozor came over to us. Now the only light in the room came from our helmet lamps, casting a warm brassy glow instead of the former yellow. Fura opened the bag fully and took out one of the quoins.

"They've gone back to how they were," she said, sounding less as if she believed it than if she were presenting the statement for our validation, more in hope than expectation.

"Let me see," Prozor said, taking the quoin.

She examined it between her gloves.

"We were in time," Fura said. "Something began, some reaction, but we broke it in time. There'll be a pile of quoins at the base of each of those tunnels, but no harm done. They can't be destroyed that easily."

"Look at the quoin," Prozor said, offering it up before her visor. "Look at it. Properly."

We did, all of us. The quoin was dull again now, no longer glowing. But it had not reverted to its former state. The pattern of bars on its surface, the interlocking arrangement that signified—according to our custom—the denomination of the quoin—that pattern was in a restless, fluttering flux. Bars were appearing and fading, the quoin's value impossible to specify from moment to moment.

"Something's happened," Lagganvor said. "Or is happening."

Prozor took another quoin from Fura's bag. The same effect was playing across the face of that one. I scooped out another and observed a similar flux.

"This had better stop," I said. "If it doesn't, these quoins are all but valueless."

"You can bet it won't be just the ones in that bag," Lagganvor said. "All the ones that were in this chamber—they'll all be affected. And not just those. Those were just the ones we saw. There'll have been others, countless others, at the bottom of those tunnels."

"No," Fura said. "I won't accept it. This wasn't our doing. We just brought some quoins together. Maybe more than was ever in one place in any bank, but Bosa had been stockpiling them here for centuries. Why didn't the ones at the bottom of those tunnels set off the same reaction?"

I did not wish to dismantle her argument, but one of us needed to say it. "We don't know what's down those tunnels, sister. Not even Lagganvor. For all we know all her quoins are stored in separate vaults, branching off down other tunnels, just as in this room. This whole rock could be riddled with sub-vaults, purely so that she never had to gather too many quoins in one place."

"No," Fura said, but with lessening conviction. "We didn't do this. This wasn't *our* fault."

"Wait," Prozor said sharply.

"What?" I asked.

"The pattern's slowing." She was still holding the quoin up to her face, her expression full of wonder and apprehension. "I think it's settlin' down again, goin' back to a fixed denomination."

I stared at the quoin, desperately hoping Prozor's suspicion to be the case. And it was, I realised. The flux was definitely slowing, and out of that shift of permutations a particular pattern of bars was beginning to reassert itself, becoming dominant.

"She's right," Lagganvor said. "They're stabilising again, regaining a fixed denomination."

"All of them?"

Fura dug through the bag, her mouth lolling open in breathless anticipation. "Yes," she answered finally. "All of them. They're all right. They're all settling down."

Prozor's quoin had stopped its fluttering completely. But she was still holding it before her, some cloud of doubt showing in the angles of her face. "It's gone back all right." She locked her eyes onto Fura. "Did you make a record of the denominations in this bag, before you brought 'em here?"

"No," my sister said. "I just...no. They must have gone back to the same denominations. They can't have changed."

"I want to agree with you, girlie. But the thing is, unless we kept a tally, we don't know what any of these was worth."

"There was a fifty-bar quoin. One of them was a fifty-bar quoin."

Prozor took the bag and delved through it quickly. After all her years on ships, she still had the keenest eye of any of us for reading denominations. "You sure about that, Fura? Cos there ain't one now."

"I swear it."

"Then the denominations have scrambled," Lagganvor said, with the reverence of someone witnessing some rare and fantastic phenomenon, perhaps for the first time. "All of them here, I'd wager it. Every quoin in The Miser, scrambled." He let out a small, desperate laugh. "Doesn't mean they're valueless, by any means. The low ones might have got higher, for all we know. But different...certainly. Whatever the net worth of this cache...we can sure it's not the same now. There'll have to be an accounting."

"What if..." I started saying, but interrupted myself before

I allowed the full flowering of the idea, the dark and terrible notion that had begun to present itself.

"What if what?" Fura asked.

I held back before answering. I did not want to give voice to the thing that had settled in my head. But sooner or later it would occur to each of us.

"What if it's not just these quoins," I said, almost stammering as I forced out the words. "What if it's every quoin. Every quoin everywhere. Every quoin in the Congregation."

"No," Fura stated, with a bold and categoric finality.

"No because you have an argument against it, or no because you don't like it?"

"We'll know," Lagganvor said. "Soon enough. We'll know. A thing like that... a scrambling of *every* quoin? It can't have happened. But if it did... we'll know. And quickly."

None too gracefully, Prozor shoved the bag of quoins back to Fura. "Here's your loot, girlie—for what it's worth. Now why don't we get back to the ship, and put our fears to bed?"

"It won't be all of them," Fura said. "It won't be all of them." As if repeating that incantation, like a prayer, might in some way make it true.

*

We winched the large trolley back up the slope of the first tunnel, passing the mute robot that I had not had—and still did not have—the courage to kill, and a few minutes later we were in the launch, on our way back to *Revenger.* While Fura worked the controls she also had the general squawk open, with the gain turned high enough to pick up the chatter and babble of the twenty thousand worlds of the Congregation. We could see it very handsomely, too, in the launch's windows. The Old Sun's spangling, shimmering light, all shades of ruby and purple, the glint and glimmer of all that was familiar, all that was homely, all that we had chosen to leave behind.

Voices scratched in and out of the speaker grille as Fura worked the squawk dial. Voices, declamations, laughter, bursts of music and song, high hysterical sports commentators, warbles and pulses of telegraphic code, banks and financial institutions muttering to each other across the intra-Congregational void.

"It's all right," she said, turning to us from her seat. "It's been half an hour since whatever happened... happened. There's nothing on any of these channels—just business as usual." But she adjusted the dial a little more and a word tumbled out of the squawk that had each and every one of us turning cold.

"Quoins."

She had gone past that channel and there were so many competing signals that there was little hope of locking in on that one transmission again. So she worked the dial a little further. The pattern of voices was starting to shift a little now. The dramas and musical broadcasts were being interrupted, the sports commentaries abandoned. The telegraphic codes were growing strident and repetitive: not routine signalling now, but urgent requests for clarification and re-transmission.

And more words, with one commonality.

*Quoins.*

*Quoins and quoins.*

*Quoins, quoins and more quoins.*

Reports of anomalies, developing rumours of unrest and confusion. The banks and chambers of commerce urging calm. Citizens being urged to conduct their business as usual. Promises that the unfolding situation was under urgent review and that normality would be restored very shortly.

"I didn't want this," Fura said, plaintively, directing her statement at me and me alone, as if I had the power to revoke the entire chain of actions that had brought us to this point. "I just wanted to know. I just *needed* to know."

"Think of it," I said, while Prozor and Lagganvor looked on, saying nothing. "Nothing's guaranteed now. If those quoins really have scrambled, then there's no continuity. The rich will probably still be quite rich, when all the accounting's done. But not all of them, and maybe never as rich as they were. Some of those fortunes, if they were tied up in a small number of high-denomination quoins…they might very well have evaporated overnight. And there are people down there, people who were poor yesterday, down to literally their last quoin, who might be as rich as we ever were on Mazarile. If not richer."

Fura swallowed. "They say they'll put things right."

"What else do you expect them to say? The word of the banks is the only thing standing between the Congregation and complete chaos. But you can bet they don't know anything more about this than we do. They're grasping for answers."

"The Crawlies will know. The aliens will know."

"They may know what's happened," I said, correcting her gently. "But that doesn't mean they're in any position to put it right. Face it, Fura. You wanted to shake things up a bit. Well, you succeeded. Whatever we're seeing the start of now…this is going to make every other financial crash look like a pleasant breeze on a summer's day."

She was still turning the dial. The clamour of voices, urgent and panicked, continued. But there were starting to be gaps in that clamour: the hiss and crackle of empty frequencies. Some of the stations were going off-air.

"This isn't it," Fura said. "This won't be the end."

"May not turn out to be the end, girlie," Prozor said, chipping in at last. "But it ain't going to be good, that I'm sure of."

Fura's hands were shaking. She was in no state to complete the final docking, so with a little persuasion I eased her from the control chair and finished the procedure myself, sliding us tail-first back into the maw of *Revenger.* After a little while, Surt and Tindouf made good the docking seal, and we were free to drift back aboard. We stripped out of our suits, barely speaking, until we gathered with the others in the galley. Doctor Eddralder and Merrix were already at the table, magnetic tankards set before them, but seemingly untouched. They had a troubled, diffident look about them. Strambli was at the squawk console, repaired now, occasionally turning the dial from one blast of static to the next.

"First, we thought the Old Sun was coughing up a storm," she said, looking no happier than her companions. "Drowning out the transmissions. But that ain't it, is it? We got snatches, just before the stations started going silent. Some talk of quoins going mad. Not just one or two, but all of them, everywhere. Suddenly no one being sure what they're worth anymore. Now, I ain't the shrewdest cove who's ever sailed—"

"It was us," Fura said, taking ownership of her deeds with a certain cocksure nobility. "It was what we did, in The Miser. What we started. What I started, I ought to say. I won't pretend otherwise. I was the one who had to know."

"And now you do," I said, in a small and quiet voice.

I expected her to explode, as she had done in a thousand similar exchanges since our childhood. But she only nodded, meeting my eyes with a sad and resigned agreement. "I do, yes. And in some ways, I'm not sorry. I got half an answer, didn't I? Whatever the quoins are, or were, it was never money. Just because we put 'em to that use..." She gave a shiver. "I can't get that screaming out of my head. I don't know if I did them a kindness or a cruelty, by bringing them together like that. But I do know that I'm not finished. I've... opened something. Like a wound. A wound wider than the Congregation, and older and deeper. And now I've got to put it right."

Surt eased in next to Strambli. "We'll know in a few days, if this is the thing we hope it ain't."

"All Occupations end," I said, thinking back to Rackamore, and his conviction that our tenancy around the Old Sun had no more guarantee of permanence than those that had preceded it. "Perhaps this is how it happens. We crawl out of rocks, set our calendars, make a civilisation, scrabble around for quoins, build our proud little empires, and then one day someone puts too many quoins in the same place and it all comes crashing down."

"I do hopes it's not the end," Tindouf said, flipping the lid of his tankard and staring dolefully into the contents. "I hasn't seen anywhere nears enough just yet." Then he looked up with an eager hopefulness. "Would you likes me to run out the sails and be ready on the ions, Captain Fura?"

"Yes," Fura said, nodding emphatically, as if nothing pleased her more than putting some distance between us and The Miser. "Whatever's begun here, I don't care to be sitting at the epicentre. Get us movin', Tindouf—quick as you can."

"I'll assist," Lagganvor said, followed quickly by: "If I may?"

"All hands welcome," Tindouf said, before there was a word from Fura or I. "And I don't s'pose I need to show you the ropeses, does I, Mister Lag?"

"I believe I can be of some tolerable assistance," Lagganvor said.

I watched the two men leave the galley. Only a minute or two later I heard the first indications of the sail-control gear being actuated: the groans, thumps and whines as the arms and winches commenced their labours. We were still close to The Miser so Tindouf would use due caution in running out the sails, but at the same time I think we all shared Fura's extreme disinclination to linger near this place. I knew nothing of the secret mechanics of quoins, how they spoke to each other across inter-Congregational distances, but it was not hard to speculate that there might be a propagation delay, a lag between the effect influencing the near worlds and its eventual effect on those further away. If that were the case, then with some great diligence it might be possible to calculate the point where the influence had originated.

"What've we started?" I asked, still confounded by the scale and oddness of what was transpiring, and our undoubted part in it. I felt as if we had plucked a flower from a hillside, only to start a landslide. "There's going to be chaos. Worse than chaos. There are grudges between some of the worlds, aren't there? Old feuds and rivalries. It'll all boil to the surface now. I wouldn't be surprised if this sparks off a few little wars."

"So long as they keep little," Prozor said.

"I do not think it will be quite the end just yet," Doctor

Eddralder said, setting his hand on Merrix's wrist, as if to include her in this reassurance, as well as the rest of us. "There will be a difficult period, I don't doubt. A readjustment. It may take months or even years, but the worlds will find a way. Wealth will redistribute itself to some degree, and there will be pain in that process. Pain as well as glory, for some. Justice and injustice alike. Wars, perhaps, as Adrana speculates. But the institutions and mechanisms that permit life on the worlds will continue to operate. There are too many vested interests for it to be otherwise—including those of our alien friends." He paused, directing his long face at each of us in turn. "But I will say one thing with confidence."

"Which is?" Lagganvor asked.

"The enemies Fura believes she has made to date? They will most assuredly connect this event to her name. And the wrath that they will wish to deliver upon her—upon us—will make all our former hardships seem like mere playground games. There will be a war, of sorts, most advisedly. But it will be gravely asymmetric. It will consist of the vested interests of the worlds marshalled against a single adversary."

"Let them try," Fura said, her fist creaking as she closed her fingers. "We'll be ready. We'll be waiting."

"We're already running," I mouthed under my breath, as the ship gave its first low grumble, signifying the rising load from those sails already run-out.

"No," she said, hearing me nonetheless. "We're moving on, and that ain't the same. We came here to learn something, and that's what we did. Maybe not what we hoped we'd learn, but that can't be helped. That was my part of the arrangement, and you honoured it fair 'n square. Now it's time for yours."

"Which would be?" Eddralder asked mildly.

"I promised Adrana that if she let me find The Miser, I'd oblige with cooperation in a matter of her own. This was something I wanted to find, and somewhere out there's something Adrana wants as well." The corner of her mouth lifted in a half-smile. "Or thinks she does."

"Perhaps now isn't the time," I ventured.

"Oh, it's exactly the time," Fura said. "Because wherever that thing of yours lies, it's going to be a long way out. Which—given that the Congregation ain't going to be the most hospitable place for us, not for a while—might suit us very well, once we've taken a prize or two for provisions."

"I am none the wiser," Eddralder said.

"You ain't alone, doc," Surt said, shaking her head.

"There's something out there," I answered, looking to each face in turn, feeling as if—despite my agreement with Fura—this might be my only chance to gain the lasting sympathy of the crew. "Something that has something to do with the Occupations; why they start, and just as importantly, what happens to 'em when they don't. It's on an orbit, a long orbit, but at the moment it can't be terribly far from the Old Sun, and I think we might have a chance of locating it."

"And then what?" Surt asked.

"I don't know. We don't know where to look, how far to sail, even if it's within the reach of a ship like this, even if we could sail for a lifetime."

"And if it isn't?" Eddralder asked.

"I'd find a way."

The doctor's look was sympathetic. "Sounds like something of a hopeless cause to me."

"Maybe it is," I replied, with a deliberate earnestness. "But Paladin's barely scratched the surface of what's on this ship, in the records and private journals. There's no telling what information Bosa gathered over the years; the secrets she barely knew she was carrying. We have to look, is all I'm saying. And now more than ever, because of what's started today." I drew in a breath, squaring my shoulders and lacing my hands before me. "Maybe this will all over blow over, like you say. But one thing we do know for certain is that there've been twelve Occupations before our own, and they all came to an end eventually. That frightens me, and I think it ought to frighten us all." I directed a significant look at Fura. "I know it put the shivers up

Pol Rackamore. But there's no law that says we have to accept it. And if there's something out there that explains the Occupations, maybe it can also help us keep this one going."

"Are you committed to this?" Eddralder asked Fura.

"We set out to save a household," Fura said, after a moment's consideration. "Not civilisation." Then she shrugged. "But plans change." She reached over and closed her cold metal hand around my own. "I'm with her. It may be a hopeless cause, but we pursue it."

"And we get a say in this little jolly, do we?" Surt asked.

"The time to leave us was when we were in port," Fura stated, with a magnificent imperiousness. "Besides, we're all accomplices now. You think there's a one of us who'd get a fair hearing in any court on any world in the Congregation? That wasn't the case before this trouble with the quoins, and you can bet your life today won't have improved matters. No, we're all in this, coves, each and every one of us." Her hand squeezed tighter around my own. It was a sisterly gesture, or one that appeared so, but beneath that grip I was already starting to feel my bones pop. Whether she meant it to hurt, or was just too carried away by the moment to think about what she was doing, I dared not speculate.

Luckily, Tindouf chose that moment to push his head back into the galley. "We's set for a few thousand leagues. Once we's further out, I'll runs out the rest of 'em."

"Thank you," Fura acknowledged, slackening her grip, and making to leave the galley. "Paladin and I will continue to review the transmissions. If anyone needs me, I'll be in my quarters."

I shifted my hand beneath the table and rubbed at the bruised flesh. As she departed I thought of correcting her on the matter of the joint ownership of the captain's room, but after some deliberation decided that I would be well advised to pick some other occasion, preferably when we were without an audience. We had just presented a united front, and—daring to believe that Fura was honest in her intention of meeting my side of the bargain—I had no wish to undermine that fragile concordance, however slight my confidence in it.

Let it be so, I thought. Let it be so.

"Miss Adrana?" Tindouf asked gently, touching a knuckle to his lips. "Might I's a word, seein' as your sister's occupied?"

I smiled with only the slightest of misgivings.

"Of course, Tindouf."

I left Eddralder, Merrix, Surt and Strambli to their mutual affairs and followed Tindouf into the warrens of the ship. Tindouf was not nearly as simple as he liked to present himself, but I believed him to be straightfoward, uncomplicated, and largely incapable of concealing a significant truth. If he informed us that the sails had been run out satisfactorily and the ship was making good headway from The Miser, then I accepted this as the case.

What, then, could demand my attention?

I soon learned.

Lagganvor was waiting at one of the sail-control stations. He had an aimless, distracted look about him, his hands folded at his waist, just like a cove passing the time at a tram stop.

"What is it, Tindouf?"

"I told 'im to waits here, miss, and that's what he did."

"And why did you tell him to wait?"

"You tells her," Tindouf said, in a tone that was more threatening than encouraging. "You tells her, then I'll tells her what I thinks."

I had quite forgotten about the ache in my hand. Now my neck bristled and a living chill seeped its way down my spine, like a worm made of ice. "Tell me what, Lagganvor?"

"Mister Tindouf seems to be..." Lagganvor paused, grimacing, as if he had already set off on what he knew to be the wrong tack. "He believes that I was doing something untoward."

"Tell her."

"He believes I was using the sail-control gear to deflect our course."

"And were you?"

Lagganvor's one birth-given eye flicked onto Tindouf, then back to me. Meanwhile his artificial eye gleamed with an implacable calm. "No, but I can understand his thinking. It's just that—and no disrespect—there's nobody on this ship who better understands her trimming than I. The sails were set quite well, a credit to Tindouf, but as I was passing this station I remembered that we always relaxed the strain on these port preventers, so that she hauled truer, and I couldn't resist making the alteration." He unlaced his hands and gestured at the control gear. "The strain-gauge is out of calibration; has been for years. If you trust it, she'll limp by one or two degrees."

"She don't limpses," Tindouf said.

"No, because you—and Paladin—will have absorbed the error with a multitude of small adjustments elsewhere. The ship will sail very well—as, to your credit, it must have done—but it won't have sailed quite as well as it could..."

I absorbed these words, finding in them the same slippery plausibility that I had already come to recognise where Lagganvor was concerned. An effortless disruption of doubts; an easy quelling of suspicions.

But I turned to our Master of Ions. "It's all right, Tindouf. Mister Lagganvor had already expressed some concerns along these lines to me. He said he'd like to take a look at our gauge-calibration when the time was right. The fault was mine for not remembering to mention it." Not wishing Tindouf to feel put-out, I added: "You were right to question his actions, though. We've taken on some new guests and it behoves us all to treat them with caution, as well as respect." I directed the full force of my stare onto Lagganvor. "You'll bear Tindouf no malice for this incident, will you?"

Lagganvor was calculating his position by the second. I could feel it whirring in him like some over-wound clockwork. Spinning from a moment of exposure, to a moment of salvation, however perilous.

"I can understand his reaction. It was silly of me not to mention what I was about to do."

Tindouf grunted. He seemed ameliorated, but how thoroughly, and how permanently, I could not say.

"Then I'll be on with my businesses, I s'pose."

"It's all right, Tindouf," I said, touching his sleeve by way of friendly assurance. "No harm was done here. Quite the opposite."

I waited until he was gone, then waited a little longer until I was certain Lagganvor and I had this part of the ship to ourselves. The hull grumbled and groaned around us, like a monster that had eaten too much dinner. Beyond that, there was no great disturbance. We were much too far from the galley to hear the squawk, if indeed it was still receiving reports from around the Congregation.

"Well?" Lagganvor asked finally.

"I know who you are," I answered.

"I have never made any secret of it."

"No—your true identity, not the one of the man you stole a name from. You are not Lagganvor. You know a great deal about him, and a great deal about this ship and Bosa Sennen, but that doesn't make you him. I believe you reached Lagganvor ahead of us; that you learned things from him—perhaps under pain of interrogation, or worse—and took his place."

His nod conveyed admiration, but it might just as well have been for the audacity of my speculation, as to its accuracy.

"Then I would be... whom, precisely?"

"You are the brother of Pol Rackamore. You are Brysca Rackamore, and you have come to avenge Pol by infiltrating and exposing the crew of Bosa Sennen." I tilted my head at the sail-control gear. "I don't know what Tindouf caught you doing, but I am willing to guess. You were trying to initiate sail-flash."

Some flicker of interest or amusement perturbed his expression, but it was there and gone just as fleetingly as an instant of sail-flash itself.

"And why would I do that?"

"Because all other signalling options are closed to you. The skull is broken, even if you had the aptitude, and you cannot risk using the squawk. You would be found out immediately, by Paladin if not one of us. But a pre-arranged code to your employers, delivered by sail-flash? The perfect means. You could not, of course, deliver this signal until you were certain of The Miser's nature. Now you are, and now you have acted."

"You are very sure of your position."

"I have not arrived at it by accident. I knew you, Brysca. There's too much of Pol in you, even with the eye. I commend you. It must have been a considerable sacrifice, to give up a good eye for that toy."

At last something gave way, some last barrier being torn down with a certain weary relief. "It has its compensations."

"Do you deny your nature?"

"It would seem fruitless."

"You are very lucky Prozor hasn't made the same connection I did. Perhaps she will, in time."

"Does it matter, since you must be intent on exposing me to your sister?"

"I see no other option. I let Tindouf go, but only because I wished to speak to you privately, to have my suspicions validated. Fura will see your true self, when the facts are laid out. She wants you to be Lagganvor, but she's not so blinded by her own glory that she won't admit the truth, however much it pains her."

"You overstate my value to her now. I gave her The Miser; what use am I henceforth?"

"She would kill you. My sister is not a born murderess, but there is something in her just as there is something in me."

"I would not care to cross either one of you. Her with her glowy, you with the traces *she* left in you."

"If you think I am Bosa, and that eye still functions, you could have your vengeance on me this instant."

"Ah," he said carefully, "but you are not Bosa, not exactly. You were the shadow she hoped would become the solid embodiment of her, but the process did not run its course, as I now understand. Bosa Sennen is dead. I am denied my vengeance."

I frowned. "Then... what is your purpose?"

"It was as it seemed, to begin with. I wished to find you and kill you. Find Bosa, I mean. But I know her to be no more. The trouble is, in coming to this state of understanding, I appear to have dug myself into something of a hole." He reached up to touch his collar, as if fingering a stage garment that would never feel entirely natural about his person. "I cannot easily dismantle this disguise."

"You were seeking to expose us, with the sail-flash."

"No, I was seeking to save you both. My position—my revised position—is very plain. I know what you are and how you have reached this state. But my employers are much less confident that Bosa Sennen is really dead. I'm afraid that your own actions—well meant, I don't doubt—have only added to the confusion."

"We don't need spelling out how much trouble we're in." Then I thought back to the words he had started with. "What do you mean, save us both?"

"I meant that I will do my utmost to keep you alive. So long as I am known to be present on this ship, they won't attempt to destroy it. Stalk and capture it, if they are able, but they'll risk nothing that might result in my death. That was the intended nature of the sail-flash: merely a signal that I remain alive."

I allowed a warning edge into my voice. "I don't care to be captured, Brysca. Neither will Fura. They won't treat us fairly."

"With my testimony, your chances would be improved. My employers would accept that Bosa Sennen is really dead; that her influence over you—the both of you, I should add—is at best tenuous, and entirely explicable given the circumstances into which you fell. I would expect a period of detention, some rather thorough questioning—but at the end of it, they would understand that you are as much victims as my own brother, or poor Trusko, or for that matter Illyria herself."

"And then what?"

"Some process of readjustment, for both of you. The flushing out of the glowy, in Fura's case. The elimination of residual psychological conditioning, in your own. Mild custodial sentencing, at worst, and then rehabilitation." His tone firmed. "But not death. Not terror, not pain, not mutilation, not one of the thousand bad deaths that they could easily visit on you from afar, if you permit them to believe that I am dead."

"So we should allow you to live."

"It's not so difficult. I'll just keep on in the role to which I've found myself."

I nodded slowly. "Being Lagganvor."

"It is the simplest course, Adrana. The only logical decision."

"So logical, that my sister won't have any difficulty seeing your point of view?"

He smiled with the haste of a man who knew he was only one misstep from fatal condemnation. "No... I do not think it would be wise to involve Fura, not just now. You are cooler-headed. You grasp the larger panorama. Fura would be... capricious. We have all seen evidence of her temper."

"I won't lie to her."

His look told me that he found that rather doubtful, given the evident betrayals and counter-betrayals we had already visited upon each other; the falsehoods and concealments. But he opted to take me at my word.

"You won't need to. She has no cause to question my nature; I will give her none. I will play my part excellently. Go along with this quest of yours... which I admit does intrigue me, as it would have intrigued Pol. I will subsume myself in Lagganvor so thoroughly that you'll hardly remember this conversation."

"So simple."

"Yes."

"But with the slight catch that you will be using every opportunity to signal your employers. Every opportunity to draw them nearer."

"So long as I am known to be alive, and gathering intelligence, they will be content to keep their distance."

I looked to the sail-control gear, imagining the secondary purpose to which it would now be put. Not constantly, but frequently enough to serve his needs. And with each illicit use carrying with it the risk of exposure, which would in turn lead to the possibility of my own implication.

"You are asking me to become a traitor to my own ship, Brysca. A traitor to the crew, a traitor to *Revenger*, a traitor to my own sister."

"No," he said softly. "None of those things. I am asking you to become an accomplice in their salvation. Fundamentally, it boils down to a very straightforward question. Do you still love your sister enough to save her?"

I answered him. But not before I'd given his question all the careful consideration it merited.

# Acknowledgements

Love and gratitude to my wife, for putting up with me during the long process of writing a novel, and in particular for once again reading and commenting on an early draft. My friend and colleague Paul McAuley was also kind enough to read the book at an intermediate stage, and provided much useful feedback. They are not responsible for such faults and deficiencies that remain in the published edition, but the end result is undoubtedly the better for their guidance.

The Revenger books have benefited greatly from the hard work of the publishing teams at Orion in the U.K. and Orbit in the U.S. Gillian Redfearn, who has been with the Ness sisters from the start, has at times understood the story I was trying to tell rather more clearly than I did, and the books would be poorer without her insight. I am also indebted to the sharp eye of Abigail Nathan, whose close reading of the text spared me (and not for the first time) considerable embarrassment, and to Craig Leyenaar, for making sense of my editorial responses. In America, Brit Hvide's enthusiasm has helped the books find an audience, something no writer takes for granted. Thank you to all involved in the production, design and marketing of these novels—your efforts are greatly appreciated.

Although he played no part in the writing of my novels, I would like to record my indebtedness to Gardner Dozois, who died in 2018. Gardner was the first American editor to take notice of my work and his continued endorsement of my short fiction meant a tremendous amount to me over the ensuing decades. The Revenger books arose from a plan for a series of linked short stories that were never actually written, but I hope Gardner would have approved of them if they had ever come about.

Last, but not least, my agent Robert Kirby has kept me on the straight and narrow for the better part of twenty years, and I could not ask for a better champion of my work.

Last again—no, *really* this time—I'd like to salute those readers who have gone along for the voyage with Fura and Adrana, even though it may have taken them into slightly unexpected waters, and hope they will remain on board the not-so-good ship *Revenger*...

Alastair Reynolds
South Wales, September 2018

# meet the author

Photo Credit: Barbara Bella

ALASTAIR REYNOLDS was born in Barry, South Wales, in 1966. He studied at Newcastle and St. Andrews universities and has a PhD in astronomy. He stopped working as an astrophysicist for the European Space Agency to become a full-time writer. *Revelation Space* and *Pushing Ice* were shortlisted for the Arthur C. Clarke Award; *Revelation Space*; *Absolution Gap*; *Diamond Dogs, Turquoise Days*; and *Century Rain* were shortlisted for the British Science Fiction Award, and *Chasm City* won the British Science Fiction Award.